Also by R.W Peake

Marching with Caesar®-Conquest of Gaul

Marching with Caesar-Civil War

Marching with Caesar-Antony and Cleopatra, Parts I & II

Marching With Caesar-Rise of Augustus

Marching With Caesar-Last Campaign

Caesar Triumphant

Critical praise for the Marching with Caesar series:

Marching With Caesar-Antony and Cleopatra: Part I-Antony
"Peake has become a master of depicting Roman military life and action, and in this latest novel he proves adept at evoking the subtleties of his characters, often with an understated humour and surprising pathos. Very highly recommended."

Marching With Caesar-Civil War
"Fans of the author will be delighted that Peake's writing has gone from strength to strength in this, the second volume...Peake manages to portray Pullus and all his fellow soldiers with a marvelous feeling of reality quite apart from the star historical name... There's history here, and character, and action enough for three novels, and all of it can be enjoyed even if readers haven't seen the first volume yet. Very highly recommended."
~The Historical Novel Society

"The hinge of history pivoted on the career of Julius Caesar, as Rome's Republic became an Empire, but the muscle to swing that gateway came from soldiers like Titus Pullus. What an amazing story from a student now become the master of historical fiction at its best."
~Professor Frank Holt, University of Houston

MARCHING WITH CAESAR

Birth of the 10th Legion

By R.W. Peake

Marching with Caesar® –Birth of the 10th Legion by R.W. Peake
Copyright © 2014 by R.W. Peake
Cover Artwork by Marina Shipova
Illustrations by Marina Shipova
Cover Artwork Copyright © 2013 by R.W. Peake
Maps of Hispania reprinted with permission from "The Barrington Atlas of the Greek and Roman World"; Richard J.A. Talbert (Editor); © 2000 Princeton University Press
Author Photo © David Conklin

Printed in the United States of America
First Printing, 2014

Foreword

My, what a strange but wonderful trip it's been since I decided to ignore the obvious signs, in the form of around 25 rejections, and self-publish what is now the first book of the six-part Marching with Caesar ® series in March of 2012, Marching with Caesar-Conquest of Gaul. I had no idea what to expect, but what I can simply say is that even in my secret imaginings, I never, ever conjured up what has turned out to be a reality, in the form of several bestsellers. But even now, as of this writing, the first book that's just short of its second anniversary spent more than 30 days back at the top of the Ancient Rome genre on Amazon, dropping out of that spot just two days ago now. Little by little, reader by reader, the story of Titus Pullus is reaching more people every day, and I owe it all to you readers who have helped spread the word about this grunt's tale.

What is even more astonishing, at least to me, is how quickly it's all happened, and again, I owe it to the readers for giving me the validation and the freedom to continue pursuing what has now become my fifth, and definitely final career. I receive a lot of comments about how "prolific" I am, and I suppose that's true; what I know is that I love my "job," and I think nothing of spending 10 to 12 hours a day visiting Ancient Rome. It's a subject of endless fascination for me, and I'm thankful that there are so many people like me who love Rome as much as I do.

Which brings us to this book, *Marching with Caesar-Birth of the 10th Legion*, and why it exists. Although it's true that it contains previously released material that is currently in Conquest of Gaul, it's equally true that there is new material, in the form of the origin of the Titus Pullus story.

When I decided to publish *Conquest of Gaul* on my own, I faced a number of challenges and even more questions. Being a complete unknown, with no audience, my thought process was that I needed to let the reader get to the "good stuff" more quickly, leading me to cut out this part of Titus' story that didn't have a direct connection to his career in the Legions. In addition, as one critic has pointed out, I have a problem with "prolixity" and, considering that in its current form, *Conquest of Gaul* comes in at 660 printed pages, the length of the book was also an issue. Hence, readers only learned of how Titus and Vibius Domitius met indirectly, or the tension between Titus and his best friend that was caused by their mutual love of Juno. No, I reasoned, I needed to get the readers to the part where the pair, and their comrades of the Legions were lopping off barbarian heads. In fact, I was so worried that some readers wouldn't be interested enough in the training of the Legions that, literally two days before I published, I added what is now the prologue of *Conquest of Gaul*, the dream sequence involving the Usipetes and Tencteri.

But a funny thing happened on the way to Gaul. Although the vast majority of readers have responded positively, and enjoyed the first book in its current form, there was a fair number of readers who complained that they didn't feel like they really knew Titus. Very early in the process of turning myself into a full-time, bestselling author (sorry for repeating that, but I just really like the sound of it!), I made what has become the beginning of this book available as a download on Smashwords for free. Much to my surprise, it was downloaded some 400 times before I made the decision that culminates in what you're reading right now. Even more surprising, at least to me, is the high percentage of female readers I have; according to what data I have available, it appears that almost forty percent of my readership are female. And they have been instrumental in alerting me that a large proportion of the readers of this series view Titus' story as more than just a "sword and sandals" tale, that they invested themselves in Titus the man, not just Titus the Roman killing machine.

Another factor in my decision is the knowledge that there are readers who are scared off by the length of *Conquest of Gaul* in its current form. It is the longest book of the entire series, none of which, as those of you who have read them can attest, are lightweights by themselves. Also, for those readers who need a bit of transition before jumping straight to the blood and guts, I hope that this will suffice. More than anything, though, although I've always viewed Titus' story as more than straightforward action fiction set in Ancient Rome, the response from all you readers has confirmed that belief, that this is a story about a man's life and all that comes with that. Titus Pullus isn't just a man of the Legions; he's a brother, an uncle, a husband, and a father.

Perhaps the biggest change lies in the fact that I am undoing what I can only call a rookie mistake, and that's my shamefaced admission that the editor of *Conquest of Gaul* was...me. Yes, I violated what I've determined is the *only* thing that the indie author community agrees on as far as being a foundation for success, and that is paying a professional editor. I know that Beth Lynne, who has been my editor since the second book, has been dying to get her hands on *Conquest*, so I'm sure readers will be just as happy as she is that the many mistakes that have caused a fair amount of comment will be corrected.

This leads me to something that I've debated in bringing up. However, I want to set expectations for all readers from the start. When it comes to critical comments, one of the most common complaints is in the stilted language and somewhat awkward phrasing. That, dear reader, is intentional, and while I'm more than happy to correct errors in things like subject-verb agreement, there are going to be "whos" that are supposed to be "whoms," and I will use "lie" instead of "lay." And although I have no intention of changing this, allow me to explain why. *(Note from RW's Editor: It is true. My master has forbidden me from changing "who" to "whom" and has threatened to use the scourge if I change Titus' voice in any way.)*

From the very first day on March 29, 2008, when I typed the first words of what would become this series, I have strived to maintain a fidelity and authenticity that even the most critical reviewers have acknowledged. And part of that is to be faithful to who I believe Titus is: an uneducated, but very intelligent man who may lack formal schooling, but because of his abilities has elevated himself to a status where his counterparts are generally more learned than he is, and received more tutoring than he did, which is virtually nonexistent, except for what he learns from first Scribonius, then Diocles. He's acutely aware of this, and it colors every part of this story, from beginning to end. Even now, at the beginning that's really the end, Titus' Pullus still has a chip on his shoulder. And since this is, in essence, a verbal account, albeit transcribed by his servant, scribe, and friend, Diocles, I wanted the story to read that way, as if you are listening to someone tell a story in your head. So for those new readers who are expecting something other than this, I apologize in advance, but it ain't changing. My hope is that if you are a stickler for perfect grammar and syntax that the power of the story enables you to suspend that requirement. Additionally, there have been some questions about Titus' "bragging" a lot; one reader compared him to John Wayne, but not in a good way. Again, this is intentional and isn't going to change, mainly for the same reason Titus' grammar is what it is, and that is for the sake of authenticity. This concept of false modesty, where one is supposed to kick at the dirt and say, "Aw shucks, I got lucky" is a modern one, and it has no place in the ancient world. As proof, I would point out to *"Veni, vidi, vici."* In the ancient world, if a man accomplished something, noteworthy or not, he proclaimed it for the world to hear.

Again, I want to thank you, the reader, for embracing Titus' story, and for validating my belief that his story is timeless. In particular, I want to express my gratitude to my fellow veterans, who make up a substantial proportion of the readership of the Marching with Caesar series, and who have expressed to me their appreciation that, in telling Titus' story, I am also telling theirs. Of all the accolades and positive comments I receive, those mean the most to me, for reasons that are probably obvious. Because of them, *Titus Pullus Vivit!*

Semper Fidelis,

R.W. Peake
January, 2014

Historical Note

Of all the campaigns conducted by Gaius Julius Caesar, the first one he led as sole commander of an army in Hispania is the least documented by the ancient sources. There is very little mention made of it in any source, although Napoleon III in his *History of Julius Caesar*, published in 1865, does devote perhaps three or four pages to it.

As an author of historical fiction, that's a double-edged sword. While it gives an author more latitude than one might otherwise have when dealing with the campaign in Gaul, for example, for someone who wants to strive to be as historically accurate as possible, it makes matters extremely difficult.

What is known is that the campaign originated in Scallabis, or modern day Santarem, Portugal, which the newly designated Praetor of the province, Gaius Julius Caesar, named as the new provincial capital. From Scallabis, Caesar and his army moved northward, moving more or less along the coast. As far as landmarks go, the most prominently mentioned are the rivers that he and his army cross, and in *Marching with Caesar®-Birth of the 10ᵗʰ Legion*, you will see the ancient names, except for the first time they are mentioned, when I put the modern name in parentheses. I do this as well for those settlements and towns that have a modern-day counterpart. After this first mention, I use the ancient names in all cases.

I have also made a change from the current series, although in the spirit of full disclosure, I am actually reverting back to my original conception of Marching with Caesar, and that is referring to the weapons and equipment by their original Latin terms. But not only am I including a glossary, thanks to my superb cover artist Marina Shipova, there are line drawings of each item, in the form that they would have appeared to the Legionaries of the late Republican era, in 61 B.C., and each one is labeled with the Latin term.

Finally, in order to help readers visualize the progress of this first campaign of Caesar's and, more specifically, Titus and the 10th Legion, I am including a map from the superb *Barrington Atlas Of The Greek And Roman World,* published by the Princeton Press. For those of you with a serious passion for Rome, or Greece for that matter, and who have extra cash on hand, I can't recommend this outstanding resource highly enough. Despite its steep price (around four hundred dollars), for me it was worth every penny, and in a very short time, it's become my most valuable resource, especially when I couple it with Google Earth, which allows me to "walk" the ground and get a sense of what it's like.

And with that, I hope you enjoy *Marching with Caesar-Birth of the 10th Legion.*

Marching with Caesar: Birth of the 10th Legion

Prologue

I have always been intrigued by the way a man's memory works. I learned fairly early in my life that I seem to be blessed with one that surpasses that of most people's, yet even I cannot possibly remember every conversation or action that I have taken in my sixty-plus years. The aspect of memory that intrigues me is how a man's inner mind chooses what to remember, and what to forget. Because every moment of my life that I desperately want to forget, I remember, and yet there are events in my life that I distinctly recall at the time telling myself I would remember, but my only recollection of it is that I thought it noteworthy at the time. These memories, usually more pleasant ones, I am barely able to get a sense of, as if I'm peering through a dense fog at a dark shape that is tantalizingly close, but just not enough to recognize. How can a man's mind dictate to his will that the events he wants to record in his memory are, in fact, the ones he will forget, no matter how much he wants to retain them? Yet, there are moments that reappear with a frequency that I would give almost anything to stop altogether, horrible moments of my life that I cannot seem to stop from playing over and over in my mind. No matter how much I try to banish them, these memories keep showing up, like an unwanted toothache from a tooth that is slowly rotting away.

Fortunately, at least so I believe, there are still a substantial number of good memories, and the fact that so many of them are of moments that I thought neither important nor worth remembering at the time, is just another example of what keeps me awake at night as I try to solve the riddle of why this is so. I suppose that it is understandable, here near the end of the strand of life that has been given me by the Fates, a great number of these concern my earliest days, of my childhood. In particular, I recall with great fondness adventures with my then-best friend Vibius Domitius, moments that I believed I had long since forgotten, but for whatever reason I now remember with great clarity.

I cannot say that I had a happy childhood, but many of those moments of joy I did experience revolve around my times with Vibius. He was my fellow adventurer, and sometime partner in crime as we managed to get into the kind of mischief that I believe only boys can conjure up. Roaming around the countryside outside of Astigi, the town nearest to my farm, in the province of Baetica in Hispania, I do not believe there was a fold of ground or nook that we did not explore. And naturally, in doing so, we sometimes found ourselves in situations where I suppose one could say we were trespassing. Not that it meant much to us; when you are a boy, concepts of property lines and ownership have very little meaning. Unless, of course, it is *your* property. Still, I cannot say that we were malicious in our snooping, nor did we set out with larceny in our hearts; for the most part, we were just exceedingly curious about any and all manner of things. It was a trait that both Vibius and I shared, and I suppose that is one reason we had become such good friends.

One of those adventures that come back to me fairly regularly concerns a two-boy campaign that we planned against the man whose farm bordered the one owned by my father. His name was Aulus Gabinius Plancus, and he was the only person I knew who came close to my father when it came to being disagreeable. And I was not the only one who held this opinion; he held the distinction of being the most disliked man in our area. And while my father Lucius Pomponius Pullus was a contender for that prize, unlike him, Plancus was a sharp dealer when it came to business. In fact, if the gossip around the forum of Astigi were to be believed, he was a bit too sharp, if one takes my meaning. In fact, there was a long line of men who, to this day, I am sure would have applauded the planned efforts of Vibius and me to take him down a notch had they been made aware of our identities. He was also very high-handed, and quick to point out the flaws of others, and even as a boy, I saw that, his other failings aside, he was an astute judge of character. Now, in the fullness of my age and whatever wisdom I have acquired over the years, I can see that at least part of the ill will that most inhabitants of Astigi held towards Plancus was due to the fact that he was, simply put, smarter than the majority of its citizens. And if the truth were known, it was not until an incident in the forum of Astigi that my own enmity towards Plancus began, when he committed what was, even now, an unpardonable sin in my eyes. He compared me to my father.

It was on the day that Vibius and I treated ourselves to one of the meat pies sold by a vendor who had a stall at the southern edge of the forum. It was run by an older woman, and I suppose we reminded her of her own sons, who I knew were grown and had moved away, but she treated us with an indulgent amusement, laced with a fair amount of disapproval at our antics. Our talent was making her laugh in spite of herself, which we tried to do every time we visited, because it meant that the meat pies were sometimes provided free of charge. And for me in particular, "finding" the copper obol to buy a pie was not always easy. Fortunately, my father spent so much time drunk that it was less a case of avoiding being caught as the fact that he rarely had that much money on him.

"Here comes Plancus," the vendor muttered, and before I turned to look over my shoulder, I saw the scowl cross her face at the sight of the heavy farmer.

However, when I turned back after ascertaining that it was indeed the man in question, I saw that she had her falsest proprietor's smile on her face, calling out with a gaiety that I am sure she did not feel.

"*Ave*, Aulus Plancus! Come to sample the finest meat pies in Astigi? Or perhaps a sweet pastry?"

"Finest?" Plancus had a harsh sounding voice under the best of circumstance, but now it was scornful. "Hardly. But Ovidia's stall is closed for some reason. Probably Ovidius beat her again last night and she can't walk. Not that I blame him; her mouth is almost as bad as yours! No," he shook his head, "I'm only here because I'm famished, and you're all that's left."

I gasped in shock, but I imagine my voice was drowned out by Vibius, the vendor, and everyone else within hearing distance. The insulted woman's mouth had dropped open, but no words came out, and I remember being struck by the thought that she looked very much like a fish I had once caught out of the stream that ran across our farm as it gasped its last breaths. Finally, she turned about to put the pies he had ordered into the oven for the last baking. This meant that there were going to be several awkward moments, since neither Vibius nor I were finished with our own pies, and being honest, I could see he was no more inclined to leave than I was. There is not much that passes for entertainment in towns like Astigi, so there was no way we were going to miss any of this. Plancus must have caught us staring at him, because he turned to examine the two of us, starting with Vibius.

"Gods, you must be the runt of your litter." Plancus gave that mocking laugh again, and as usual, he scored a direct hit on his target. There was nothing that Vibius was more sensitive about than his size, and I saw his face flush with the embarrassment of having it pointed out. "If I were your father, I would have left you for the wolves to eat. You're not going to be much use to him, even if he is a tanner." He said this last word like it was the worst epithet with which he could come up.

I began to grow alarmed, because I recognized the look that came over Vibius' face at this last insult; it was the same one I saw when we had first become friends, in our battle with two of the local bullies. He was opening his mouth to say something, and I suppose I either made some sort of movement or sound that drew the attention of Plancus. And if he had been scornful before, now he made no attempt to hide his contempt.

"Oh, it's you, Pullus' boy. You're certainly bigger than that one." He jerked a thumb over at Vibius. "But you better hope that you're not as stupid as your father." By this point, the vendor had retrieved the pies from their last step, wrapping them in cloth and was holding them out to Plancus. As he turned away from me to toss a coin contemptuously onto the wooden board that served as the counter, he made one last parting remark. "Or you'll turn into a drunk like he is." Without another word, he turned to leave.

I have been large my whole life, and because of the hard work on my father's farm, I was, and still am exceptionally strong, even in my dotage. I also have a horrific temper, and while time has served to wear down its edge, back then it was as if I was riding the back of a huge beast that was barely under my control. And when it got loose, I could no more stop it from doing whatever damage it could than I could have stopped a stampeding herd of cattle who are panicked by lightning. Before I had any conscious thought, my legs were pumping, the remnants of the pie in the dirt and forgotten, and he had gotten just far enough away that I was able to get up to full speed. I lowered my shoulder, driving it right into the small of his back, and I was rewarded by a massive explosion of air as it was forced out of his lungs by the impact of him hitting the ground with me on top of him. I was no more than twelve years old, but I was already the size of many full-grown men, and he is fortunate that I was as yet untrained in the ways of hurting another human being and was just a ball of unfocused rage. There is a vague memory of meat pies tumbling through the air as we went crashing to the ground and, unskilled I may have been, I knew enough to understand that I had not yet won the battle. I immediately began pummeling him about the head, barely noticing that smashing my fist into his skull hurt my hands at least as much as it was hurting him. I have no idea how long I was flailing away at him before I was suddenly, and very roughly, jerked from my position of straddling his prone body. Someone had hold of the back of my tunic, and although they had exerted enough force to pull me off Plancus and more or less upright, they had no idea how strong I was. My tunic, one of two that I owned, ripped away from my upper body, and I would have completely yanked myself out of it except that my belt held it in place. Plancus was just then rolling over, shaking his head like a bull that had been stunned, and I suppose that was what he was in some ways, and I felt a sense of savage satisfaction when I saw that his face was covered in blood. I did not know it then, but he looked very much like a general of Rome who is celebrating a triumph. Lunging at him again, I was only stopped when I was tackled, hard, and knocked off my feet, and out of the corner of my vision, I saw the face of one of the town watch, understanding that he had been the one who was now pinning me to the ground. This gave Plancus the opportunity to regain his feet, and while he was unsteady, he immediately staggered toward me with a bellow of rage. The watchman, seeing Plancus come, scrambled to his feet, but I had no time to regain my own. Somehow, I managed to dodge the heavy kick that Plancus aimed at me. I was not so lucky the second time; I had just come to my knees when his next blow hit me squarely in the chest, his foot knocking the wind out of me and putting me flat on my back. Since I was staring skyward, I did not see what happened next, although Vibius was more than happy to give me the details. Hearing another bellow, I assumed it was Plancus and I closed my eyes, knowing that I was about to receive the most severe beating of my life. But when the next blow did not fall, only then did my mind recognize that the shout of Plancus had been more of pain than rage or triumph. His first cry was immediately followed by another, another one of pain, but it gave me the time to roll off my back and onto all fours as I gasped to regain the breath he had knocked out of me. Plancus was standing there, but he had his hands up around his head, and while I recognized that he was trying to protect himself, I had no idea why. Until the third paving stone in perhaps as many heartbeats came flying from somewhere beyond my vision, striking him in the hip.

I had been saved. Not by Vibius, not by the watchman, but by the citizens of Astigi who, over the years, I suppose had suffered more insults and outrages from Plancus than I had. They did not do it for me; I knew that even then, but the fact that I was saved at all was more than enough. Our last sight of Plancus that day was, with his face still covered in blood, backing out of the forum while pointing at me, howling that he would have revenge.

"That was the bravest thing I've ever seen." The vendor had bustled out from behind her stall, and while I was thankful for her praise, I was even happier because in her hand, she held two steaming pies.

"That was the dumbest thing I've ever seen," was the opinion of the watchman, but he offered me a hand, pulling to me my feet. "Plancus is nothing if he's not a vengeful man. I don't envy you a bit. Although," I suppose he thought he meant this as a chastisement, "it's probably your poor father who's going to suffer the most."

That idea actually cheered me a great deal.

It did not take long for Plancus to act. He started by damming off the stream that ran across our property, which he was able to do because his own farm was upstream. Fortunately, that scheme of his was short-lived, as he quickly ended up flooding his most valuable pasture. My father, as addled as he was by his wine consumption, never considered that Plancus was the cause of this; he was blissfully unaware of what had happened in Astigi, which I was determined would remain the case. Instead, he attributed it to some quirk of the gods, and was just another sign to him that he was cursed, which I suppose was one of the few things he had the rights of in his whole life. I had confided in our male slave Phocas who, although worried about Plancus, knowing the farmer not just by reputation, but in his own dealings with the man, was also proud of what I had done. I, on the other hand, was not so sure about my actions once I had cooled off and had the opportunity to think about it. My reaction had had nothing to do with the slur against my father; it was the insinuation that I would end up like him that had enraged me. Now I had brought down consequences on the heads of my entire family, and I would be lying if I said I did not have conflicting feelings about it, because despite how harsh it was, Plancus had uttered no less than a truth. My father was a drunkard; that was about the best that I could say about him, and the reason I had been so angry at what Plancus said was that, even at my young age, I somehow recognized that my following down the same road as my father was a distinct possibility. It was because of my hatred towards my father that a secret part of me was happy that he would be inflicted with some sort of punishment, even if this particular time he had done nothing to cause it. However, that satisfaction was far outweighed by the idea that my sisters, and our slaves Phocas and Gaia, who I viewed more as parents than my own blood, would be suffering because of my temper. After Plancus dammed the stream, although it did not last long, I knew more was coming, and that is what kept me awake nights.

Perhaps a week after the incident, I was roused by a visibly upset Phocas, who curtly told me to get out of bed and follow him. It was sufficiently unusual for him to speak to me in such a manner that my alarm drowned out any irritation I might have felt at a slave spoke to me in such a manner. Hurrying to catch up, we went outside, and I followed him to the small shed that served as our barn that held our mule, milk cow, chickens, and the sow that my father had paid to mate with, ironically enough, Plancus' hog and had just borne its litter. Even as I walked into the barn, I had a premonition of what I would see, but even so, I was unprepared for the scene that met my eyes. Because it was still early, just after dawn, Phocas had brought an oil lamp, and its flickering light contributed to the macabre vision. In the enclosure where the piglets and their mother had been contained, it looked much like a scene with which I would become all too familiar as an adult, although I had no way of knowing that then. Blood was literally everywhere, splashed on the plank walls, and in congealed pools surrounding the corpses of the sow and every piglet. I could not stop myself from letting out a horrified gasp, and my heart started hammering in my chest as I stared down at the grisly sight, knowing without any doubt that I had been the unwitting cause of what was a devastating blow, not just to my father, but my entire family. Because my father had a lack of interest and skill in farming, those piglets represented a large portion of our food supply for the coming winter. Naturally, despite the manner in which the sow had been slaughtered, Phocas would salvage every scrap of meat, along with those of the piglets, but they were still many months away from providing more than a mouthful of meat. Having been born and raised on this farm, I had become accustomed to the sight of slaughtered animals, and in fact helped Phocas in the yearly task, but I had never seen anything of this nature before. And in the lamplight, I could see by Phocas' face that neither had he, as his face was paler than normal, even in the dim light.

"Fucking Plancus," he muttered under his breath. "He did this." Phocas turned to look at me, and while his gaze held no censure, I could see that he held me at least partially responsible. "Titus," he said quietly, "I know why you did what you did. And a part of me is proud of you for standing up to a bully like that man. But your temper," he shook his head, "is going to get you in serious trouble."

Even now as I recall this, I have to give a rueful laugh; he was more right than he could possibly have known. But in that moment, I felt a peculiar mixture of shame and rage…and a cold, hard lump in my chest as I swore that I would come up with a way to stop Plancus. Because the one thing I was sure of was that he would not stop.

Not surprisingly, I did not even think of mentioning this to Phocas; my only confidante was Vibius, and it is still to his eternal credit that he did not flinch when I told him I planned on exacting retribution on the farmer. Equally unsurprising, and for once understandably, my father's reaction was one of rage at this devastating blow, not just to our family's fortunes, meager as they were, but to his own *dignitas*, which was equally skimpy. Until, that is, Phocas finally revealed the identity of the culprit and resulting cause of Plancus' actions…himself. Yes, gentle reader, a man who was our slave had the courage to tell my father that he had unwittingly caused Plancus' offense, on one of Phocas' trips to town. As I sat at the table and listened to Phocas calmly relay what, to my ears anyway, was a fantastic tale where Phocas had not been looking where he was going and, turning a corner, had knocked Plancus into a particularly nasty mud puddle, I did not see how even someone as drunk as my father could possibly believe it. Yet, to my astonishment and contempt, he not only accepted Phocas' tale, when he learned that it was Aulus Plancus, he turned even greener than his normal coloring, and for a horrified moment I thought he would vomit all over himself, and us.

"You did *what?*" he screeched, his already reedy voice coming out as a shrill blast that felt like an awl was being punched into my ears. "You...imbecile! You stupid, incompetent idiot!" He pointed a shaking finger at Phocas. "I am going to whip you bloody for giving him offense, do you hear me?"

Phocas sat there, and while I could see that he was afraid, he looked steadily at my father, then inclined his head.

"As you say, master," he replied, his voice husky. "I deserve to be punished, and I humbly beg your apology."

"Well, you don't have it," my father snapped, his lips pulled back in a sneer, which gave me a perfect view of a row of rotting teeth. "I'm going to give you a striping you'll never forget, you *cunnus!*"

I sat there, waiting for him to turn his wrath on Plancus, but he turned his attention to his wine cup, draining it greedily and, as usual, I had to watch as he drank so deeply that two thin streams of the liquid came out on either side of the cup, running down and staining his already filthy tunic.

Finally, I could take it no longer, and I asked incredulously, "Is that all you have to say? What about Plancus?"

"What about him?" my father replied, eyeing me with a wary hostility.

"He slaughtered our pigs!" I shot back. "No matter what...Phocas may have done, he has to pay for that!"

"Shut your mouth, boy," my father did his best to growl at me, but to my ears, it was a surly whine. "How I handle this is none of your affair. I am the *paterfamilias*! So it's my business and not yours!"

"Which means you're not going to do anything." I could match my father when it came to surliness, and I made no attempt to hide my scorn.

"I said *shut up!*"

I know that from his perspective, his hand shot out with the speed of a lightning bolt, but it had been many years since my father had been quick enough that he could catch me with a blow, and I dodged this one easily. I was not so quick that I dodged the kick he aimed at me from underneath the table, catching me in the shin. Staggering to his feet, he raised his hand to try to actually land a blow, but I dodged out of the way and stood myself, facing him and, as I remember it, this was the first time I realized that, even at twelve years old, I was as tall as my father already. This was a dance we had done before, and it was one that later my sisters and I would laugh about, as he lurched around the kitchen trying to catch me, bellowing with rage as I capered just out of reach. Apparently, he remembered this as well, because he only took a step or two before dismissing me with a disgusted wave and collapsing back into his chair. Within another moment, he was again sucking wine from his cup, and my disgust for my father raised yet another notch.

Phocas was never whipped, although none of us expected my father to follow through with it. But neither did he do anything about Plancus. That was left to me, and to Vibius.

"We need to do something that sends a message that if he tries anything like that again, we're going to answer back, even worse than what he did. And we won't stop until there's nothing left."

I can say now that I uttered these words with all the callow assurance of a boy who was certain that he would never fail at anything he set his mind to, but I now understand how much stupid luck was involved. The plan we came up with was ambitious, and that is putting it mildly. Over a period of perhaps a week, Vibius and I planned a campaign of terror that was restrained only by our imaginations, and those imaginations were very vivid. None of his property would be left untouched or unscathed; our first target were the olive trees that accounted for a large proportion of the olive oil supply of Astigi. We would girdle the trees, stripping a section of bark all the way around, knowing that within a season the trees would stop bearing their fruit. His chickens would be fed feed that we had soaked in our own urine, and although we had no idea whether this would kill them, we were fairly certain that they would at the very least become sick and stop laying. He had a herd of goats, and while at first, our scheme involved hamstringing them and crippling them, neither of us were particularly enthused about this idea, so we settled on killing the rams. Our final blow would be our most ambitious one, and it involved Plancus' prize bull. The bull, named Hercules, was a local legend, supposedly siring fully half of the cattle belonging to several farmers. But being honest, both Vibius and I bore a grudge against that bull that was only slightly less vehemently held than the one against his owner. One day, after a particularly tiring adventure that I have forgotten, I urged Vibius to take a shortcut, across the pasture where Hercules was lord and master, as it offered the shortest path back to my farm. Vibius wanted nothing to do with the idea; part of the legend of Hercules the bull included goring at least two men that we knew about, and he was as bad-tempered as his owner. However, there is no better way to overcome one's trepidation than being goaded by one's best friend, which was exactly what I did, finally making Vibius mad enough that his anger overwhelmed his very sensible caution. And although we both escaped the wrath of Hercules more or less intact, in Vibius' case it was not without the bull offering him an extra boost over the stone fence that surrounded my farm. I had just hopped over and landed with a heavy thud when I saw Vibius sail past me, over my head, to land in a heap at my feet, the bull tossing him over the fence to safety. And yet, despite this close call, with the short memory that comes with boyhood, we had convinced ourselves that we would somehow be able to rope Hercules, snub him to a tree, and turn him into a steer. A very large, very angry steer certainly, but neither Vibius nor I doubted that this act alone would avenge the insult done to my family and our honor. I still believe that to this day, but as matters turned out, we would never find out.

If I still had any congress with the gods, I would ascribe what happened to their blessing and protection, because now I have no doubt that the plan Vibius and I concocted would have not only been a spectacular failure, it would have made a bad situation worse.

However, on the very day before the first attack on the olive trees that Vibius and I had planned, setting out that night, when Phocas returned from Astigi on some errands, he radiated an air of suppressed excitement. Whatever it was, he deemed it sufficient cause to rouse my father from what he called his afternoon nap, but was in fact his drunken stupor.

"Pluto's cock, this better be good," he growled as he staggered into the kitchen, collapsing at the table and in a gesture that I knew was automatic, reached for the amphora of wine that was always there.

As he filled his cup, I idly wondered how much of what our farm produced, little as it was, went into trade for wine, somehow understanding that I probably did not want to know the answer.

"I think you will forgive me, master," Phocas assured him. And with his next statement, he proved to be as good as his word. "Plancus is dead."

For a moment, none of us spoke; I had been standing in the doorway, and I suddenly felt the need to grab it in order to steady myself as I gaped at Phocas in amazement.

My father did not react immediately, just stared at Phocas vacantly before finally saying, "Dead? Plancus?"

Neither Phocas' face nor manner betrayed any impatience, but I knew him well, and I could sense his irritation as he repeated to my father, "Yes, master. I am speaking of Aulus Plancus, our neighbor. He is dead."

Before my father could say anything, I blurted out, "But how? When did it happen?"

For the first time, Phocas' expression changed as a smile crossed his lips, and there was no mistaking the satisfaction in his voice as he supplied the information.

"It appears that he was gored and trampled to death."

I stared at him incredulously, and I could feel my mouth hanging open as I gasped, "Gored? Not by…"

I did not finish; there was no need, but it was a peculiar feeling when I saw Phocas' head nod up and down.

"Yes," he confirmed. "Apparently, Hercules didn't appreciate being taken to stud again. Plancus was trying to rope him and tie him to a wagon, and the bull charged him. When he tried to get away, he stumbled and fell, and before any of his slaves could stop him, the bull gored him and stepped on him several times. By the time they got Hercules drawn off, it was too late."

There was a silence for several moments, then my father uttered something that I will never forget, if only because it was one of the only times he ever said anything worth remembering.

"Well," he said as he raised his cup in a mock salute, "maybe there is some justice to be had for men like me."

Then, without another word, he got up and stumbled back to his bedroom. I was not surprised to see he took the amphora with him. Then it was just Phocas, Gaia, and I, and I walked slowly to the table, taking a seat as I tried to grasp what this meant. I could sense Phocas' gaze on me, but I was too absorbed at the moment to notice. Finally, I looked up at him, and he was regarding me with a peculiar expression.

"What? Why are you looking at me like that?" I asked suspiciously.

"Well, there was one thing that someone mentioned when they were talking about Plancus'…accident," he replied carefully. His mouth kept twitching, and if I did not know better, I would have sworn he was trying to suppress a laugh. "But according to the slaves, Hercules did this all the time, and Plancus was always too light on his feet to get caught by the bull. Except this time, they swore that his luck finally ran out because he had been favoring one leg for the past couple of weeks. Ever since his last trip to Astigi, apparently."

I stared at Phocas for several long moments, then despite myself, I burst out laughing. Before more than one or two heartbeats had passed, Phocas joined in and before much longer, we were overcome with laughter.

As my father said, perhaps there is some justice in the world.

Chapter 1- Who Is Titus Pullus?

These are the words of Titus Pullus, formerly Legionary, Optio, Pilus Prior and Primus Pilus of Caesar's 10th Legion Equestris, now known as 10th Gemina, Primus Pilus of the 6th Ferrata, and Camp Prefect, as dictated to his faithful former slave, scribe, and friend, Diocles.

This is being written in my 61st year, three years after my retirement as Camp Prefect, in the tenth year of the reign of Augustus, and 489 years after the founding of the Roman Republic. I have more than 40 military decorations, including three gold torqs, three set of phalarae, two coronae *civica*, three coronae *murales*, and a *corona vallaris*. I have more than 20 battle scars on my body, all of them in the front, and my back is clean, never having been flogged in my 42 years in the Legions, nor turning my back to the enemy. Although my record is not as great as the revered Dentatus, I am well known in the Legions, and I have given the bulk of my life and blood to Rome.

My goal is straightforward; with these words, I plan to record all of the momentous events that I participated in as a member of Rome's Legions, during a period that changed the very foundations of Rome itself.

When I was young, Rome was ruled by the *Senatus et Populus Que Romanum*, the Senate and People of Rome. Every year, two Consuls were elected from the Senate to run Rome for that year; now, only one man rules, the members of the Senate are his pets, and Rome has never been stronger or mightier than it is right now. The letters SPQR are now famous throughout all of the world, known and unknown.

Although it is no longer in my nature to express excessive pride that some have called hubris in the same way as I did in my youth, it is with some justification that I lay claim to playing a small role in expanding Rome's fortunes. However, I do so in the name of my fellow Legionaries, those still living and those long or recently dead. For it was with our strong right arms and our sharp blades that such titanic changes were made possible; our legs that carried us as the agent of change to be used by a great man, a man who saw what needed to be done in order to ensure the future prosperity of the city and country he loved more than life itself. His work was unfinished when he was struck down, and it is the very same man known now as Augustus, whom, under a different name, that of his adopted father, picked up the ivory baton of imperium and carried it forward to complete what the great man started.

If, dear reader, you are looking for elegant and witty prose, know this now; I am a simple soldier, and have a simple soldier's story to tell. Despite being literate and possessing a fair hand for simple letters and documents, I have no training or experience in these matters. That is why I am dictating this account to my former slave, scribe, and friend, Diocles, who is trying his best to keep up with me as I talk. My purpose is to offer an account of these great events, and a viewpoint of the great men of our day, as I saw them and lived through them. I make no claim to be an intimate of all of the First Men of Rome, yet I can say that most of them of whom I speak in this account knew me by name. I saw them at their finest, and some I saw at their lowest point, but most importantly, I saw them as they appeared to the eyes of their Legions.

Also in this account, I will endeavor to recall conversations and events as exactly as possible, and I must beg the reader's forgiveness because of the coarseness and crudity of some of the conversations, because they are the words of soldiers and are not the manner of speech one would normally use in polite company. However, I have broken what is a promise to myself that I have kept for many years now and made a vow to Jupiter Optimus Maximus that I will recount as faithfully as I can all that transpired in those days. One might ask, how is it possible that I will be able to remember conversations that occurred thirty or forty years earlier? First, I have been blessed with the type of memory that seems to retain more than others, and second, even as events were transpiring, I had an idea that they were noteworthy. Perhaps I even had it in the back of my mind that I would one day want to record the events of the day, although I had no idea how I could accomplish this. When I enlisted in the Legions, I was barely literate, able to write my name, and to read very simple instructions and the like, meaning the idea of writing this down would have been nonsense. However, I somehow always knew that one day, I would be in the position where I either had the ability myself, or I would be able to use someone to create this record. In fact, that was the great, burning ambition of my life, to elevate not only myself, but those who follow, bearing my name into the equestrian class, an ambition that has been fulfilled.

Now, as I look back on my life, I know that I am nearer to the end than to the beginning, and despite being in good health, only the gods know how much longer I will live. Therefore, I have decided to start this last mission of mine, and will devote almost all of my time to it. In truth, I have nothing much else to do; I am a wealthy man, and while I hold office here in Arelate, it is mainly a ceremonial post, leaving me free to come and go as I please, just as long as I am present to march at the head of the procession on festival days. Truth be told, I am bored. I know that I no longer have the strength of body to continue in the Legions, but my spirit is still as if I were a sixteen-year-old-lad, on the lookout for adventure and a way to improve my station in life. Such is the cruel humor of the gods; ability may wane, but desire never does.

And I am lonely; I miss my comrades, I miss the Legions and the life of the Legions. I will find myself staring at my *lorica hamata*, my *galea*, *scutum*, and *gladius*, and thinking, *if only I could stop time*. But I cannot, so there is no use in dwelling on it. Perhaps that is why those few comrades of mine who managed to survive as long as I have drink as much as they do. In particular, I miss my friends Vibius and Scribonius, but Vibius is dead more than ten years now and, while Scribonius is alive, he is far, far away and with his nose buried in a book, I am sure. Thinking of Vibius in particular only makes me more melancholy, both for his death and for all that transpired between us. When all is said and done, I am a warrior without a war to march to, and I fear that this fact alone, not any sickness of the body or just plain old age will finally send me to the afterlife.

Before I go, however, I have one last job to do, not dissimilar to some of the jobs I had to do in the Legions. It will take patience and endurance, but most importantly, it will require me to relive certain memories that I have not thought of in many, many years. Nevertheless, now I must turn my mind's eye to the past, moving back over the years, and the miles, and the battles, to find the young man that I was, the young man who was looking for adventure and a way out of his life, along with his best friend.

I was born in the province of Baetica, what was known as Hispania Ulterior at that time, near the town of Astigi, south of the provincial capital of Corduba, in the year of the consulships of Publius Servilius Vatia and Appius Claudius Pulcher, on April 20th, as it is calculated under the calendar of the Great Man, Gaius Julius Caesar, my former commander. The only reason I know for sure is that my father would remind me on that day, for as long as I can remember, that this was the anniversary of the day I killed my mother.

You see, I was, and am a rather large man and I was born a large baby. Why this is so is a mystery, since my father was not large and, obviously, neither was my mother. Whatever the cause, my passage into the world was sufficiently traumatic for my poor mother that she bled to death. I suspect that this was the primary reason that my father hated me; I know that he hated me to be true because he told me so, even more than he told me that I killed my mother. I was the only boy; I have one sister still alive, Valeria, and it was Valeria who took care of me during my youth. Despite the fact that she is only five years older than I am, I viewed her then as more my mother than a sister. It was Valeria who would hide me from my father when he would be in the throes of one of his drunken rages, which grew in frequency with every passing year. And it is the children of Valeria, especially her son Gaius, who will inherit all that I have when I die, save the portions I am leaving for her maintenance, as well as the small stipend I am leaving for my slaves.

(Note by Diocles: My former master's "small" stipend to his slaves was the sum of 2,000 sesterces, a not altogether small sum, but more importantly, to each slave save one they received

documents of manumission, even those Gallic slaves he was awarded by Caesar for his role in the Gallic Campaign. The lone exception is the slave Simeon, who came into my master's household late in his career, part of the paltry bounty that those men who survived Marcus Antonius' disastrous campaign in Parthia received the next year when they invaded Armenia. Simeon represents a very bitter and disappointing period of time in my master's life; besides, he is an excellent horseman and is responsible for the care of my master's most prized possession, the horse, Ocelus.)

As far as my father is concerned, his name was Lucius, and he was a Roman citizen and settler in the province of Baetica, migrating from Campania as the third son of a Roman farmer who was not going to inherit any of his father's land. This lack of inheritance was another source of bitterness for Lucius, who was a small, bitter man in every sense of the word. He viewed the world and all that was in it as his enemy, always suspicious that those he had dealings with were trying to cheat him in some way. I suspect that it was this quality, more than any injustice on the part of my grandfather that caused Lucius to be left out of any inheritance. It is more likely that my grandfather simply did not want Lucius to be anywhere in the area because of the foulness of his disposition. You may notice, gentle reader, that I refer to my father as Lucius; that is simply because I have no familial feelings towards him whatsoever. I suspect that if it were not for the combination of my size and strength, even as an infant and small boy, and the intercession by my sister Valeria, that I would never have lived long enough to relate this story. He viewed me as little more than one of his mules, and treated me as such as soon as I was old enough and strong enough to provide labor for his farm. It would probably not surprise you that Lucius was not a good farmer, and barely kept his three children and two slaves fed and clothed. In fact, if you, gentle reader, were to be magically transported to Lucius' farm, you would be hard pressed to discern who among our sorry lot were the slaves, and who were the Roman citizens!

Our two slaves were a man and woman, married for all intents and purposes. Their names given to them were Phocas and Gaia, and they were born slaves, although they claimed that their people originally came from Thrace. They were not a couple when Lucius purchased them, but given their lot in life, and their somewhat limited options, they became married, at least in their eyes. It was from Phocas that I learned more about what it is to be a man than from Lucius. And Gaia loved me as much as if she were my mother, for Gaia was barren and never had children of her own. It was not until I was grown that I learned that she was barren only in the sense that she never had children; not because she was unable to do so, but because she and Phocas had made a vow to one of their gods that they would not have a child born as a slave in the same manner they had been. One of my regrets in life is that by the time I was in a position to offer them their freedom, it was too late for them to enjoy the fruits of having children, in more ways than one.

As far as the farm itself, it had originally been granted to a retiring Legionary who found he had no stomach for farming. My grandfather gave Lucius a stake to purchase the land, a couple of slaves, and the essentials needed for starting a farm. I suspect that one of the conditions for this gift was that Lucius move as far away from my grandfather and the rest of Lucius' family as possible, which suited Lucius just as well. As farmland went, it was much better suited for what most of the other settlers in the area did, using the land for vineyards and olive groves, but Lucius had no knowledge of such affairs, and he was much too stubborn and thickheaded to learn. So, he scratched out an extremely modest living, albeit on the backs of Phocas and later me, as I grew old enough to pitch in. We tried to grow corn, enough to feed ourselves, with hopefully just enough as surplus to barter in exchange for the essentials we needed to get by. My earliest memories involve carrying rocks, something our land had in extreme abundance and which were used to build a stone fence, marking off the boundaries of our land. It was the only one of its kind in the area at the time, a fact of which Lucius was extremely proud, and was one of the local curiosities that brought people from the surrounding area to come and gawk. In point of fact, the reason they were gawking was that of all the farmers in the area, he was the only one stupid and stubborn enough to try and raise corn. He misused the land as it was meant to be, to raise olives and grapes, which was something that was completely lost on him. As he grew older, so did his pride in his fence, to the point that whenever he went into town, he would look for the slightest excuse to bring it up in conversation with other citizens, for which they began avoiding him as if he carried the plague.

I realize that I am being harsh regarding my father, but if you had lived as I did, being raised by him, I daresay that you would feel the same way. To me, that fence was a symbol of Lucius' foolish and stubborn pride, and I hated it with a passion, one that has only recently diminished as I have grown older. In fact, when my father died, I prevailed upon my sister Valeria, to whom he had left the land, to tear down that fence, stone by stone. It took almost two weeks for a group of my slaves to finish. At that time, Phocas was still alive, and I had bought his freedom, but he was much too frail to help. My father had never been able to afford more slaves after Phocas and Gaia, as by that time, he had drunk every sesterce that came his way. If he had been able to get his hands on the money I sent to Valeria, he would have drunk that as well. The stones that were left from the fence I used to have a true villa built, in the style that I had seen in the countryside outside Rome, albeit on a more modest scale. But it was a huge improvement over the hovel that I had grown up in, and I was proud and happy that my sister and her husband had one of the nicest homes in the area.

One of the puzzles of my life is how, from such modest stock as my father and mother, I grew to be the size and strength that I am. The strength I earned myself, but I had a frame to pack on muscle in a manner that few others I have met, before or since, have been able to match. As I said, Lucius was a scrawny little thing, although he was wiry strong. It has been such a matter of curiosity for me that whenever I have met another man of almost equal size and strength, if appropriate I have questioned him closely, in order to try to understand if there are some commonalities between us. Of course, the only place where I have regularly met men of my size was on the battlefield, particularly when fighting the Germans, who as a race seem to be almost completely composed of men whose average size is comparable to mine. They usually were not of a mind to speak of it, given that they were most often dead by the time it came to discuss such matters. However, what I have been able to gather from the information I have received over the years seems to point back to a peculiar aspect of my childhood. You see, when I enlisted in the Legions, I was subjected to a diet, that up to that point, I had no experience with whatsoever. As I mentioned, we barely scratched a living out of the soil and had to supplement what grains we did manage to grow with other fare, and that other fare usually meant meat, a lot of meat. Chickens mostly, but there was a fair amount of game. Phocas was a skilled hunter, learning from his father, who

Phocas claimed was a great warrior and hunter in his tribe. I had no reason to doubt him at the time, but in the intervening years, it has been my experience that, when asked, most slaves either claim to have been one themselves, or to be descended from great warriors and the like. It makes me wonder who was around to do the drudgery work in those tribes, since I seem to have met nothing but chiefs and sons and daughters of chiefs.

The truth is that we were ashamed to be eating as much meat as we were because it meant that we could not afford to buy any surplus grain to make bread – something that the other children from the surrounding farms were always quick to point out to us; mocking and ridiculing the children of Lucius Pullus as little better than slaves themselves. And it was true, but it did not mean it hurt any less. Now, however, I have come to the conclusion that it is that very diet we were so ashamed of as children that gave me the size and strength to improve not just my own lot in life, but that of my sister and, most importantly, her son – my nephew and now my adopted son. My strong right arm has also helped shake Rome to its very foundations, and ushered in an age of change that not only rivals, but surpasses any of the great civilizations of the past. But that story is for later.

* * * *

The way I met Vibius Domitius is something that, all these years later, still brings a smile to my face. I was about ten or so, and I had been sent by Phocas to town to fetch a sack of nails to be used to repair one of the sheds on the farm. I suspect that it was just as much to get me out of my father's way as anything else, since by this time, he had taken to starting his drinking before midday and was usually roaring drunk by dinner. When he was in that state, he was even more liable to lash out at me and because I was still recovering from a particularly severe beating from him, administered just a couple of days before, I think Phocas decided that the best thing for me was to get out of the way. He handed me a coin that he had gotten from Lucius' pitifully small hoard, smiled at me, and winked.

"Titus, you need to run to town to get some nails and, if I were you, I wouldn't run there and back."

At this age, I was still deathly afraid of Lucius, and I gulped hard.

"But what if he asks where I am?"

Phocas looked over his shoulder at my father, who was stumbling around. Phocas looked as if he were the master and Lucius the slave as he tried to contain his disdain.

"Don't worry about him; when he gets like this, he has no sense of time. When you come back, I'll insist that you've only been gone for a short time."

Patting me on the back to reassure me, he sent me on my way. The road to town ran directly in front of our property, and if it were not for a series of low hills between our farm and there, it would have been in eyesight. It was a little more than a mile, and as I grew older and Lucius grew drunker, I would find my feet carrying me down that road more and more. This day, the weather was its usually sunny self; a warm breeze helped ease the temperature somewhat, but I was born in this climate and I knew nothing else. Therefore, I loved it. Many years later, as I would stand shivering in some remote place in Gaul, I would think back to the weather with great fondness. As I walked, I imagined what those faraway lands would be like, wondering if I would ever be able to see them or if I was doomed to spend my days on that accursed farm. While I had not started thinking of soldiering at that point, I was already dreaming of ways to get away from Lucius, and I would pass the time on the walk, picking up small rocks and throwing them at an image of my father as I went.

Despite Phocas' instructions, I went immediately to get the nails, instead of passing time in the town. While Astigi would grow a great deal and become better known as Colonia Firma Astigi, at this point, it was still a dusty little settlers' town. There was a small forum with market stalls surrounding it, which is where I would spend most of my time, looking at the goods and wares for sale, but mostly just listening to the adults talk. When you are a child, it is amazing the places you can go and things you can hear because you are more or less invisible to adults, as long as you do not do anything to draw attention to yourself. Although I was only ten, I was still almost as tall as a lot of the adults, but my youth was obvious and only the merchants watched me with a wary eye to make sure I did not steal anything. For some odd reason, despite my poverty, it never really occurred to me to do so. I wandered around aimlessly, holding the bag of nails, taking in the sights and sounds of a small but bustling town. I wandered a bit away from the forum, moving into the area of town where the townspeople lived, marveling as I did every visit at the size and splendor of the buildings that people called their homes. Of course, they were nothing of the sort, but compared to what I lived in, they were definitely very fine homes.

I was drawn to a sound that attracts all children; I heard other children laughing. Excited, because I rarely had contact with children of my own age, I hurried around a corner to see what fun thing was happening, stopping short at what I saw. There were children all right; about a half-dozen or so, mostly boys, but also a couple of girls, but that was not what stopped me. What caught my eye and immediately got my heart pounding was the sight of two of the boys, each one of them holding the leg of another, smaller boy who was dangling upside down, suspended only by the two boys holding his legs. But it was where the poor boy's head was that was responsible for the reaction that I had; it was fully lowered into a chamber pot, one that was obviously full from the stench that reached me where I was standing several feet away. I could hear the poor boy choking on the contents, and it was at that moment that something happened to me that had never happened before. Even with all my father's abuse, I had never once lost my temper, but for some reason, seeing that poor boy, thrashing about as he was being drowned in *cac*, made me very, very angry. So angry that I completely forgot that there were more of them than there were of me; although they were all older than I was, I was still larger than they were, which I am sure had something to do with my bravery.

"Stop that!" I yelled at the top of my voice, with all the power my ten-year-old lungs could muster.

For a matter of perhaps a couple of heartbeats, it appeared as if it worked; both boys holding the other looked up at me in astonishment and, in doing so, brought the boy's head out of the bucket. I could not see anything but the whites of his eyes; his face was covered in excrement and he had tightly pursed his lips to avoid getting it in his mouth. But it did only work for a moment; the two boys glanced at each other, then at their friends, then back at me. Only this time, they were smiling, an evil smile that only youngsters can give each other.

"What?" called one of them. "Did you want to join this little *mentula*?"

They evidently thought the use of profanity was a great joke, because they all guffawed, even one of the girls, although the second remained silent. Suddenly, I felt my knees shaking, but whatever fear I felt was still overruled by my anger.

"Put him down," I said slowly, drawing out the words as if that would have more of an impact.

It did not, at least not in the way that I had hoped. Because they did indeed put him down; by silent consent, they took a step back, pulling the poor boy's head out of the pot, then unceremoniously dumped him on the ground, where he lay gagging and frantically wiping his face.

Menacingly, the boys started to approach me and, for a moment, I was unsure what to do. The thought of running occurred to me, but I immediately dismissed it. They would catch me most likely, I reasoned. I was sure they knew the town better than I did. And even if they did not catch me then, I would have to watch my back every time I came to town. No, I would stand and fight, so I dropped the sack of nails. Up to that time, my only experience with violence had been at the hands of Lucius, but I had made my decision, come what may. The two boys who were holding the other boy's legs were obviously the leaders, and they slowly advanced towards me, one on either side.

Without taking their eyes off of me, one said to the other, "What do you say, Aulus? Do you want to beat this *cunnus*, or shall I?"

The boy who spoke was the taller of the two, with gapped teeth and wearing a filthy tunic, dirty even by my standards.

The other boy laughed and shook his head. "No, Marcus. Why would I want to deprive you of all the fun?"

Marcus laughed at this as well, and suddenly lunged at me, catching me completely by surprise. He lowered his head and tackled me around the midsection, no doubt with the intent of driving me to the ground, but he seriously underestimated my weight and strength. It was now that I saw the benefit of carrying all those rocks, as I barely budged when he crashed into me. Without thinking, I reached down with my left arm, encircled his neck, then proceeded to hit him across his exposed back with my other fist. He let out a yelp of pain, prompting Aulus to growl at me and charge as well, except instead of using the same tactic as Marcus had, he stopped short and swung his fist. It connected squarely on my cheek. As lights burst inside my skull, I staggered a step back, shaking my head to clear it. Aulus clearly expected me to fall, but although it did send me back a step, I maintained my balance. I stopped hitting Marcus and, still with my arm around his neck, I flung him directly into Aulus, sending them both tumbling to the ground.

It was then the other two boys who had been watching decided to pitch in and take me to the ground, because they both came running at me. Instead of trying to meet them head on, I dropped to one knee just as they launched themselves at me, and they both went flying over my head, landing on top of each other.

One of them let out a yelp of pain, followed by a string of oaths.

"My arm! You broke my arm, you cocksucker!"

"I didn't do it," the other exclaimed indignantly. "That *cunnus* did it, not me."

Aulus and Marcus had regained their feet and I waited for them, a mistake, I know, but it *was* my first battle! I would not make the same mistake again. Warily this time, they approached me, looking for an opening. Realizing that I was surrounded, I retreated a few steps and put my back to the wall. I looked over the two boys' shoulders to see the boy I had rescued, his face somewhat cleaner, standing unsteadily and gazing around him as if looking for something. I hoped he had not been knocked silly before they dunked him, I thought. Suddenly, the three remaining boys rushed me at the same time, this time with fists flailing, and I lashed out in the same manner. I was hit a number of times, but I had been toughened by the beatings that Lucius had inflicted on me; having children hitting me was almost a relief. Almost. I connected squarely with the third boy's nose, squashing it flat and forcing blood to squirt out from under my fist, as if I had hit a ripe plum. It startled me for a moment, it being the first time I had ever drawn blood, although it would be far, far from the last. Even so, my second's hesitation cost me dearly, as one of the other boys drove his fist into my stomach, almost knocking the wind out of me. My knees buckled and I felt myself starting to lose my balance, so I lashed out and grabbed Marcus by the throat, determined to pull him down with me if I fell.

It was at that precise moment I heard what I can only describe as the kind of screeching a *numen* must make when you violate its sanctity, and I felt more than saw Marcus suddenly knocked to the ground, his throat jerking out of my hand. A second later, Aulus suffered the same fate, and I realized what the boy had been looking for, as he stood over them with a stave from a barrel of some sort.

Shaking with rage, he began to strike the two boys on the ground, over and over, all the while screaming out, "Who's the *cunnus* now, huh, Marcus? Who's the *mentula* now, Aulus?"

Both boys were now crying like babies, blubbering for the other boy to stop beating them, but he did not look like he was in any hurry to stop.

Careful not to be hit by him myself, I stepped towards him and said as nicely as I could, "I think they've learned their lesson, don't you?"

He stopped with the stave above his head, still ready to strike down, and looked at me, then down at the boys. The third boy had crawled off with his friend with the broken arm, skulking off to lick their wounds, leaving Marcus and Aulus to their fates. The stave hovered in midair as the boy tried to decide whether to continue or not.

Then he asked them, in a much calmer voice than before, "What say you? Have you two learned your lesson?"

Both boys immediately began groveling, insisting that they had absolutely learned their lesson, and would be model citizens from this point forward.

Shaking his head gravely, clearly beginning to enjoy himself, he said dubiously, "I don't know. I think that you might be lying to me, that you're going to run off and plot some sort of revenge."

"No, no, Vibius," they said, and I learned the boy's name for the first time. "We'll swear on anything. We've learned our lesson and will never bother you again."

"Swear on Jupiter's Stone," Vibius answered instantly, and I am sure you know, gentle reader, that this is the most sacred oath a Roman can swear by.

Both boys immediately began babbling, but Vibius stopped them, insisting that they get on their knees before him as he held the stave, ready to strike.

"Say it like you mean it," Vibius said, and both boys solemnly swore by Jupiter's Stone that Vibius would never be troubled by Marcus and Aulus for as long as they all lived.

They were lying, of course, and both Vibius and I knew it; anyone who would stick another's head into *cac* is not to be trusted in the slightest. But the battle was won for the day.

Once they had sworn, Vibius said, "Now get out of here," and they jumped to their feet and started to slink past me.

I do not know what possessed me, but I called out to them, "If you lie, *I* swear by Jupiter's Stone that I'll beat you both worse than you've ever been beaten."

They glared at me with undisguised hatred, but said nothing and just kept walking. As it turned out, one of us was telling the truth that day, but that is for later.

It was then that I turned to face the boy who would become my greatest friend and companion, growing to be a man I would fight beside, bleed beside, and love more than any man can love a brother. He was smaller than I was, of course, but he was even small for his age. However, even then, he had a barrel chest that made his arms stick out at an angle from his body. He was typical of almost every small man that I have ever known, which is no surprise, given how life has treated them, in that he was quick to offend and slow to back down. He had serious brown eyes, and a thatch of wiry hair that looked unkempt, no matter how he tried to tame it. I am no judge of another man's looks, but judging by the way women fell at his feet, I would have to say that he was very handsome, with a winning smile and a quick wit, coupled with a big mouth that got him, and us, in our share of trouble. We stood for a moment, eyeing each other, not noticing that one of the girls was still there, and slowly walking up to us. Despite the obvious smell coming from Vibius, she smiled at him, and somehow I knew that what I had witnessed involved her in some way.

"Thank you, Vibius, for…" She chose her words. "…trying to defend me."

She was a vision; I felt my heart jump, immediately thinking she was even more beautiful than my own Valeria, who, until that point, I believed was absolutely the most beautiful girl in the world. But this girl was in a different class; golden hair with smooth white skin, and she had beautifully luminescent blue eyes that always seemed to be laughing, no matter what her mood. Vibius was suddenly overtaken by some *numen* that stole his tongue, and the silence became awkward as he looked at the ground.

Finally, he spoke. "I just wish I had been able to do more."

"But you did," she exclaimed. "They left me alone after you stepped in!"

"Only because they were dipping my head in a bucket of *cac,*" he mumbled, and despite myself, I laughed out loud. He whirled on me and looked at me for a moment, then started laughing himself.

"I guess that was funny," he admitted.

"It's only because they outnumbered you," the girl said diplomatically.

Still chuckling, despite his appearance, Vibius responded, "I doubt it. Anyway," he suddenly looked shy again, "Thank you, Juno."

Looking mischievous, she said, "I would give you a kiss," blushing as she said it, and hurriedly added, "on the cheek, of course, if you weren't.....you weren't, you know."

Embarrassed, she looked away.

Vibius stood there as if he had been struck mute and, after a moment, Juno said, "Well, I need to go. I'm sure *tata* is wondering where I am."

Waving to us, she departed, leaving two love-struck boys in her wake. After she disappeared from sight, I stuck my hand out in the manner that I had seen Lucius do when he was concluding a deal to sell his surplus grain.

"I am Titus Pullus," I said. It was not until he looked down at his hand ashamedly that I realized my error. He could not shake my hand because it was covered in filth, so I hurriedly said, "Let's go find a place for you to clean up."

When he agreed with me, I turned to pick up my sack of nails, and my heart sank. One of those *cunni* had stolen the bag, and I would now have to go back to Lucius empty-handed. I was doomed.

It was a long walk home, one that Vibius volunteered to walk with me, as he had nothing better to do. Now that he smelled better, I found his company very enjoyable. I had not really had much contact with other children of my age, and Vibius would become my best and longest friend. We found that we had much in common, despite our disparity in size. Like me, he was not particularly liked by his father; however, it was for exactly the opposite reason. Vibius was the runt of the litter; he had four brothers and three sisters alive at that point, and he was the youngest. He was viewed as basically useless by his father for doing any of the heavy work as a tanner, his father's profession. This was something of a blessing, however, because it gave Vibius more freedom than his other brothers had, a fact that they were quick to remind him of with a swift kick in his rear if he got close enough. As we walked, I noticed that Vibius almost had to run to keep up with me, but he did not seem to mind. Aside from our upbringing, we also found we had a common desire to see things and do great deeds that were not available to us here in Hispania Ulterior. As we got closer to my farm, we tried to think up a reasonable excuse for my returning empty-handed, but really could not come up with anything. We stood at the path from the road that led to our farm, and once again, he thanked me for intervening that day. We shook hands solemnly, and I turned to face my fate.

In times such as this, it was in my best interest to go find Phocas before I faced Lucius, since he generally knew what to do in order to soften my father's punishment. After my father's beatings, I usually went to either Valeria or Gaia for comfort, but before the fact, I always sought out Phocas. I found him at the shed, and I could tell he was irritated himself, which did not bode well for me. No matter how much he despised my father, he was still a slave and, as a slave, had to put up with Lucius' abuse of him. From appearances, it looked as if Lucius was in rare form this day, although I did not see him anywhere around.

Phocas glanced up and saw me coming, and a hint of impatience showed in his face as he held his hand out and snapped, "I didn't tell you to be gone THAT long." I gulped hard, and only shook my head, which made him even angrier. "What, are you mute as well now? Where are the nails?"

"I...they were stolen from me," I stammered out.

Phocas' eyes narrowed as he asked, "What do you mean stolen from you? How could they be stolen from you? You had to carry them."

"I...I set them down for a moment." He cut me off angrily.

"Boy, why would you do something stupid like that? Haven't I told you that you have to watch every step you make when you go into town?"

I held my hands up, mutely asking him for a space so that I could explain. He quieted, and then motioned for me to proceed. I told him what had happened, how I had met Vibius, and how I had gotten in a fight. His expression changed as I told him, and he had a look of concern when I got to the part about the fight, and he stepped closer to examine me. Seeing a bruise forming on my cheek, his anger evaporated as quickly as it had come.

"Titus, are you all right?"

He began pulling my tunic this way and that, looking for other marks, but I protested that I was fine. Once I finished, he stood there thoughtfully, trying to think what to do to replace the nails and, presumably, to keep me from being beaten by Lucius.

Finally, he said, "All right. I know what I can tell your father; don't worry about him. You need to go have Gaia see to that bruise, and get cleaned up. It's almost time for dinner anyway."

I turned to leave, and then Phocas called me back. I turned to him, and he had a strange expression on his face.

"I...I'm proud of you, Titus. It does my heart good to see that you're willing to protect those weaker than you. Even if your father wouldn't be proud, I am."

To that moment, it had never occurred to me that I had done anything remotely noteworthy; I had seen an injustice perpetrated, and I had stepped in to stop it. But I realized that Phocas was right; Lucius would have called me a fool. The one person who treated me as a son was a slave, not my own father. I left the shed in a thoughtful mood.

Vibius and I became inseparable over the next several weeks. Every chance I got, I snuck away and went into town, and would go to Vibius' father's tanning shop, where Vibius would be waiting for me, trying to avoid being underfoot with his father. As soon as he saw me come up the alleyway where his father's shop was located, he would scamper out and we would go roaming around, looking for mischief and adventure. In the beginning of our friendship, we still had the enmity of Marcus, Aulus, and their gang, but now that I had tasted combat, I found that I was eager for more. No doubt, it was a consequence of being the biggest and strongest child, and having absolutely no fear because, in my mind, I was invincible. It would not be until I was much older that I would learn the hard way how wrong I was. But at the time, I enjoyed the feeling I got after we had one more incident with Marcus and Aulus and their gang.

Vibius and I were walking near the forum, closely examining an interesting rock that I had found on my walk into town, convinced that because of its uniqueness, it had to be fabulously valuable. We were gloating and talking about what we would do with the riches that would come from our sale of it, when I was struck in the head by a broken-off piece of paving stone. It was a glancing blow, not hitting me squarely, but it was enough to knock me to my knees, with my ears ringing and seeing all sorts of lights in my head. Marcus, Aulus, and their friends came bursting out of the places where they were hiding, behind some empty crates, whooping with excitement. I heard Vibius gasp in surprise, and I noticed that when I touched my hand to my head where I had been hit, it came away bloody. I looked up and there seemed to be twice as many boys as last time, and I would have sworn on Jupiter's Stone that Marcus and Aulus had twins. This time, I was the one in trouble, but Vibius, instead of running away as he should have, let out a howl of outrage and charged directly at the other boys, picking up the stone that had hit me and hurling it as he charged. Caught off guard, the boys hesitated for a moment before they realized that they still outnumbered us. Vibius charged directly at Marcus, fists flailing, and the larger boy found himself trying to protect himself from my friend. This gave me time to gather my wits, pull myself to my feet and, within a few heartbeats, I hurled myself at Aulus, swinging wildly.

The resulting melee did not last long, but the outcome was such that neither Marcus, Aulus, nor any of the other boys bothered us ever again; in particular, I beat Aulus severely as a reminder that he had broken his oath. Whenever they saw us, they would steer a wide path around us, which amused Vibius and me every time it happened.

It was that battle that first got Vibius and me talking about the idea of joining the Legions. Like most boys, we idolized the Legions, and because there were a number of retired Legionaries in town and the nearby farms, we began pestering them about life in the army. Most of them were happy to talk about it, and we could tell they missed it. Some were not so happy, however, and we soon learned to avoid these dark and bitter men. Besides, we had no use for tales of woe; we wanted to hear only of adventures and battles, heroism and glory, which most of these men were happy to supply. We were relentless in our quest to learn as much as we could, and begged them to show us their *gladii, pila, scuta,* and the mementoes of their campaigns. We saw human teeth, strung together on a necklace, the owner of which claimed was one tooth from every man he had killed in battle. As we were to learn later, it was just as likely that he bought the necklace from another Legionary, or won it at dice, but at the time, we believed every word. We asked them to show their scars and tell us the stories behind them, and they had a rapt audience as they spun wild tales of charging elephants, scythed chariots mowing men down like wheat, and the brave Legionaries who brought all of their enemies crashing to defeat. Several of the Legionaries had served with Pompey Magnus, and it was clear that they still revered their general all these years later. At that time, Pompey was the First Man of Rome, and his former Legionaries basked in the reflected glow of his accomplishments. All of them had been *triarii,* or at least claimed to be, but when I boasted that one day I would be a *triarii,* they informed me that the army was no longer using the division of *hastati, principes, triarii, velites,* and the like. Now, you were either a Legionary or you were an auxiliary, the auxiliary being non-citizens. Both Vibius and I had been born Roman citizens, so that meant that we could serve in the Legions, which excited us immensely.

We soon found that the best place to find retired Legionnaires was at one of the local taverns, of which there were three in the town then. Although they were retired and supposed to be farmers, it seemed to me that most of the "farmers" spent the bulk of their time sitting with others like them, swapping stories of their time in the Legions. Just a few years before, when I was only six or seven, there was a great slave rebellion, led by a slave named Spartacus. One of the men in the town had been in the army led by Crassus that finally put down the revolt, and he told lurid tales of mass slaughter, vividly describing the sights and sounds of the final battle that saw the defeat of Spartacus. The man's name was Tertorius, and Vibius and I could tell that, despite his hatred for the army of slaves, he had a grudging respect for Spartacus. He claimed to have been present nearby when Spartacus fell, slashing and killing a path through the Romans, all with the goal of getting to Crassus personally and killing him.

He never made it; he was cut down by members of Crassus' bodyguard, but as Tertorius said, "He may have been a slave, but he certainly didn't die like one."

He shuddered as he said this, then hastily drained his cup of wine before calling for another. Tertorius seemed to be in a state of perpetual inebriation, and as much as we enjoyed his stories, both Vibius and I were looking for more than just tales; we wanted someone to show us how to BE a soldier.

The revolt of Sertorius had only been quelled a couple of years before, and although there was fighting all around the area where I grew up, it never touched our farm or the town. Several men in the region served with Sertorius, and once the rebellion was crushed by Pompey, and after the death of Sertorius, those who survived came back home to resume their lives. There was one man in particular, nicknamed Cyclops because, like Sertorius, he had only one eye, and was rumored to have been one of the greatest soldiers in Sertorius' army, but unlike most of the other retired Legionnaires, he did not spend time in the taverns. He was of average height, and his dark hair was just beginning to show streaks of gray, and if one could look past the great, puckering hole where his eye had been, he could have been considered as handsome, with a fine aquiline nose and strong chin.

He was rarely seen in town, and it was only through a stroke of fate that Vibius and I got to meet him. It was from Cyclops, whose real name was Quintus Ausonius, that we learned the most about what it meant to be in the Legions. He had come to my father's farm when he heard that our mule had died, and he had a couple for sale. Normally, Lucius would never allow me or either of my sisters to watch him conduct business, but this time was different for some reason. Lucius introduced me to Cyclops, whose good eye looked me up and down, as if he were appraising another mule he was thinking of buying. He did not offer his hand, but merely nodded at me once he had finished his inspection, and turned back to Lucius. I watched as Cyclops practically skinned my father alive on the deal, which raised Cyclops a great deal in my esteem. He seemed to sense the weakness in Lucius, and showed no mercy to him, arranging to take not only all of the surplus of that year's crop, but the hand of my sister Livia, who had just turned thirteen years of age. Cyclops was a shrewd judge of character, that I saw immediately, because somehow he had divined that Lucius greatly treasured Livia, and not in the normal way that a father treasures a daughter. Valeria and I knew the things my father did to my younger sister, and I am ashamed to say that, while I was happy for Livia that she would be out of my father's clutches, I was more worried about the fate of Valeria now that Livia was going to leave, and wished for that reason that my father had said no. For, although Valeria at this point was almost sixteen, and in my eyes just as beautiful as Livia, for some reason, my father never violated her the way he did Livia, or at least so I believed. At the time, my best surmise is that he knew how close we were and, being the coward that he was, he worried that one day I would become old enough and strong enough to exact vengeance upon him for hurting the one person I loved more than any other in this world. But that is just a guess; who knows what goes on in the minds of sad little men like Lucius?

But Lucius needed a mule more than he needed a bedmate. Perhaps in his thinking, he knew that Valeria would be a fitting substitute. For Livia, her fate was a mixed blessing indeed; while she was even happier about escaping Lucius, the very sight of Cyclops, which struck fear into the hearts of grown men on the battlefield, had to be all the more terrifying for my sister. For his part, Cyclops appeared no more pleased than if he had purchased a fine breeding stallion to make more mules, but as we learned, his looks were deceiving. Although he was a fierce warrior, he turned out to be a very loving husband for Livia, and though she was destined to die as my mother did, bearing a child for Cyclops, the years that she lived with him were the happiest of her life. Livia had not experienced her womanly flow yet, so the deal was made that upon the onset of her monthly time, only then would she come to Cyclops.

That event happened some three months later, and for reasons I can only guess at, I was given the task by Lucius of escorting her to the farm of Cyclops. Perhaps he was afraid that he would have second thoughts, or that somehow he would betray his true feelings for Livia and expose the fact that he thought of her as a lover, not a daughter. Whatever the reason, I was as happy as I always was when presented with an excuse to leave our farm. The way to Cyclops' farm passed through the town, so I collected Vibius as we passed through, and we began talking excitedly of the chance to talk to Cyclops, completely oblivious to my poor sister's state of anxiety. I am afraid that we did not help matters much, talking as we were about some of the bloodier exploits that had been attributed to him, so that by the time we arrived at his farm, Livia was in a state of acute panic and fear.

The farm was small, but the property was very well maintained, with the outbuildings that housed the animals and the feed sturdily built and in good repair. While Vibius and Livia waited out on the road, with Livia holding all of her worldly possessions, I went to the house to announce our arrival and our purpose. I must admit, I was somewhat nervous as well; after all, this was a very adult thing that I was doing, and I was still just shy of eleven years old.

Cyclops was seated at the table, working on a piece of tack when I knocked on his open door. As he looked up, I noticed that his right hand dropped to the handle of a *gladius*, sheathed but lying on the bench next to him. He stared at me for a second, his good eye narrowing as he tried to place who I was, then he realized that I was the son of Lucius. He also realized why I was here, and his look changed to one that I was unable to identify at that tender age, but looking back now, I realize it was that look that expresses both anticipation and a little unease. It never occurred to me that a man such as Cyclops would be nervous about anything, much less meeting my sister for the first time, but now I understand. For men like Cyclops and for the man I would become, the terrors of battle are nothing compared to the terror of facing a woman who you are going to spend your future with; the problems that the matter of marriage poses are much more difficult to solve than facing a problem in combat. In battle, the most direct way of solving a problem is to kill it and, although technically, one could do that to his wife as long as he had just cause, I do not think any man enters

48

the state of matrimony thinking that he will have to avail himself of that choice at some point. Looking back, I am sure that this was what was running through Cyclops' mind, but all I could see was some sort of hesitation that I did not understand, and frankly, with which I was growing impatient. If this was how he froze up when meeting a girl, especially my sister, it was hard for me to imagine him being the great warrior that we had been told so much about.

When he did not speak, I finally cleared my throat and announced, in as grown up a voice as I could manage, "*Salve, Cyc…er, I mean, Quintus Ausonius,*" repeating the lines that had been drilled into me by Lucius. "I am Titus Pullus, come to bring you my sister for marriage, in accordance with the agreement struck by you and my father, Lucius Pullus. My sister has reached the time of her…" I must confess that I had to suppress a very unworthy giggle at this point. "…womanhood, and is therefore now ready to be your wife."

Turning back to the outside, where Livia was standing, shaking like a leaf in a gale, with Vibius beside her, wide-eyed and looking everywhere around him, I motioned her to step inside. For a moment, she hesitated and appeared as if she was ready to bolt, but a look passed between us and, in that look, we communicated perfectly. This was her only chance to avoid the horrible fate of carrying her father's child, and bringing eternal shame to our entire family line, all the way back to our ancestors. Standing erect and pulling her shoulders back, Livia stepped through the doorway with the confidence of a queen, and I was prouder than I had ever been that she was my sister.

She entered the house, then went to her knees with her head bowed, saying quietly but strongly, "*Salve,* Quintus Ausonius. I am Livia, daughter of Lucius Pullus and," what she said next surprised me because it was not part of the ritual, "sister to my beloved brother, Titus Pullus. I am here to be your wife."

At the mention of my name, my vision started to blur, and I felt a quite unaccustomed lump in my throat. I could not remember crying for no reason before this, and I felt shamefully weak. I bit my lip to stop it from quivering and forced myself to look directly at Cyclops, challenging him to mock me, despite my age. But he had no eyes for me; he was looking down at Livia, as at the same instant he stepped forward, holding out his hands to take hers in them. I was struck by how much larger his hands were than hers, and how much darker and weather-beaten.

In a surprisingly soft and gentle voice, Cyclops responded, "*Salve,* Livia, daughter of Lucius. Welcome to my home, my hearth, and to my life. I will always treat you with the honor and respect you deserve, and together we will build a life, with many children and much happiness."

Livia looked up then, in surprise, and I watched a flush start from her neck, going all the way to the roots of her hair. Keeping her hands in his, she rose and stood facing him as they gazed at each other, and now I was getting uncomfortable. I might have been only eleven, but I knew what that look meant, and I think what shocked me more than seeing it on Cyclops was the fact that Livia shared that same look. They had completely forgotten I was there. Finally, I cleared my throat, pulling them from their inspection of each other. Startled, they both looked at me and gave a little laugh, which then caused them to laugh even more, once they realized that they had shared the same reaction.

"I must leave now," I stammered. "I will tell Luc....Father that you have arrived unharmed." I turned to leave, then remembered the last line I was supposed to utter. "May the gods smile on this house and this marriage," I mumbled, then turned heel and left.

Vibius was standing just outside the door, straining to see what was happening, and I ran right into him, bowling him head over heels in the dust, and staggering me so that I fell against the doorjamb. Mortally embarrassed, I grabbed Vibius off the ground and gave him a great kick in his rear, which sent him tumbling yet again. He howled in protest, but seeing the look in my eye, scrambled to his feet and ran headlong towards the road, with me in hot pursuit.

We ran for maybe a mile, long enough for the anger to leave me so that when I caught up with him, I was laughing at the memory of his panic-stricken face, looking over his shoulder as I chased him. Hearing me laugh, he slowed down and looked back, scowling suspiciously, suspecting some trick on my part. I had my hands on my knees and was panting for breath, and laughing at the same time.

I pointed at him and howled, "You should have seen your face! You would have thought Cerberus was after you!"

Still scowling, but having stopped running, Vibius shot back, "It may as well have been Cerberus, when you get like that. I was sure you were going to kill me!"

I continued to laugh, but pulled myself upright, and walked towards Vibius. Immediately, his eyes narrowed, and he began to move away from me, ready to break out in a run.

Putting my hands out towards him, I cried, "*Pax,* Vibius, *pax*! I'm not mad anymore. I promise."

Still unconvinced, he said, "You promise?"

I nodded. "I promise."

"Swear on Jupiter's Stone that you're not mad."

"*Bona Dea*," I said in exasperation. Then, seeing he was not budging, I raised my right hand in the air, and said, "I swear on Jupiter's Stone I'm not mad, and I won't try to hurt you in any way." Dropping my hand, I asked, "There. Satisfied?"

Nodding, he waited for me to catch up. Before we had gone much farther, we were both laughing hysterically again.

My sister's marriage to Cyclops gave Vibius and me the perfect excuse to spend time at his farm. What we learned was that Cyclops was not surly; he was in fact rather shy, made more so because of his disfigurement. Once he got used to our constant company, and resigned himself to the fact that we were not going anywhere, he began talking to us; not as boys, but as men. It made us enormously proud that he would deign to speak to us in such a manner, never realizing that we were the only friends he had. At least, the only ones still alive. Livia blossomed almost immediately, and it was clear for all to see how happy she was. There was a double bonus to us because her happiness was the direct cause of Lucius' discontent; I think, in his heart of hearts, he was hoping that she would come running home. Instead, it gave me a much-welcomed sanctuary from my father's coldness and hostility, and it became a second home for me. I do not believe at first that Cyclops was too thrilled about it, but I think Vibius and I grew on him, and slowly he began to open up with us. He was extremely reluctant to talk about his experiences in the Legions, which he had served in before fighting for Sertorius, and would never discuss it in front of Livia, but there is nothing quite as persistent as a boy with glory on his mind so that slowly but surely, he began to share more and more with us.

The next couple of years passed in this manner; I spent as little time around Lucius as I could, which suited him fine, as long as I got my daily chores done. I would wake up before dawn, go through my morning chores, then well before midday, I would be at Cyclops' farm, helping him as well. For some reason, I did not begrudge the fact that he put me to work, doing so willingly, as did Vibius, who was in much the same position I was in. As long as he did the minimum his father expected, there were plenty of other, stronger sons to help with the work of tanning. I would meet Vibius next to the forum almost every day and, once a week, we would buy a meat pie or some treat from money that we had "found." I was growing rapidly, and was in the stage where my clothes and, more importantly, my shoes never fit, so I tended to go barefoot everywhere. One day in particular I remember, because Vibius and I had decided that the time for talk had passed; it was time for Cyclops to start showing us what a Legionary needed to know in order to survive in battle. Vibius had turned fourteen the month before, and I was another month away from turning thirteen, but already I was taller than a lot of adults, and if truth be known, I was stronger as well. What I lacked at this point was coordination; I was just as likely to trip over my own feet as over any obstacle, and I was desperately embarrassed by my clumsiness. I was hoping that Cyclops would be able to give me some exercises that would help make me more coordinated and graceful, enabling me to move without being a danger to myself. Vibius hoped for lessons as well, but for different reasons. He had grown tired of living under my shadow, relying on me for protection. Nobody had touched him in years, but that did not stop them from mocking him for needing my help to keep the other boys of the village at bay. While he was filling out, he was still painfully short, and he was afraid that unless he grew more, he would be considered too small for the Legions. If that happened, we would both be crushed, but with the typical naïve optimism of youth, we had decided that with the help of Cyclops, we would be sufficiently trained so that if the moment came where the *conquisitores* turned him down, he would be able to show them such prowess that somehow the rules would be bent for us. As I said, we were very naïve, but as it turned out, that very summer, Vibius grew several inches, making it over the minimum height by more than an inch.

When we arrived at Cyclops' that fateful day, we found him currying the mules. We had gotten into such a routine that, without a word, Vibius and I would begin pitching in, knowing what needed to be done without being asked.

We would usually pass the first little while in this way, in silence, waiting for Cyclops to heave a sigh and ask with mock weariness, "All right, what do you want to know today?"

We had decided that Vibius would make the request when the moment came, because it was usually me who did the talking for us, and we thought that by changing this routine, it would be clear to Cyclops how much this meant to both of us.

He did seem surprised when Vibius spoke, and I could hear the slight tremor in my friend's voice as he said, "Cyclops, Titus and I have decided that we're old enough and ready for you to actually show us things we need to know for when we join the Legions."

If Cyclops was surprised, he did not show it. I imagine he had probably been expecting such a request, because without a word, he turned and left the shed, leaving Vibius and me puzzled, although, by this time, we had become used to some of his odd ways. We were not sure whether to follow or wait, so we decided to stay in the shed.

After a few moments, Cyclops poked his head in and asked irritably, "Well? Are you going to stay in there or come out? We're wasting time."

We came barreling out of the shed to find Cyclops, standing in front of a pile of armor. The gear had obviously seen action, but it was still oiled and well cared for. We stood dumbly, staring at it, not sure what we were supposed to do, but I know we both had idiot grins on our face at the sight of the stuff on the ground. Motioning to us to come to him, Cyclops reached down and picked up a vest made of chain mail, known as the *lorica hamata*, the piece of equipment we wear to protect our bodies, which is just now being phased out for the *lorica segmentata*, or segmented armor, and motioned me to come closer. I approached, and he had me lift my arms, then dropped the mail shirt onto my shoulders. I almost fell down from the weight; it felt like it weighed as much as I did, but it was really only about twenty-two pounds. I grimaced and straightened up, not wanting to show how much of a strain it was, and stood there, hoping that the trembling I felt in my legs was not visible. It was Vibius' turn, as Cyclops held out another shirt, this one much shabbier and harder used than the one I had been given. There were several links missing where wire had been used to keep things together, and it was a little longer than mine, which led me to believe that this was not Roman. Cyclops did the same thing to Vibius, dropping it onto his shoulders, but poor Vibius collapsed into a heap immediately, and lay there, unable to get up. I could not help laughing, but one look from Cyclops' good eye shut me up immediately.

Cyclops nudged Vibius with a toe and said quietly, "Quit your squawking. Stand up."

"I can't," gasped Vibius as he struggled to get his feet under him.

"I said, stand up," repeated Cyclops, just as quietly, but with a new undertone in his voice that made me begin to feel apprehensive.

"I'm trying, but I can't get my feet…" Vibius never finished the sentence.

With amazing speed, Cyclops launched a kick at Vibius that hit him square in the chest, knocking him flat. I gasped and moved to help Vibius, and before I knew it, I was flying through the air from another kick, landing a few feet away, the wind knocked out of me. Cyclops aimed another kick at Vibius, catching him in the side, causing Vibius to let out a moan of pain. However, when Cyclops took a step to launch another kick, somehow Vibius found the strength to roll quickly out of the way, then to climb almost as quickly to his feet. Meanwhile, I had regained my feet as well, and we both stood there unsteadily, glaring at Cyclops, who looked placidly at us, a half-smile on his face.

"Why in Hades did you do that?" I demanded, also ready to bolt if my question was not well received.

"You said you wanted to learn to be in the Legions," Cyclops responded calmly. "And that's what it will be like."

So began our tutelage with Cyclops. Before we ever picked up a weapon, we had to learn to move around in our *loricae*, no matter what tasks we were assigned to do. We started just wearing the *hamata* and doing the normal things we helped Cyclops with. The first couple of weeks, Vibius and I would trudge home, swearing as we left that we had suffered enough, then talking ourselves into returning by the next day. Every day I left my farm and went into the village, I half-expected Vibius not to show up; as hard as it was on me, it was even harder on poor Vibius. But every morning, he was there, more out of the fear of being shamed in front of me, his best friend, than anything else. And if truth be known, it was exactly the same reason that kept me walking down that road every day. That and the secret knowledge that every day, as I got stronger, it made Lucius fear me more and more. I was now taller than he was, and broader in the shoulders, although I had just turned but thirteen years of age. It was only because I knew that anything I did to Lucius would cause him to exact retribution on Valeria, Phocas, and Gaia that kept me from striking him down when he made one of his sour, bitter comments to me. I swore that I would have my vengeance for all the insults, but that I would bide my time until I could do so without worrying about those I loved. I think Lucius knew that as well, and was just as unwilling to force a reckoning as I was, for different reasons.

Slowly, Vibius and I became accustomed to the extra weight and how it changed our sense of balance. As soon as Cyclops saw that we had gotten somewhat acclimated, he produced two *galeae* and plopped them on our heads. It may not seem like much, but the extra weight of the helmet, in some ways, was harder to deal with than the *lorica*. With the mail, it was spread over a wider area of the body, so that although it weighed more, it was more evenly distributed, especially once he allowed us to start wearing the *baltea*, the Legionary's belt that allows the mail to ride better on your hips. With the helmet, it was all resting on our necks, and it was not long on that first day before they felt the strain. Also, the *galeae* were large and we had not felt caps underneath the *galeae*; Livia ended up making us each a cap, but that took a few days. In the meantime, the accursed thing kept sliding all around, particularly if we had to execute a sudden or violent movement. I think that was the most I ever saw Cyclops laugh, when he would suddenly bark out a command that forced us to turn in another direction, or jump one way or another, causing our bodies to face one way, while the *galeae* would sit stock still, facing in the original direction. Vibius and I would stand there, peering out around the dangling cheekguard of the helmet, seething with embarrassment, while Cyclops would howl with laughter.

However, we learned quickly not to reach up and correct the position of our helmet, because even while still laughing, Cyclops would suddenly bash us on top of the helmet and roar, "Nobody told you to correct yourself!"

The first week we wore the *galeae*, we both had headaches by the end of the day, both from the strain of wearing them and from the bashing that Cyclops would give us for some offense, real or imagined.

Despite this, Vibius and I continued trudging back and forth, alternately hating and loving what we were going through. Because despite the pain involved, we could both tell that we were getting stronger, and we were making progress. We fancied ourselves almost as good as in the Legions already, and we would excitedly talk about the possibility of another insurrection occurring, one in which Rome was so desperate that they sent out a call for volunteers. In our fevered imaginations, the Praetor would be in such peril that he could not afford to turn anyone away, even a couple of raw youths like ourselves. We would gloat at the idea of the surprise of our fellow Legionaries and all of Rome when Vibius and Titus stood in the first line of battle, and acquitted themselves as well as any full-grown soldier of Rome! We would argue back and forth as to who would make the first kill of an enemy, and how many we would slay, arriving at Cyclops in such a frenzy of patriotism and zeal that we could not wait to start the next phase of our training. Finally, one day, Cyclops was happy to oblige, depositing a *scutum* for each of us, emblazoned with the symbol of Sertorius' army. These were Spanish *scuta*, being flat instead of the curved shape that we would carry in the Legions, but it was made of thicker wood as a result, and was a bit heavier than the Roman version. Again, we started using muscles in ways that they were not accustomed to working, as we tried to carry the *scuta* everywhere, only putting them down to perform tasks that required two hands.

Cyclops would wait until we were the most absorbed in what we were doing, then roar, "*Porta arma, porta arma!*" requiring us each to grab our *scutum* and run to an imaginary muster field and fall in, side by side.

I can only imagine how ridiculous we looked, wearing oversized *loricae* and *galeae*, each carrying a *scutum* more than half his size. I say "we" to be kind; because I was of adult size, it was really Vibius who provided the more comical sight, but we shared everything, so I was perfectly willing to accept that I looked as silly as he did. We still had no weapons at this point, so, at best, we looked like raw *tirones* in their first month and not true Legionaries. We got so that we could stop whatever we were doing and fall in with enough speed that Cyclops could find no fault with us, and he finally grunted that we were not the worst he had seen, causing our spirits to soar to the heavens.

* * * *

It was about this time that Valeria and I had a conversation. She had been watching my comings and goings with quiet amusement, having long since grown accustomed to my games and fantasies of glory. But I was approaching the age when enlisting in the Legions was not that far off, and I think when she saw how quickly I was taking to the work of being a soldier that it scared her. Although I did not yet know it, starting with the formation of the 10th Legion by the Praetor of the province, enlistments were going to be raised from twelve to a minimum of sixteen years, and Rome was in a period of almost constant warfare, as she has been most of my life. Valeria was just like any female; while she knew that men thirsted for glory, she could never understand why. For Valeria, the idea of getting married and raising a family meant that her husband should be there by her side, and it worried her that all men felt the way I did about going to war. And as much as I loved Valeria, and still do to this day, I knew that she was jealous of Livia's happiness, so that every day that went by that saw Lucius refuse yet another suitor for her, she saw her chance for happiness dwindling day by day. She was now close to eighteen years old, well past time to marry, and she was very beautiful. This is not just a brother's blind love; I knew she was beautiful because every time I was in town, I was constantly being approached by young and old men, begging for an introduction to her, and they would wax poetically about how she was as Aphrodite in their eyes. Frankly, it made me a little nauseous; she was my sister and I loved her, but they had never seen her in the mornings, a fact which I gleefully relayed to them until she found out about it and hit me with a piece of firewood.

That day, as I remember it, we were sitting at our table; Lucius had gone to the village on some business, and Phocas had gone with him. Gaia was working in the kitchen, preparing the meal. Valeria sat there for a moment, staring at me with her gray-blue eyes, which were flecked with little pieces of gold, and I imagined that this must have been what my mother looked like. I seldom thought such things, because it made me feel very sad, but for some reason that day, it was comforting to think that there was part of my mother in that steady gaze, that maybe she was looking out at me through Valeria. The light played through the window by the kitchen, the curtains pulled back to let in the light, and I could see the motes of dust dancing in the ray of light. We sat facing each other on one of the two benches that we sat at for meals and, before she spoke, she used her hand to pull her hair out of her face, tucking it unconsciously behind her ear. For some reason, every time she did that, I loved my sister even more, and this time was no different.

She frowned as she thought, then asked me, "Titus, what do you want out of life?"

I was surprised by this, since we seldom talked about such things in my house, but I curbed my normal tendency to reply with some sort of teasing or lighthearted remark, as I could tell she was serious. Although I had never consciously thought about it, I surprised myself with how easily and quickly the answer came from my lips.

"I want to make a career in the Legions, and I want to elevate myself and my family to the equestrian order. I want to be famous throughout Rome as one of her finest Legionaries."

If she was surprised, she did not show it, and I will always bless her for taking me seriously and not laughing outright. I would have been crushed if she had.

Nodding, she simply said, "Why?"

Now I *was* surprised, and I looked around at our house, then at her, as if that action would be enough to answer her.

But she waited, and I responded, "Because I don't want to be anything like *him*."

I didn't have to say who "him" was; we both knew.

Again, she nodded. "Good. Well, know this. If there's ever anything I can do to help you reach your goal, I will do so. I swear by holy oath that I'll do that for you."

Tears leapt to my eyes, completely unbidden. The way she had said it, with such quiet conviction and…vehemence, told me that she felt as acutely as I did the weight of my father's contempt for me.

But she was not finished.

"Now," she said, taking my hands in hers and leaning forward, "I'm going to ask something of you."

"Anything," I replied instantly, meaning it with all my heart.

"I know that you aren't happy with the idea of me marrying and going away…."

Before she could continue, I started to protest. But she silenced me with a look, and I could feel the heat rise in my face because of the shame. She knew me too well.

"Titus, listen to me. I know that you're not happy, and I know why. I know that you don't want to be left alone with *him*, but have you ever stopped to think about when *you* leave? That I'll be the one alone?"

Now I was even more ashamed, because it had never even occurred to me. I was so focused on Valeria being there for me, to be the mother that I had never had, that I never stopped to think about what would happen when I left.

Gulping, I slowly nodded my head and said, "You're right, sister, and I beg your forgiveness. I didn't think of it like that."

Smiling, she replied, "There's nothing to forgive, Titus. You're still a boy," and hurriedly added when she saw my head come up, ready to speak angrily, "I mean in years, not in size or strength. Or courage." This immediately mollified me; Valeria always knew what to say.

"What do you want me to do, sister? Name it and I'll do it."

"I only want you to stop trying to chase suitors away." She laughed. Turning serious, she added, "I have enough problems with that from *him*. I don't want to have to worry about you as well."

"I'll do that no more, I swear it," I said, happy to do something that made Valeria happy also.

"I know I had but to say a word to you, Titus. You're truly the best brother any sister could have," she said, and kissed me on the cheek, something I had started to rebel against as I grew older, but was happy to let happen on that occasion.

"And hear this, Titus. I *know* that you'll accomplish your dream. I'll make a sacrifice to Mars every day to make it so."

I left the house, feeling ten feet tall and as if I could slay all of Carthage by myself.

That day marked a turning point in my attitude, and instead of trying to stop the men courting Valeria, I sang her praises to anyone I thought would make her a good husband. Before long, a man came to our farm that, for some reason, was different from the others, at least in Valeria's eyes. He was somewhat older than Valeria, but had never married because he had served an enlistment in the army of Sertorius before coming back to take over his father's farm, which was about twenty miles from our farm. His name was Gaius Porcinus, and only the gods know why Valeria found him more pleasing than any of the other men hanging around, but she looked like a moonstruck cow when she laid eyes on him for the first time. In my eyes, he was not much to look at, yet he was the spitting image of Apollo to her. As soon as I saw that, I made an effort to become friendly with Gaius, who stayed at his cousin's house in town while the courtship took place. As I spent time with him, I realized that despite his bland exterior, there was something there behind it that made me realize that somehow perhaps Valeria had seen it immediately. He was on the short side, but he was stocky, strongly muscled in the chest and shoulders, a sign of the hard life on a farm that had no slaves. Porcinus had a shock of dark hair that seemed to perpetually fall into his eyes that he would impatiently brush aside, and while his features were plain as far as I was concerned, I was not going to have to wake up to them every morning for the rest of my life. What I liked about him was that he did not seem to have any bitterness or malice in him, cheerfully accepting his lot in life, and not covetous of others. He also had a good sense of humor, with a sense of the absurd that I identified with immediately.

I began splitting time between training with Cyclops and with Porcinus and Valeria, acting as the chaperone. I did not really know why Lucius was so insistent on a proper courtship between Porcinus and Valeria, when he had allowed Cyclops to just come to the farm and take Livia away for the price of a mule, but I suspected it was because he was out of daughters, and he did not have a pressing need for another animal or implement. As I had come to learn, the trade for Livia involved the mule; her dowry was the portion of surplus grain that he had promised to Cyclops. Because Porcinus had come after the harvest and the sale of our grain, Lucius had nothing substantial to offer. I think he was hoping that allowing Porcinus to spend time with Valeria would cause him to fall so madly in love he was willing to forego the traditional payment made by the bride's father. In this, Lucius proved to be right for one of the few times in his life. Porcinus had arrived to court Valeria around the Kalends of February; by the Ides of March, he had agreed to marry Valeria without any payment of a dowry, taking her as a love match. Once more, I found myself escorting a beloved sister to her future husband, with Porcinus going on ahead to prepare his farm for her arrival. The journey took almost two days, partially because of the distance, but more because despite her relief to be away from the clutches of Lucius, she knew that she was leaving me behind. I was of a similar mind; I was genuinely happy that she had escaped, yet I would be lying if I said that I was not apprehensive at being the only child of Lucius left, particularly the child that he blamed for the death of his wife. If Lucius had one redeeming quality, it was that he truly had loved my mother, and I would like to think that her death was the major cause of his cruelty to me, that he had been driven half-mad with grief. Perhaps that is the truth, or perhaps I am just grasping at straws; nobody wants to believe that their parent hates them without some external cause.

We camped for the night a distance from the road. Although I was carrying a *gladius* borrowed from Cyclops, and I was sure that I could protect my sister, there was no need to tempt fortune by not taking other precautions. I made a fire to heat our meal, then doused it to avoid drawing attention. There was a full moon, and as is normal for that part of the world, there were no clouds, so there was plenty of light for us to see each other as we talked. Of course, it was of a different quality than what we were accustomed to, and I thought Valeria looked particularly beautiful in the silvery light, her face looking as if it had been chiseled from the finest marble. I looked at her fondly, and as she looked back at me, the smile on her face gradually changed, until before I realized it, she had begun to sob. Thinking to comfort her, I moved to her to put my arm around her, but she shoved me roughly away, shaking her head and burying it in her arms. Confused, I sat there, and I'm not sure how much time passed before I could see her shoulders stop shuddering, her sobs becoming more of a whimper.

Not sure what to say, I tried, "I know you're nervous, but there's nothing to be worried about. Look how happy Livia is."

"Livia's lot has nothing to do with me," Valeria snapped. I was shocked; she had never expressed anything but happiness about our sister's marriage.

Not sure where this was coming from, I replied, "But I thought you were happy to marry Porcinus."

She shook her head, refusing to look at me as she said, "I am. That's not the problem. I'm just worried that he won't be happy with me."

I laughed. "Nonsense! Look at you! You're much more beautiful than he deserves! You…"

Before I could continue, she shouted, "Shut up, you stupid boy! You don't have any idea what I'm talking about."

Her referral to me as a boy was the one thing guaranteed to hurt me and, as usual, she hit her target unerringly. I could feel the heat rising to my face and I began to rise and storm off, but she stopped me with a hand on my arm.

"Please, Titus, I'm truly sorry. I'm not angry at you in any way. It was unforgivable for me to say that I know, but please forgive me anyway."

Not willing to be mollified, I continued to rise and walk away.

I had gone no more than a pace or two when she said softly, "I'm not what you think I am, Titus."

That stopped me short. Turning, I sat back down, looking at her and somehow knowing to keep my mouth shut.

I will not relate the total of the conversation, as it would bring shame to my sister, a woman who is completely undeserving of such a fate. But what I learned that night hardened my heart even more towards Lucius, and I think it was then that I first began to foster a terrible hatred for him, a hatred that made my earlier dislike for him pale in comparison. His poisonous touch had defiled everything that I loved most in the world, and that night I swore by Dis that I would somehow exact a revenge on the man who had sired me.

I delivered Valeria to Porcinus, going through the same ritual that I had performed with Livia. Valeria was just as nervous as Livia had been, but upon seeing Porcinus standing there and the look on Valeria's face, I saw how much she had come to love him, just in the short time they had known each other. Porcinus turned out to be as good a husband as Cyclops was; in that, my sisters were extremely fortunate. Fortune favored Valeria as well, more so than Livia. She is alive and well even now, and has lived to see most of her children and so far, all of her grandchildren survive, even if they are very far away. Her oldest son will inherit all that I have to give, other than those portions I have set aside for my sister and slaves. I do so because it was not my fate that I pass them to my own son, or to my wife, as I have none, but that is a story for later.

* * * *

Once Cyclops had judged that Vibius and I were no longer a continuing menace to ourselves, and had learned to move about and operate with *lorica* and *scutum*, he introduced us to the training version of the *gladius,* called the *rudis*, made of wood and weighted with lead. I was surprised at its heaviness when I first picked it up, and Cyclops explained to us the purpose for it.

"Once you get used to handling the weight, when you use the real thing, it helps you perform your movements more quickly."

It made sense to us, but that did not mean our arms ached any less. Cyclops erected a set of wooden stakes for us, which are standard training tools in the Legion. Demonstrating first, then having us repeat his actions, we began to learn the moves that would make us effective at killing our enemies. The *gladius* that we use is much shorter and shaped differently than those used by every tribe of Gauls that I fought, or any of the Eastern peoples, for that matter. Whereas their blades are longer and give them an extended reach, their points are pointed in name only. More rounded than ours, they rely on the length of the blade to cut. While it gives them more area to inflict damage, the problem for them is twofold; it requires more room to swing, forcing the gaps between each warrior to be wider than our Legions, but slashing someone to the point where they die takes quite a bit of doing. Since most of our internal organs are buried deeply within our bodies, it leaves that type of *gladius* fewer targets. The reality is that the throat and head are the only target that bring instant death, but that means the size of, the target is much smaller and harder to hit. With our blades however, which come to a needle point, the goal is to thrust it into the body of your opponent, where you are more likely to hit a vital organ. Besides that, there is the horror of having a blade sink deeply into the body that is more likely to remove the thought of further combat from the mind of your enemy than a simple slash will. The superiority of our *gladii* have been proven against all enemies of Rome over the years, and yet, very few of our enemies have been smart enough to copy what we do. I believe that this is one of the reasons Rome prevails over all others. We will copy and adapt those tactics of our enemies that prove to be useful; our *gladius* is a case in point. Supposedly, it came from the Iberian tribes in the very area of my childhood, because when Rome first faced them, we suffered horrible casualties from the *gladius Hispanensis*, and it did not take long for Rome to copy it for their own use. Now, even in my old age, I still spend at least a third of a watch a day at the stakes, keeping up the skills that have served me so well.

However, in those days, as I first began my training, I cursed the *rudis* I was wielding with every stroke. My arms would soon be on fire as I thrust and cut, thrust and cut, over and over. Vibius was in worse shape than I was, but we were both grimly determined to continue; we had come this far in our training, and we were not about to give up. Besides, from our perspective, the use of the *gladius* was the most important skill a Legionary could have. As it would turn out, it was the second most important skill; the ability to carry a burden for long distances without collapsing is the most crucial, but we were to learn that. We had learned to be patient when it came to moving to the next phase of our training, as Cyclops would not budge in his decision until he thought we were ready, no matter how much we whined and begged. So we gritted our teeth and took out our frustration on those wooden stakes, bashing them over and over. I would finish each session completely exhausted despite my strength and endurance, so I can only imagine how Vibius did it, but he proved his mettle day in and day out, as determined, I think, not to show weakness in front of me as anything. He had experienced his growth spurt by then, so he was substantially taller, but still on the short side of average and much shorter than I was, despite the fact that he was a full year older.

My life on our farm was getting worse, just as Valeria and I had feared. Without the buffer of my sister, my father's abuse, verbally at least, increased dramatically. He still would not touch me, and as I grew stronger and harder, the chance of that became more remote every day. I sometimes think that my contempt for him would have been much less if he had at least shown the courage to strike me, but his cowardice was complete, and it never happened. I would be less than honest if I were to not mention that I did give him cause; every week would see me become more insolent to his face, which of course only made the situation worse. But by then, after what I had learned from Valeria, my heart had been hardened and I would never have considered giving in, although I had yet to confront him with what I knew. I may have been large and strong, but he was still my father and the *paterfamilias* and obedience is strongly ingrained in the Roman people. It may make us great, but it has its price as well. Phocas tried his best to interpose, and it succeeded as far as the physical abuse; rarely a week passed where my father did not apply a rod to his back, which he bore without any complaint, at least to Lucius' face. It only served to fuel my hatred of Lucius, along with my contempt for him, because I knew that what he was doing was beating me, not Phocas; he just didn't have the courage. I should have been wise enough to cease in baiting Lucius, since he kept taking it out on Phocas, but when have the words wisdom and teenager ever gone together in the same sentence? Unless your name is Octavian, who proved to have a very wise head on his shoulders indeed, but again, that is for later.

Once we had satisfied Cyclops with our work with the *gladius*, he began sparring sessions with Vibius and me. The first session he bade us to pick up our arms and motioned that we both come at him, as he stood there with his own weapon and holding one of the *scuta*. Looking at each other, Vibius and I grinned, arriving at the same thought simultaneously. This would be our revenge on all the things that Cyclops had forced on us, all the insults, the bruises, everything. Now would be the moment of our revenge. Not saying a word to each other, we somehow knew to work in opposite directions, Vibius going towards the side where Cyclops held the *scutum*, with me heading towards the opposite side, watching his *gladius*, which he held closely to his side at the ready position. We approached slowly; we may have been confident, but we also respected Cyclops, who had proven in the last months that he knew what he was about. Keeping my feet the proper width apart, I shuffled towards him, watching Vibius out of the corner of my eye, waiting for him to make a move that I would match. Vibius went wide, so that he was almost perpendicular to Cyclops before suddenly lunging forward with a shout, signaling me to begin my attack. I lunged forward as well, although I was slightly behind, having moved a bit more slowly. As we both lunged, Cyclops, instead of retreating as we had expected, took a sudden step forward and towards Vibius, who was now a little behind him on his left. This moved him away from Vibius' blade, while at the same time, Cyclops whirled his *scutum* and bashed Vibius hard on his left shoulder with the *scuta*'s boss, the metal protuberance in the center. Vibius went flying, which by reflex, I watched, while Cyclops, in a move that I do not think I even saw, leaped the few feet between us and, before I knew what was happening, smacked me hard in the solar plexus with his *gladius*. The blow knocked me to my knees, forcing me to drop my own blade to clutch my stomach and gasp for air. Before Vibius could regain his feet, Cyclops moved to his side and did the same thing, jabbing him in the breadbasket and dropping him back prone on the ground, where he lay, retching violently. Cyclops stood, waiting for us to gather our wits, barely out of breath, his *scutum* grounded. He twirled the *gladius* as if it were a stick. Slowly pulling myself to my feet, I glared at him with murder in my eyes and heart, while he looked placidly at me with his good eye. Vibius was a bit slower to recover, rubbing his stomach and his shoulder at the same time, but soon enough, he was standing as well.

"Well?" I demanded, knowing that he would not mince words.

I was surprised when he said, "Not bad, actually. You were right to work as a team. That, more than anything, is the secret of our success in battle. We work as a unit, and the unit is composed of two-man teams that work in concert. You understood that immediately, but your inexperience showed."

I was nonplussed; I had expected scorn, but he genuinely seemed to think that we had done a decent job for our first attempt.

"So where did we go wrong?" I asked, mollified by his words.

"You came at me separately, not as a team. That allowed me to dispatch each of you, as long as I moved quickly and decisively enough."

I thought for a moment; that seemed to defy common sense, but I slowly began to see what he was talking about.

Continuing, he said, "What would I have done if you had come at me from the same side? What *could* I have done if you had come at me on the same side? One of you I could defend against, but the instant I do that, it leaves me vulnerable to the attack of the other. I only have one *scutum*, but as long as you come at me so that I can employ both my weapons at the same time on one of you, it evens my odds."

Once explained, I saw the sense of this, because to this point, I had only seen the *scutum* as a strictly defensive weapon.

As if he sensed my thoughts, Cyclops continued, "Your *scutum* is both a defense and a weapon. This," he pointed to the boss, "is there precisely so that you use it as I employed it. It's as much of a weapon as it is for defense."

With that, and taking what he had told us, we attacked again, but both of us approached from the same side, shoulder to shoulder. This time, when we closed, Cyclops did the unexpected. Leaping to Vibius' left side, he smashed his *scutum* directly into him, putting his weight behind it. Vibius flew into me, knocking him down, and forcing me to stagger backwards, which Cyclops used to his advantage, smacking Vibius in the gut yet again on his way down. Before I could regain my balance, Cyclops was on top of me, swinging the *gladius* in a short arc, smashing into my stomach once more and knocking me flat. Resuming his waiting position, the only consolation I had was that he seemed to be breathing a bit heavier.

Climbing to my feet, I asked wearily, "So what did we do wrong this time?"

"You were too close together," he said instantly. "All I had to do was to knock Vibius down and the same was bound to happen with you. I chose to attack Vibius' side because he was smaller," he said matter-of-factly. This did not please Vibius, but it was the truth, no matter how brutal. "And trust me, when given the choice of attacking you or attacking Vibius first, no matter who you face, they're always going to choose Vibius first."

He turned to Vibius and pointed his *gladius*. "That means that you have to be exceptionally skillful, Vibius. You'll be considered the weak link. But," he turned to face both of us, "that also means you can use it to your advantage." He shook his head. "Of course, that's assuming that you'll be standing side by side in the line." Continuing, he said, "When you go to enlist, they'll tell you to select a friend that will be your counterpart. Each of you will watch the other's back; you'll hold the other's wills, you'll be responsible for his safety. When that moment comes, you need to choose each other, because that will give you the most out of what I'm teaching you."

This made eminent sense to both of us, and we readily agreed. We knew already that we were friends for life, that nothing would come between us. What little we knew then.

It took a couple of weeks, but we were finally able to defeat Cyclops, and it was a great day for Vibius and me. Once we did that, only then did he turn us loose on him one on one. I would watch as he thrashed Vibius, and Vibius would watch as he did the same to me. I wish I could say that I was the first to finally best him, but that would not be true. One day, Vibius, taking a page from Cyclops' own book of tricks, got his *scutum* inside of Cyclops' and wrenched it from Cyclops' grasp. Even then, it took Vibius some time to score a killing blow, which was signified by the blotch of red paint that Cyclops coated on the tip and first few inches of the *gladius*. Finally, Vibius just wore him down and managed to jab his *gladius* into Cyclops' chest when he was not quick enough to bring his own up to parry Vibius' thrust. We both whooped in triumph and I yelled just as loudly as if I had been the one that made the kill, happy both for

Vibius and for the event itself. Cyclops took it gracefully, seemingly as happy for us as we were, hard as it was to imagine for me.

Whatever the truth, he got to his feet and clapped Vibius on the back, saying, "Well done, Vibius. You may survive your first battle yet."

It took me a couple more days before I was able to defeat Cyclops; one problem of my size was that I could not move as quickly as Vibius could, although the force behind my blows was stronger. Still, Cyclops said that I moved very well despite my size, and this rare praise made me feel much better. Finally, he deemed us ready to go after each other, which we did with gusto. I had no end of trouble trying to corner Vibius so that I could bring my superior strength to bear, and he was more dexterous in his use of the *scutum* than I was, causing several bruises all over my upper body. My biggest problem was giving in to frustration and impatience, but slowly, I began to get his measure and learn his tendencies. For instance, he would dip his *scutum* slightly just before launching an attack; once I learned that, I was able to counter his attack with one of my own, often catching him off-balance. However, he was devilishly quick to recover at all times, so I quickly learned that once on the attack in such a case, I had to continue pressing forward. Slowly, over a measure of days, I was able to get to a point where I beat him six times out of ten, which was the best I was ever able to do against him, at least back then. Cyclops, for his part, would merely stand watching us circle each other, making quiet comments about our position, or chastise us for an error. It was in this manner that we learned one of the most basic skills of the Legionary.

Once Cyclops had deemed us well enough trained in the *gladius*, he introduced us to the *pilum*. Because of the fragility of the regular *pilum*, with its soft metal shaft that is designed to bend on contact with whatever it hits, we only worked with the practice *pila*, which are somewhat heavier because of their stouter metal shaft. It took some time to get accustomed to the proper way to throw it so that the point would imbed, or at least strike what we were aiming at. For some reason, I had more trouble mastering it than Vibius did; perhaps it was my greater height, but to this day, it is the weakest of my skills, although I eventually became passably fair at throwing it.

While our bodies had become accustomed to the strain and stress of the *loricae*, the *scutum* and the *gladius*, throwing the *pilum* used different muscles and, after the first day, we could barely lift our throwing arms. But that did not concern Cyclops the next day, when he had us continue where we left off, throwing at the stakes, which had become scarred and battered from our previous training. After a week, we were both able to hit the stake most of the time from a distance of thirty paces, whereupon Cyclops immediately had us move ten paces back. After three or four weeks, we were very accurate from a number of distances, although Vibius was much better at it than I was. If I would hit the target eight out of ten times, Vibius never missed, and he was just as accurate at the longer ranges. Since, by this time, I had gotten the upper hand, albeit a slight one, in our training with the *gladius*, his supremacy in this did his confidence a world of good. And it irritated me to no end, I must confess; I am nothing if not extremely competitive, and the fact that in my view that Vibius liked to gloat a little too much about it did not help matters. All the way back to the town, where I would leave him to continue on to my farm, he would chatter about it like a bird, using every excuse to bring it up in conversation, particularly around Juno.

Ah, Juno. The source of the first falling out between Vibius and me. As the months passed and turned into years, by the time I was fifteen and Vibius sixteen, Juno was blossoming, from a mud-spattered urchin to what, in our eyes, was the image of Aphrodite. I think that must be the way all of us remember our first love, or lust, as the case may be. Juno was always waiting for us to come back from Cyclops', hanging by the forum where her father was a baker, selling his daily allotment of bread. I cannot actually name the day or time that she sprang up before us as a woman, and not just a somewhat tiresome girl who hung on our every word, no matter how flattering it may have been. But it seemed to happen to Vibius and me simultaneously, and it was somewhere around the time we had started working with the *pila*, because that is my first conscious memory of her as a woman. Vibius had done exceptionally well that day, and was crowing about it, as he was wont to do, while I was growing more irritated by the moment. By the time we got to the town and approached the forum, I was in a sour mood, which immediately got blacker on the appearance of Juno. Vibius waved to her and she came skipping over to us, and perhaps it was the fact that underneath her shift, things were bouncing about that I had never noticed bouncing before. I glanced over at Vibius, and I caught the same look I suspected I had on my own face, a mixture of surprise and...something else. Unbidden, I felt a heat in my groin, which immediately made its way to my cheeks, and I felt flushed and unsteady in a way that I had not experienced much at that point.

Juno seemed oblivious, teasing us, "So how many Carthaginians did you big, bad Legionaries slay today?"

Vibius immediately used that as an excuse to brag about how he had bested me with the *pila*, causing me to snap, "That may be true today, but we'll see how things play out tomorrow."

"And tomorrow, I'll still be better than you," Vibius mocked, oblivious to my growing anger.

Juno turned to me, her eyes wide with feigned surprise, since this had been the same story for the last few days, and I knew that my rejoinder was becoming weaker every time I said it.

"Again, Titus? Vibius beat you again?"

Smiling, she reached out and grabbed Vibius' bicep, squeezing it, gasping and cooing as if she were touching the right arm of Mars himself. My anger was growing by the second, and I could feel it building in me, but did not know how to stop it.

"Well, I can still take you with the *gladius*," I declared.

"That may be true, but you'll never get close enough to me to use it before I'd turn you into a pin cushion."

Growling, I took a step towards him, his face showing surprise and alarm for the first time as he looked into my eyes and saw how truly angry I was. "It looks like I'm close enough now, eh?"

Scrambling backward, he tripped over a loose stone, falling on his backside, and I broke out into a harsh laugh. "Not so mighty now, are we, Vibius?"

Vibius scrambled to his feet and charged me, fists swinging wildly. I must say I was surprised and he caught me with a right fist on my cheek, which snapped my head back. I realized that I was not the only one who had gotten stronger with all the exercise that Cyclops had put us through, but it still was not enough to do more than make my head move. With a roar of rage, I grabbed Vibius by his tunic with my left hand, picking him up as if he was made of straw and threw him against a wall of one of the buildings surrounding the forum. By this point, everyone had stopped conducting their business, most of them grinning at the sight of the two of us fighting. Life in a small town is boring and people will look at anything out of the ordinary as a source of entertainment. A fight was a perfect excuse to stop working to watch. Vibius thudded against the building, sliding down to a sitting position, shaking his head to clear it as I walked towards him, still at the height of my anger. Juno stepped in front of me, putting her hand on my chest, her eyes wide with fright.

"Please, Titus! I didn't mean to start a fight between you. It was my fault, not Vibius', truly! You should be angry with me, not him."

That deflated me instantly, and her words cut me as if they were made of knives. She was taking his side! I suddenly felt as if I could not breathe, as my chest constricted, and I could feel unwanted tears threatening to well up and unman me. There was nothing that could have hurt me worse than this, and it was at that moment that I realized that I loved Juno, or at least thought I did. After all, what does a fifteen-year-old truly know of love? Regardless, my anger dissipated, but I was still not willing to do anything like apologize.

Through clenched teeth, I muttered, "Fine. I'll go home and you two can stay here together. I'm sure it's what you want anyway."

Without waiting for a reply, I turned heel and pushed my way through the crowd, my size and anger enough to keep anyone from saying something unwise.

I cooled off on the walk home so that by the time I got back to our farm, I was more sad and heartbroken than anything else. The fact that I held feelings for Juno had come to me as a complete surprise; I had always seen her as just another child like us, but somewhere along the way, things had changed. Coupled with that was a sense of shame in the way I had behaved towards Vibius. Truly, he was not to blame for the way Juno felt. After all, he had not done anything any different than I had, and I realized that I was in the wrong. Yet, I was as stubborn as most teenage lads are, and I did not know how to get out of my predicament without losing what was more important to me than anything, my *dignitas*. Even then, I had a very clear picture of who I was and who I wanted to be, and such doings as I had perpetrated at the forum were beneath me, but I could not decide which the worst fate was: apologizing or not saying anything. If I were to apologize, while it would smooth things over with Juno and, more importantly, Vibius, it would be an admission that I had done wrong, which would damage my *dignitas*. However, if I did not apologize, I would be bothered because deep down, I knew I was wrong. So, I did nothing. I did not leave the farm the next day, nor the day after that, nor the day after that. Finally, Phocas came to me as I sat brooding on Lucius' stone wall, looking down the road towards town.

"I don't think I've seen you spend all day here for this long since, well, since I can remember." Phocas always had an indirect way of approaching sensitive topics; rather than just coming out and asking me what was bothering me, he made a comment that would get me to talking.

I shrugged. "I just thought I should spend more time here…"

He laughed abruptly at that, so transparent was the lie. At first, I got irritated, but looking at him, I found myself laughing too. The thought was too ludicrous even for the one who had uttered it.

"All right," I admitted. "It's not that. I got into a…disagreement with Vibius."

He raised an eyebrow in surprise.

"Really? I thought you two were as close to brothers as anyone could be."

I nodded glumly, but did not answer.

"So..." he said gently. "What is this great matter that caused you to disagree so much that you sit as if you're part of this stone wall?"

I shrugged again, hesitant to discuss the matter, mainly because I was not sure myself.

Finally, I said, "He was bragging about having beaten me with the *pilum* and it made me mad."

"Ah." Phocas nodded. "And that made you angry that he was doing so? Or was it the way he was doing it?"

Shaking my head, I said, "No, that's not it. It was..." I trailed off, not knowing what to say.

"I see." I did not know how he could see, but when he spoke next, he proved me wrong.

"If it wasn't what he said, or how he said it, then could it have been who he said it in front of?"

I looked at him in surprise, then quickly looked away, feeling my cheeks burning.

Nodding, he said, "That is it, isn't it? He said it in front of someone whose opinion is important to you."

"I don't care what she thinks," I blurted out, then immediately realized my error, causing a new wave of heat to rise to my face.

Now it was Phocas' turn to be surprised.

"So this is about a girl?"

He threw back his head and laughed, and I scowled at him, angry that he seemed to be mocking my pain and confusion.

He put his hand on my shoulder, and I immediately shrugged it off, and he said in a conciliatory tone, "Truly, Titus. I didn't mean to make light. It's just that you're experiencing the same thing that all men experience at one time or another."

Somewhat mollified, mainly because he had referred to me as a man, I asked, "Really?"

Nodding, he continued, "Yes, really. Every man who's ever been born has felt the pain of either being ignored or being mocked in front of a woman that he cares about."

"I didn't even know I *did* care about her," I replied.

"That's the worst kind," Phocas said wryly. "The kind that sneaks up on you. One moment, you're going along about your business and all is right with the world, and then BAM!" He clapped his hands together. "Cupid sends an arrow that lodges deep in your heart, and you suddenly are some changed being. Nothing makes any sense anymore. Down seems to be up, light seems to be dark, nothing tastes right…"

"Yes!" I cried. "That's exactly how I feel! I was perfectly happy, but now I can't think about anything else. I can't sleep, I can't eat."

Phocas put his hand on my shoulder again; this time, I let it stay there, as it provided me with comfort. These were the sort of matters that a boy is supposed to discuss with his father, but it had never even occurred to me to talk to Lucius about this.

"Welcome to manhood, Titus. Welcome to manhood."

* * * *

On the fourth day, after receiving Phocas' counsel, I walked into town, my heart thudding loudly as I walked, much faster than my pace would normally dictate. I was positively frantic with worry about what I was going to say, and how it would be received. I resolved that I must speak to Vibius first, since he was my best friend, and frankly, that talk I had less trepidation about. Juno, on the other hand, was a different matter entirely and, as I walked, I tried out and discarded dozens of approaches. Finally, I offered a prayer to the gods that I would know what to say when the time came and continued walking.

Because it was the normal time of day where I usually met Vibius, I was not surprised to see him standing there, as if he were waiting. What did surprise me was that Juno was standing next to him, and there was something about the way they stood that caused my stomach to churn and tie into a knot. They were doing nothing overt, but there was some sort of energy between them that I would swear had not been there before. They saw me coming at the same time, and when they both gave me the same nervous and furtive look, my apprehension deepened.

As I approached, Juno called out, "*Salve*, Titus. We were hoping to see you today. We've been waiting every day."

We? What was with this "we" business, I wondered, but I was determined to maintain my composure, and calmly returned the greeting.

"*Salve* Juno, *salve* Vibius. Yes, I apologize. I was…detained for these past days, helping my father."

This was a bald-faced lie, but I was determined to salvage something of my *dignitas*, and it was with relief on all of our parts that they seemed to accept this fiction with a simple nod. Together, both of them nodding together, I thought, as if they were one person, as if they were a…And that was when I knew why they were so nervous.

They had become a couple. As if reading my thoughts, Vibius cleared his throat and said nervously, "Titus, there's something I want to tell you, and I don't know how to begin."

He looked at me hopefully, as if I were going to save him the trouble by announcing what I now knew to be the case, but I was not willing to be so accommodating at that point.

I said nothing, and he continued, "It's just that, well, I'm not sure how you'll take it."

Looking at him in mock surprise, I replied, hoping that my voice did not betray me, "Why, Vibius, we're best friends, aren't we?" He nodded vigorously. "Then all you need to do is to come out with it."

Screwing his face up, he blurted, "It's just that Juno and I have become…fond of one another."

At this moment, Juno interrupted, looking at me, and said, "We're more than fond of each other, Titus. We're in love."

Even though I had guessed as much in the last few moments, hearing it still came as a shock. For an instant, I felt a red-hot anger start to build, immediately followed by shame. What right did I have to such feelings? It was clear enough; Juno liked Vibius more than she did me. If I were being honest, I would have told myself that I had deep down always known this to be the case. After all, the day I had rescued him, it had been because he had in turn been trying to save Juno. But I was in no mood to be honest, although I was resolved to handle this news with as much grace as I could muster.

"Congratulations," I said stiffly, and stopped there.

There was an awkward silence as they waited for me to say more, but I was not disposed to do so, forcing Juno to say, "It's just that, well, we didn't want it to cause any problems between you and Vibius."

Raising my eyebrow in feigned surprise, I replied, "Why on Gaia's earth would it cause us any problems? Truly, I'm happy for you both."

Turning to Vibius, I changed the subject. "Are you ready to get back to work? I'm sure Cyclops' been wondering where we've been."

"Absolutely," Vibius replied, but made no move to go.

Puzzled, I asked, "Is there something else?"

Looking flustered, Vibius replied, "Well, not really. All right, yes there is. Juno's asked if she can go along with us to watch us train."

I was certainly not prepared for this, and I stood there, speechless for a moment, trying to come up with a proper reason she should not come.

Turning to her, I asked, "Won't your father refuse for you to go unescorted?"

"Not if it's with Vibius," she said softly.

So, they were more than in love, I thought. They must be betrothed. That would be the only way I could see her father agreeing for her to go out into the countryside with a boy. But Vibius was no longer a boy; he had donned the *toga virilis* several months ago. I still had almost four months to wait before it was my turn, and I tended to look at everyone else through my own experiences, so it had not occurred to me that Vibius was eligible to marry because I was not eligible.

"Well, by all means," I said with as much good humor as I could muster.

Secretly, however, I was planning on a different reaction, once we got to Cyclops and squared off against each other.

If Cyclops was surprised at the sight of Juno accompanying us, he hid it well and Livia was happy for some female company. Usually, she would tend to chores while Cyclops worked with us, but would always manage to find time to watch occasionally. Now, she and Juno chattered away about whatever it is that women talk about amongst themselves, while Vibius and I stood to face each other for our first bout. At Cyclops' signal, I charged Vibius with all the pent-up anger that had been building as we walked to Cyclops' farm, anger at being passed over by Juno for Vibius, and anger at myself for feeling badly about it. Vibius was surprised, but recovered quickly. However, I was in a different state than normal this day and I gave him no chance to regain his wits or composure. I could have finished him with a killing blow almost immediately, but instead I chose to toy with him, striking him about the arms and legs, depending on what opening he gave me. Desperately, he parried as many of my blows as he could, catching quite a few with his *scutum*, but a large number landed, causing him to gasp in pain whenever I got through his defenses. I sensed more than heard that Juno and Livia had stopped talking; good, I thought, now Juno will see that she made a poor choice, as if her entire basis for choosing who to love was based on how well they could kill. Such is the thinking of the young man who is incapable of understanding the way a woman thinks. I will be the first to tell you, gentle reader, that while I have finally understood how a woman thinks, I still have no idea why. It is one of the great mysteries of life.

Finally, I struck Vibius a killing blow, a hard thrust right under his ribcage that laid him flat and knocked the wind out of him. I had never hit him that hard before and as suddenly as it happened, I was ashamed of myself for doing so, but was still unwilling to show that I was sorry. I glanced over at Juno and Livia and my shame deepened, because I saw in Juno's eyes that she knew exactly why I had done what I did, and so did Livia. I wondered if, in the short time they had been talking while we were preparing for training, Juno had told Livia exactly what had transpired, and about her love for Vibius. As I pondered this, Vibius slowly climbed to his feet, his cheeks splotched an angry red as he glared at me. For my part, I refused to meet his eye, instead motioning to him to step back into the middle of the area that we used for our contests. Vibius spat on the ground, then a look of grim determination came over his face as he stepped into the middle. I closed on him, and Cyclops, who had remained silent this whole time, just observing what was taking place, gave us the signal to re-commence. This time, it was my turn to be on the defensive, as Vibius was a blur of motion, using his superior speed to bob and weave, using his *scutum* to knock mine to the side. I was able to block his blows, but just barely, and I knew that if he kept up this pace, at some point, he would get through my defenses and score a killing blow. A thought flashed through my mind that this might be the best course of action, as a way to make peace with him. If I let him score a killing blow on me, we would be even and things could go back to normal. Even as I thought this, however, I rejected it, out of pride mostly, I imagine. He might have won the girl, but I did not have to let him win anything else, and I gritted my teeth and began to counter-attack. Again, it was Vibius' turn to be on the defensive and I could see that the toll of his earlier pace was beginning to tell on him. Slowly, his *scutum* was dropping, and it was then I tried something that I had been thinking about, a maneuver that has since served me well in many, many battles. Stepping to my right, so that my *scutum* was directly across from his, I shoved it at his in a downward, chopping-type motion, so that the bottom edge of my *scutum* hit the bottom edge of his at an angle that drove it backwards and down. This served to drop the *scutum* and tip the top of it forward just a matter of a couple of inches, but it was enough to expose his face and neck. Instantly, I lashed out with my *gladius*, ignoring the rule of no blows to the head. Despite wearing our *galeae*, the wooden blade caught him square on the nose, causing it to spew a fountain of blood as it split. I let out a savage cry of delight as, once again, he fell to the ground, completely oblivious to the fact that I could have killed my best friend, wooden blade or not. Instantly, I felt a tremendous blow from behind that knocked me to my knees, followed by another kick to my side, causing me to drop the *gladius* and grunt in pain. I fell over, panting for breath, and as I lay there, I saw Cyclops' boots in front of me, and I squinted up at him. He was as angry as I had ever seen him, before or since that day.

"What in the name of Dis do you think you're doing? You could have killed Vibius," he snarled at me, lifting his leg as if to kick me again.

Despite my size and strength, I was still scared of the man and knew that he could thrash me within an inch of my life, or worse, so I flinched and put my hands out in supplication, dropping my *scutum* as I did so.

"*Pax*, Cyclops! I'm sorry! I forgot myself," I said as quickly as I could get the words out, anxious to appease him.

His foot hovered there, still ready to strike, but he stayed it, at least for the moment.

"How many times have I told you that there are to be no blows to the head?" he asked rhetorically because it was a number too high to accurately count.

Keeping my hands out in a posture of supplication, I replied, "I know, I know. I was just…carried away, I guess. I swear on Jupiter's Stone that I won't do that again."

Grudgingly, he dropped his foot. "It's not me you need to apologize to, you *cunnus*. It's him." He motioned to Vibius, who was sitting up with his head between his knees, while Juno and Livia tried to stanch the flow of blood.

My heart sank when I saw him in that state; I alone had done this, for no better reason than I was jealous that he had found someone to love him. I gazed at Vibius, and Juno turned to look at me. I braced for the look of hatred that I was sure she would send me, but it was worse. She looked as if it had been she herself who had been bashed in the nose, not Vibius, and that look of hurt and pain scarred me to the quick. Gulping, I drew myself up to all fours, and crawled like an animal over to Vibius, who, sensing that I was approaching, looked up, his face partially obscured by a rag that had already turned scarlet with his blood.

His eyes were flinty hard, and he was silent as I crawled over to him.

"Vibius," I began, "I am *so* sorry that I did this to you."

He did not reply, but continued looking at me, as did Juno and Livia. Apparently, I was going to have to do more than this.

"I don't know what came over me," I continued, but before I could finish, he broke in.

"Yes, you do." His voice was muffled by the rag and had a nasal quality because of all the blood, I supposed. "You know exactly why you did it. You're jealous of me."

There. He had said it, aloud for all to hear, and if he had punched me in the stomach, it would not have felt any worse. I thought for a moment; I could deny it, but what purpose would that serve?

Swallowing hard, I said quietly, "You're right. I am jealous."

He had obviously not expected me to capitulate so quickly, judging by the look of surprise on his face. He was not the only one; I had surprised myself too, by being so forthright about what was bothering me. I think it was a measure of how much I needed his friendship that I was willing to do so, no matter how difficult.

Continuing, I said, "Vibius, you're the one true friend I have. And I think that I am jealous, not because you're happy, but because I fear that we'll no longer be friends, at least as we are now. When you and Juno are married, I'm afraid you'll no longer have time to spend with me. And," I added, "you know that if you're married, you won't be able to join the Legions with me."

I stared at the ground, ashamed to meet his eyes. What I said was the truth, but not the whole truth; I was not yet willing to admit I had feelings for Juno myself.

There was a silence for a moment, then Vibius heaved a sigh. "You're truly a *mentula,* Titus, if you think that whatever happens between Juno and me will change our friendship. Besides, just because we're betrothed, doesn't mean that we'll be getting married right away." I looked up at him in surprise, to see him looking at Juno and she at him. With great affection, he said, "Juno knows that my dream is the same as yours, to serve with you in the Legions, and she's agreed to wait for me."

I was incredulous. Wait for him? That was sixteen years of waiting! Was she mad? Had Cupid struck both of them silly?

Seeing my look, Juno interjected, "It's true, Titus. And we know it's a long time, but the truth is," now it was her turn to lower her eyes, "I've loved Vibius for as long as I can remember. I've waited this long, I can wait longer."

Vibius and I patched things up and, soon enough, all was right as rain again between us. The fact was that neither of us could stay mad at the other for very long; I wish it could still be true to this day. My feelings for Juno were something that I never shared with him, locking them away in a secret place in my heart, and I lived for the moments when I would see her, even if she was with Vibius.

My birthday came and Lucius, very grudgingly, presented me with the *toga virilis*, signifying that I was a man. There was no ceremony; he just handed it to me with a grunt and had Phocas show me how to wear it. I still have trouble making it drape correctly, even now. I much prefer a simple soldier's tunic, but my status now forbids that. But I have to say that I was pretty proud of myself as I strutted into town, my left arm holding up the drapes as I gestured with my right hand, as if I were addressing an adoring crowd. Vibius and Juno gave me a gift, an amulet for Mars, which I hung about my neck and still have to this day, on a leather cord, although the cord has been replaced many times since. But it was the other news they had that changed the course I had set out for myself.

Without any preamble, Vibius said excitedly, "There are recruiting parties in the area. Legions are being raised for the new Praetor, and they're looking for men to join!"

This was news, indeed! For a moment, my heart quickened in excitement, but just as suddenly, I was brought low. I had just turned sixteen; that was a year too young for the Legions. And what was worse, Vibius was already seventeen, and of the age for acceptance. He had grown enough to make the height qualifications, if only just, and I knew his father would not disapprove since it solved the problem of one less mouth to feed, not to mention that Vibius' father already had more than enough heirs to take over his tanning business, which Vibius had never shown the slightest interest in pursuing. Vibius saw the look on my face, and his own became troubled.

"Gods, I forgot. You're still but sixteen. I always forget because you're so big and strong." Biting his lip, he pondered, and it was with genuine sadness that he said, "But, Titus, you know that there's no telling when they'll be raising a Legion in this area. If I don't join now…"

He did not have to finish; if he did not join now, there was no telling when he would be able to. Back in those days, all the Legionaries in a Legion came from the same area, and replacements were never provided as the years passed. If a young man missed his chance, his only hope was to either wait for another call for raising a Legion in his area, or move to a place that was raising Legions, once he heard of it. The problem with the latter was that if he was not quick, he might arrive after the complement for the Legion had already been filled. Neither of these problems meant that a man could not join the army; if the Legions were full, there was always a place in the auxiliary, but that was beneath any true Roman citizen, as both of us were. Besides, we had set our hearts on the Legions and nothing else, so I could not with any good conscience hold it against Vibius, but I was still sorely disappointed. However, I gritted my teeth and tried to put a good face on it.

"Eh, I guess the gods didn't want me to overshadow you, Vibius. I understand that you have to go immediately and enlist, but I won't lie. I'll miss you, and I curse the Fates for making me too young to go with you. But," I forced a smile, "perhaps there'll be another call soon. I've heard that this new Praetor has some ambitions to be more than that. The only way for that to happen is for him to fight a war and, with a war, he'll need an army and, with an army, he'll need Legions."

Vibius nodded, but I could see that he was genuinely as hurt as I was, and my affection for him threatened to unman me in front of him and Juno, so touched was I at the sight. Juno had been silent this whole time, and when I looked over at her, I was shocked to see tears. While I knew that she would miss Vibius, she had to know that this meant that their marriage would happen sooner, now that an opportunity to join had arisen. But that was not what was making her sad.

"It breaks my heart to see that you two, who are closer than Vibius is to any of his brothers, separated in this way. There has to be something…"

I shook my head, as I had been thinking along those lines.

"I'm simply not old enough, Juno," I replied.

"Says who?" This came from Vibius, and I looked at him in surprise to see the beginning of a smile on his face.

"What do you mean, Vibius? Says the fact of my birth being sixteen years ago today, that's who."

"Really?" he responded immediately. "Who would dispute you if you claimed to be seventeen instead of your actual age? Look at you," he said excitedly. "Who would ever know that you're not seventeen, or even twenty, for that matter?"

I shook my head. "It doesn't matter how old I look. I have to be able to prove my age, and the only way to do that is..."

"For your father to swear to it," Vibius interrupted. Grabbing my arm, he said, "Think about it, Titus. Your father has never wanted you around. Why would he object to you being out of the house earlier?"

"Because then there's one less to do the work on the farm while he drinks all day," I retorted bitterly.

And it was true; Lucius had long since stopped lifting a finger to help Phocas and Gaia. The only thing that kept the farm together was the commitment of Phocas and Gaia, which, while I did not understand it, I was thankful for, because if I was being honest, my contribution in terms of labor was not that much. My major work came when it was time to plow the field, which I did but twice a year, and while it was hard work, I did not find it altogether unpleasant. That thought stuck in my mind, as I began to see just the faintest glimmer of hope.

Voicing what I was thinking, I said, "Truth be known, the only real work I do is the plowing, and that only happens twice a year. Perhaps," I said slowly, "I should talk with Phocas, at least, and get his opinion of what I should do."

Vibius clapped me on the shoulder. "Absolutely! Talk to him; I think you might be surprised that this isn't impossible after all."

For the remainder of the time I was in town, I stood and let others admire me, knowing that my size and frame kept the toga from looking like a flapping bunch of fabric thrown onto a chair. I had filled out every month that Vibius and I trained with Cyclops, so that I looked much older than my actual age when seen from a distance. However, up close, I was still waiting for my full beard to grow in, but while my hair is brown and wavy, the fuzz on my cheeks was still so light yellow that it was visible only if I squinted in the right light when I looked in the brass mirror. Even so, I was not blind to the admiring glances from some of the young ladies who frequented the forum, but even as they batted their eyes at me, I was looking sidelong to see if Juno was noticing that I had other admirers. If she was, her face did not betray it in any way, but I thought I saw a flicker of what I knew was her look when she was irritated when one of the young ladies called my name in greeting.

After my stroll around the town, I walked back to the farm, careful not to let the folds of my toga drag on the ground and get dirty. A spotless white toga is a very hard thing to keep in the same condition, and I did not look forward to the kind of comments Lucius would make if I did not return with it in the same condition as I had left. My head was full of conflicting thoughts, and not a little fear at the idea of what I was going to attempt. But as I walked, my resolve grew, and so did my anger. I began to think of all the slights, the injustices, and the hurts inflicted on me by the man who was supposed to love me, his only son, above all others. With each furlong, I became angrier and more resolved that I would make my father give me what I was convinced was the least he owed me, freedom from his rule. He had never wanted me, he made that plain on every occasion he could think of, so why should he not give me what we both wanted? By the time I reached the farm, I was filled with a terrible resolve that one way or another, my father and I would have a reckoning of accounts. What better day than the one in which I became a man? I thought.

Despite my resolution, I still wanted to talk to Phocas first, although now it was more to solicit ideas about the best way to gain what I wanted from Lucius. However, there was also some guilt there at the thought of leaving Phocas and Gaia behind to face not only my father, but the extra work that my absence would create. I found him at the barn, mending a harness that we used to hitch the mule to the plow. I stood and just looked at him for a moment, realizing with some surprise that somewhere along the way, he had aged. He was no longer as arrow-straight in his posture as he had been in my childhood; there was a slight stoop that I suspected was from all the amount of time he spent bending over and tending to the crops. His hair, which had been as black as a raven's wing, was now liberally sprinkled with strands of silver that gave his appearance something of an aura as the light reflected from it. His hands were careworn, becoming what can only be called gnarled, but they were still strong hands, and I was struck by the sudden thought that, slave or no, I would have been much happier if he had been my father instead of Lucius. And now, as I look back, I realize that he indeed *was* my father, in all the ways that mattered. I learned more from a slave on how to be a man than I did from that bitter, pathetic hulk of flesh that was my father.

Phocas sensed my presence and looked up, smiling when he saw me standing there in my *toga virilis*, which I had not even taken the time to change from before seeking him out. I struck a pose as if I were one of the statues of the great men that one saw in the larger cities like Corduba, and he burst out laughing at the sight. It warmed my heart to make him laugh, and I had always tried to do as much my whole life, with silly jokes and comical stunts that I would perform for his and Gaia's amusement. Whether or not they were truly funny, they both laughed at whatever I said or did. Again, I was struck by the thought that this was the sort of thing a son did for his parents, not slaves. Pushing the thought away, I immediately became serious. Looking about first, I made sure that Lucius was not in earshot, which would have been unlikely. Usually, by this time of day, he had drunk himself into a stupor that he would only rouse from to eat the evening meal, then he would go back to worship Bacchus. Still, given what I wanted to talk to Phocas about, it was better to be safe. Seeing how serious I had become, Phocas put the tack down and walked to me, a concerned look on his face.

"What is it, Titus? What troubles you? Did something happen in town?"

Choosing my words carefully, I replied, "Yes and no, Phocas. There's a matter of utmost seriousness I wish to speak to you about."

Putting his hand on my shoulder, he answered, "Of course, young Master. What can I help you with?"

"You know I hate being called that, so for one, please don't refer to me in that manner, especially today," I snapped, which I was instantly sorry for.

Phocas looked wounded, but answered calmly, "Of course, Titus. My apologies."

I shook my head. "No, I should be the one apologizing, Phocas. It's just that I learned something today, and now I face a decision."

I went on to explain what I had learned, watching his face as I went on to tell him what I was thinking of doing. When I was finished, he was silent for a long time, but despite the impatience of youth, I knew better than to try to force him to speak before he was ready.

Finally, he said gravely, "What you seek to do is a very large thing, Titus. Are you sure this is what you want?"

I nodded. "Yes, I'm sure. I can't think of any other course at this point, and I think that this is the best thing. The one thing I'm worried about," I added, "is that I'll be leaving you and Gaia behind. It's not just the added work, it's..." I paused as I searched for words, but I was stopped by Phocas' hand, laid gently on my arm.

"Don't worry about us, Titus. We may look old and worn out, but Gaia and I are more than capable of handling the extra burden. As for the other thing you worry about, don't. I've learned how to handle Lucius. Besides," he added with a grin, "I think you overestimate how much work you actually perform around here."

Despite the seriousness, I could not help laughing at that, for it was true. If, gentle reader, you are surprised by such a bold statement by a slave, I would bid you to think again. In fact, I say that if you were willing to look at your own situation honestly, you would have to agree that it is indeed the slaves who control the masters, such has our dependence on them become. I know that in my own case, I defer to Diocles in almost every matter pertaining to my affairs, as he knows the minutiae of them much better than I do. (*Diocles' note: My master does not speak the entire truth. While it is true that he does rely on me to inform him of conditions with his estate, he is always the one making the decisions. There has never been any question, at least in my mind, who is the slave and who is the master. Such is the condition of a slave; no matter how exalted one's position may be, the fact that one is a slave is never far from mind.*)

I looked at Phocas fondly, unable to speak because I was not sure what I should say.

Phocas continued, "And it does my heart good to know that you, the last of Lucius' children, may be free of his poisonous influence. Master of me he may be, but just because I'm a slave doesn't mean that I can't see what's right and what's wrong. And you've suffered grievously at the hands of your father because of something that you had no control over. Gaia and I have prayed many times for your deliverance, and this step you take means that our prayers weren't in vain. Just tell me what you need me to do, Titus, and I'll do it. Even if it means my life."

Now I could not hold the tears back, and they came bursting out of me like a dam. Here in one conversation, this gentle man, this slave had shown me more love than my own father had in the previous sixteen years. When I broke down, he took a step towards me and I grabbed for him, put my head on his shoulder, and cried as I had not cried in many, many years. All of the pain and sorrow that I felt spilled out, as he just stood, holding my shoulders as I let it all out.

After I had regained my composure, Phocas took me to Gaia and, talking quietly, in order not to disturb my father's inebriated slumber, told her of my decision. She began to cry, which set me off again, and for a short time, we huddled together, all of us weeping. This, I thought, is what it means to be loved, to be part of a family. I swore then to all the gods that I would somehow repay these two kinds souls. Alas, by the time I was in such a position that I could, it was too late for Gaia. But that night, Gaia was very much alive and warm, patting me on the back as she tried to ease my own grief while she suffered her own.

Finally, I pulled myself away and, with an effort, I said, "Enough of this crying. I need to make ready to talk to Lucius. I expect I'll remain clothed as I am, but I do need to pack some things. I won't stay here for more than this night."

Gaia shooed me away, saying that she would pack my things; I needed at that time to eat something to regain the strength I would need for what was to come. So Phocas and I sat and talked quietly as I ate some cold meat and bread, and waited for my father to arise.

I do not know how long had passed, no more than a third of a watch, but the sun was just touching the top of the hills to the west of our farm, signaling that dark would be arriving in about the same amount of time when Lucius came staggering from his private room. Even several feet away, I could smell the sour stench of wine, not just wine spilled on clothes or coming from one's breath, but from the pores of the man himself, so saturated was he with the grape. He squinted as he struggled to focus on the sight of his son and slave, sitting at the table, and groaned as his accustomed headache made itself known.

"What are you doing still dressed in that getup?" he muttered as he staggered past us and headed for the amphora that held his wine.

I looked at Phocas and nodded my head, the prearranged signal for him to leave, so that he rose as he said casually, "Master, I must go finish mending the harness."

"Why haven't you finished already, you lazy *cunnus*?" my father snarled, and I felt my fist clench reflexively.

But Phocas was accustomed to Lucius, and said placidly, "Many apologies, Master. I'm sorry to disappoint you. I'll try to do a better job."

"Make sure that you do, or by the gods, I'll whip you."

That raised an eyebrow, not just from me, but from Phocas as well. As unpleasant as my father was, he did not usually speak of matters such as whipping. It made me wonder what the cause was for his change of behavior; perhaps his hangover was particularly bad, or perhaps he sensed that something was afoot. Phocas left the house, but he was going nowhere far. We had arranged that he would step outside but stay in earshot, in order to be able to intervene should things turn uglier than we anticipated, before he was supposed to enter as we had planned.

I sat, trying to remain as calm as I could, but my heart was threatening to beat out of its spot under my ribs. Even now, I cannot recall ever being more nervous than I was that day, even with all the battles and skirmishes of which I have been a part. But the first time one acts as a man is always the most momentous and the hardest.

Lucius, seeing that I was still sitting there and had not moved, snapped, "I told you to go change, damn you."

"Before I do, there's something I need to speak with you about." I was surprised how calm I sounded.

As I looked down, I saw that despite my anxiety and the rapidity of my heartbeat, my hands were steady, which encouraged me.

Stopping short, unaccustomed as he was to a son who did not immediately obey, he repeated dumbly, "You have something you want to talk to *me* about? What could that possibly be, boy?"

"First, that I'm no longer a boy. As of today, I'm a man."

This elicited a hoot of laughter, a harsh, rasping sound that was as grating to me as anything I had ever heard.

"Is that so, *boy*," he mocked. "So it's a man now, is it? Well, well." Making a mocking bow in my direction, which caused him to stumble forward a step, which he caught just in time before pitching forward, he said, "Then out with it. What's this matter that you need to speak to me about?"

Calmly, I said, "There's a *dilectus* in the area, looking for men for the Legions that the new Praetor is raising. Vibius is joining, and I am too."

It took a moment for this to register, his wine-addled brain struggling to put this idea in some coherent form.

Finally, he asked with true puzzlement, "What has this got to do with me? You're but sixteen and you can't enlist for another year."

"Exactly," I replied calmly, "but I wish to enlist now. And in order to enlist, I'll need you to go with me to swear that I'm seventeen, not sixteen."

Again, it took a moment to register, but when it did, he began whooping with laughter, a harsh, mocking laughter that lacerated me to the quick.

"And why on Pluto's thorny *cock* would I want to do that?" He asked this with a malicious grin, as if he could not wait to have something else to laugh at.

But when I responded, the smile stopped, as did the laughter.

"Because if you don't, you'll never be able to sleep soundly again, because I swear on Jupiter's Stone that I'll kill you."

I could not believe that I had said it so easily, but I realized as I said it that I was serious. I would kill this man if I needed to.

He staggered back a pace, his eyes wide with shock, then attempted to recover, drawing himself to his full, pathetic height, his scrawny chest puffed out as he declared with all the bravado that the wine could give him, "You'll do no such thing, boy. I am the *paterfamilias* in this house, not you. And as long as I am such, you will obey me!"

He tried to thunder this last bit, but it came out as a squawk.

I stood up, and stepped towards him, knowing that I did not have to posture in order to tower over him.

Still, I did flex my muscles a bit as I replied pleasantly, "You're only *paterfamilias* while you're alive. Once you're dead, I become the head of the family. Look around." I motioned with my head. "What do you see? Where are the nearest neighbors? Who would hear you scream as I killed you? Where would you run?"

I kept approaching him as I talked and, suddenly terrified, he stepped backwards, tripping over his own feet to fall heavily to the floor on his backside, where he stared up at me in abject fear. I never felt so powerful and ashamed at the same time; not shame because it was my father, but shame at him, that he was so pathetic and weak. I was being a bully, nothing more.

"You wouldn't dare," he squeaked, his voice gone high with fear. I could tell that at least all inebriation had been banished, as if it was never there. "Phocas and Gaia wouldn't allow it! They would report you. You may have no love for me," he at least had the rights of it there, "but you care for them. You know what happens to slaves when their master is dead under suspicious circumstances, don't you? They're tortured in order to gain a truthful account."

As you know, what he said is true; in the event of any suspicion of foul play, the slaves of the victim are put under torture as a matter of course, in order that they give a truthful account. While I understand the reasoning, I have often wondered how effective it is. This was what had troubled me when I first thought of approaching Lucius with this ultimatum, but after talking it over with Phocas and Gaia, I was no longer worried. It was at this moment that Phocas stepped back in the door, as we had planned.

Sensing him come in, I said, "But that's only the case if there's foul play suspected. And as I'm your only son, and the only one of your children left alive who lives here, who's going to doubt me when I say that you died in some sort of accident? Or even in your sleep?"

Lucius immediately looked over my shoulder at Phocas, who then spoke the piece that we had agreed on.

"No, Master. I wouldn't betray Titus. I'll corroborate his story, as will Gaia."

He walked up to Lucius, who was still huddled on the floor, and squatted down opposite him so that he could look Lucius in the eye, something that a slave was expressly forbidden to do, although it was rarely enforced, except at my house.

"And if I have to endure torture, I'll do so gladly, knowing that Titus is at last free from you. And you will still be dead."

I was both sickened and fascinated at what happened next. Simultaneously, Lucius' eyes filled with tears, and he lost control of his bladder, a dark stain growing on the floor. I smelled it before I saw it, and I made no attempt to hide my revulsion.

"Look at you," I snarled. "You who dare to call ME 'boy'? You are pathetic, and you are weak. I curse the Fates that made me your son." Now that I had started, I was unable to stop. Stepping closer, I continued, pouring at all the hate and scorn I had built up. "Do you want to know one of the reasons I'm joining the Legion, *Father*? So that I can restore some honor to our family name, honor that you've pissed away, honor that you never had! YOU," I roared, "are the reason my mother died, not me. Gods only know what she saw in you, but I firmly believe that the reason she died was because she had come to learn what kind of man you really are, and she couldn't live with the shame of it."

As I had hoped, these words had a visible impact, and for the first and only time, my father tried to act like a man.

"Liar!" He screeched this at me, making the sign of the evil eye. Despite myself, I took a step back. "YOU, Titus Pullus, are the one who killed your mother. I loved her! I loved her more than any man alive has loved a woman! And you," he pulled himself to his knees, the puddle underneath him ignored, "you took her from me! So that's right! I hate you! I have always hated you, and I will always hate you!"

For the first time in our lives, my father and I had been completely honest with each other.

* * * *

His show of bravado over, Lucius quickly collapsed on himself, spent and drained of what little courage he had possessed. However, I had gained what I had come for; Lucius agreed that he would accompany me to wherever the recruiting party was, take the appropriate vows as to my citizenship and age, and hopefully, neither of us would see the other ever again. Although he had agreed, I felt compelled to add one more term to it.

"If you harm a hair on either Phocas' or Gaia's head, I will come back and I'll teach you all that I've learned in the Legions. I swear to you that your death won't be quick, but it will be exceptionally painful. Do you understand?"

Sullenly, he nodded, but said nothing. Gods know that I have no reason to say anything good about my father, but I will say that he lived up to his word. I had no doubt that it was the fear of me who prevented it. Once this was settled, it suddenly seemed a little silly that I would leave the farm, so I made the decision to stay there instead of leaving. But I will say that my remaining nights were spent sleeping very lightly. I did not need to worry; if anything, Lucius seemed determined to drink himself into an even deeper stupor, earlier in the day. This fact kept me from fulfilling my promise to end his days, and then come up with a new plan for joining the Legions.

Lucius agreed to take me to Corduba, along with Vibius and his father two days after our "agreement," and we would be accompanied by Phocas and Gaia, as any trip to the capital was an occasion. Not mentioned but obvious to everyone involved was the other reason for both of our slaves' company was so that nothing untoward happened to either Phocas or me. While I was unafraid of Lucius, Phocas was more circumspect; his main fear was that Lucius would pay some thugs to exact revenge along the way, as we had to stay at inns during the three-day journey. I was appreciative of Phocas' caution, but I was sure that Lucius was too much of a coward to try anything. Since we had some time, Vibius and I went to tell Cyclops the news, and to bid farewell to Livia. I was somewhat upset that I would not have time to go visit Valeria and Porcinus, but I was going to leave a letter to be delivered to my sister. I paid a sesterce out of the hoard of coins that I had managed to save to a scribe in town who did such things, since while I knew my letters and could write my name, at that time that was about the extent of my literacy. I knew she would understand my haste.

Vibius and I arrived at Cyclops' farm and ended up in a mock wrestling match, rolling in the dirt as each of us competed to be the first to tell Cyclops the news. Naturally, I won, and as I sat panting, straddling Vibius' chest to keep him pinned to the ground, I told Cyclops and Livia, who had been attracted by all the commotion and was standing next to her husband, the news that we were off to join the Legion.

"But you're too young," Livia protested, and I acknowledged that was true, then told her all that had transpired.

After I finished, by which time I had gotten back to my feet and hauled up Vibius, who was busy dusting himself off, I could tell Livia was torn between happiness for me, made even sweeter by the humiliation of my father, the hatred of whom made the Pullus children even closer than most siblings, and her natural apprehension at seeing her brother march off to the army. But I was sixteen and immortal, as all young men are at that age, and I laughed at her fears.

"You're not being very complimentary to your husband," I teased. "After all, he did teach us everything we need to know."

"Not everything," Cyclops interrupted, these being the first words he had spoken since we gave them the news. Turning on his heel, he walked into the house, leaving Vibius, Livia, and me looking mystified. He certainly did not seem happy about this.

We followed him into the house, finding him sitting at the table, pouring a cup of wine, then offering the amphora to us.

We both sat with him, while Livia returned to her chores and, without preamble, Cyclops told us, "I have shown you everything I can about the individual skills you'll need to be a Legionary. Everything else will only come when you're actually in the Legion."

"What sort of things?" I asked.

"Unit formations, for your Century, your Maniple, your Cohort, and for the whole Legion, for one. You'll have to learn to march in column and in square, and that's just one thing."

I had an idea of what column meant, but I was puzzled about the other term.

"What do you mean by 'marching in square'?"

"You'll march in square when you're in enemy territory, and it's a possibility that you'll be attacked. It's basically marching in a battle formation, with three Cohorts marching in the front, two Cohorts on each side, and three Cohorts in the rear, all marching as if you were formed for battle."

I nodded as if I understood, but I really did not. I thought to myself that I would just have to wait until it happened and then I would understand. Then Vibius asked a question that, as hard as it is to believe, we had never asked before, at least I do not remember doing so. It might have been that we had asked, but Cyclops chose not to answer until this day, now that we had made the decision to join the Legions.

For a moment, it was quiet as Cyclops sat there, looking into his cup with his good eye, and I thought that he had either not heard, or was choosing not to answer. He looked up at us, and there was a look in his eye that I had never seen before, a look of almost unfathomable sadness and…something else. I know now that he had the look of a man who has killed in battle, something that changes a man forever, no matter what they might say otherwise. No matter how much you may hate your enemy, when you look across your *scutum* and look into his eyes, it is impossible not to recognize that he is a man, a man just like yourself, and no matter how hard you try, thoughts enter your mind that you do not want there. Does he have a woman? Does he have children? What is he like? It is impossible not to think those thoughts; the best one can do is put them away in the moment, and only think about them after the battle is done and you survive. You look at that man as the blade of your *gladius* sinks into his gut or chest, and you can hear the breath escape from him as you watch the life drain out of his eyes, right in front of you. Almost without exception, the men I have killed all had a shocked look on their face, as if they were surprised that this was their fate, despite the fact that they must have known it was possible as they lined up across a field from us to do battle. I have come to believe that this is the essence of being a human being; no matter what the circumstances, there is always this thought in the back of one's mind that you will be the one that cheats the gods and achieve immortality, that you of all the people who have come and gone are the one destined not to experience death. And then it happens, and you are surprised. But I knew none of this then; I was just impatient for Cyclops to talk to us.

Before he began speaking to us, he turned to Livia and asked her softly, "*Meum mel*, would you go outside to milk the goats? I don't think that you should hear what I'm about to speak of."

Even as he said it, I tried to contain a smile; they still were newlyweds and did not know each other that well. Livia was not the type to meekly obey any man, at least I had never seen it, so I could not hide my shock when she simply nodded her head, gave him a fond smile, and left the house.

I looked at him and blurted, "How in the name of Dis did you do that?"

He looked at me blandly and asked, "Do what?"

I motioned in the direction of her retreating back. "Get her just to do what you say without fighting about it? Luc....my father could never get her to do anything by telling her one time."

"That's because I didn't tell her; I asked her to do that," he responded.

I was mystified; who had ever heard of such a thing, actually asking your wife, or any woman, for that matter, to do something? As much as I despised Lucius, I had obviously been conditioned by him in these matters, and I sat there with my mouth agape as Cyclops ignored me, and answered Vibius' question.

"So you want to know what going into battle is like? You want to know what it is to kill a man?"

Put as starkly as that, it made the both of us gulp a bit, but we both nodded.

"Very well," he said, swirling the contents of his cup around as he stared into it. "The first thing that you notice when you prepare for battle is the smell, at least that was how it was for me. Men who are afraid have a different smell about them."

He was cut off by Vibius, who laughed in disbelief. "Scared? Since when are Legionaries in the Roman army scared?"

The look he gave Cyclops was one of pure scorn, and I had just enough time to choke back the very same laugh, as I was just as disbelieving as Vibius was.

"Any man who tells you that he's not scared before going into battle is either a fool or a liar, and in either case, you want nothing to do with him," he said quietly, but with a vehemence that gave us no doubt that he was serious. "All men feel fear; it's what one does with it, how one controls it that makes the difference between acquitting yourself honorably, or bringing unending shame on you and your entire line." We said nothing to this, so he continued, "As I was saying, the thing you notice on the day of battle is the smell. Men's sweat smells different, their *cac* smells different; it's a smell that from that moment on, you will always associate with the fear that you felt when you first went into battle." He sipped at his wine before continuing; he had our undivided attention now, and he knew it. "The other thing you remember is the sounds. By the gods, it's a terrible racket, two armies about to clash. At least, when you're facing barbarians; they get ready for battle by whipping themselves into a frenzy, screaming all sorts of insults in their ridiculous language. We would always laugh because it was not like we could understand what they were saying, and our laughter would just whip them into a further frenzy. Then, they start beating their weapons against their *scuta* and it gets even louder." Cyclops seemed to be warming to his subject as he began to lean forward, patting the table with one hand in a rhythmic manner; I guessed he was trying to simulate the sound of the barbarian hordes.

"Now, we're quiet, at least compared to them. We whisper to each other, but the Centurions and Optios will smash us with their *vitus* if they catch us, so mostly it's just the sound of them yelling to close the ranks, keep alignment, that sort of thing. Then, the order is given to advance, and we start out, slowly so that we can keep alignment. Sometimes, depending how far away we are, the barbarians will start running at us right then, but usually, they wait so they won't have to run as far and be winded when they reach our lines."

We were both listening intently now as I tried to imagine what the sight must look like of the Legions, perfectly aligned and marching in unison towards the enemy.

"At some point, the *cornu* sounds and we go to quick time, picking up the pace a bit. Now you can hear the boys around you, muttering the Legionary's prayer, 'Jupiter Best and Greatest, protect this Legion, soldiers all.' You find your lips moving as you say the prayer yourself, and your gut is twisted into a knot as you look ahead. If you were like me, in the fourth row of the Second Century of the Fourth Cohort, what you saw were the backs of your fellow Legionaries, and maybe a glimpse in between the spaces of the mass of men facing you." He took another swallow of wine, his voice grown hoarse, as this was the most he had said at one time since we had met him. "Then the order comes to prepare to loose, and you grab one of your *pila* that you've been carrying pinned to your *scutum*, and you notice your hand is all sweaty as you grab hold of it, and tell yourself that you've done this hundreds of times in practice. But this time is different, and you know it. Since I was in the Fourth Cohort, that meant we were in the first line of the *acies triplex*, and the way it works is that, once the command to loose is sounded, the lads in the first rank throw their *pilum*, and hunch just a bit, as the second rank launches, which then does the same as the first, until all the ranks in each Century, which are side by side, loose their first volley. As soon as we loose our first set, the command is given for double time, and we pick up the pace as we are closing with the barbarians, who have usually started their run by this time. Just a moment after we begin our double time, the second command to loose comes, which we do on the run this time. Then, as soon as we've loosed all of our *pila*, we're given the order to charge. It's only then do we make any noise, but what a noise!"

I sat spellbound, completely captivated by his description, feeling as if it were me running across that field. I could even feel a trickle of sweat run cold down my back, and I suppressed a shudder.

"We let loose with a cry from the bowels of Hades, and run headlong into the enemy, but we don't do it all haphazard, though. We try to maintain alignment as much as we can, so that the impact happens along the whole front line at the same time. Even so, it's devilishly hard to do, what with the terrain and the different strides that the men have when running."

He stopped again to take a sip, and both Vibius and I were almost beside ourselves with anticipation. This was the best part! Cyclops sensed our state and deliberately took another, slow sip of wine.

Finally, Vibius burst out, "Well? What happens?"

Looking mildly surprised, Cyclops asked innocently, "What do you mean? What happens when?"

"Don't mock us, Cyclops." I tried to sound firm, but I am sure it came out as a petulant whine.

Laughing, he said, "Oh! You want to know what happens once two opposing armies have started the charge at each other? Well, when they collide, all the sounds you've been hearing to that point are but a whisper compared to the sound of more than a thousand men wearing armor and carrying *scuta* colliding. It's a combination of metal on wood, metal on metal, flesh on flesh, and worst of all, flesh on metal as somebody makes a killing blow in their first strike. At the same time, there's a fearsome grunting and gasping, immediately followed by the screams of those who weren't fortunate enough or good enough to survive that first rush." I closed my eyes, trying to imagine the scene, as Cyclops continued. "From then on, it's the sound of metal on metal, men cursing and fighting, which you can't see because you're in the line, holding onto the back of the man in front of you as they wait their turn to move up. You can't see anything until you're just one or two men back, and then all you see is the flashing of blades as the barbarians try to split us in half with their great huge *gladii* because they're no good for stabbing."

"Then why do they continue to use them?" Vibius asked.

Cyclops shrugged. "Who knows? I'm just thankful that they do, as you should be, now that you're going to be more than likely facing them."

He filled his cup again; Vibius and I exchanged a glance as neither of us had seen him drink this much. Neither had he talked this much, but we were still hanging on his every word. For a moment, we sat there in silence as he was lost somewhere, before Vibius gently urged him to continue. Starting at the sound of Vibius' voice, it was obvious he had been far, far away. Shaking his head as if to rid himself of a bad dream, he heaved a great sigh, looking at us sadly.

"You two are in such a hurry to experience something that, once you've lived through it, will make you wonder why you ever wanted it in the first place. But," he gave a short, harsh laugh, "I was just like you. I guess every young man is as you two are today. At least every free man. So," returning to his subject, "you're standing in the line, holding onto the baldric of the man in front of you, and you can feel him shaking in anticipation and fear with every blast of the Centurion's whistle, the signal for the man in the front of the line to use his *scutum* to bash or push whoever he's battling at the moment back a step, while at the same time, he takes a quick step to the left, and the man behind him steps forward to take his place. Then the man who's been relieved moves to the back of the file to rest and everyone moves up a place. That means that you're one step closer to the fighting. When it gets really difficult is when you're second in line; you can see everything that's going on, but you're supposed to be concentrating on providing the man in front of you with support at the same time. You want to be there to brace him if he's pushed back, but you have to give him room to work and can't crowd him. Unlike all the other positions, where you're holding onto the back of the man in front of you, you can't do that here because it will restrict him too much." He sipped again to lubricate his throat and continued. "The other tricky part of being number two man is that you have to watch what's going on to either side of you as well. If a man in the front rank goes down, and the man behind him isn't quick to fill the gap, you may find yourself in a fight before you're ready when some smelly barbarian steps into the gap. It can be especially bad if it's the man to your right that goes down, because that's the unprotected side. That's why the greatest honor is to be in the Legion on the right flank, and the man farthest to the right of the first Cohort is considered to be one of the best fighters in the Legion, next to the Primus Pilus, who's the only other Roman to his right."

On hearing that, Vibius and I looked at each other and, seeing the same expression, burst out laughing, as we both knew exactly what the other was thinking.

Cyclops looked puzzled for a moment, then chuckled. "Ah, and now both of you plan on being that man, don't you?" We both nodded, still laughing, and his only reply to that was, "Be careful what you wish for, boys." Turning serious again, he said, "So you're waiting for your turn and watching around you, and by this time your body is shaking as if you were suffering the *quartan ague*, so keyed up are you. Then the whistle blows, and the man in front of you does what he's supposed to and you leap to the front, hoping that he did a good job of pushing the enemy back because there's nothing quite so difficult as beginning combat when you can smell the barbarian's stinking breath in your face. It doesn't give you any room to work and you can't use your *scutum* effectively, which means you go straight to the *gladius*. But usually, you have the space that you need to get your *scutum* up and then it's just a matter of letting the barbarian bash away at you and wait for an opening. And when it happens, you must strike quickly and, more importantly, recover quickly and get the *scutum* back up and wait for the man you just dispatched to be replaced by another who wants to kill you. All the while, they're screaming at you in that hideous language, and they try to spit on you every chance they get too. Animals," he spat himself with vehemence, I suppose to emphasize his point, before he took another sip. "If the battle goes well, you only go through one or maybe two rotations, but I've been in battles that have lasted all day, and have gone through the rotation no less than twelve times. *That* was a day, I'll tell you! By the end, I knew that if we had to go one more round, we'd lose because none of us could even raise our *scutum* off the ground. But the gods favored us yet again, and we prevailed. A lot of good men fell that day," he finished quietly.

By the time he had finished, it was almost dark, and we ate with him and Livia before making our farewells. Livia clung to me tightly, embarrassing me by the fuss she was making over me, and pleasing me at the same time.

She gave me what was to be my birthday gift, which was now my farewell gift, a small oil lamp that bore the image of Hercules Invictus slaying the Cretan bull, saying, "So you can have light to write your sisters a letter to let them know you're still alive and well."

She said it with a smile, as if it was a joke, but the shining of her eyes told me she was serious. I still have that lamp to this day.

Cyclops, looking embarrassed, had something wrapped in cloth that he handed to me, while he said apologetically to Vibius, "If I had known that we'd be saying goodbye, I would have something for you, Vibius."

Vibius waved at Cyclops, signifying that no offense had been taken. "What you've given me already, Cyclops, is a gift I'll never be able to repay. I only hope that I've learned your lessons well enough to bring you the honor that you deserve."

Cyclops' weathered features turned even darker as he flushed with pleasure.

As we embraced, he handed me the object, saying quietly, "Open it after you've left."

Nodding assent, I hugged my sister one more time, the last time as it would turn out, and then Vibius and I turned to go. Just before we left, Cyclops grabbed me, tugging at my elbow to pull me a few paces away from Livia and Vibius, clearly wanting to share a private word. The two of them continued chatting quietly while I stood, waiting for Cyclops to speak, sensing that he had something important to say.

"Titus, I just wanted to let you know that I think Vibius has the makings of a good Legionary," he began, which confused me somewhat. I was not sure why he felt the need to pull me aside to talk about Vibius, but as usual, my youthful impatience and self-absorption was total. However, with his next words, I understood why he had pulled me aside, as he finished, "But I think you have what it takes to be a *great* Legionary, Titus. One of the best, if not *the* best that's ever marched for Rome."

There was nothing that I could say to this, although I believe I sputtered some sort of thanks, which he waved away impatiently.

"I'm not telling you this to swell your head. I suspect," he added with a grin, "that you won't need any help with that." As cutting as his words might have been, even then I had recognized a boastfulness in myself, so my answer was to grin back. "No, I'm telling you because that means you have a huge burden. Men will look to you to set the example."

That was when I cut him off, suddenly disappointed.

"Because of my size," I said with more than a touch of bitterness, although I know not why since I had always been proud of my size and strength. I suppose it was just the idea that he only thought it was my size that marked me for greatness in his eyes, but he gave an impatient shake of his head.

"That's only part of it," he replied. I looked at him suspiciously, but there was nothing in his returning one-eyed gaze that indicated he was being anything but completely honest, which would have been completely out of character anyway. Not deigning to comment on my suspicious gaze, he continued, "But there's more to it than that. You don't see it yet. You're too young probably, but I think you've been touched by the gods, and that you were born to lead men in battle. If, " as always, he had to finish with a half-joking, half-mocking conclusion, "you don't let your head swell so much that it bursts."

I stood for a moment, not knowing what to say, before I finally mumbled something to the effect that I would try very hard not to let him down.

"See that you don't," he finished, suddenly thrusting his hand out, which I took.

Understanding that he had spoken his piece, I went to rejoin Vibius, who was waiting for me next to Livia. I gave my sister one final hug, then we turned to leave.

As we were walking away, Vibius turned back and suddenly asked Cyclops, "You never told us how you lost your eye, Cyclops."

"I got promoted," Cyclops responded with grim humor.

"To what?" I asked, but I had a suspicion I already knew the answer.

Cyclops answered, "To the First Cohort, first of the line on the right."

Vibius and I exchanged a glance, and as if reading our minds, Cyclops called out, "I told you boys to be careful what you wish for."

Chapter 2: Joining the Legion

I joined the Legions as part of the *dilectus* authorized by the Senate in the year of the Consulships of Marcus Piso Frugi and Marcus Mesalla Niger, journeying to the newly designated provincial capital of Scallabis, where the new Legion was gathering. I came to the capital accompanied by Vibius and his father, along with my own father and Phocas and Gaia. Our farm outside Astigi was a three days' journey southwest of Corduba, putting it about a week's journey to Scallabis.

Two days after I first donned the *toga virilis* on my sixteenth birthday in April, about a third of a watch before first light, Phocas and I hitched the mule to the wagon, with Gaia packing the food we would eat on the way, along with various other essentials. All my belongings, or at least those that I planned on taking with me, were in a bundle as part of the load, along with obligatory amphorae of wine to keep my father Lucius properly lubricated along the way. He was much more pliable and cooperative with a skin full of wine at hand, and both Phocas and I were nervous that somehow things would fall apart and my father would try to sabotage the deal we had made. He had been more sullen than usual since our agreement, yet to that point did or said nothing to indicate he was having a change of heart. To remind him of the threat I made, I had taken to wearing a *pugio*, given to me as a gift by our tutor Cyclops. The point, so to speak, was not lost on Lucius, as I saw him eying it continuously, no doubt imagining the feeling of it plunging into him should he try to betray me. Once the wagon was loaded, Phocas went to inform my father Lucius that all was ready. He walked out, wrapped in his cloak, already staggering a bit, since he had not slept but had been drinking all night. Without a word, he climbed into the back of the wagon, onto the makeshift pallet that Gaia had prepared and, within moments, was snoring loudly. Phocas and I exchanged a glance, then he mounted the wagon and, with Gaia beside him and with me walking beside the wagon, we left the only home I had ever known. I wondered as I stopped for a moment to gaze back at the modest farm, its main house not much better than some of the hovels I would come across in Gaul, if I would ever see it again and, if I did, under what circumstances. Then I turned and trotted to catch up with the wagon.

Just after dawn, we met with Vibius and his father, both of them astride mules. Vibius' father stank of lime and rawhide, marks of his trade as a tanner, but he was pleasant enough. His good spirits, I suspected, came from the relief he felt at having solved a dilemma without lifting a finger, increasing his family fortunes by subtraction since Vibius was one less mouth to feed. I also believe our choice absolved his conscience of having to make a decision about Vibius' future, since he was not going to inherit the business. Despite that, I could also sense some genuine affection on the part of Vibius' father towards his youngest son, a feeling only strengthened by what I witnessed on our journey to Scallabis. At least I could see a resemblance between the two; Vibius was the image of his father, the same short but powerful frame and bandy legs, as if they had been born astride a mule, with pigeon chests and muscular forearms. And they had more similarities than physical, as I was to learn on the journey. Juno was standing there, her eyes red-rimmed and puffy, signs that she had spent the last night with Vibius in a state other than connubial bliss. Despite the fact that they were as yet unmarried, their love for each other, and the ardor that young men and women all suffer from combined to make any idea of Juno's maidenhead remaining intact, as by rights it should have, an impossible burden for the both of them to bear. Normally, this might have caused Juno's father to exercise his rights as *paterfamilias* and kill Juno while demanding some sort of punishment from Vibius and his family, except their love for each other and the affection that Juno's father had, not just for his daughter, but for Vibius as well, all worked to cause him to turn a blind eye to their passion. I knew that Vibius and Juno were having sexual relations, but Vibius was kind enough and cared enough about Juno to avoid the normal boasting a man does to his best friend about his conquests. Although we never spoke of it, I believe that Vibius knew I loved Juno as he did, and it was a mark of his friendship that he did whatever he could to avoid rubbing what was in effect a failure in my face. Regardless, it hurt; nevertheless, I smiled as I went to Juno to give her a farewell hug. Putting my arms around her, I could feel my heart racing, the unbidden and unwelcome thought coming of what it would be like if there were no clothes between us, if we were alone and…I shook my head, trying to banish the thoughts that were bound to make my feelings known if I allowed them to continue.

Juno, for her part, seemed oblivious to my struggle, stood on her tiptoes to whisper in my ear, "Titus, please take care of Vibius. Make sure he comes home to me."

"I will," I promised, and I meant it sincerely.

Despite my feelings for her, they were still overridden by my love for Vibius. Suddenly grabbing both of my arms, in a grip that was surprisingly strong for a girl her size, she whispered urgently, "Swear it on Jupiter's Stone, Titus. Swear that you'll bring him back to me alive."

Flattered that she put that kind of faith in my ability, and somewhat unnerved by her passion, I made the oath, which calmed her down. While I was making my farewells to Juno, Vibius' father had ridden his mule over to our wagon, where he saw Lucius sprawled in the back of it, snoring away.

Glancing over at me, I could feel the heat in my face rising, but before I could speak, Phocas said smoothly, "My master has been suffering from ague and flux, and it's weakened him considerably. But despite his illness, he didn't want to deprive his only son of his greatest wish to join the Legions."

Vibius' father nodded gravely, clearly not convinced in the slightest, but not wishing to make a fuss about it either. Farewells done, we turned our little caravan towards the road out of town leading towards Scallabis.

The trip was pleasant enough; the weather cooperated, and Vibius' father turned out to be a veritable fount of chatter, telling awful jokes and fantastic tales of the exciting life in the tanning business. He was not that bad, truth be known, and as we talked, I could see where Vibius got his sense of humor and buoyant nature. Lucius regained consciousness a watch or so into the journey, leaning over the side of the wagon to retch violently. Phocas handed the reins to Gaia in order to aid Lucius, his help being in the form of handing him an amphora of wine.

Seeing Vibius and his father watching and unable to ignore what was taking place, Phocas announced, "This is a potion that's served to ease my master's suffering in the past. We paid a Greek doctor for a large quantity since it's proven so effective."

I silently thanked the gods for Phocas and his quick thinking; despite the transparency of the fiction, neither Vibius nor his father seemed inclined to dispute it, and given that Lucius' sickness seemed to pass as soon as he drank of the "potion," there was no unpleasantness. In fact, once Lucius was fully conscious, he began a conversation with Vibius' father, who rode beside our wagon as they talked. They began discussing the current political situation, with the aftermath of the Catiline conspiracy still fresh on every citizen's mind. While they talked, it gave Vibius and me the opportunity to drop back a ways, he riding and I walking as we talked. The only topic of interest was our immediate future, and we both speculated on what was facing us. As much as Cyclops had told us, there was as much and more that we did not know, of which we both were all too aware.

We arrived in Scallabis after almost a week of hard travel; it was the first time I had been to the provincial capital. To my country-boy eyes, it was the height of glamour and excitement, a bustling metropolis that always seemed to be buzzing with activity as farmers, muleteers, merchants, whores, and all sorts of shady characters flocked to the city. Of course, it was not a metropolis, but I had yet to see Rome or Alexandria, another point about which Lucius was only too happy to remind me, seeing it as one more sign of my inadequacy. Just as our party entered the city through the main gate, my father made a loud declamation how this pile of *cac* was nothing when compared to Rome, going on to relate how his father, who had loved him well, took him and his brothers to the eternal city to see none other than Pompey Magnus. His words immediately drew hostile stares from the others around us, and I felt my face turn red from embarrassment, with Phocas turning to give Lucius a warning look as he sat in the back of the wagon, swilling wine and running his mouth, completely ignoring the both of us.

Vibius and his father looked equally embarrassed at this display, and finally I dropped back to the wagon to hiss, "By the Furies, if you don't shut your mouth, I'll kill you on the spot!"

He opened his mouth to say something back to me, but evidently, the look on my face stopped him, because he snapped his mouth shut and remained quiet, sullenly sucking on his wine skin.

We made our way to the Praetor's residence; this was the site of the *dilectus*, the *dilectus* being the official recruiting effort for the Legion. Because it was just after midday, there was a line of young men, accompanied by the men who would vouch for them, waiting for their turns in front of the *conquisitores*, the group of officials charged with finding qualified enlistees to enroll in the name of the Praetor. It was in this line that I first heard the name of the Praetor, a name that every citizen of Rome and probably every human being in the known world has heard of by now. It was by way of overhearing a couple of the older men, obviously the fathers of other boys.

"So do you know anything of the new Praetor, since you're recently arrived from Campania?" asked one of the men, some sort of artisan, by the look of him. The man he was asking was dressed as a member of the equestrian class, although it was clear that his toga had seen better days.

The equestrian nodded and said, "I know of him. Gaius Julius Caesar is his name, of the Julii."

The artisan shrugged, responding, "Never heard of him. What do you know?"

The equestrian gave a snort of derision. "He's ambitious, I'll give him that. He's so ambitious," he said with a sly grin, "that he supposedly became Nicomede's 'woman' when he was serving under Marcus Thermus in Bithynia."

This caused the other man to hoot with laughter; it has always been the case that the lower classes love any hint of scandal attached to their social betters.

The equestrian became serious. "Whether or not that's true, that's what's said. But what I do know is that Caesar is well loved by the people of your class."

He did not say this as a compliment, yet if the other man took offense, he gave no sign.

"Well," the artisan grunted, "what I care about most is whether or not he can properly lead a Legion. The gods know, in my day, it was hit or miss."

The equestrian looked at the other man in some surprise. "You were in the Legions, citizen?"

"One of Marius' mules," the other replied with quiet pride, as well he should have.

The men of Marius' Head Count Legions were the first of their kind, and showed their supposed betters that they could fight just as well as anyone in the higher classes, better perhaps. In fact, it was the reforms of Marius that opened the door for those of my class to enter the Legions and perhaps advance their own fortunes. For the rest of the time we stood in line, the equestrian was completely respectful of the artisan, and indeed began plying him with questions about Gaius Marius.

Such was the nature of the conversations all along the line as we shuffled slowly towards the entrance to the building, which even I could see was not much more than a large villa. It served as the headquarters and the living space for the Praetor sent by Rome to govern the province and, as I was to learn, carries the same name as the headquarters tent of a Roman military camp, the *Praetorium*. While we waited, we saw much bustling about, with couriers coming and going, jumping from their horses to walk quickly into the building, then reappearing in a matter of moments, their dispatch bag full, either of answers to the original dispatch they had delivered, or some sort of counter-orders or further questions, or at least so I imagined. Phocas was monitoring Lucius carefully, to ensure that while he was sated enough to be lucid and appear to have all of his faculties, my father was not allowed to render himself insensible. With the day passing and the sun sinking lower, I began to worry that we would be out of luck, since my father had not remained this sober for this long in some time and, despite my threats, I was worried that he would bring ruin to all Vibius and I had planned because of his thirst. Finally, it became our turn; Vibius and his father would follow us, and I took my father by the elbow, applying extra pressure just before the impatient guard made a comment, giving him a look that was meant to convey exactly what awaited him if he failed. His fear was palpable, but he nodded his head and we entered the building.

There were a series of tables, where not one, but three *conquisitores* were actually standing, each behind a slave who was working as a scribe, writing down the necessary information dictated to them by the *conquisitores*. The third table to the farthest side of the room was empty, and the *Conquisitore* behind it waved to us impatiently.

"You're here to enlist, no doubt," he said briskly, but I could only nod dumbly. Turning to my father, the official spoke just as briskly. "And you're here to swear to his citizenship and age, aren't you?"

For a moment, my father did not speak, and my heart began to hammer even harder. Glancing out of the corner of my eye, I could see his lips working but nothing came out.

Finally, his words came in a hoarse whisper. "Yes, your Excellency."

Obviously unimpressed with my father's oratory skills, the *Conquisitore*, a middle-aged man wearing a toga with the badge of his office worn around his neck, snapped, "Out with it, citizen. Who are you?"

Finally given a question he could answer, my father replied, with just a hint of pride, "I am Lucius Pomponius Pullus, citizen of Rome and a member of the tribe Pupinia, of the gens of the Pomponii."

Nodding, the *Conquisitore* pointed at me, and asked, "This is your son? Is he the one joining the Legion?"

I spoke up with the rehearsed answer that we were told to give by Cyclops when he explained the process to us.

"Yes, I am Titus Pomponius Pullus, also a citizen of Rome by virtue of my father and his father and grandfathers before him. I am also of the gens of the Pomponii, and my mother was a citizen as well, of the tribe Galeria, and of the gens of the Asinia."

The *Conquisitore* indicated to his scribe to write down the appropriate information.

Once completed, the *Conquisitore* looked at Lucius and asked, "And his age?"

Here was the moment of truth; we had rehearsed this many times. As you know, gentle reader, the years of the birth of Roman citizens are recorded by the number of years from the founding of Rome and the Consuls for that year. It had been drilled into me that I was born in the year of the Consulship of Publius Servilius Vatia and Appius Claudius Pulcher but now, in order to perpetrate this fiction, we were forced to consult the annals to determine the Consuls for the year before. I could feel the sweat beginning to trickle down my back as I waited for what seemed to be the week that it took my father to answer.

However, it must not have been long because I detected no change in the expression of the *Conquisitore* or the scribe when my father finally said, "My son, Titus Pomponius Pullus, was born in the year of 430, as reckoned from the founding of Rome, under the Consulship of the dictator Lucius Cornelius Sulla and Quintus Caecilia Metellus Pius, may the gods favor both of their memories, on the date of April twentieth."

This raised an eyebrow from the *Conquisitore*, though not in a suspicious manner.

"Just a couple weeks ago, eh, boy? Couldn't wait to join the Legions, could you?"

Finally, an answer that I could give honestly!

"No, Your Excellency, I couldn't. It's been my dream since I was a boy to serve."

"Good," the *Conquisitore* replied. "Would that all of your fellow citizens had your patriotism. But it's auspicious, your birth date, because you'll be assigned to the 10th Legion, and its symbol has already been established."

Looking at me, smiling, he added, "It's the sign of the bull, the symbol under which you were born. It must be that the Fates have brought you here."

And with that, my father's part was essentially done. The scribe used his stylus to write down the relevant information on a beeswax tablet, then handed it to me, instructing me to go through a door on the left to be examined by a fellow who would determine that I was fit enough to join the Legion. Lucius was told by the scribe to wait, pointing him to the back of the room where other fathers were standing, while I went into the other room for my physical examination. There, another man waited, quickly identified as a doctor and with his own scribe standing next to him, to whom I handed the tablet. I was told to disrobe for the doctor to examine me, if that is what one could call it, asking me a few questions about my overall health, telling the scribe to write that I was physically fit and had no identifying marks. In particular, they apparently were looking for any marks to indicate that I was once a slave. Passing the examination with no other comment than the physician's exclamation about my size and musculature, I was ordered to dress, then handed the tablet and told to go back into the original room, where Lucius was still waiting. The process took no more than a few moments. My father was presented with a document, written on vellum, containing the information that we gave concerning my birth, with the extra information provided by my physical examination, which he signed, his hand barely shaking at all. It was done. The *Conquisitore* told us what would happen next.

"Lucius Pullus, your part is done. Titus Pullus, you're now a *probatio*, and as such will take an oath before you're sent to the camp of the 10th Legion. It's not the full oath that all Legionaries must take; that will only be administered once you're considered to be worthy to be a soldier of Rome."

I bristled a bit at that; if he only knew who he was dealing with! However, he either missed my irritation or ignored it and continued with, "You're to report at first light at the camp of the 10th Legion. Until then, you may spend your last evening as you wish. The scribe will give you the directions to the camp. It's just outside of the city walls."

Whereupon he had me swear an oath to Mars, Jupiter, and Roma, then, once completed, he motioned to the door, indicating that our business was finished. By this time, Vibius and his father had entered and were in the same process I had just endured, and we grinned at each other as I walked out the door.

Phocas was waiting for us; when I told him that our ruse had worked, he whooped with joy, ignoring decorum as he hugged me with all his might. While he did so, I was reminded that this was a moment I should be sharing with my father, except he had made a straight line for the wagon and the amphora, ignoring the celebration. For a moment, just one, I experienced a terrible sadness as I watched my father make his supplication to the only god he truly worshiped, or for whom he had any feeling, for that matter. Then I shook it off, enjoying the moment Phocas and I were having. Presently, Vibius and his father emerged from the villa, Vibius' face plastered with what must have been the same silly grin that was on my face, and we embraced. We had done it! We had joined the Legions together. The thought that this was merely a first step never entered our minds; as far as we were concerned, we were both as good as Legionaries. Fortunately, the gods did not disagree with our assessment.

We spent the night at an inn; it turned out to be the last night either Vibius or I would spend under a roof for some time to come, although we did not yet know that. There was a tavern attached to the inn, and Vibius' father at least was determined to give us a proper send-off, which my father was only too happy to participate in, since it meant that the wine would be flowing. I was ashamed at Lucius' obviously naked desire to suck up all the wine that Vibius' father was willing to pay for, but thankfully, Vibius' father was gracious, despite his modest means. By this point, enough time had passed for me to witness that, despite Vibius' lowly status in their family, there was real affection between father and son, and I mused about what that must feel like. Despite the convivial atmosphere, I drank just enough wine, watering it at that, to keep from appearing ungracious. I was not much of a drinker of wine in those days, and although I am not much of one now, I certainly have experienced moments of which Bacchus would be proud, including a period of several weeks when I stayed more or less perpetually drunk, but that happened much, much later in my life. The evening progressed, and Vibius, his father, and my father got drunker, even as I grew more impatient.

At some point, one of the whores that can always be found in such establishments made her way to our table, and Vibius' father poked his son in the ribs and winked. "Well, son? How about your father giving you a real going-away present, huh?"

Vibius' face flushed immediately, a combination of embarrassment and anger.

"Father, I'm sworn to Juno, and she's the only woman I want."

"Just wait, that'll change." His father laughed, which Lucius found equally amusing.

"No it won't," Vibius snapped, and I could see he was very angry now.

So could his father, who made a placating gesture.

"*Pax*, son. I was only joking. Forgive a father for trying to give his son something to remember," he said.

Vibius softened immediately. "No, Father. I should be begging your forgiveness. I know you meant well; it's just that I already miss Juno."

Vibius' father put his arm around his son and nodded. "I understand, Vibius. You're just like me. I've been with your mother going on twenty-four years, and she's still the only woman for me." He paused. "Most of the time."

He said this last with a roar of laughter, and even Vibius could not remain upset.

The evening passed by quickly enough, but once it was time to retire, I found I could not sleep, being much too excited. For a moment, I envied Vibius, who lay across the room, snoring peacefully, making me think that perhaps more wine would not have been a bad idea. Lying on my cloak that I threw over the pallet of straw, I stared at the sky through the small window placed high on the wall, wondering how different my life would be one short day from now. It was with this thought in my head that somehow, I finally fell asleep.

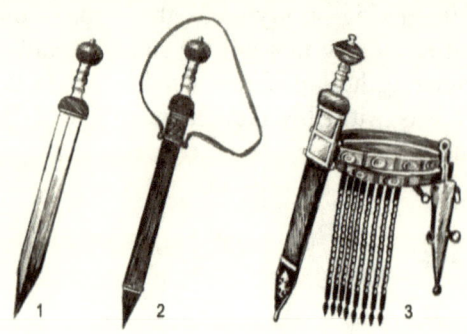

Roman *gladius; (pl.)gladii* suspended from the *baltea (Drawing on right)*

Roman *galea; (pl.) galeae* of the Late Republican period

Roman *scutum; (pl.) scuta* of Late Republic with *pilum; (pl.) pila*

Tools and cooking equipment carried by a Legionary. From top: Cooking pot and wicker basket; ladle. Tools from left to right are: sickle; pickaxe; turf cutter; palisade stake, of which two were issued per Legionary.

Chapter 3: *Tirones*

Any regret from the night before about not partaking of wine was immediately dismissed when I saw poor Vibius, who looked slightly green, his eyes rimmed red, and his breath smelling like my father's in the morning. We had paid the slave maintaining the watch to wake us two parts of a watch before dawn, despite it being only a short walk to the camp. Neither of us could rouse our respective fathers, which was fine with me, but I felt a pang about not going to the slave quarters to wake Phocas and Gaia. Making our way down to the main room of the inn, we rummaged around until we found a loaf of bread and some oil that was close to turning rancid, and split the loaf, soaking it in the oil. Carrying our portions out the door, we began to make our way in the dark, the few belongings we were bringing with us slung over our shoulders, along with the appropriate token that we were to hand to the soldier at the gate to show that we were now part of the Legion. Walking slowly, neither of us said much. Despite our eagerness, we also knew that we were embarking on something momentous. After all, we were still boys to a large degree, and I would be lying if I said we did not have any fear of what we were headed into.

Arriving at the gate, we stopped a short distance away, not wanting just to walk up on some guard who might be half-asleep and would kill us before our career even started, so we sat on the ground, waiting for the light to become strong enough so that we could approach without fear. While sitting there, we made out other shapes of men approaching, then heard them talking quietly, as the others who enlisted the day before began to show up. Vibius and I smugly but quietly congratulated ourselves for being the first to arrive, making no sound to alert the others to our presence, although I do not know why. Instead, we sat listening, learning about our fellow *tiros* as they talked among themselves.

"So what do you think it'll be like?"

This from a high-pitched, nervous-sounding voice.

"It'll be the hardest thing we've ever done," came the response from a grim-sounding, deeper voice.

"By the gods," came another. "I can't wait to kill some barbarian scum! I bet I have the most kills of anyone in this Legion!"

Vibius and I glanced at each other and, despite barely seeing the other in the gloom, I could tell we were both making a mental note of that voice. We wanted to see this mighty warrior for ourselves as soon as it was light.

"*Gerrae!* That's awfully big talk," replied the grim-sounding voice, which I could just begin to make out as a shape against the slowly lightening sky.

It was hard to tell from my vantage point, sitting on the ground, but he seemed to be nearly as tall as I was, but as I learned later that was not the case, and was simply because I was sitting down.

"You'll probably be the first one to piss yourself the instant one of those barbarians looks at you cross-eyed." This came from yet another voice and, following the sound, I could just make out what looked like a pair, but sitting very closely together, making it impossible to tell which one of them actually offered the challenge.

"Watch your tone, you! I've beaten better than you, I swear by Hercules I have!"

This from the great warrior, although I sensed a note of uncertainty, despite the brave words.

"That's easy to say," said the other coolly.

"Easy, boys." This came from a previously unheard voice. "There'll be plenty of time enough for everyone to get as much fighting in as any man could want."

This voice sounded older, more confident. The others seemed to sense it as well, and consequently, there was no more bickering. Besides, the light was growing, so that what were indistinct shapes before took on more definite form, and the areas of the camp that were not illuminated by torchlight earlier could now be made out. At that, Vibius and I stood from where we were sitting completely silent, causing our new companions to yelp in alarm and jump away. I could not help noticing that the one who yelped the loudest was also the one bragging, but I held my peace. No need to make enemies so early, I thought. One day, I might be fighting beside that man. Stepping forward, I called to the other men; I could now see that there were a total of six other men standing there.

"*Salve*, citizens," I called with what I hoped was a tone of friendliness.

They returned the greeting in a ragged chorus.

As I got closer, one of the other men exclaimed, "Gods, you ARE a big one, aren't you? Remind me to stand next to you, Ajax."

This brought laughter from the others, and I joined in since I had been teased about my size my whole life. The only man near my height was tall, although nowhere near as tall as I was; I had a good two to three inches on him. Standing for a moment, we surveyed each other now that the light was strong enough, but before we could speak, we heard the sound of a call inside the camp, then the gates opened, each half pushed open by a man dressed in *lorica* and full kit.

"Well," I said. "I guess that means they're ready to receive us."

And without waiting, I began walking towards the gate, where a third man appeared, standing in the middle of the gateway, hands on his hips. As we drew closer, I could see that while he was in basically the same uniform as the other two, his helmet was different. He wore a crest of horsehair, transverse across the helmet, going from ear to ear. His face looked like wrinkled leather, the kind one sees after wearing a set of shoes for a long time in all types of weather. In one hand was clutched a stick of some sort, which he was slowly twitching against his leg as he watched us approach. He was short, but very stocky, and once I got close enough, I could see that on one arm a livid scar ran from his elbow all the way down his forearm, slowly twisting until it stopped just above his wrist. I had trouble taking my eyes off of it, but when I did and looked the man in the eye, I saw no welcome in his expression. In fact, if I were to characterize the look on his face, the best I can conjure is to ask you to imagine that a *numen* or other invisible shade is hovering just in front of him, holding a huge, steaming pile of *cac* under his nose, *cac* that only he can smell. That was how he looked at us, and I was soon to find out that my description was not far off from the truth, except that the pile of *cac* was actually us.

"All of you fall in, in a single line starting right here, with the tallest first to my left." He pointed to a spot with his stick, and I headed that way, knowing already that this would be my spot.

His voice sounded like he had eaten gravel for breakfast, with his tone matching the look on his face, and he obviously was not pleased with what he saw. We struggled to get into the proper order; my part was easy, but the others had to gauge each other to determine exactly where they were supposed to be. After a couple of moments, we were more or less settled into a line, and I looked over to my left to see where Vibius had ended up. Suddenly, I was slammed in the stomach by something that felt very much like a *pugio*, except it was blunt and the wind rushed out of my lungs as I dropped immediately to my knees, gasping for breath and clutching my stomach, expecting to feel blood, so sure I was that I had been stabbed. Seeing a pair of boots in front of me, much like the pair that Cyclops wore, I looked up to see the Legionary with the stick in one hand, tapping the other end of it into the palm of his other hand as he looked down at me with a sneer on his face.

"Nobody told you to look around, did they, you *cunnus*?" he snarled, his voice even more gravelly than before because he pitched it loudly enough for all to hear.

Not sure what to say, I shook my head. Instantly, the stick lashed out, catching me just above my ear, causing stars to explode in my head.

"I asked you a question, boy," he roared, and now more afraid than any time I could remember in my life, I answered quickly, "No, sir...I mean, Your Excellency."

WHAM! Another blow, this time on the top of my head, and now I felt something more than fear as I began to get angry. Was there no pleasing this man?

"I work for a living, you *cunnus*," he bellowed at an even louder level, which I had not thought possible if I had not heard it. "I'm no Excellency! You'll address me by my proper title."

Suddenly, his voice dropped back to normal, and he continued talking, as if there was nothing untoward taking place an instant before.

"On your feet, boy. And look straight ahead, you got that?"

I pulled myself to my feet, a little unsteadily, but before I could answer, he continued.

"Of course, none of you know what my proper title or my name is, because you haven't been taught such things. So we'll begin with that. My name is Lucius Favonius, and I'm the Primus Pilus of the Tenth Legion. I know that the title means nothing to you now, but you'll learn what it means in time. Right now, all you need to know is that as far as you're concerned, I, and anyone who wears this," he pointed to his helmet, "are to be considered on the same level as the gods you worship, because like the gods, we exercise the power of life and death over each of you."

I gulped; this was not going exactly as I had seen it in my mind's eye, and I wondered how Vibius was taking this. My gut was still throbbing, and my head still ringing, so it was hard to pay attention, but I knew that what I was being told was important.

"I'll escort you to the *Praetorium*." He turned and pointed at a huge tent, dead in the middle of the camp, several hundred feet away.

Without waiting for an answer, he turned to stride away, with all of us following quickly behind him. When we drew close, he stopped us several paces away from the entrance. Standing in front of it were two Legionaries, obviously on guard duty, and similarly to the Praetor's residence, the area around the tent was a bustle of activity as soldiers and civilians came and went into it. As I was to learn, anywhere our commanding general, the Praetor Julius Caesar, was located, it was always like a beehive.

"You'll hand in those tokens, and you'll then return to that spot outside the *Praetorium*, where you'll get into the exact same line you're in now, facing the tent, and you'll wait for me. Is that clear?"

"Yes, Primus Pilus," I answered quickly, before anyone else had a chance to answer, catching him a bit by surprise.

He looked at me for a moment before giving a harsh chuckle.

"Maybe you're not as stupid as you look, boy."

You have no idea, I thought grimly, but I am going to take your job, old man.

Turning in our tokens to a clerk, we gave our names, which were matched up to the documents that were created as part of our records and sent from the Praetor's residence the day before. On turning in our tokens, we were informed that we were now no longer *probationes*, but had achieved the lofty status of *tirones*, or *tiros* as we were more commonly called, when of course we were not called all manner of other names. None of us had any idea what the distinction was, or why it mattered, although we would learn, and the difference was actually quite important. As *probationes*, while subject to some of the rules and regulations governing the army, it was not the complete set, so that if we ran afoul of one of those rules during our brief time in that status, the range of our punishment was limited. The status of *probatio* usually lasted longer because normally the *conquisitores* were out in the countryside and would march groups of new recruits to the training camp, but it was not necessary in our case. However, as *tirones*, we were now under the full authority of the Roman Legion, meaning that we could be flogged, or worse, executed for a breach of the rules, if deemed serious enough. We were then presented with another document that we were told to sign, something I found impossible to read because it seemed to be in some sort of language that I did not understand. I would come to master it and read it as easily as I read any document written in the normal fashion, but it would take some time. Back then, I just signed like everyone else and was informed that this involved our pay.

"So when do we get our pay?" piped up the one I had marked as being the loudmouthed great warrior.

His name was Spurius Didius, and he was also on the tall side, standing third from the end where I stood. He had a sly look about him, always peering about like he was searching for something to steal, which as it turned out, was exactly what he was doing, but that is for later. The clerk looked up in surprise at the question, then burst out laughing.

"Why don't you ask the Primus Pilus about that?" he replied, and I sensed that this would not be a good idea, something that Didius obviously did not pick up on, as he exclaimed loudly, "I'll do just that."

Once we turned in our tokens and signed our documents, we went outside and fell into our positions in line more quickly than the first time. There was just enough time for Vibius to whisper a quick question about how I was doing, and I reassured him that I was fine, if still hurting a bit. However, I was determined that I had learned my lesson and would let someone else make the mistakes from here on in. Standing in line again, we waited for what seemed like a full watch and I sensed, as did some of the others, that this was some sort of test, so I made sure to stand as still as I could and not look around.

The waiting turned out to be too much for some, and I heard someone whisper loudly, "Pluto's cock, what are they waiting for?"

Instantly, I heard quick footsteps, followed by the sound of what had to be a stick smashing into someone's body, then a thud as the man fell to the ground, the unfortunate gasping for air much like I had.

"Did anyone tell you to speak, *cunnus*?" It was the voice of the Primus Pilus.

"N-no, Primus Pilus," the man managed to gasp.

"Then on your feet, you pathetic piece of *cac*," the Primus Pilus spoke scornfully. "I didn't hit you near as hard as I did the oaf on the end, so get up and quit sniveling like a woman."

The Primus Pilus reappeared in front of us, but instead of turning my head to look again, I watched him out of the corner of my eye. He wore the same expression on his face, except this time, he was not alone. Standing next to him, in identical uniform, though without quite as many phalarae, torqs, and arm rings, was a slightly taller, slender man, who also looked a bit younger. He bore a scar down the right side of his face, from the middle of his ear to midway down his jaw, giving him a look of wickedness, and he too was carrying the same kind of stick as Primus Pilus Favonius, although he stood slightly behind the Primus Pilus.

Indicating the second Centurion, Primus Pilus Favonius announced, "This is Secundus Pilus Prior Gaius Crastinus. He's the commander of the Second Cohort of the Tenth Legion. You'll accompany him to the quartermaster, where you'll be issued your equipment. You'll obey him in the same manner you obey me, or you'll wish you had never been born. Is that understood?"

This time, we responded in a more unified manner, although it still did not impress the Primus Pilus, or the Pilus Prior for that matter. The two Centurions exchanged a quiet word before the Primus Pilus disappeared into the *Praetorium*, leaving us to the tender mercy of Pilus Prior Crastinus.

"Right," he called out. "The first thing we're going to learn is how to go from one point to another without looking like a mob. Understood?"

"Yes, Pilus Prior," we answered.

"The first thing you *cunni* need to know is how to stand correctly," he continued.

I was somewhat surprised; I did not know until that moment that there was a right and wrong way to stand!

As if reading my mind, he said, "As you'll learn, there are only two ways of doing things in the Legions. The Legion way and the wrong way. When you hear the command *intente*, you'll come to the position that I'm about to show you."

He demonstrated; pulling himself erect, he looked straight ahead, pulling his chin in, with his chest out, his feet together and his arms straight down by his sides.

Holding that position for a moment so that we could see it, he broke the position, then immediately snapped, "*Intente!*"

Instantly, we tried to emulate the position he had just shown us, as he walked up and down, inspecting us, correcting my comrades with a quick smack to the part of the body that was not in the proper position. His progress was punctuated by grunts and groans as he made his way to me, and I prayed to every god I knew that I had done it correctly because I was still sore from my earlier lesson. Once he reached me, I concentrated on looking straight ahead, despite my natural inclination to look at him. This was one time where my height actually helped, since I could look directly at his horsehair device and not in his eyes. Luckily, he just rapped my knuckles to make me put my hands into the correctly curled position before he returned to the front of our group.

"That is pathetic, truly pathetic," he sighed, with what sounded like genuine sadness, "but since we have so much to do today, we'll have to work on this another time. Now, I'm going to give another command, to tell you to turn to the right. When this command is given, you'll all immediately pivot, like so." He demonstrated by pivoting on the ball of his left foot, while simultaneously turning on his right heel, then, after turning, bringing his left foot back to its original position next to his right foot. "You will not move until you hear the last word of the command," he commanded next, which confused me.

How would we know which was the last word?

However, it became clear that this was yet another trick, when he called out, "*Ad GLADIUM*," putting the emphasis on the second word, causing at least three of the others to turn in the manner he had demonstrated. For some reason, I did not move; I think I was already beginning to understand how things worked, or so I thought at the time.

Immediately, the Pilus Prior screamed, "Do not move!" Then he ran over to the unfortunates and roared at one of them, "You miserable bag of *cac*! I said to wait for the FINAL word of the command."

"But, Pilus Prior," the man replied in a whining, wheedling voice that I recognized immediately as belonging to Didius.

Before he could get another word out, however, the thud of the stick smashing into his gut sounded, and I heard him fall, choking.

"But what? There is no but, you *cunnus*, you piece of filth! You'll wait for the command!"

Before Didius could give any response, Pilus Prior Crastinus leaped to the other two, administering the same type of punishment to them that he had doled out to Didius. It turned out that one of them was Vibius, although I did not find out until later, because he was at the farther end of the line, towards what would become known as the "little end."

Once the three recovered and were at the original position of *intente*, the Pilus Prior again commanded, "*Ad Gladium…Clina!*"

Immediately, we all turned in the manner we had been taught, except that now, one of our group, while he had indeed turned in the exact manner that was specified, turned to the left instead of the right. This sent Pilus Prior Crastinus into an ecstasy of rage.

"By the gods, what has been sent to me?" he asked rhetorically.

Running over to the man standing facing the one to his left, instead of staring at the back of the man to his right as he should have, I could hear by the tone of voice that this had taken the anger of the Pilus Prior to a new level.

"Are you daring to tell me that you don't know your left from your right?"

"N-n-no, Pilus Prior," came the answer, almost forcing me to look down the line to see who could possibly not know their left from their right.

The response obviously caught the Pilus Prior by surprise as well, because there was silence for a moment, then he asked in a deceptively calm voice, "What's your name, boy?"

"Q-Q-Quintus Artorius, Pilus Prior," came the answer in a quaking voice.

"Well, Quintus Artorius, seeing as your whore of a mother and slave of a father never bothered to teach you your left from right, let me show you."

SMACK!

"That's the left side of your face."

SMACK!

"That's the right side of your face. Which hand do you eat with?"

"Th-this hand, Pilus Prior," came the answer.

SMACK!

"That's your right hand! That's the hand you'll hold a *gladius* in, do you understand? So when I give you the command, *Ad Gladium, Clina*, which direction do you suppose you'll turn towards? No, don't tell me, point."

A silence, where Artorius obviously pointed in the right direction.

"Very good, Artorius. Now, turn around and face the way everyone else is facing. And remember, if you obey an order and find yourself as you just were, you were wrong. Got it?"

"Yes, Pilus Prior."

Once we were faced the correct way, he taught us the command to march, starting on the left foot first, which made sense because it automatically put our *scuta* side first, and would be how we would fight. After a few fits and starts, and more beatings, we finally got it right, then marched to the section of the camp, behind the *Praetorium,* but still part of the headquarters area, where the quartermasters were housed in their own tent, almost as large as the *Praetorium.* Inevitably, we bungled the halting when the order came, which was of course by design of the Pilus Prior, to whom we were taking a healthy dislike at this point. After more beatings, and practice of starting and stopping, we were then told to go into the tent, where we would be issued our basic necessities as a Legionary. I was first in line, and immediately ran into trouble because of my size, when I was handed a tunic, the soldier's tunic, plus a spare and told to try it on. Instead of hanging loosely in the proper manner, it was fairly tight, particularly across the shoulders. The first pair of boots I was handed were too small as well, as were the next few pairs. Finally, after rummaging around, the Legionary assigned as *immunes* for the quartermaster found a pair that almost fit.

"You'll have to have one of the cobblers outside of camp make you a pair, special."

"How much will that cost?" I asked, dismayed.

The Legionary shrugged. "No more than a few sesterces, I expect. I wouldn't know."

He immediately moved on to the others, passing out their own set of boots, all of which fit, I noted dismally. This was not shaping up to be a great day for me. While the *lorica* I was handed fit, it was also a little snug. Fortunately, it was not enough to restrict my movement, and I gave a quiet thanks to the gods for that small favor. Some of the other lads looked lost, and more than one staggered when they were handed the *lorica* and told to put it on over the tunic.

We were told by the *immune* to invest in a padded undershirt that was not issued, but could be made by one of the merchants dealing in such items who were a permanent fixture outside the camp. Handing us our belts and harnesses next, he showed us how to bunch the mail of our *loricae* above the belt so that it would distribute the weight better. Next came the helmet, and once again, I presented a problem, although this was more my problem than for the *immunes*. The helmet fit, except that it fit more tightly than it did on the others, so that the felt padded cap that the others wore was useless to me, at least with its normal thickness. I was sure that this too would require a trip outside camp at the first opportunity. In the meantime, the helmet was riding on my head with nothing in between it but my hair, which kept catching on some of the internal fittings. Because of that discomfort, I resolved that I would cut my hair as short as I could, a style that I wear to this day. Hair may be the pride of a woman, but it is the shame of a warrior, at least that was what I told the others when they teased me about being practically bald. A hidden benefit of shaving my head was that it gave the normal cap just enough room to fit, saving me a few sesterces. Even so, it was still a snug fit, but I learned fairly quickly that this was an advantage; it kept the helmet from slipping down over my eyes or turning sideways, which was a constant problem for a lot of my comrades. Once the *galeae* were passed out, we were given our *scuta*, not the real one, but the one made of wicker with which Cyclops had trained Vibius and me. Having held a *scutum* many times by this point, Vibius and I had no trouble, something that did not go unnoticed by the *immune*, who narrowed his eyes, although he did not say anything. The others had some trouble, handling it awkwardly, not sure how to grasp it correctly. One of the others even dropped his, causing a string of curses to be launched by the *immune*, yet thankfully, there was no beating, the Pilus Prior not being nearby at the time.

There were a number of other pieces of equipment; a spade, which was handed to us by the *immune* with a smirk and a comment. "You're going to get to know that piece of equipment very well."

We stared at him blankly, not knowing exactly what he meant, but he was right. Along with the spade came the turf cutter, our *patera* from which we would prepare and eat our meals, a basket to put the smaller items in, the pack and a grinding mill that was to be shared by our tent section, along with spare thongs and other odds and ends. Finally, we were left with just two pieces of gear to be handed to us, and again Vibius and I thanked the gods that we knew what to expect. Alone out of our group, we knew that we would not be getting the real *gladius* or *pilum* that day, just the *rudis* and practice *pilum*. Therefore, when we were handed our wooden weapons, we made not a sound, which was fortunate, because the Pilus Prior had just entered the tent behind us, although we did not yet know it.

"What's this?" demanded none other than Didius. "Are we children that we don't get a real *gladius*?"

"Exactly," exclaimed one of the others, someone in the middle of the line, a somewhat swarthy lad standing next to someone who looked remarkably similar to him, although not close enough to be twins. "Aren't we good enough to rate having a real weapon?"

For the second time that day, Didius was struck down by the Pilus Prior, followed closely by his fellow complainant, and then was joined by the man that had to be his brother, who out of reflex, I suppose, had reached down to help him.

"Nobody told you to touch him," the Pilus Prior snarled.

It was beginning to become clear to us that nobody was going to do anything unless they were specifically told to do so, and I made a mental note of it.

"Sorry, Pilus Prior. He's my broth…" He did not get a chance to finish his sentence, struck again by that infernal stick.

"And nobody asked you for an explanation, you *cunnus*," the Pilus Prior snapped. "On your feet, the lot of you."

Once they climbed back to their feet and came to the correct position of *intente*, which the rest of us had immediately assumed, the Pilus Prior spoke to the rest of us.

"So, is there anyone else who feels like complaining about not being handed a real *gladius*?" he asked in a deceptively pleasant voice. Fortunately, this did not fool anyone, even Artorius, into answering. "You *cunni* can barely walk in a straight line, so you don't really expect that we'd hand you a real weapon, do you? You have a LONG way to go before you reach that point."

Seeing that we had received our basic allotment of gear, he indicated that we should leave the tent, carrying the gear that we were not wearing in our basket or stacked on top of it, along with the possessions we had brought with us. He gave the order to *ad signa*, to get back into our assigned places in line. It did not take us as long fortunately, or perhaps the Pilus Prior had just resigned himself to our ineptitude, so we only had to do it once. Giving us the order to turn to the right again, he started us marching towards the far side of the camp. As we marched, we passed by other men, apparently in different stages of training, which I watched only out of the corner of my eye, not daring to turn my head. After a few moments, we reached the far corner of the camp, near the *Porta Praetoria*, the main gate. There were several rows of tents arranged in a square, all of the outermost tents facing the walls of the camp. Immediately behind each tent, facing the walls, was the back of another tent, whose opening faced in the opposite direction, away from the wall. Across a wide pathway from those tents was another line of tents, whose openings faced in the direction of the tents closest towards the wall. The effect was that there was a series of streets, with rows of tents acting as the houses, although it was much more neatly arranged than most cities. Such is the camp of the Roman army, even to this day. The camp we were at housed a total of four Legions, the 7th, 8th, 9th, and 10th. Normally, the most experienced Legions are placed closest to the walls, but since we were in friendly territory and had no fear of attack, placing was not as important. This was to be our new home for most of the time we were in the Legions.

Indicating a tent, the Pilus Prior told us, "This is where all of you will be living. There are eight of you here; your Sergeant has already been selected, and one man will be joining you shortly. This is your tent section; look around at each of these men, because they'll be the ones you're living with from here until your time in the Legion is up. Or until you die, whichever happens first."

He gave a short, barking laugh at this, which none of us found particularly amusing. Before he dismissed us to arrange ourselves, he gave us one last instruction.

"Before you go in, each of you needs to select one other man from your tent section. This'll be your companion, your closest companion and friend for the time you're in the Legion. He'll be the holder of your will, he'll be the man who watches your back wherever you go. Whenever possible, you'll go together, even when you go out into town, so choose wisely. I'll give you a few moments to do that, then you're to go into your tent, and with your choice in mind, you'll select the spot where you'll be sleeping. The cot that your Sergeant occupies is the one closest to the entrance; you'll be able to tell because it's already occupied with his gear. Now, I'll return in a sixth part of the watch. Or maybe sooner," he said this last with quiet menace, "just to make sure that you're doing what you're supposed to be doing and not already fucking off."

Turning and stalking off, he left us standing there a bit bewildered, if I am to be honest.

The man next to me, the second tallest man who I had judged to have some intelligence, nodded to me. "My name's Sextus Scribonius. You seem to have your wits about you, like me." He grinned as he said this. "What do you say we pair up?"

Somewhat regretfully, I told him that I could not because I already had someone, and since my hands were full, I nodded in the direction of Vibius, already walking towards me with a smile on his face. Scribonius was clearly disappointed, but he took it well, especially when I explained that we had been best friends for so many years. Immediately, he turned to his left, but that was Didius, with whom he clearly had no intention of pairing.

Vibius whispered, "Well, at least this part is easy. Why don't we duck in now and claim our spots while the rest of them are arguing?"

Which we immediately did, to the protests of some of the others, Didius most notably and unsurprisingly. However, the two brothers, seeing us, quickly followed. I selected the spot across from the Sergeant nearest to the door, with Vibius taking the spot next to me, the second man to the left. The brothers headed for the two cots directly across the doorway from Vibius and placed their gear on them, claiming the space as theirs. They were followed by two others, who claimed the spots at the back, next to the brothers, and it was then I began to notice something that did not make sense. There were a total of eight cots, but there were eight of us already, plus the unnamed Sergeant, and the Pilus Prior had told us that one more would be joining us. That made ten men, but only eight spots. Vibius caught on as well, and we were looking at each other in a puzzled manner when we heard a new voice at the entrance to the tent. We both turned to see another Legionary, wearing a uniform identical to ours, with the exception that his helmet had a flowing black horsetail on top of it, the tail spilling down near his shoulders.

"So, apparently someone can count," he said laconically as he stood in the doorway.

He was a well-built man, in his mid-twenties it appeared, with even features and cool grey eyes that appraised each of us. His gaze lingered on me, taking in my size and he pursed his lips in a silent whistle, but he did not say anything to me. Instead, he turned to the whole group and announced, "In case you haven't guessed, my name is Lucius Calienus, and I'm the Sergeant of this tent section. I was a member of Pompey's 1st Legion, and was promoted to help fill this Legion out with some men who knew their asses from their elbows. And judging from what I'm seeing in this lot, I might as well kiss my ass goodbye because I'm as good as dead the moment we go into battle."

This did not set well with me, but I kept my mouth shut.

Calienus walked into the tent, standing in the narrow area between the cots and said, "So I see that you, or at least some of you," he turned to nod in the direction of Vibius and me, "were catching on that there seems to be a problem with the numbers in this tent."

Not sure how to address him at this point, we contented ourselves with just nodding.

"Well, you'll be happy to know that you're correct in your assumption, so there may be hope for some of you yet."

Turning to the outside to the remaining man, he motioned him to come inside. Having seen that Scribonius had grabbed Artorius, despite the early signs that Artorius might be a weakling, I assumed that Scribonius must have decided that Artorius was the lesser of two evils. Didius walked in, and I have to say that he looked a little upset that he was not picked, although he did not say anything about it.

Calienus said to Didius, "So you're the odd man out, neh?"

Didius nodded, and Calienus laughed, but while it was not necessarily a cruel laugh, it still obviously rankled Didius.

"Maybe you're just slow to make friends. Or," he became serious, "it means that you're someone I have to keep an eye on. Either way, you're out of luck, neh?" Without waiting for an answer, Calienus turned to the rest of us, and explained the mystery of the two missing cots.

They were not missing at all. Instead, it meant that at any given time, there would be two men on some sort of duty, at least once we finished training. Even during training, there would be at least one man on watch on our assigned sector of wall, so that at some point, someone was sleeping in your cot while you were out on duty. During training, only one would be missing, requiring that someone slept on the ground, but in order to be fair, it was rotated evenly, even Calienus participating. Also, while the sleeping arrangements would change, the area where we stored our gear, under our cots, would remain the same. Didius and the unknown tenth man were given two corners of the tent as their area, making it somewhat inconvenient for them, but was designed to stop gear from being "accidentally" mixed up, a practice that turned out to be a very good precaution with Didius in our tent, although we did not know that then.

Once that was explained to us, Calienus showed us the proper way to stow our gear underneath our cots, taking the remainder of the time allotted to us by the Pilus Prior. I imagine it was a sixth part to the instant when we heard a shrill whistle sound outside. Vibius and I knew what the whistle meant, even if we had never actually heard one, thanks to Cyclops, so we immediately grabbed our *scuta*, put our *galeae* back on, picked up our *rudis*, and hurried outside. Falling into our places at the opposite ends of the line, we were followed in a matter of moments by the rest of the group, who seemed to follow our lead, and came out carrying their weapons and *scuta*. They got in line quickly, but none of us were sure how to stand at *intente* holding our *scutum* or *rudis*. That we assembled in this fashion clearly surprised the Pilus Prior, but he made no comment about it, and fortunately, we were not penalized, for whatever reason. Instead, the Pilus Prior showed us how to hold the *rudis* vertically; normally, our *gladii* would be sheathed, but since we had not been issued them yet, and the *rudis* would not fit in the scabbard anyway, we were taught this method. Then he told us to go stow the gear in our tents and come back outside.

Once we did so, he marched us over to the forum, which in an army camp is the large clear area next to the *Praetorium* where the Legions are mustered when they are to be issued orders en masse, or some other event occurs that requires everyone's presence. The rest of the time, at least in the early days of the Legion, it was being used by us *tiros* as we were taught how to march and perform close order drill. There were other small groups, along with a couple of large ones, composed of a full Century, normally eighty men. However, in the case of our Legions, and in every Legion raised by Caesar from that point forward, he made a change by commanding that a Century would consist of a hundred men, which was changed back to eighty men by the man now known as Augustus. This was why we had the unusual sleeping arrangements in our tent; normally eight cots were sufficient, since the Century of traditional size consisted of ten sections of men, one section to each tent. Of course, we did not know this was unusual, and would not learn otherwise until much later in our careers. Now, these Centuries were all marching about under the order of their respective Centurions. Assisting them was the Centurion's Optio, the second in command of each Century; we had yet to meet ours because he was working with the rest of the Century. As it turned out, we were the last of the First Century of the Second Cohort to be added, explaining why we were getting the undivided attention of the Pilus Prior and not the Optio. The Pilus Prior had us watch the other groups marching for a moment, and even to our untrained eyes, we could see that they were in different stages of training. Smaller groups like ours still displayed a tendency to look like they were shambling along, and they were being "encouraged" with the Centurion's stick more often than the others. It was also plain to see that being smacked with that stick was going to be a regular part of our lives for some time to come.

After a few moments, the Pilus Prior said, "You can see that you'll be spending a great deal of your time just learning how to march in the proper manner, and obey the commands given you while you march. And know this, you *cunni*," he finished, "my Cohort will be the tightest, best drilled Cohort in this Legion, or you'll all die trying."

He laughed at his own joke, if indeed it was. For ourselves, we were not sure. The rest of the day was spent marching about, with a liberal amount of bashing with the stick, which we learned was called the *vitus* and is a symbol of the Centurion rank. Up and down, we marched, learning the basic commands, and I never suspected one could become so tired from just walking around, yet by the time we were through, I was exhausted. So were the others if the looks of them were any indication. We marched through at least two watches; the watch is divided into increments of three hours each, and the end of each watch is signaled by the sounding of a horn. I could not tell which horn it was, but as I learned later, the change of the watch is sounded by the *bucina*. Either the Pilus Prior thought we had been through enough, or we were at a point where we would not have improved, but either way, we were thankful for the break.

We were marched back to our tent and put in the charge of Sergeant Calienus, who informed us that it was almost time for the evening meal, so he spent the time waiting showing us the proper way to stow our gear under our cots. As one might surmise, everything had to be arranged just so, and although he did not have to do so, Sergeant Calienus explained why.

"Let's say it's the middle of the night, and you're all sound asleep, thinking of the women you're missing back home," he said, drawing a chuckle from us, which he did not seem to mind. "Then, out of nowhere, the horns are blasting and men are shouting because an attack on the walls has started. It's pitch black, and you have to fall to your defensive station, which," he added, "I'll show you where it is on the wall on the way to draw our meal. Anyway, everyone's screaming and shouting, there's a horrible racket coming from the barbarian horde outside the walls, and it's utter chaos and confusion."

While he was talking, he was seated on his cot, facing us, except he was demonstrating as he spoke, pulling out first his *lorica* and putting it on as he continued explaining. "So you've got just a moment to get your gear on and stand to on the wall, or there'll be Hades to pay, or worse. What if the breach to the wall happens in your area, because you couldn't get armed and ready in the proper amount of time?"

By the time he was finished, he had put on his helmet, donned his *lorica*, strapped on his baldric, grabbed his *scutum*, and was ready to go, all without looking for any piece of his gear. We were all suitably impressed, and I at least saw the immediate sense of what he had said. As we were to learn, this was the way of Sergeant Calienus; while the Pilus Prior used his *vitus* and the most inventive cursing I had ever heard in my life to that point, Sergeant Calienus talked to us like we were already Legionaries. I supposed it was because he was not as far removed from having been like us as Pilus Prior Crastinus was, although I was hard pressed to imagine that Crastinus was ever a *tiro*. In fact, I imagined that he had been born in his *lorica*, fully formed and ready for battle from the day he was born, an image that I was to learn was carefully cultivated by him, and one that I would come to use myself.

Sergeant Calienus marched us back to the *quaestorium*, the tent that is located next to the *Praetorium* and serves the quartermaster, where we each were given our flat loaf of *panis castrenis*, had the small-stoppered bottle for our olive oil filled, and watered wine put into our flask. Some of the boys looked at what they were being handed with a combination of puzzlement and distaste; for me, it was nothing since I had always been indifferent to food as far as what it tasted like. I did miss my meat, although I did not say anything, since that would have exposed my poverty to the others. Over the years, I have developed a belief that one reason I was so large was due in part to my father's lack of success as a farmer. Because we did not have much grain with which to make our bread, we ate more meat than was normal for most Romans, and I have since seen people like the Germans who are my size and whose diet is composed mostly of meat, which seems to support my idea. Still, it was not something I liked to talk about with the others, so I pretended that I liked the diet of bread and chickpeas just as much as everyone else did.

"We get bacon every other day, a nice salted chunk of it, but today's not the day. And you're lucky that we're in camp and only training, or it would be straight water, no wine," Calienus explained.

Once we were given our rations, we marched back to our tent, where Calienus had us sit on the ground outside, and we began eating our evening meal. While we ate, Calienus gave us more information.

"If I were you, boys, I'd save a bit of the bread and oil for the morning, because we only get our one ration a day."

Granted, the loaf, which was round and flat and about four inches high by about one foot in diameter was a good size, but I still wondered how we were to survive on this alone, even with the bacon as supplement.

"Once we begin marching, our rations will increase," explained Calienus, who obviously was a mind reader.

Or, he had once been a *tiro* and wondered the same thing.

"But while all we're doing right now is drill and weapons training, the general doesn't want us getting fat and lazy."

I did not see how that could happen, but I was content to take him at his word. Calienus then went around the group, asking questions of each of us in order to learn more about them. It was in this manner that I learned the names and basic information of the men I would spend the next several years with, some of them at least. Along with Vibius and me, there was Sextus Scribonius, the man who stood next to me when we were arranged by height. Scribonius said he came from Corduba, yet he was vague about what his father did or anything else about his family, for that matter. It was a subject that he rarely discussed, and it would not be until many years later that I would learn that he was lying about where he was from, but that is for later.

Then there was Quintus Artorius, and his story was a fairly common one, not unlike mine. His father was a blacksmith and they could not get along, so after a particularly bitter argument, Artorius threatened that he would go join the Legion, whereupon his father called his bluff. It was clear to all of us that he seemed to be having second thoughts, an impression that was only reinforced as time went by. His was the nervous voice I heard in the pre-dawn of that day when we all reported. He was also the smallest member of our group, which I do not imagine helped his outlook.

The two who looked alike were indeed brothers, Marcus and Quintus Mallius, and it was a common occurrence for all of us to mix them up. Before long, they each earned nicknames, but until they did, it was a source of exasperation for all of us. They were sons of a farmer in the province, outside the town of Illurco and were quick to point out that there was a pretty good chance that the olive oil we were dipping our bread in came from their farm, since they had accompanied their father making a delivery to the army. The brothers decided to enlist because there was a multitude of brothers Mallius. Marcus was the older by a year, although they could have almost passed for twins. Both had a cheerful disposition generally, although Quintus possessed a fearsome temper, which got him in trouble more than once during our time together.

Next was Publius Vellusius, who stood to the right of Vibius in our line, and up to that point from who I had barely heard a word. His story was similar to Marcus and Quintus, and Vibius for that matter; an excess of sons, with Vellusius being the excess. His father had a farm in the far northwest of the province in Nertobriga (Badajoz); it took him a week to arrive at Corduba and he had gotten a later start like we had, accounting for his relatively late arrival along with the rest of us. He was about as tall as Vibius, but built much more slightly, with a bristle of black hair that seemed to stick straight up, no matter how much oil he used to keep it flat. To me, he looked a bit like a bird, with the same kind of nervous movement and constant peering at his surroundings, as if waiting for a cat to come along, but he turned out to be a good soldier, though, one of the best in our Century.

Finally, there was Didius, who had calmed his mouth somewhat, just not enough to suit me or the others. Despite being shorter than I was, he was built similarly to me, and indeed, he turned out to be quite strong, perhaps as strong as I was, something I had not encountered before. Perhaps, if I am being honest, that is one of the reasons that I disliked him as much as I did, although if that is true, it does not adequately explain the hatred the others held for him before much time would pass from this first day. Still, at that moment, we were willing to give him a chance, despite his bragging and generally unpleasant attitude. Didius told us that he was born to be in the Legions, like his father and grandfather before him, who were great heroes in their own right, although he would outshine them, and the rest of us. I took care to hide my feelings, munching on my bread with what I hoped was a bland expression.

Calienus just gave a slight grin, as if he had heard it all before, which he had. Once we were done, he told us about himself. He was twenty-eight, and had been in the Legion for ten years, but re-enlisted for the full sixteen-year term that Caesar set as the length for this enlistment of the 10th Legion, all for the chance of promotion to Sergeant. He was also *immune*, having skill as an armorer, his father being one before him and teaching him his craft. That meant that he was exempt from most of the other duties, with the exception of standing watch during the night hours, when he would not have been working anyway. Calienus was in Pompey's 1st Legion, a fact that gave him instant respect, and had been with Pompey during his short but sharp campaign against the pirates, recently returning from the war against Mithridates, which was the talk of the Roman world ever since. He fought in over thirty engagements, and had been wounded four times, once so seriously that he almost died from the infection. Calienus was a hardcore Pompeian, and I sometimes wondered that if things had worked out differently, what road he would have traveled.

But I am ahead of myself again; forgive me, gentle reader, it is the prerogative of the elderly to sometimes meander. Introductions done, with the light beginning to fade, we continued talking and asking questions of Calienus, all of which he answered with great patience. Finally, the horn blew that signaled it was time to retire, and we entered the tent to make preparations for sleep. Because it was our first night, we were not entered as part of the duty rotation, though that would change the next day when the last member of the tent section joined us. It was just as well; we were all exhausted and I think even if Hannibal himself had risen from the dead to mount an attack on the camp, it would have been impossible to rouse us from our slumber. I do not even remember lying on my cot, and in the morning, I awoke in the exact same position in which I had fallen asleep, something that would become a common occurrence over the next few weeks.

The next morning, we were roused, again before daylight, to start our day, being given just a few moments to eat what we saved from the night before, then forming up outside the tent. Pilus Prior Crastinus came striding up, with the same invisible *numen* waving the same invisible turd under his nose.

"Well, you *cunni*," he snarled by way of greeting, "I was expecting half of you to be gone like the sorry specimens you replaced."

This was a shock; it was the first we heard that we were not just original drafts, but instead had replaced others. As we learned the story over the next few days, we were added to the Legion to replace *tiros* in the Second Cohort that failed to measure up, for one reason or another. Rather than sprinkling us into the Centuries of the Cohort that lost men, they instead consolidated by moving the men who were in our Century out to the ones that had missing men. The logic was obvious; at least, once it was explained to us. The other Centuries were all at more advanced stages of training, and dropping in a brand new *tiro* into one of them would have been a hardship that compromised the training of the other Centuries. Instead, our Century, the First Century, was selected to be the one to dole out men to make a hole to fill, with members of the First Century serving as replacements for those who had fallen out. Like with most things in the army, once explained, it made perfect sense. It was just relatively rare that things were clarified for us, especially as time passed. The more experienced we were, the less it was considered important to at least give us an idea of what was going on or why we were doing something; we were just expected to obey as if the order came from Jupiter's mouth directly to our ears. Again, if one thinks about it, it makes some sense. By that time, you are indoctrinated in the ways of the Legion. In your first days, you are still more citizen than Legionary, and as part of the process, there is a certain amount of explanation that is given to you. Not much, but a little, which is more than more experienced Legionaries got.

This also explained why we were in the First Century, so we could have the undivided attention of the Pilus Prior, not that we were very appreciative. He marched us over to the forum, and we picked up where we left off the day before, learning the basic drill movements and commands. Over and over, with the word "*Repitate*" ringing in our ears, along with the sting of his *vitus* to help remind us, we marched up and down, up and down. The only break in the monotony was in mid-morning, when the last member of our tent section joined us, having drawn his gear and been escorted by either Sergeant Calienus or the Optio to our tent. He was introduced to us as Marcus Atilius, and he slotted into our line between Scribonius and Didius, much to the relief of Scribonius. Atilius appeared to be somewhat older than the rest of us, with the exception of Calienus, although it turned out to be more a case of hard living. When he joined us, he wore the same look as Vibius had the morning before, somewhat pale and a little unsteady on his feet, the result of a particularly festive farewell party, or so we thought at the time. However, we would learn that every day was an occasion for a festival as far as Atilius was concerned. Because he was also behind in learning the basic movements, we were told to run around the camp along the *Via Sagularis*, the road that runs around the inside perimeter of the camp along the walls, while he received personal instruction.

When we all hesitated for a moment, confused, the Pilus Prior snapped, "Well? What are you waiting for?"

"How many times, Pilus Prior?"

This came from Scribonius, which was exactly what I wanted to know, but thank the gods he beat me to it, because it earned nothing more than a smack with the *vitus* and a snarled, "Until I tell you to stop, you idiot."

With that pleasant admonition, we began to run. Being in the lead, I set what I thought would be a pace that everyone could keep up with, yet would be sufficiently quick enough not to earn a beating from the Pilus Prior. However, I miscalculated, badly. While

Cyclops made Vibius and me do plenty of exercises that helped our dexterity and overall endurance wearing helmet and *lorica*, he never had us do any running, so very quickly I found that what I thought would be a comfortable pace was putting me into difficulty. However, I was also too proud to slow down, and I continued on, trying to ignore the pain in my side and the feeling that I was breathing pure fire. Leading the way for one circuit, then two, I never looked back, now afraid that since nobody behind me asked to slow down, I was running slower than they would have had they been leading.

It was not until I was halfway through the second lap of the camp that I heard a gasping shout, "*Eho,* Pullus! By the gods, man, are you trying to kill us all?"

Startled, I looked around to see Scribonius, his face as red as our new *sagum*, the soldier's cloak, staggering as he caught up to me now that I had slowed down. Looking over my shoulder, I saw to my dismay that the others were far, far behind, barely visible just turning the second corner of the second circuit of the camp. Scribonius, hands on his knees as he sucked in air, began to gag, making me feel horrible and good all at the same time.

In between retches, he gasped, "Didn't you hear us shouting for you to slow down? I swear that all of us were begging you to slow your pace, but you just ran along like you were Mercury himself."

Despite the fact that I was breathing as hard as he was, and was fighting the urge to vomit as well, I tried to sound nonchalant as I replied, "Really? No, Scribonius, I'm truly sorry. I didn't hear a thing. I just thought I was running at a pace that wouldn't get us in trouble with Pilus Prior Crastinus."

He looked up at me to see if I was joking, but in that, at least, I was telling the truth; by this time, the others had joined us, and all assumed the same position as Scribonius, each of them cursing my name, my father, and my ancestors. Even Vibius was angry with me, and I wavered between embarrassment and anger at the invectives they were using against me.

Defensively, I protested, "I already told Scribonius I was sorry. I didn't realize I was running so fast."

"Well, clean your ears out, damn you," spat Didius, pushing my mood immediately to anger.

"If you can't keep up, that's not my problem," I retorted, and he stood up straight, making a move towards me as if he had more to say, but before he could, Vibius stepped in between us and grabbed my arm. "None of us could keep up, Titus," he spoke sharply, "because you forget that you have these great long legs."

That it was Vibius talking so immediately deflated me and I apologized again, this time more humbly, which seemed to satisfy everyone except for Didius, who continued to glare at me. That was when I knew that he and I were destined for trouble at some point. To make matters worse, the Pilus Prior happened to look up and saw us standing in a group, and we could hear his booming voice, over all the other noise of camp, and we jumped a little in panic.

"I don't believe I told you *cunni* to stop," he roared. "The next time I look around, you had better be running, ladies."

We looked at each other, and then Scribonius said, "The Pilus Prior didn't tell us what order to run in, did he?" When we shook our heads, he continued quickly, "Well then, let's run with the little end at the front. That way, we won't have to worry about Pullus galloping off on us."

This was immediately accepted, even by me, not wanting to draw the ire of the others any more than I already had, although I now knew that I could run more slowly without being afraid of being seen as weak. Quickly reversing our order, we started up again with Artorius leading us off. Almost immediately, we could all see that while this was a good idea in theory, Artorius was so weak and slow, the chances of evading the wrath of the Pilus Prior was practically non-existent. Fairly quickly, we rearranged yet again, putting Vibius in front, who set a pace that most of us could follow with a moderate effort, except for Artorius. I assumed that the reason he was so far behind was that he was at the little end of our line, but it turned out that not only was he the smallest physically, he was the weakest, in more ways than one. We made a couple more circuits before we heard the Pilus Prior yell at us to stop, which we did, heading back to where he and Atilius were standing. Poor Atilius, being the only focus of the Pilus Prior, already had several large red welts on his arms and legs, but his face showed no emotion as he stood there at *intente*. It became apparent that Atilius had taken his personal lessons to heart, because he immediately matched us in terms of our skill level. Once more, the rest of the day was spent in drill, and it was a weary group that trooped to the tent. Sergeant Calienus joined us shortly, and informed us that we were going to be put into the rotation for guard duty, starting that night. During our *tiro* period, we would only be standing watch at night so that we could get all the training in possible. The brothers drew the first watch, followed by Scribonius and Artorius, then Vibius and me. In this manner, everyone would be able to sleep through the night on a cot, although there would have to be some shifting around.

"But as soon as we finish our meal, I'm taking you boys to the bathhouse," Calienus told us, wrinkling his nose, "because you stink. And I'm not going to share a tent with a bunch of animals."

This was my first experience with regular bathing; on the farm, we bathed at most once a week, usually on the market day, using a large wooden tub for the purpose, after which Phocas or Gaia would oil us down. Actually, I stopped allowing Gaia to bathe me when I was perhaps ten or eleven, but I certainly had never heard of bathing in the middle of the week; it was at least three more days to market day! Nevertheless, I quickly grew accustomed to it and, to this day, I bathe every day, at least whenever possible. Back then, though, I was just a country boy who thought such refinements a waste of time. After the meal, Calienus took us to a large tent near the *quaestorium*, where a line of men stood, all waiting for their turn. This was our first time actually mingling with the other Legionaries, and we obviously looked as green as grass because almost immediately we were jeered and teased. When I heard those mocking words, I felt the heat in my face and my anger starting to rise, when a gentle but firm hand on my elbow stopped me; I was not aware, but I had begun moving towards one particularly mouthy man who looked about the same age as Calienus, just softer. Turning, I saw that was in fact who was grabbing my elbow, giving me a stern look as he shook his head.

"Hold, Pullus. You can't go getting upset when someone runs his mouth at you. Besides," he grinned, "you are fresh meat, and the boys are just having some fun. Soon enough, you'll be doing the same to poor *tiros* like you are now."

I listened and obeyed, except I did not believe him, promising myself that when I was in their shoes, I would not be so callous. It was just one more promise broken in a life full of them. The interior of the tent was lit by oil lamps, and there was a buzz of laughter and conversation, ribald jokes, and the kind of complaining that only soldiers can do. There were a couple of dozen slaves who rubbed down each man with oil, then scraped him clean.

Seeing that there were no bathtubs, I looked to our Sergeant, and Calienus explained. "No, we don't have proper baths in camp; that only happens in winter quarters when we build more permanent facilities. Here, we just have the oil and scraping."

Like other things I had been told, it made perfect sense to me. Not only was it time spent, it was a matter of resources; we should not be wasting water on luxuries like baths. Even so, it was refreshing, and I left feeling like a new man, invigorated by the skilled hands of the slave who rubbed down my tired and sore muscles. It may seem like a small thing, yet I firmly believe that one reason we are invincible is because not only are we well trained, we are well cared for and well fed. There is no doubt in my mind that the rubdowns that we receive help us recover from our exertions more quickly and thoroughly, so that we are revitalized and able to do more work than our enemies, in every phase and facet of warfare.

Just like the night before, I was asleep before I finished lying down, and it seemed but a moment before I was being shaken awake by Scribonius, while Artorius did the same for Vibius.

"Your turn," Scribonius whispered, and I came awake immediately, something that I somehow managed to teach myself, and it has served me well throughout my career. I can be sound asleep, but at a word, I am instantly awake. This night, I sat up and, copying what Calienus showed us, tried to do the same thing, pulling my gear from underneath my cot from memory. Instead, I immediately dropped my helmet, making a horrible racket and earning me a round of curses from my comrades. Finally stumbling out, I waited for Vibius, who managed to equip himself without making a sound, then we headed to the wall that was our sector. I could see in the darkness the same thing happening up and down the wall as the guard changed. Stifling a yawn, I climbed the rampart, feeling somewhat ridiculous not properly armed. I had not yet seen the view from the wall and, despite it being dark, there was enough light from the moon and the nearby torches that remained lit throughout the night hours to see the disposition of the outside of the camp. About thirty feet away was a ditch, although from the gloom, I could not tell its depth. It was in fact twelve feet deep, different from the standard nine feet, but with Caesar as our general, he favored ditches that were twelve feet deep by fifteen feet wide, versus the nine-foot by twelve-foot wide standard. This in turn allows for a higher wall, therefore the camp of a Caesar-led Legion was always harder to storm than those of other generals.

We stood behind a crenellated palisade made of wood; as I was to learn, two of those stakes belonged to me, and I would carry them everywhere we went, or more accurately, our section mule did, along with those of every other Legionary, giving them up to form the wall that protected us. The earthen rampart that I stood on was the product of the dirt that came from the ditch, making the rampart six feet wide. It was tamped down to give us a solid footing and wide enough to allow men to move behind others, manning the walls in the event they had to run to a trouble spot. The rest of the dirt formed a ramp leading to the rampart, allowing us to run up to the wall without having to worry about climbing ladders. The Roman camp is second to none of its kind and for as long as anyone could remember, this was how a camp was built, almost every single night on the march, with very few exceptions and only slight variations depending on the threat level. In our long-ago past, some unfortunate army did not go to the trouble and was massacred, so from that time on, this was the standard. While Vibius and I stood there, shivering in the damp despite our *sagum* wrapped around our shoulders, we could hear the low buzz of voices from the other Legionaries on the wall. Vibius and I glanced at each other; the Pilus Prior had been very specific about the prohibition on talking on guard duty, but it seemed that there were others who did not get that warning from him, or were ignoring it. However, we were still too new to even consider disregarding the rules at this point, so we just shrugged and turned back to stare out into the blackness.

All I can say about my first turn on guard duty is that I wish the hundreds and hundreds of times that I have done since then had passed as quickly as that one. I think it must have been the novelty, because before I could believe that the proper amount of time had passed, the horn was blowing, and I could see a very faint lightening in the sky. Since we stood the last watch, we at least had the advantage of being fully dressed and returned to our tent as the more experienced Legionaries who had the day watch relieved us, giving us the proper password. There is a new password and countersign issued every full day, and our shift would be the last to use the old one. Now, the commander of the guard Cohort would go to each station and issue the new password and countersign. Like the camps, this was done without exception, no matter where the Legion was located; as I would learn, even on the Campus Martius just outside Rome, we would have to learn and remember the password and countersign. I would also learn that the method of relief that we used the night before was not the norm; the relief of the guard, especially when on campaign, is much more formalized and is done by the commander of the guard that shift, who marches the men of the relief to their specific spot on the rampart. Those being relieved then fall into the marching formation, taking the place of the men who relieved them, continuing in formation to the next post, where the process is repeated. Only after a complete circuit of the camp is made do those that were relieved get dismissed to go back to sleep, or resume their other duties. That morning, the others were just getting dressed and, while we waited, Vibius and I gnawed on the small piece of bacon and bread left over from the night before. By this time, our third day, we knew enough to immediately form up outside the tent and, before long, the Pilus Prior showed up, snarling his usual cheery morning greeting. Then we went marching off to begin another day.

Thus set the pattern for the next week, where every day seemed to blur together into one long continuous day of marching and the command *Repitate* ringing in our ears over and over and over. Of course, the command was almost always accompanied with the smack of the *vitus*, and although I was a bit farther ahead than the others, as was Vibius, I received my fair share of blows. Our days became measured by the sounds of the tromping of our feet and the blowing of the *bucina* marking the change of watch, yet slowly, we began to at least look like Legionaries, even if the Pilus Prior kept insisting that we were the worst collection of *tiros* that he had ever seen. Finally, the day arrived for which all of us, particularly Vibius and I, had been waiting. The morning started in the usual manner, but we were told to carry our *rudii*, and instead of being marched to the forum, we marched past it, took a right turn and headed out the *Porta Principalis Sinistra*, the side gate on the left hand side of every camp, exiting it and stopping on the other side of the ditches. Arrayed before us were a huge number of stakes, the same type on which Cyclops had trained Vibius and me, and despite Vibius being a few men down from me, I was sure that he was fighting the urge to smile as well. Finally! We would get our chance to show that we were not as raw as the others, and I could feel my stomach twist in excitement at the thought of finally doing something with which I was familiar.

Of course, it was not going to be so easy. They were not going to just turn us loose to start whacking away, and for this task, we were formally introduced for the first time to our Optio, who acted as our Cohort's weapons instructor. He was a bit taller than average and at first glance looked rather pudgy, but as I would learn, that was extremely misleading. Although I did not yet know it, he was the only man in the Legion clearly stronger than I was by a good margin. That was not the only deceptive thing about the man; the other impression that one came away with just by looking at him was that he might have been a bit on the slow side. He wore a somewhat slack expression on his round face, with a tendency for his mouth to hang open slightly when he was not engaged. However, once he took up a weapon, he became something entirely different, a blur of motion and controlled savagery the likes of which none of us had ever seen before. Unlike most of the more experienced men, he bore no visible marks or scars, which I supposed was a testament to his fighting prowess. Still, I would be lying if I said that the first day we met, I was particularly impressed, and I wondered if this man would actually have anything that he could possibly teach me after my tutelage with Cyclops.

"This is Optio Aulus Vinicius," the Pilus Prior announced.

Vinicius gave the slightest nod in our direction as we stood examining him.

"He's the second in command of this Century, and he's also our Cohort's weapons instructor. Today, he'll begin to show you *cunni* what it truly means to be in the Legions."

Turning to Optio Vinicius, he said loudly enough so that we could hear, "Good luck, Vinicius. You're going to need it with this lot." Returning his attention to us, Crastinus finished, "You'll spend the day with the Optio. I'll be by to check on you, so don't think I won't know if any of you are slacking off! All the marching and drill is fine, but this is what your real purpose is, to fight and kill for Rome. And die, if that's the will of the gods," he added superfluously, in my opinion.

With that ominous warning, he left us to the Optio, who was still standing there, not having said a word. It was almost as if he were in a trance, although when the Pilus Prior left the area, he snapped out of whatever fog he had been in.

"All right," he announced, "first thing is for you to gather round that stake right there." He pointed to one a little distance off.

We assembled around it as he took my *rudis* from me, then had us maneuver so that our backs were turned to the other men who were training on the stakes around us. My first thought was that was smart because we were a little distracted watching other men working on the stakes, but as I came to find out, Optio Vinicius also did not want us infected by what he considered the bad habits that the other Cohort's weapons instructors were instilling in their pupils. He held a very high opinion of his abilities, and all I can say is that I am still alive after more than forty years in the Legions because of what I learned from him, in addition to what Cyclops taught me. There must have been truth to his opinion. Once he had us arrayed like he wanted, he showed us the basic positions that we would use in training. These were exactly the same positions that Cyclops had shown us, making it a struggle to appear interested. Inwardly, I was chafing to get started, yet Vinicius had his own pace, and he was not going to be rushed by a bunch of *tiros*, particularly a couple who thought they knew what they were doing. He also took time to show

157

us how he wanted us to grip our *rudis*. As I watched, I saw that it was not the way that Cyclops had taught us, so I dismissed it as unimportant, confident that once I demonstrated my skill that some quibbling thing like the way I held it would not be an issue.

Finally, after what seemed like a full watch, he had us each stand in front of a stake and he returned my *rudis* to me. Then he walked from one of us to the other, checking our stance, kicking a foot wider here, turning a set of hips there. Finally, he returned to me, and I felt a flush of pride when he looked at my position and found it satisfactory.

Then he saw the way that I was holding the *rudis*, but instead of hitting me, he just said quietly, "You're not holding the weapon the way I demonstrated."

"No, Optio," I answered, yet I made no move to change, instead just waiting for the chance to show off to him, sure that he would desist from this lunacy.

"And why aren't you holding it the way I showed you?" he asked, as if he were truly interested.

"I...I've had training, Optio, from a man who was in the Legions, and this is the way I was taught to hold it."

I winced in anticipation of a smack of some sort, but instead, Vinicius merely nodded.

"You're right; that's the way the majority of the Legions are taught to hold the weapon, but that's not the way I teach it," he explained.

Unsure what to do, I stood there, but still did not change the grip.

Sighing, he simply said, "All right, I can see you need some convincing. So, turn and face me and assume the first position."

This is the position that makes us ready to strike, with the blade held parallel to the ground, the arm pulled back, ready to strike and with the hips twisted slightly. That was the position he had told us to get in originally, so I dropped back into it, facing him.

"Now, strike me. As hard as you can. Give me a killing blow."

I was confused and very apprehensive. Confident as I was in my strength and ability, I was sure that even with the *rudis* I would impale the man, or at the very least break his ribs when I struck.

If he was worried, he certainly did not seem to be, and he repeated, a little impatiently, "I said, strike me. Give me all that you've got." As if sensing my concern, he added, "And don't worry. If you land the blow, I'll absolve you with my dying breath."

He said this last with enough sarcasm that it made me angry, so I immediately struck my blow, punching the *rudis* forward hard as I twisted my hips with as much force and speed as I could. To this day, I am sure that if he were any other man, I would have killed him, wooden blade or no. Instead, with a speed that I had never seen before, he lashed out with his bare left hand, using a sweeping motion across his body to make contact with the wooden blade before it touched him, sending the *rudis* flying from my hand. Even as my eyes tried to comprehend what was happening, he made his own move, stepping forward to strike me hard in the stomach with the end of his *vitus*, which he held in his right hand. Now I was the one who was sure that I was going to die, despite wearing my *lorica*, and I dropped to the ground as if I had been ordered to fling myself down, so violently did I hit the ground. I am not sure how long I was out; it could not have been that long because everyone was still clustered around me, leaning over with a combination of worry and malicious glee. Vibius looked worried, while Didius grinned like it was the happiest day of his life. Optio Vinicius was the only one not bent over. Instead, he stared down at me impassively, hands behind his back, watching as I slowly crawled to my feet.

"I thought for sure you were dead," Vibius exclaimed, thumping me on the back in relief.

"So did I," I answered honestly, slowly pulling myself erect, my pride fighting to overcome the searing pain in the pit of my stomach where he had hit me. That night, when I removed my *lorica* and pulled up my tunic, I sported a huge bruise as big around as my fist on my stomach, which stayed with me for several weeks, turning all sorts of interesting colors.

"Do you know why I was able to do that?" Optio Vinicius asked politely.

I considered the question. To me, the answer was obvious; he was simply quicker than I had been, yet I knew that was not the answer he was looking for, so I thought carefully. Slowly, the answer came to me, and as the look of understanding came to my face, he smiled slightly.

"Because my thumb was exposed," I answered, and he rewarded me with a nod.

And therein lay the secret. The thumb is the weakest part of the hand. The normal method of holding the *gladius* is by wrapping the hand around the hilt, with the thumb on the outside of the fingers. When pressure is applied in the right direction by a sudden violent force, against the base of the thumb, it is too weak to maintain its position. By wrapping the fingers over the thumb, the thumb is supported and protected. While it is true that if one were to fight barehanded in this manner, it would break the thumb, the pommel and guard of the *gladius* provide enough protection to prevent this from happening on those occasions you use that end of the *gladius* in a fight. Despite the obvious evidence, I was still not convinced, because there was one disadvantage that I could see. I debated opening my mouth, yet to this point, he was almost gentle with us, despite the ache in my stomach, which I had asked for, after all.

"But..." I started, unsure of how to continue, and again I was rewarded with that slight smile.

"But," he finished for me, "the problem with that grip is that it restricts your blade from moving laterally, so that you don't have the same freedom of movement. Is that what you were about to say?"

"Yes, Optio," I answered excitedly, although to be honest, I was not sure that was what I was going to say until he did it for me.

He nodded again, and replied, "You're correct, *tiro*...?"

"Pullus, Optio. Titus Pullus."

"You're correct, *tiro* Pullus, that at first, your movement is more restricted. But," he said this with the quiet confidence of a man who knew what he was about, "you'll regain that with practice. By the time I'm finished with you, nobody will be able to tell how you grip your weapon."

He turned to the others and finished, "Except that you'll be alive, and your enemy dead."

Of course, he was right. And it did not take nearly as long as I thought it would. By the end of the second day, I felt almost as comfortable using the new grip as I had the old. The only men who experienced difficulty with it were the men with smaller hands, who did not have as much length in their fingers to wrap around their thumbs sufficiently. To compensate for this, Optio Vinicius prescribed special exercises for them to strengthen their hands, exercises that once I saw them performing, I began as well. Vinicius had them thrust their hands into a bucket of sand, with their fingers splayed out. Once their hands were buried in the sand, they drew their fingers in as if they were grabbing a handful of sand. It is an extremely effective exercise, and my hands are still strong because of those exercises. In addition, I know that some men actually shaved down the handle, making it slightly smaller in diameter than a standard issue *gladius*. Once we became accustomed to the new grip, Vibius and I started demonstrating that we were indeed more skilled than our comrades, a fact that did not escape the notice of Pilus Prior Crastinus. It was toward the end of the third day working on the stakes that I became aware of the Pilus Prior standing nearby, watching me with narrowed eyes. Unnerved, I struggled to concentrate on my work, the sweat running freely off of me while my arms, having been hardened and conditioned to such labor, still contained a great deal of energy, reflected in my thrusts.

"This isn't the first time you've held a *rudis*, is it, Pullus?"

The question, posed in what passed for a conversational tone by the Pilus Prior, completely flustered me. Unsure what to do, I stopped, snapped to *intente* and replied, "No, Pilus Prior."

"Who trained you?" he asked with some interest.

"Quintus Ausonius, Pilus Prior," I answered, which was immediately met with a roar of laughter.

"*Edepol*! You were trained by old Cyclops himself? He swore that he'd never pick up a weapon for the rest of his life, the bastard."

I was so shocked that you could have knocked me over with the lightest touch, although I should not have been. Back then, the Legions were still relatively few and small; men such as Cyclops who gained renown were known throughout the Legions. The fact that he was my brother-in-law meant that it never occurred to me to think of him in this manner.

"And how, by Pluto's cock, do you know Cyclops?" Pilus Prior Crastinus demanded.

"He's married to my sister," I said, which drew another roar of laughter.

"By the gods, he's married too! Well, maybe there's hope for an old bastard like me yet." He chuckled.

And then he did something that amazed me even more. Stepping up to me, he slapped me on the back as if I were a comrade and finished, "Well, Pullus. You couldn't have had a better teacher. I'm going to keep an eye on you."

And with that, he turned and walked over to Optio Vinicius, who was standing there looking as bemused as I felt. The Pilus Prior whispered something in his ear that I could not catch, but Vibius did.

Later that night, Vibius relayed to me excitedly, "You know what that old knob Crastinus said to Vinicius?" Without waiting for me to answer, he continued, "'Watch out for Pullus, Vinicius,' he said, 'he may take your job.'"

I felt like I was ten feet tall. Those words, however, had the opposite effect than I expected. Looking back, however, I felt that perhaps the Pilus Prior understood me better than I thought. From that day, I was pushed much harder by Optio Vinicius than any of the other *tiros*, and was subjected to scathing critique of everything I did. The night of the incident, Vibius and I discussed the idea that Vibius should point out that he too was trained by the legendary Cyclops, but luckily, for him anyway, before he got a chance to open his mouth, the next day, he saw the lay of the land. Indeed, not only did he keep his mouth shut, he also endeavored to hold back a bit so that he would not be singled out for special attention in the same manner that I was. It seemed I could not do anything right; my thrusts were sloppy, my slashes were weak, my recoveries were atrocious. Indeed, if Vinicius were to be believed, I would be lucky to survive the first contact of the first battle I was in. If the goal were to take me down a peg, it had the opposite effect. Instead, it just spurred me to work harder and prove him wrong, and I looked forward to the day where we would finally be allowed to pair off.

After a week, we began working with the *scuta* as well, and we were beginning to pick up on the rhythm of training. Everything appeared to work in cycles of a week, with a new skill being added to the training each cycle. That did not hold for everyone, however. It was after the first week of work on the stakes that Artorius was held back a couple of extra days because he was not considered adept enough with just the *rudis* to move forward with the more advanced work. This was when Vibius first started showing signs of being more than just the average Legionary, because he stepped in and offered to work with Artorius in the evenings, after our meal. It would have been perfect if Artorius showed any enthusiasm, but after the first few days, it became apparent to all of us that Artorius' heart was not in learning to become a Legionary. The fight with his father seemed a long-past event; he even admitted to us one night that he could no longer remember what it was about. It was not that he was necessarily a bad Legionary; I just believe that some of us are born to be one thing, others are born to be another, and Artorius was clearly not born to be a Legionary. He did make an effort, so that he was not quite bad enough to be one of the *tiros* dismissed as unfit for duty, yet not only was he clearly the weakest in our tent section, he was the weakest in our Century and may have been the weakest in the Cohort. However, that discovery was still in the future, so Vibius spent his spare time with Artorius, working with him tirelessly. I marveled that Vibius had the energy, because I was still exhausted at the end of every day, but my friend had always been blessed with more vitality, much to my dismay at times.

While the rest of us would sit and take care of the myriad little things that occupy a Legionary's free time while watching Vibius and Artorius, it was during those periods that we got to know each other. For some reason, I found that I spent more time with Scribonius than the others, at least during those times I was not with Vibius. He was somewhat quiet, with a thoughtful manner about him, yet I discovered that his placid exterior masked a razor-sharp wit and a sense of the absurd that I enjoyed immensely. Meanwhile, Didius introduced the other boys to dice, and he had to be the luckiest man I had ever seen, or he was an extremely good cheater. Either way, most of the others, with the exception of Scribonius, Vibius, and me ended up owing him things like their next day's rations, something that was expressly forbidden for Legionaries to wager. It is also one of the more flouted rules in the Legions my entire time in the ranks. However, Didius was smart, I will give him that. He did not actually take the others' rations; instead, he traded them back for favors, things like mending his gear or standing watches for him. I do not know that the three of us were smarter than the others. I think it was more our mutual dislike of Didius than anything, which meant that of our tent section, we were the only ones who never owed Didius anything, something that he did not like at all.

Also by this point, we had been integrated into our Century in terms of marching and drill, on which we still spent a portion of the day working. Since we were the last to join the Century, we were the very back rank, a fact that bothered me to no end. That meant that the battles would all be over before I got to have my turn, I fumed to myself, and where would the glory be for me? Being the tallest and the biggest in my Century, and one of the largest in the Cohort, I was sure that I would be placed in the front rank. However, the system that has operated in the Roman army for hundreds of years by that point did not allow for the vanity of a young man. That is how I thought of myself, a young man, despite easily being the youngest in the Legion because of my deception. Later, I was to learn that there were several others who were sixteen; they were just older than I was by months and, in a couple of cases, weeks. Even so, I was still sure that I was bound for glory, and I was eager to show what I was made of.

It was not until a full month passed that we began working together as a whole Legion, with every Cohort, and we were full strength for the first time and one of the last Centuries to be so. I am not sure, but I would guess that we started losing men within the first three to four months of our existence, by virtue of illness or desertion, and it is only just now becoming standard practice, forty years later, that replacements are placed within a particular Legion. However, back then, once we attained our full complement of men, every one lost from that point was one less in the Legion. Even so, it was an amazing sight to see upwards of 6,000 men standing in formation, rank after rank, Century after Century, the Cohorts lined up in their order. We, being the First Century of the Second Cohort, were privileged to be fairly close to the front of the formation, giving us a better view of the proceedings when the Tribunes and the other officers gathered together. My height also helped with the view, except when we were in full dress uniform with everyone wearing their horsehair plumes, which was nothing but a damn nuisance. I am as proud of being a Legionary as any man who has ever served Rome, but I was never much for the pomp and polish, and I always hated those formations where some prig of a Tribune or Legate decided to flex his muscle and call for a dress inspection for no other reason than he could. Luckily for us, once Caesar took command and we began fighting, that sort of nonsense was kept to a minimum. Ironically, the times we wore our full dress uniform the most often were going into battle under Caesar, because he believed it helped the men fight harder. This I did not mind as much because it had a point to it.

Speaking of Caesar, the occasion of our first full formation as a Legion, carrying all of our gear, no less, was also where I first laid eyes on the man. I must say that I was somewhat disappointed. He was shorter than I was by a few inches and somewhat slight, with very fair complexion and features. I did not know it at the time, but no matter how much time in the sun he spent, and he was in the elements as much as we were, he never turned brown the way we did. Some of the boys said it was proof of his noble birth; there were others who were not so gracious, saying it proved that he was womanish and that the rumors of his liaison with the king of

Bithynia were true as well. I was not yet confident enough in those days, but before long, any man who uttered such nonsense in my presence would have trouble on their hands of a sort that they did not want.

However, that day, I was not impressed, to say the least. Caesar mounted the rostra, giving a speech of welcome to us, noting that although we had been here for varying lengths of time, we gathered as a Legion just that day, making welcoming us appropriate. Despite my lack of awe at his appearance, I will say that he gave very good speeches. He was not like some of the patricians that took a turn at leading us, who would talk to us like we were children or spoke to us of high-flown principles and ideals, for which none of us gave a rotten fig. No, Caesar spoke plainly, and I could see that I was not the only one who appreciated it. He did spend some time telling us how we were upholding the finest traditions of Rome, and how, under his command, we would make our ancestors proud, yet it was not overdone. Such rhetoric is like adding spice to a stew; the right amount, and it makes for a memorable meal, one that you will tell others about for days to come. Too much, however, ruins it, and while it still is memorable, it is for the wrong reasons. So we stood and listened while he told us that he would always lead from the front, indeed starting that day, then when he was finished, he stepped down from the rostra, turning over command to the Tribune in nominal command of the Legion. Such was my first physical contact with the man who would lead us down the path to our destiny.

After he stepped down, he strode to the *Porta Praetorium*, the main gate of the camp and, leading us, took us on our first long march. To that point, once we were integrated with our Century and our Century with our Cohort, we had started forced marches, but they were all out a certain distance, then back to the camp. All this was done with the goal of building us up to this moment when we were going to put in a full day's march, then make a marching camp for the first time. None of my tent section had been present for the building of the camp that we were staying in at that time, with the exception of Sergeant Calienus; because it was a semi-permanent camp, we had only been involved in work details making improvements. Although we had never stayed outside of the camp at the end of a march, we always carried all of our gear, some of it put in the wicker basket that is then attached to the pack, which we carried over our shoulder using a stick with a crossbar called a *furca*, to which we attached everything. Our *scuta*, in its leather cover, was strapped to our back, our helmet attached to that. We wore our arms and *loricae*, carrying a *pilum* in our left hand to serve as a staff, while our second *pilum* we held in the same hand as our *furca*. For the *tiros,* it meant carrying the *rudis*, which was attached to our belt with a leather thong instead of a scabbard, and practice *pilum*, and it was only when we were arrayed in such a manner that we could finally tell exactly how many veterans were among our comrades. It turned out that all of the leaders of each Century were veterans, along with the Sergeants of each tent section and a few *Gregarii* in each Century, so almost a quarter of the Legion appeared to be veterans.

Taking our spot in the column, we marched in the lead spot just behind the command group, with the First Cohort serving as the vanguard, meaning that we did not have to worry about eating as much dust. This was something that we would learn to treasure, although on this first march, we were more worried about how we would bear up, this being our first real test. The fact that just in front of us marched our commanding general, along with his bodyguard, all of whom rode while he walked, did not help with the pressure that we felt. And he set a cracking pace, quite a bit quicker than what we were accustomed to on our other marches and, for once, I was thankful for my long legs. Normally, in standard close order drill, I had to pay particular attention to avoid stepping on the back of the man in front of me, but with this type of route march, we could stretch our legs a bit more.

The weather was pleasant; it was still late spring, but my country is warmer than most places, and what felt pleasant to me, I have learned is unbearably hot for others, mostly Gauls or people who come from those areas farther north. The first few miles passed easily enough, yet I could see others were struggling to varying degrees, the worst of them being Artorius. Both Pilus Prior Crastinus and Optio Vinicius roamed up and down the length of the Century, using their *viti* to encourage laggards. Between them, they must have easily covered twice the distance of our march. My admiration was tempered by the knowledge that they did not carry the same loads that we did, their gear being carried on one of the pack mules attached to our Century. Our tent section not only had its own pack mule but its own slave, a miserable little creature we called Lucco, who was responsible for guiding the mule to our final destination, wherever that was, among a variety of other duties. We stopped every two parts of a watch for a short break, during which we were allowed to ground our gear, yet not allowed to sit down.

"Once you sit down, we'll never be able to get you up," Sergeant Calienus explained, whose spot when we were in full formation was actually right in the middle of our rank.

We were allowed to place our hands on our knees and bend over a bit in order to relieve some of the strain on our backs brought on by the weight of our *scuta* and *galeae*, but that was all. As we would find out later, once sufficiently conditioned, we would be allowed to sprawl out in any position we chose, although someone would always be on guard, but until we reached that point, we had to content ourselves with standing there. Despite being only slightly fatigued at this point, I could feel the strain of the load I was carrying and wondered how I would feel after more miles. During our rest, most of us talked quietly; Scribonius and I discussed our new general.

"What did you think?"

He eyed me curiously as he asked me, yet all I could think to say was, "He gives a good speech. Why, what did you think?"

He frowned, something I noticed that he did a lot, then shook his head. "I don't know, really. All I do know is that I've seen him somewhere before, but I can't remember where."

The *bucina* cut our conversation short, and I thought no more about it.

By the time we made our second stop, I was beginning to feel true fatigue, and the weaker men like Artorius were clearly at the end of their tether, barely managing to make it to this point because their fear of the wrath of the Centurions was greater than their fatigue, yet I could not help wondering how much longer that would last. As we rested again, I looked over at the general, standing talking to the Primus Pilus of our Legion, who had fallen back to talk to him, I supposed, from his place up in the vanguard. Neither of them seemed to be in the slightest bit fatigued, something that angered me more than anything else. How could they appear as if they were just out for a daily stroll, without a care in the world? Well, I was determined that I would not falter in front of them, no matter what! When we set out for the final leg of our march, I was grimly determined to appear just as fresh as they did now, no matter how much of a sham it might have been. The idea that they would even notice a lowly *tiro* in his private struggle never occurred to me; like all youngsters, I was still of the opinion that somehow the world revolved around me.

It was with a great amount of relief to the *tiros* when we arrived at the site of the evening camp, which the advance party had already marked and staked out. That feeling was short-lived, however, when after just a few moments' respite, we were told to ground our gear, and the real work began. The Centurions and Optios began running about as each Century of each Cohort was assigned with a task. To our inexperienced eyes, it was chaos, yet as we were to learn, that was deceiving; everyone had a role to play, and once assigned their tasks, the seeming chaos would disappear.

The Pilus Prior, after a brief conference with the command group, came to us and said without any ceremony, "Right, we've been assigned the ditch," which was greeted by groans from the experienced men, to which the Pilus Prior snarled, "Shut your mouths, you lazy bastards! Now, I expect the Sergeants to take their tent section and give these fresh young things a quick lesson on what they're to do. I'll give you some time to explain and then," he pointed with his *vitus* to a point a distance away where some stakes were placed, "get to work. That's our section. I'll be around to make sure that you don't make a complete mess of things."

And with that, he strode off to do whatever it was that Centurions do while the rest of us worked, which as I was to learn, was to walk about keeping a sharp eye out for the inevitable lagging.

Sergeant Calienus stood in front of us. "You'll need your turf cutter and your spades," he said simply, waiting while we pulled them from our baskets. "Follow me," he called over his shoulder once we produced them, as he headed over to the area that the Pilus

Prior had pointed out. "All right, what we're going to do is to dig our section of the ditch."

As he talked, each tent section was receiving its instructions all around us, so it was somewhat difficult to understand him over the babble of other voices, but it soon became clear what was expected of us. Our section was going to be one of the ones digging; another tent section was tasked with carrying the dirt that we produced in their wicker basket to create the rampart that formed the internal boundary of the camp. Another group was tasked with collecting our two stakes apiece, which were loaded on our pack mule, to form the palisade. While this was all new to us, this is the manner in which Roman camps have been constructed for as long as anyone could remember and, soon enough, it would become second nature for us.

Turning to our task, we first used the turf cutter to cut out squares of sod. These would be used as foundations for some of the structures in the camp, along with serving as the surface of the rampart. Once that was done, we began to dig. Despite my fatigue, this was work that I was used to, but some of the others began having trouble, the most surprising to me being Vibius. However, as he explained later, working as a tanner did not involve the use of a spade or turf cutter. There was one piece of luck, although we would not understand it for some time to come. As I explained earlier, Caesar required the ditches to be deeper and wider across than any other general did; fortunately for us, we did not know any better, so the work we were doing did not seem to be any more onerous than what any other Legion endured. It took us the better part of two parts of a watch to make our section of ditch, no more than ten feet of the total, the proper depth and width, and we were utterly exhausted, but as I turned around, what I saw amazed me. The wall, made of the combination of our stakes and the spoil from the ditch, was almost completely up in our sector, with the men in that area putting the finishing touches on the rampart. Other parties who went out into the surrounding area came back with enough timber to create the guard towers that are placed on each corner of the camp, and although not finished, their form was plainly visible. Despite the dust, noise, and bustling activity, it was clear that we knew what we were about, or at least our leaders did. At this point, we were no more than just brute labor, although after a few more of these camps, as we rotated in our duties, we would all learn our parts and, by the end of a year, each of us would be able to build one of these camps in our sleep.

Finally finished, we staggered back to our area, at least knowing where we were located in the camp because it was the same as back at our home base. The slaves of each tent section in the Century, working together, had erected our tents and dragged our equipment into them, placing our gear in our accustomed place, knowing where to put it by the names inscribed on the leather covers of our *scutas*. They had also started a fire, and Sergeant Calienus proceeded to show us how to turn our rations of grain into bread, this being the first time it was not baked for us. Each of us took our ration and ground it in our section's grinder before contributing it to the community pot, where Sergeant Calienus showed us how to make bread, using the *panera* that we had been issued. I know I was looking forward to falling into a deep sleep as soon as we were finished eating, but my hopes were dashed by the Pilus Prior, who came and announced that we were the guard Cohort for the night. We all groaned, prompting the Pilus Prior to walk among us, lashing out with his *vitus* and snarling at us to keep quiet. His progress was marked by the same sounds as he relayed the word to the rest of the Cohort, something that gave us a little solace that we were not the only whiners.

I was never more thankful for Vibius than that evening on watch, because without him, I would surely have fallen asleep on guard duty, although I think he was as thankful for the same reason. Even so, a decent number of *tiros* were caught asleep, and if it had happened in enemy territory, it would have meant death, but since it was in training, it still called for a flogging. Luckily, only one poor soul was selected for that punishment, which was administered when we returned to base camp, only because he had been caught not once but twice. Since it was our first such march, I guessed, the Centurions were content with administering a particularly severe session with their *vitus* to the men caught asleep. In our case, Pilus Prior Crastinus, Optio Vinicius, and even the Tesseraurius, a man named Titus Cordius, who was our designated man to receive the challenge and password every day, came to check on us at regular intervals. Somehow, even Artorius managed to stay awake, by virtue of being paired with Scribonius, I expect, so that we were one of the few tent sections who did not have anyone fall asleep.

The next morning, if that was what it could be called, it being at least two parts of a watch before first light, I was as sore as I had ever been during my training with Cyclops and, judging from the slow movements and groans of my comrades, I was not alone. I had used muscles previously unstrained, at least to this extent, and I was hard pressed to determine where the soreness came from, the marching or the digging. Either way, we were awakened by the call of the *bucina*, whereupon we got up and packed the gear that we would be carrying, leaving the striking of the tents to the slaves, who performed this task while we ate our morning meal. We were now going to march back to the base camp, except this time, we would not be in the lead. It was our turn in fact to take up the rear; it is in this manner that no Cohort can complain that they are mistreated. Everyone shares equally in all the unpleasant duties in the army, which is one of the things that makes us stronger and bonds us together as much as, if not more than, combat itself. There is no glue like shared misery.

The march back was going to be an ordeal, since we were still sore from the day before, the only slightly cheerful thought being that because the camp back home already existed, at least we would not have to dig. At least, so we thought, until we were informed that before we began the march back, we were going to go to the spot where we had dug the ditch the day before, and fill it back in. This was not a punishment, because every other Century involved in digging the ditch was doing the same thing. Fortunately, it did not take nearly as long to fill it in as it did to dig it. As we marched away, the early morning sky was lit by fire as the guard towers and the wooden structures that were not part of the palisade made by our carried stakes was put to the torch. It was on the occasion of this first march that we were introduced to this practice, one that, if the truth be known, bothered us probably more than anything. On the march during a campaign, we never left a camp intact, and despite the fact we could all see the sense in doing so, it still pained us to see the fruits of our sweat and labor destroyed every day. Speaking only for myself, it was something I never became accustomed to, despite the hundreds, maybe thousands of times I have done so.

On the way back, Artorius fell out of the ranks and, despite the curses of the Pilus Prior, could not be induced to keep his place in the march. Finally, he was abandoned, to the disgust of the Pilus

Prior, Optio and, truth be known, the rest of us. Weakness is not tolerated in the Legion, and no matter how we might have sympathized to a degree, none of us were doing any more or any less than Artorius was. The fact that he was weak physically was not his crime, at least in my mind. It was his mental weakness that I found most damning. I know now that I was being unkind; I tended, and still tend, to view others as if they were me, that they were born as big and strong as I was, and that is not usually the case. It is a failing, the gods know, and I hope that I have mellowed with age. It also did not help that we were the tail end of the column, eating the dust of the rest of the Legion, yet I suspect that he would have fallen out even if we were in our place of the day before. He finally came staggering into camp a full third of a watch after we arrived, and he was warned that two more such failures would result in his dismissal from the Legion, a fate that he did not seem to be entirely unhappy about.

Our general, meanwhile, had marched at the head of the Legion both days, never showing any sign of fatigue and, as we were to learn, this was not just a case of Caesar showing off. He would always walk when we walked, and live as we lived, as much as it was possible for him to do so; being a general, there are certain requirements when dealing with others that elevate him above the rest of us. However, he ate what we ate, drank what we drank, and, in his actions, began to form a bond with us that is famous to this day. Never before, even in the days of Pompey Magnus or the great Scipio Africanus, has a general been loved in the way we in the 10th loved Caesar, and the foundation for that love was formed on that first march, and strengthened in the months to come. Although as it would turn out, not all of us shared the same feelings about our general.

Our training continued; we learned the battle formations, the *acies triplex*, the *acies duplex*, down to the formations that only Centuries used, such as the famous *testudo*, which is known and feared throughout the world. Our weapons training continued as well, now with the *scuta*, and we also began work throwing the *pilum*. Once we got over the slight bump in the beginning of our relationship, Optio Vinicius and I seemed to form a bond. Perhaps he recognized in me someone as devoted to the learning of the skills of arms as he was, yet whatever the reason, I became his star pupil, something that did not please Didius. I was still constantly scrutinized and criticized, but not only had I become accustomed to it, I recognized what it meant. However, along with the status came the responsibility. I was always the subject for the new lessons to be learned so that I took the bumps and bruises first, something that was lost on Didius. He began muttering choice names for me under his breath, loud enough for the others to hear but not me, some of them finding what he was saying witty enough to laugh. Growing more and more in my dislike for Didius, I consoled myself with the idea that soon enough, we would be squaring off one on one with the *rudis*. Then we would see who was laughing.

Proving that the Optio was not oblivious to what was going on, the very first day that we finally had progressed enough that we could begin beating on each other, he pitted me against Didius. Of course, the way it was expressed to us was not that we had progressed, but that Rome could not afford to wait the ten years it would take us to know the sharp end of a *gladius* before we continued in the pursuit of our enemies.

Still, when the Optio beckoned to me and Didius and told us to square off, he whispered in my ear, "I'm not deaf. The only thing I'll tell you is that you're forbidden to kill him. Understand?"

I nodded, but I had to swallow down the lump that suddenly formed in my throat. Despite my confidence, any time you face an adversary that you have never faced before, there is some trepidation. I cursed myself that I had not paid any attention to Didius' work on the stakes so that I would have an idea of his weaknesses, but that vessel was already broken and could not be mended now. For his part, Didius did not appear to be his usual blustery, confident self, for which I was grimly satisfied. Approaching each other, both of us in the first position, I instantly saw that Didius showed a weakness in his grip of the *scuta*, holding it in a slightly tilted manner and not in the direct vertical way that we were taught. I tucked that away, because I had decided that I did not want a quick kill. No, my goal that day was to completely dominate him, embarrass him, and leave no doubt who was the master.

Looking back on that decision now, with the blessing of hindsight and age, I wonder if I had been satisfied with just a straightforward end to our bout whether things would have been different. Somehow, I think that Didius and I were destined to clash, but the truth is that this might be the wishful thinking of an old man; only the gods truly know. In the moment, however, I slowly circled Didius, taking the role of the attacker and, observing him, I could see he was actually afraid.

Grinning, I called out to him loudly enough for the others to hear, "*Ave,* Didius. How long will it take me to make you my whore?"

This taunt brought a chorus of gasps and chuckles, and I saw Didius' eyes narrow in anger.

"Why don't you come and find out, you *cunnus*?" he snarled, to which I laughed and replied, "Be careful what you ask for, Didius."

And before I finished saying his name, I struck. Despite the fact I was not as quick as Vibius was, I was very fast, deceptively so, probably because of my size. Using the *scutum*, I banged into Didius hard enough to send him stumbling back a few feet, while I pressed the attack, slashing with the *rudis* instead of thrusting in the manner we were taught, smacking him hard on the arms and shoulders, causing him to roar in pain and anger. Lashing out wildly, he attempted to restore his equilibrium as I parried his blows contemptuously with my *rudis*, not even bothering to use my *scutum*.

This drew a comment from the Optio. "Careful about showing off, Pullus," he said evenly. "It's sloppy and it can become a habit."

Nodding that I heard him, I relented enough to allow Didius to regain his position, happy to hear that the cheering from the others was clearly in my favor. I decided to use that to my advantage.

"Hear that, Didius?" I asked, while I continued to circle him. "It sounds like your comrades don't care for you too much."

"What do I care about those *cunni* for?" he growled, which was met with the howls of derision that I expected it would invoke.

"Oh, I don't know." I kept my tone casual. "Maybe because one day you'll have to rely on them to save your life."

Again, as I finished speaking, I attacked, but this time Didius was prepared, managing to bring his *scutum* up to meet mine and we crashed into each other, *scutum* to *scutum*, neither of us giving an inch. He was strong, I had to give him that, and I resolved that I would go ahead and show him that I was indeed stronger. Dropping my hips a bit before uncoiling my whole body, I let out a roar as I did so, and once again, Didius went backwards, except this time, instead of stumbling, he fell flat. Immediately, I leaped astride him, putting the point of the *rudis* under his throat.

"You make this too easy," I told him contemptuously, then stepped away to turn to my comrades, raising my arms as if I were a victorious gladiator.

The blow was completely unexpected, and I dropped to my knees, my lower back on fire from where Didius hit me hard along the kidneys. I would piss blood for a week from the blow, but he made a fatal mistake in not following it up, allowing me to get to my feet. Spinning around, I was angrier than I think I had ever been to that point, and there was complete silence as we faced each other.

"Who's the whore now?" Didius taunted with an evil grin on his face.

When I looked over at the Optio, he gazed back at me with an impassive face, but almost imperceptibly, I saw him nod. Taking this as permission to continue the fight, I did not bother to talk. Instead, I launched a massive attack, using both *scutum* and *rudis* as offensive weapons, completely disdaining the defense and relying on the fury of my attack to protect me. Didius desperately parried my blows, backing up and giving ground, the only sound the thuds of wood hitting against wicker and wood and our harsh breathing. I was inhaling heavily, yet Didius was positively panting from the exertion of trying to meet my blows and keeping them from landing. Finally relenting, I waited for the moment I had planned when I first saw his telltale tilting of the *scutum*. Now, because of his fatigue, it was tipped outward even more, for which he tried to compensate by pulling the top of the *scutum* even closer to his face. Using the move that I had once used on Vibius, I smashed down on the bottom edge of his *scutum* with my own, pushing the top of his *scutum* even farther out and down to expose Didius' head, then once again I lashed out, smashing Didius' nose with a backward slash to the face. And just like Vibius, his nose exploded blood as it was smashed flat against his face, whereupon he dropped his *scutum* and *rudis*, falling to his knees and screaming in pain. At least, I thought to myself with satisfaction, Vibius had not acted like a little girl. Turning and walking back to my comrades, still panting with exertion and blood lust, this time I knew that he would not be getting back up. Our friends were still quiet; half of them seemed to be entranced by the sight of Didius, who was on his knees with his hands to his face, trying to stanch the flow of blood with little success. The others were looking at me, with expressions that were hard for me to place, a mixture of respect and....something else. Vibius was the only one who approached me, gently taking my weapons from me, then patting me on the back.

"As much as I hate him, I do sympathize," he said wryly. "I know what it's like to be hit like that by you."

"I hit him harder," I replied simply, and he nodded his understanding.

"Thank the gods that you did that to him and not me."

Scribonius came up to us with a grin. "Remind me never to make you angry."

The Optio had gone to Didius, trying to help him to his feet, which Didius angrily refused, getting to his feet on his own. Despite his voice being muffled by his hands, we could hear him clearly when he asked the Optio, "Well, are you going to do something? Isn't there some sort of charge you can write against him?"

I was shocked, and apparently, so was everyone else. The Optio asked with mild amazement in his voice, "And what, pray tell, would I write him up for?"

"What for?" Didius retorted. "You saw what he did to me. There are rules against striking the face and head in training."

He was right; we had been briefed about the penalties for striking blows to the head and face of a fellow Legionary in training. For a moment, my stomach began to twist.

"There are also rules against striking a fellow Legionary when he's not prepared," replied the Optio calmly. "You had been knocked down, *tiro* Pullus bested you, and the bout was over."

"I didn't capitulate," Didius protested angrily, and now I could see that the Optio was beginning to get irritated himself.

"More fool you," Vinicius retorted, "because Pullus had finished you. The fact that you're too stupid to know it isn't his or my fault. Now, follow me to the *medici*."

He turned to lead Didius away, and as Didius was passing, he stared at me with undisguised hatred. "This isn't over," he hissed, although it was hard to understand him because he was still clutching his face.

I merely smiled and replied, "Any time you want another beating, I'm more than happy to oblige."

He did not say anything else, instead following the Optio to the *quaestorium* where the doctors and *medici* were constantly busy patching men up. Our training is supposed to be bloodless combat, and our battle bloody drills, but sometimes, at least with the former, accidents happened and blood did flow.

As we watched them leave, Scribonius said quietly, "I'd watch your back if I were you."

I nodded, and Vibius answered for me, "I'll be there to do it, don't worry about that."

The pace of training picked up; we began doing a march three times a week, both to condition us and also to teach us how to make a camp, rotating the various jobs of building so that we learned everything we needed to about building one. We also began battle drills, Century against Century, which we all enjoyed the most, despite it also giving us the most bumps and bruises. Slowly but surely, we were beginning to look more like a real Legion and not a great gaggle of fools who happened to be wearing the uniform of a Legionary. That was not the message that was being relayed to us by our Centurion, yet even so, we could detect the slightest change in his tone with us. We were not raw *tiros* anymore, but not quite full *Gregarii* either, yet for most of us, the idea had become solidified that we would make it to the final swearing in ceremony. Most of us, anyway.

Artorius was still struggling mightily, and while he seemed to put in the extra work willingly to correct his deficiencies, of which there were many, I, for one, suspected that he was going through the motions rather than putting any real effort into his training. However, when I asked Vibius this question, he bristled at the suggestion; apparently, he had taken his tutoring of Artorius to heart.

"I believe he's putting everything he has into his extra work," Vibius snapped, his swarthy face flushing darker. "He can't help it if he's not as strong as you, Titus. Not everyone is; in fact, few people are, yet you seem to think everything should come as easily to them as it does to you."

That surprised me quite a bit. In my mind, I was struggling just as much as anyone else was, and this was the first I learned that there was a perception that the opposite was true.

I could not hide my surprise when I answered, "*Edepol!* Who says that things come easily to me? I have to work just as hard as anyone else."

Vibius looked at me steadily for a moment before replying quietly, "I know you think you do, but I don't think you have the slightest idea just how much stronger and better you are than the rest of us. Haven't you seen not just us, but the other men in the Century, stop to watch you when you're going through the drills?"

I shrugged. "What of it? I'm sure that they're just watching me because I stick out, being so large."

And that was truly what I thought at the time; I had been stared at most of my life because of my size, and it was simply something to which I had become accustomed.

Vibius shook his head vigorously and, using his finger for emphasis, pointed to my chest and replied, "That's not why at all, Titus. You make these drills look easy. I know; I hear the other men talking. There are even men betting on how many barbarians you'll kill in our first battle."

Now I was shocked. It is true that men in the Legions will bet on absolutely anything, but I had no idea that the others, including the veterans apparently, saw me in this light. My chest constricted as the thought settled into my mind and I realized the implications of it. Suddenly, I had a reputation to uphold, and I had yet to fight my first battle!

This revelation from Vibius rocked me, so I began surreptitiously watching others when they looked in my direction, trying to discern what their true thoughts were. I began feeling an enormous amount of pressure, whether it was warranted or not, and soon found myself fretting about what might happen when we actually did go into battle. There had been rumblings for some time that the Legions were about to move out and begin campaigning. It was already late May, and the campaigning season was open for some time now, meaning a late start for us, but Caesar was forced to spend that time training us because we were a new Legion. Despite that, the word around the fires was that we would be moving soon, and it would be north, into the wilds of Hispania north of the Tanis River, to pacify the remaining tribe in the area, the Lusitani, who had revolted again. To that end, we were finally equipped with our real weapons, the *gladius* that most of us would carry for as long as it lasted, and our two *pila*, along with our *scuta*, emblazoned with the symbol of the 10th Legion, the bull. My first thought was how ridiculously light the weapons were compared to the training weapons we had been using, but that was the point of our training. As I examined my blade, still unmarked from where I would work it with the sharpening stone to put as fine an edge on it as I could, I hefted its balance, trying to imagine thrusting it into the body of another man, rather than a stake. Glancing about, I could see all of my tent mates doing the same thing, and I wondered if I wore the same grin on my face.

It was about that time that Artorius fell out of his third march, despite Vibius' almost frantic efforts to help him keep up, even as it caused the Pilus Prior to give Vibius a good thrashing for doing so. It did not help; less than halfway along our march back to our base camp, Artorius fell out. We had suspected this as a likely event, it becoming clear to all of us that the effort of the extra training, along with the burden of our normal regimen, was steadily wearing him down. He was barely able to eat the evening meal, sitting listlessly and chewing his bread with the same vigor as a cow chewing its cud. The next morning, as we broke camp and made ready to begin the march back, he moved like a man sleepwalking, and it was so noticeable that the Pilus Prior came over to him to smack him in the face. That seemed to stir him a bit, and he was responsive when we formed up to begin the march back, then at some point after the first break, he dropped from the ranks. Vibius did not notice straight away, but when he did, he immediately fell out himself, trotting back to find Artorius, despite the cursed warning directed at him by the Pilus Prior. Optio Vinicius then went back to retrieve both of them and he returned shortly, along with Vibius carrying his own pack and Artorius' as well, trying to balance both *furcae*, one on each shoulder, his face shining with perspiration from the exertion and strain. Artorius was being dragged by the arm by the Optio, who was trying to use encouragement instead of the threats that the Pilus Prior favored. All of this was taking place amid the normal noise and chaos of a march; the dust swirling all around from the tramping of thousands of feet, the clinking and clanking of gear as it bounced against each other, the steady underlying hum of the men talking to each other in snatched conversations, trying to pass the time. I will say that even for me it was hard to breathe and I was higher up than Artorius, so I could imagine how choking it was in his spot, which could not have helped. Looking over at him, I could see that his face was white as chalk, with a clammy look about it that we had learned indicated someone who was having trouble coping with the heat. His mouth hung open as he gasped for air, while his eyes would seem to focus for a moment, as if he was conscious of his surroundings, then begin wavering before rolling back in his head, whereupon he started stumbling again. The Optio would shake his arm, he would snap back to the present, then after a moment would drift off again. It was almost like he was falling asleep as he walked, something I had never seen before. Over the years, I would be on marches where all of us looked like that, but to that point, he was the first to exhibit these signs, and I was morbidly fascinated.

By the time we made it to the second break, Artorius was nowhere to be seen, even when the *bucina* sounded the signal to begin the start of the last leg of the march. Vibius stood to the side until the last moment, looking to the rear of the column before getting another whack from the Pilus Prior and a snarled order to get into the ranks. Vibius was obviously hoping that Artorius would somehow come staggering up, but he did not. Continuing on, we finished the march, almost all of us not very fatigued from the effort except for Vibius, who had carried Artorius' gear most of the way back. The last few miles, Romulus and Remus, the nicknames we gave to the Mallius brothers, tried to relieve Vibius of his load, but he would have none of it and in fact got downright nasty about it.

"I don't need any of you *cunni* helping me," he snarled at Marcus, who we called Romulus, and I swear that if Vibius did not have his hands full, he would have punched Romulus in the face.

For his part, Romulus did not appreciate having his offer spurned in such a manner.

"Prick! I'm sorry I asked," he snapped back, "and see if I ever offer to help you again."

He turned away to complain to Remus about Vibius' brutish behavior, the whole exchange drawing the jeers and catcalls of the men around us, prompting the Pilus Prior to suddenly appear in our midst and lash out with his *vitus*. There were times I really wanted to take that thing away from him and break it over his head.

Artorius was brought in on one of the wagons of the baggage train, a Centurion in the Cohort marching behind it having thrown him in the back. By this time, we were already finished with our evening routine, having our bath and meal, and were in fact just a few moments away from the call to retire. I began to treasure these quiet moments around the fire, listening to the wild tales of the veterans and watching the inevitable dice game, which was a feature at almost every tent. I always thought it somewhat interesting that men would almost always gamble with other tent sections but not with their own tent mates, unless there was no other choice. The only exception to this was Didius, but he was already starting to be shunned by our section and was therefore forced to look elsewhere. I believe that for most of the men, besides Didius, it had something to do with the idea of not wanting to cause any bad blood between such close comrades. Whatever the reason, the idea seemed to be that fleecing men from other Legions was always best; if not other Legions, then other Cohorts, and if not other Cohorts, at least other Centuries. However, many times not even this was possible, and nothing stops a Legionary from gambling, so it was inevitable that there would be disagreements among the closest of friends. Personally, I was never much for gambling. It is not that I had anything against it; I could take it or leave it, not to mention I had big dreams that only a large amount of money would fulfill, so it was not a fever with me the way it was with other men like Vibius, who I swear would wager on anything, no matter how ridiculous. For a while, he was trying to make wagers on which of the men in the tent would break wind next, yet soon enough he found out that there was cheating going on, because in the dark, one cannot tell whether the sound was true or made by using our mouth, and he was terribly put out that we ruined such an exciting game for him.

However, there was nothing exotic this evening; it was dice and, as usual, the next day's wine ration was up for wager, something that was strictly forbidden but always ignored, when Artorius came stumbling up. He was not wearing his helmet or *lorica*, carrying them instead, and his head was down as he approached, refusing to meet our eyes. There was an awkward silence as he approached, because we had already been told that since this was his third failure, he was being dismissed from the Legion. He came to get all of his gear and return it to the Legion quartermaster, where he would be issued a civilian's tunic and shoes, then given a small amount of money along with a document that he was to carry with him that detailed his disgrace. Because he had committed no crime, unless one considered failing to make it as a Legionary a crime, as I did, he was not punished in any way other than having to carry the shame of his failure back to his family, if he did indeed go back to his family. Many young men were too ashamed to do so, making their way to the nearest big city to try and seek some sort of life there. Despite feeling badly for him, there was also a sense of relief that we would not have to worry any longer about whether or not he would hold up in the trials of combat. It also created some relief to the problem of space in our tent, now having one less body to shift around. Still, it was difficult; we did not know what to say to him, only offering a sympathetic pat on the back instead. While he looked relieved, there was also a new look of fear in his eyes, undoubtedly caused by the dread of what was facing him, the uncertainty of a life that no longer held any particular value to the rest of the world. His only hope lay in his father forgiving him and both of them patching up their differences; otherwise, he was all alone in the world, with no real skills. Knowing what I know now, I should have realized that he would most likely turn to a life of crime. He was not cut out to be a highwayman, the type of hard man that lies in wait for unsuspecting travelers. Because of his temperament and his slight build, he probably went into a life of petty crime, stealing what he needed to survive, at least until he got caught. Most of those types eventually do, and ours is not a forgiving society like some of the others I have encountered in my travels. Once he gathered up his gear, Optio Vinicius escorted him to the *quaestorium*, our last view of him struggling to carry all his equipment, with the Optio walking beside him.

Before we went into the final phase of our training, we held the lustration ceremony, a sacred rite that calls for the gods' favor onto the standards of the Legion and the Legion itself. Because of its sacred nature, I cannot speak of it. I will say that it is a rite that is usually performed at the beginning of the new campaign season. However, since we were new *tiros,* it was not seen as fitting for us to participate until we were deemed worthy of being called Legionaries. After the ceremony for the rest of the army, we *tiros* were ordered to remain in our places in formation, where we were faced by the Praetor, who was standing on the rostra, dressed in his cuirass and his general's *paludamentum*, the scarlet cloak of general rank. Arrayed in front of him, also facing us, were all sixty of our Centurions, all wearing their dress uniforms, with their phalarae, torqs, and other badges of office and decoration gleaming with the strength of a hundred suns.

"Soldiers," Caesar addressed us, causing a stir in our ranks because this was the first time we were spoken to in this manner, and it took a moment for the meaning to sink in.

We had done it! We were being addressed as soldiers by Caesar because that was what we were. All of the pain and sweat of the last almost four months was as if it never happened, just like the last mist of a bad dream dissolving when you awake because of the brilliance of the new day.

"Today is a great day for you, and for Rome," he continued, using what I would learn was his oratorical voice, which he pitched higher when addressing large crowds so that it would carry farther.

"You are about to be entered into the rolls of the brave men who have served Rome so well in the past, covering both our eternal city and themselves in glory."

He indicated the Centurions standing in front of him.

"Perhaps some of you will elevate yourself to the glory and rank of the men you see standing before you. Perhaps not."

He paused for a moment before continuing in a way that sounded as if he was speaking quietly, yet somehow still pitching his voice loud enough for all to hear, at least in the first few ranks.

"What is certain is that some of you will die, if that is the will of the gods."

This had our complete attention.

"But if it is the will of the gods that you die, it is still up to each of you to choose *how* to die. And in dying well, you add even more glory and fame to Rome, to your tribe, to your family, and to yourselves."

It is a curious characteristic of young men, at least in my lifetime, so I suppose that it has always been so and always will be. As Caesar talked of the possibility of death, while I was at the position of *intente,* I still looked at the others out of the corners of my eyes, and I remember thinking to myself, poor bastards, I wonder which of them will die? As I was to learn later when we talked about the speech, every one of my comrades claimed that they had the exact same thought, for it never occurs to the young that they might be one of those unlucky souls who fall before they live to a ripe old age. It is not until one of us actually falls that it becomes real, and from that moment, nothing in one's life is the same. But at that moment, we were still young, full of bright hopes and brash courage, and it was the greatest sense of pride I had ever known in my short life when we finished the oath to finally become *Miles Gregarii*, the common Legionary in the service of Rome. We were dismissed for the rest of the day, as those of the Legion who were veterans came to congratulate us. Perhaps the biggest shock was the change in the demeanor of Pilus Prior Crastinus, who was the first man to stand us to a round of drinks at one of the shabby, ramshackle inns that had been thrown up outside the camp.

"Welcome home, boys," he roared, the color of his face showing a hint that he might have started the celebrations ahead of us.

Passing among us, he shook each of our hands, gave us a slap on the back, and made some sort of comment about something we did in training that either had amused him or angered him, although he still relayed the latter with a laugh.

When he got to me, he looked up at me and shouted, "Well! Here's the hero! Hasn't seen a battle yet, but he already has those Lusitani *cunni* shaking in their tracks!"

I could feel the blush moving up my neck to my face, and I quickly glanced around. Of course, I was the center of attention, but I could not determine what the looks I was receiving meant. Some of the men were grinning at me, apparently delighted at my discomfort; some were not smiling, yet still looked friendly. There was only one whose countenance I could not mistake; Didius glowered at me, the bruises under his eyes still slightly visible, making him look like he badly needed a night of sleep. Seeing his displeasure made me feel somewhat better and I grinned, first in his direction, then back down to the Pilus Prior.

"I certainly hope that I can live up to your belief in me, Pilus Prior," I said honestly.

He laughed and replied, "You will, boy. You will. I have no doubt of that. Once I saw you working the *rudis*, I knew that you'd be one to watch. Just save some for the rest of the boys, eh?"

With another slap on my shoulder, he moved on to the next man, leaving me to stare bemusedly into my wine cup. I was glad that he possessed no doubts; that made one of us. Vibius saw my thoughtful expression and came over to me, leaning against the wall of the crude hut that served to shelter all of the carousers who found their way there every night.

"Aaah," he cried cheerfully, "quit moping about, you big ox. You'll be fine and you know it. He's right; you'll probably kill so many of those barbarians that there won't be enough left for the rest of us."

Despite his jovial tone, I was still not willing to give up my contemplative mood.

Shrugging, I could only reply, "I hope it works out like that. But the truth is, none of us really know, do we? I mean," I continued, lowering my voice, "nobody truly knows how they'll react until it happens, neh? So for all I know, I may find that my knees turn to water, and I piss myself like a girl."

Having gotten it out at last, I hurriedly took a swallow of my wine so I could hide my face and shame at having made such an admission.

"That much is true," a quiet voice sounded next to me, and I swiveled my head to see Calienus standing there.

Obviously, he had heard what I said, so I saw no point in pretending otherwise. He examined me with a kindly expression, one that I imagined a big brother would use when his little brother came to confide in him some wrong done to him. Without waiting for me to answer, he continued, "Nobody really knows what they'll do the first time they face the enemy, unless they're a liar or fool like him." He jerked his head in the direction of Didius, who had managed to draw a crowd around him, no doubt boasting of the glory he was going to earn. "All you can do is this; rely on your training, and put your trust in the man next to you." Grabbing me by the shoulder, he turned me about so that he could look me in the eye as he spoke. "The rest will come much easier than you think. When the moment comes, trust me, you'll know what to do." Turning to Vibius then, he finished, "And both of you need to watch each other's back at all times."

"All right, Sergeant, but we haven't started the fighting yet," protested Vibius with a laugh, which died in his throat when he saw that Calienus was not joining him. "I wasn't talking about the Lusitani," he replied in a voice pitched just loudly enough to be heard over the din, but not any farther than where we were standing. "I'm talking about with him."

He nodded his head, again in the direction of Didius. Perhaps it was a coincidence, perhaps not, but when we looked over in the direction that Calienus had indicated, we both saw Didius drinking from his cup, staring straight at us.

I had never drunk so much in my young life as I did that night, and truthfully, I do not remember much of what transpired. However, I vividly remember the next day, when we were roused by the Pilus Prior, who amazingly seemed none the worse for wear, and was in his normally loud state.

"On your feet, you *cunni*," he roared when he shoved his face into our tent, his customary morning greeting. If we were expecting that the goodwill that he had shown to us the night before would be present this morning, we were disappointed. Indeed, as the day progressed, it was as if the day before had never happened, which we found not only puzzling, but a little disturbing.

Going to Calienus for guidance, he explained to us, "It's going to be like this a little while longer, at least until we're blooded. The Pilus Prior is going to keep pushing us until he knows exactly what we can do in battle. If we do well, then you'll see more of what you saw last night, although not that often and not as much as last night."

I, for one, despite understanding what he was saying, still did not like it. We were *Gregarii* now, after all; that was what the whole ceremony had been about the day before, and I expressed this to Calienus, who shook his head.

"What happened yesterday was unusual. Normally, you'd have completed your four months of training before swearing in, but Caesar's anxious to move because it's already late. So he had you sworn in earlier than usual. It didn't sit well with some of the Centurions, I'll tell you that." Before we could ask the question, Calienus added, "The Pilus Prior wasn't one of them, though. I heard him telling the Optio he thinks our Century is ready to go right now. Second Century," he rolled his eyes and we laughed, "is another story."

The conclusion of our training was a forced march of all the Legions, the 7ᵗʰ, 8ᵗʰ, 9ᵗʰ, and 10ᵗʰ, culminating in the creation of two marching camps, followed by a mock battle the next day with two Legions against two Legions, along with the cavalry and auxiliaries, now numbering about another 5,000 men, split evenly between the two sides. Particular emphasis was placed on the changing of formations; from column into line, then moving as quickly back into column as we could, simulating the march to contact, with a battle, then a pursuit of a withdrawing force. The last thing that we practiced was how to stage a fighting withdrawal, and much was made by the Centurions that although we would never likely use this, it was still good to know. We wholeheartedly agreed, taking their word for it that we would never use it, the veterans among us openly scoffing at the idea.

"I haven't taken a backward step on the battlefield yet," barked the Pilus Prior, "and with you bastards with me, I don't plan on it ever happening."

This brought a roar of approval from us, and it was clear to all of us that we were ready to march, for real this time, against a real enemy.

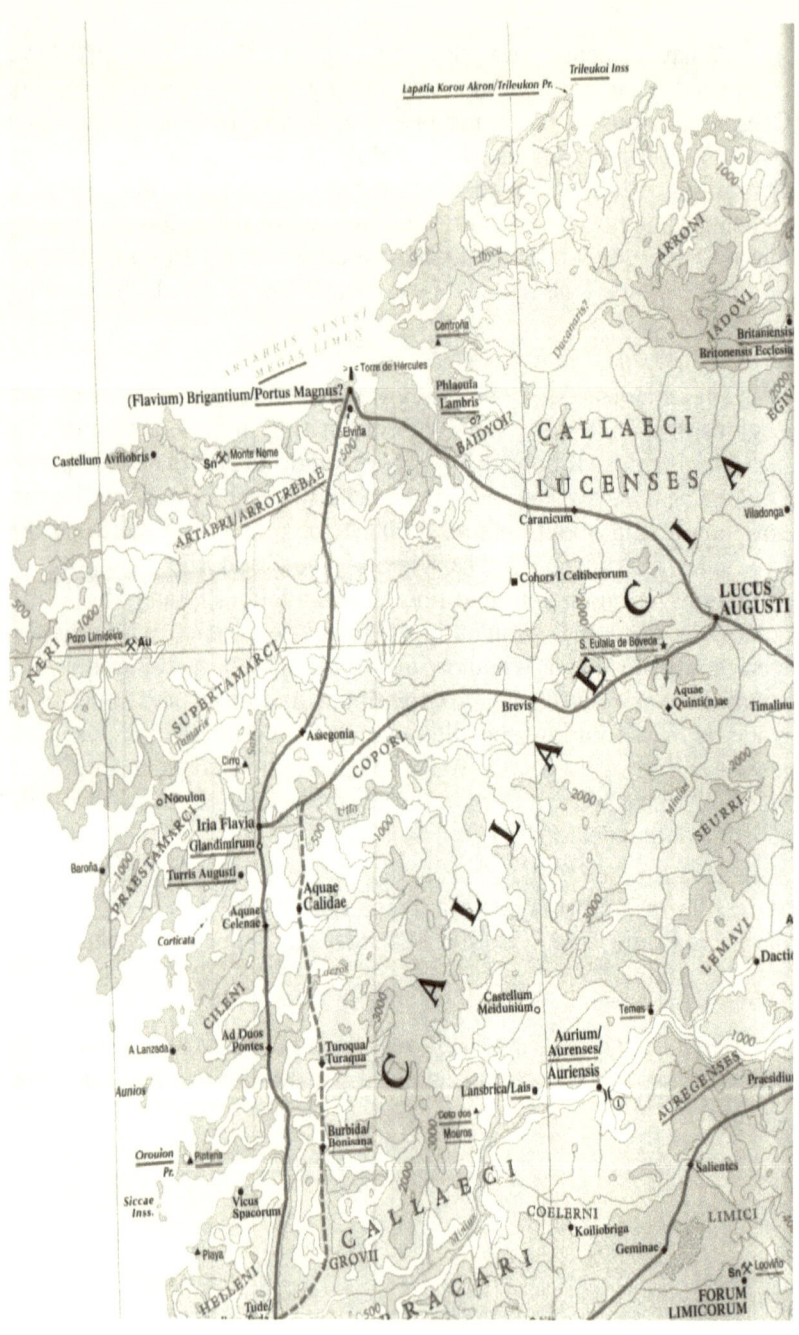

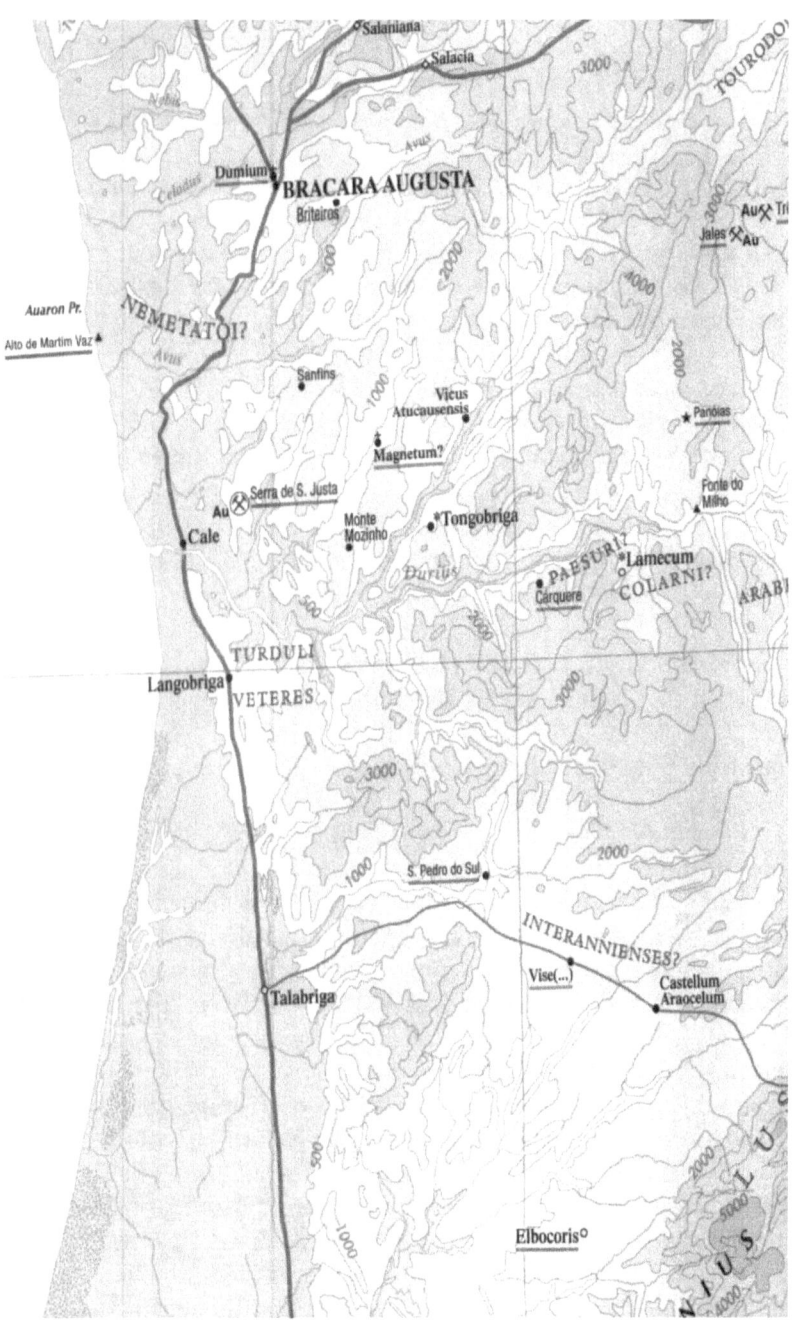

Chapter 4- Campaign in Lusitania

We were given two days in which to arrange our affairs, deposit excess baggage into stores, and put finishing touches on our weapons and uniforms. All last-moment items like the replacement of thongs that tied pieces of gear to us that had broken, or *pila* that had become unserviceable were taken care of, in anticipation of leaving the camp for good, or at least for the rest of the season. Spirits were running high, as were tempers, and there were a number of minor skirmishes among Legionaries from different Legions, Cohorts, and Centuries, yet that was to be expected. At least that was what Calienus told us.

"I don't know about you," he remarked as we were waterproofing our *scuta* covers, "but I've had enough of training. It's time for some real work."

Every one of us barked our approval at this, yet even as I joined in, I felt my stomach do a twist at the thought. Supposedly, at least according to the other men, I was the most ready of all of us and the most likely to attain glory, so why did I feel so apprehensive? If I was as good as they said I was, should I not truly be looking forward to this without any doubts or fears, which is certainly not how I felt now? These were the thoughts crammed into my head as I busied myself packing, making sure that varnish was properly applied to straps, buckles were polished, all the myriad things that occupy an army before it moves. The camp was a swarm of activity, with men running this way and that; scribes and Tribunes were marching about carrying scrolls and wax tablets, all of them trying to look like the message or order they carried involved the fate of the Republic itself. Up to this point, we had little to do with the Tribunes, but they were slowly becoming more visible as they gained a little confidence and we advanced in our training. The smart ones and, being honest, there are precious few of those in the army at any given point, let the Centurions run the Legions, and mostly stayed out of the way. However, there were an officious and arrogant few who, having read a manual, thought themselves the experts in all manners relating to the military arts. Not surprisingly, their attitude was met with barely disguised contempt by the Centurions, but fortunately for us, Caesar was the type of general who made sure that his Tribunes knew their place. Nonetheless, high and noble birth apparently makes some men a bit thickheaded, as a few, thank the gods a precious few, still sought to establish their authority over us.

There was one in particular and, being honest, I do not remember his true name; there have been so many Tribunes pass through my Legions in the last forty years that they all seem to blend together. Relatively few ever stick out in my memory, and those that do are because they are either spectacularly good at their job or spectacularly bad, and unfortunately the latter outnumbered the former by a huge margin. While I do not remember his true name, I do remember what we called him: Doughboy. He was named that by Scribonius, I believe, and it was an apt name for many reasons. For one, he had the pasty complexion of the kind of dough that graces the finest tables, while his body betrayed a fondness for sweets and pastries. It was more than just his physical attributes that led to his nickname, because he was about as useful as a lump of dough, and when heat of any sort was applied, he would puff up, just like a loaf of leavened bread, falling back on his status as a patrician of one of the old families of Rome. He was an Appius, I believe, yet for the life of me, I cannot remember his name; it is funny how the memory works sometimes as one grows older. On that day, he was the acting commander of the Legion, because in those times, it rotated daily among each of the six Tribunes assigned to our Legion, and since it was his day, this meant that there would be more than the usual silliness. He was constantly stalking among us, snapping at us about things like not coming to *intente* as he walked by, forcing us to constantly stop packing or working on our gear since he seemed to do nothing but walk in circles around and around our part of the camp. Compounding matters, he would insist on stopping to inspect our gear, then berate us for not having everything ready, polished and packed, apparently simply because he thought we should have been finished by that point.

"Doesn't he have anything better to do?" Vibius muttered in his wake, after Doughboy chastised him for not having his leathers properly varnished. Despite still being new, we had been in long enough to know that doing something stupid, like pointing out that we could only do one thing at a time, would have gotten us in more trouble than the momentary satisfaction was worth, so Vibius simply responded in his best parade ground manner, "Absolutely correct, sir. No excuse, sir. Won't happen again, sir."

Apparently expecting something else, Doughboy stood there nonplussed for a moment, his mouth hanging open, causing his second chin to quiver slightly, a sight that threatened to make me laugh so much that I was forced to bite the inside of my mouth until it bled.

Finally snapping his mouth shut, Doughboy replied in a tone I am sure that he thought was very officer-like, but to us reeked of his uncertainty, saying, "Very well, then. Just make sure that it doesn't happen again."

Then he stood there for what seemed like a full watch, although was just a few heartbeats, as if unsure what he was supposed to do next. Finally, he said, "Right. Well, then. I must go. There are many duties to attend to."

Doughboy then went wandering off, leaving us staring at his retreating back.

"Apparently, no, he doesn't have anything better to do," I spat a bloody gob on the ground. "But just make sure it doesn't happen again," I finished, in my best attempt to mimic Doughboy, which set us both to laughing as we turned back to our work,

At last, all was ready, giving us the opportunity to lie where we were to catch some sleep before we started out on the march, a real march heading towards a real enemy, making the energy definitely different from our training jaunts. One other thing that made it different was that we were all required to wear our dress uniforms. For us *Gregarii,* that was not much more than the horsehair plume, which I hated because if the wind were coming in the wrong direction, it would whip around and hit me in the face. It was the Centurions and the officers that had the most to worry about; rather, their slaves did. Still, it was a sight! The glittering array of the eagles and standards, the panoply and pomp as we were led out of the gate by Caesar himself for that first time, followed by the officers of the Legions, was a sight that will be with me until the day I die.

Wondering that Caesar would be at the very front, without a vanguard of any type, I asked Calienus, who replied, "That's only for the first mile or so. Then he and the others will pull to the side, and let the 7th lead the way."

For that was how it was that first day; we marched in the order of our numbers, so that we walked drag, ahead of only the baggage train and the rearguard. When an army of that size is on the march, it does not make any sense for the trailing Legions to even start forming up for the first watch or so, which was why once the initial formation was dismissed and the march began, we were allowed to break ranks to go stand by the gate to watch the procession. None of the veterans bothered; they lay down and immediately fell asleep again, using their packed gear as a pillow, but for those of us for whom this was the first campaign, we could not be drawn away from the spectacle. When you are young, things like sleeping or eating can be made up later, but it would not be long before we learned one of the most valuable lessons of being a soldier, that when you have the chance, you sleep and eat. However, we did not know that yet, so I stood with the rest of my tent mates, watching the first Legions go marching by.

There was the usual banter and jeering among us, the men of the 7th calling out to us, "That's right, 10th. In the rear with the gear where there is no fear!"

"They're just saving the best for last," someone shot back, which of course we cheered as the wittiest retort ever made, while the men of the 7th did the opposite.

I cannot help but think back to that day, when despite our bickering, we were all comrades, none of us knowing the great struggle that lay ahead, where we would be looking over our *scuta* across at some of these same men, preparing to kill or be killed. Such is the fickle nature of the gods and the Fates, I suppose, yet despite knowing that we are subject to their whims, it is still hard to understand how we came to that place. However, that was far in the future and, on that day, even the gods seemed pleased. The sacrifices had been made, the auspices taken, and there were eagles sighted flying over the camp in the direction of our march, so for everyone, it was seen as a sign that the gods were with us. That day, the weather was glorious, at least to me. Consequently, I reveled in the feeling of the sun on my face as I watched men just like me go marching by, and when I looked at Vibius, my grin could have split my head wide open.

"This is what we've been waiting for, Vibius," I crowed, "since we were boys. We're on the march with the Legions. Can there be anything more glorious?"

Vibius shook his head in agreement, replying, "I don't think so, Titus. I don't think so."

It was almost two parts of a watch before it was our turn to set out, and when we marched, the few men who were remaining behind, those too sick to march and a few of the marginal men who it was felt would be better suited to keep the camp open and running, were all that remained as our audience when we exited the gates. The worst part now was the horrible dust that hung in a pall over us, making the sun appear as just a hazy orb in the sky that you could actually look at without hurting your eyes, it was so heavily obscured. This meant that the choking, coughing, and cursing began at almost the same time, and despite the Centurions telling us to shut up and quit whining, soon enough they were choking, coughing, and cursing along with us, especially the cursing. Another thing that makes walking drag so unpleasant is that marching behind first the cavalry, then the officers, means that no matter how careful you are, before a couple of miles go by, your feet are covered in the deposits of dung left behind by the thousands of animals. The combination of the freshness and the heat also did not help with the smell, so it was not long before some of the more delicate stomachs were heaving, beginning a chain reaction of sorts. All in all, it was a miserable experience.

Because we could only march as fast as the baggage train, with the drag Legion being charged with guarding it and the train being slower than the rest of the Legions, the one small blessing was that this meant that the other Legions got to do the work of making the marching camp. The camp outline, the ditch walls and palisade were already finished when we arrived, with the streets and tent areas all staked out and ready for the pitching of the tents. Filing in, we were followed by the wagons, entering through the *Porta Decumana*, the rear gate of the camp, then marching to our area to erect our tents. Since there was not a bath like at our permanent camp, we had to make do the best we could to clean off the filth of the march by just oiling down and being scraped clean where we stood, performed on our section by Lucco. The one piece of good news was that we would be the vanguard the next day, so we would not have to go through the same ordeal that we endured that day. Such is the way of the Roman army, and one of the many small reasons we are so great. Everyone shares equally in both the easy duties and the onerous tasks; it is all a matter of time before it is your turn for both. The only exception is latrine duty, which is reserved for Legionaries on punishment, and I thanked the gods that there were enough men who fell afoul of the rules and regulations that it never became a regular duty, although at one point or another we all took turns mucking out the stables. For some reason, the idea of cleaning up the *cac* of an animal is not nearly as loathsome as that of a human's and although I have no idea why this is so, I just know that it is.

Falling asleep easily that night, the talk was held to a minimum by our fatigue, and this began the pattern of the next several days as we moved northwest to confront the Lusitani. Drawing closer to the enemy, the terrain became more difficult, consisting of rolling hills that were not particularly high, yet whose slopes were steep, so that we felt the effort even if it did not take particularly long to crest each hill. Crossing the Anas (Guadiana) River, we were told this marked the southern border of the Lusitani territory, and was the home of the Turdetani and Lusitani branches. While they were reputed to be the more civilized of the tribes; it was the Celtici and particularly the Vettones who were the most savage back then, the Lusitani and Turdetani were still supposed to be formidable warriors. Crossing the river took the better part of a day, there being only one narrow ford and the river bottom was sandy, meaning that the lucky lads immediately in front of the baggage train got to push and pull the wagons when they inevitably got stuck. While we were happy to march as the vanguard that second day, it also meant that we would have the most work to do constructing the camp. Now that we were officially in enemy territory, we were ordered to be even more vigilant, and part of that vigilance included making our camp more secure. The depth of the ditch was deepened a foot more, and widened another foot, making the rampart that much higher. Also, the guard was doubled, and it was also our turn for that duty, so that we made up for the easy day we had as far as eating dust and not stepping in *cac* by getting less sleep. As I said, it all evens out.

Since this was our first night in what was considered to be enemy territory, there was little trouble staying awake during our turn on the walls. The fact that there had been a sighting of the enemy as the camp was being completed just made it all the easier, not that it amounted to much. It was Rufio, one of the veterans in our Century, who spotted them first and raised the alarm. There was a bit of a hubbub as his shout got all of us scrambling for our *scuta* and *pila*; we were already wearing our *galeae*, although this was not standard when we made camp, but we were ordered to do so because we were in enemy territory. Normally, we wore our *gladii* and *pugio* at all times, on pain of punishment ranging from a flogging to execution. As it turned out, the sighting was a huge army of three men, sitting on their horses on the nearby ridge as they watched us work. They were some distance away, so it was impossible to make out details, yet I, for one, felt my pulse race. It did not matter that there were only three of them; there they were! The enemy, the barbarian horde, the feared Lusitani, the scourge of Hispania! I could tell that my friends were just as excited and even Calienus seemed to be a little more than his usual placid self. It was enough of an occasion that the Pilus Prior did not immediately start thrashing us when we stopped working to stand watching the men observing us. After a moment, we heard him yelling something about our sorry asses getting back to work, so we returned to our respective labors. This day, it was my turn to carry dirt, a job that I detested until, that is, I realized that it was a good way to keep working on my strength by trying to carry more than the others. Also, it was a chance to show off a little, I must admit. I could not help being born bigger and stronger, but I saw no reason why I should not demonstrate it from time to time, for which my tent mates would roundly jeer me. However, I could tell that they were secretly proud of the fact that I was already considered one of the strong men of the Legion. Just before we set out, we had held games, including wrestling bouts with men picked by their comrades from each Legion facing each other. Naturally, I was picked, despite never having wrestled a day in my life, and it was only due to brute strength that I won my first two matches, advancing to the penultimate round, where I was thrashed soundly by a man much smaller than I, but who was an experienced wrestler. While I had not shamed myself or my Legion, I was still determined that I would avenge that loss, deciding that when the campaigning season was over, I would learn to wrestle. If I lived, at least.

As we were breaking camp the next morning, the alarm went up once again. This time, however, it was not just three men, but several hundred, all of them mounted and who watched us from the same spot as the first three. Again, there was a stir among all of us, since this was obviously not just a scouting party, even though there was no way that they could match us in strength and were extremely unlikely to attack us. Because of the presence of these men, who one of the scouts confirmed were Lusitani, we marched out in a column of squares called an *agmentum quadratum*, which is an extremely difficult formation to control on the march. I think it was more just to show the Lusitani that we had seen them and were prepared for anything they cared to throw at us than from a fear of being attacked. We were told to continue carrying our *scuta* on our backs, but to remove the covers so that they were instantly ready should we need them. It turned out that we did not; instead, the horsemen were content to shadow us as we marched, always staying just out of reach of a sudden attack by our cavalry screen. After about two parts of a watch, the column was halted, and we were shaken out into our standard marching formation, with our Legion in the middle this time. Again, because of my normal marching place on the outside of the column, I was able to pass the time watching the men on the horses, who were split into two groups, with one group on each side of the column. Even with my lack of experience then, I could at least tell that these men were born to ride a horse; indeed, it was hard to tell where the man stopped and the horse started. Perhaps, I thought, they are really centaurs, and I let this thought occupy my mind as we marched; it is in such ways that one learns to pass the monotonous watches of marching, staring at the back of the man in front of you.

It was shortly before we were to stop for the day when it happened. Suddenly, from behind us, came the blaring of *bucina*, and then the *cornicen*, the curved round horn with a deep bass voice that carries a great distance and is used to relay orders in battle, instantly telling us that something important was going on. Craning our necks to look to the rear, it was still impossible to see, and indeed, as we learned later the sounding of the horns that we heard were merely the relayed signals sent up to the front. Whatever happened had occurred far to the rear, although we did not know that then.

"Eyes front, you *cunni*," the Pilus Prior snarled as he strode by us down the side of the column, heading towards the rear to see what was going on. "Let me find out what all this racket's about."

The column had halted, and just a few heartbeats later, Caesar and what looked like his entire staff came galloping past, heading in the same direction. Shortly after, one of the cavalry *ala* that was up front came back as well.

"What do you think it is?" Scribonius asked me, as if I would have any better idea than he would.

"The gods only know," I answered, trying to hide my irritation at being asked a question to which I obviously did not know the answer.

"My guess is that those bastards who've been following us picked off some stragglers." This came from Calienus, and we instantly accepted this as truth since Calienus was a veteran.

There was a buzz of conversation from all the men, speculating about what happened, with the consensus seeming to be what Calienus had predicted, so now it was just a matter of waiting to see what the truth was.

Vinicius came to us and ordered, "Keep alert. Don't keep your attention to the back of the column. This may be a trick to draw our attention away from some other point."

The reality of this hit me immediately, and I snapped my head to look around. My heart leaped a little when I saw that the horsemen who had been on my side of the column the whole day were gone.

"Where did those horsemen go?" I asked Vinicius, hoping that one of us was paying attention.

He had been.

"They peeled off a mile or so back, a little while before the alarm sounded," he replied.

Inexperienced I may have been, but I knew that this was not a good sign. Had they rejoined their comrades to launch an attack on the rear?

In fact, Calienus was right. One of the wagons had a mule go lame and was forced to drop from the column. A Century had been assigned to guard it while the rest of the wagons continued, a spare animal being drawn from the pool of spares and the lame beast slaughtered, meaning someone would get mule for supper. When that happened, the Lusitani obviously decided that this was the moment for which they were waiting. Apparently sending a rider to the group that had been on my side of the column, they raced back to join forces to support the attack launched by their comrades in the second group. It was a short but bitter fight, the aftermath of which we saw once the Century was escorted into the camp with the cavalry. Several men wore bandages on various parts of their body, but the most sobering sight was the wagon, its driver seat soaked in blood, with a number of spear shafts protruding from the wooden sides. However, it was the extra cargo that riveted our attention, and silenced all of us immediately. The men of the Century gently unloaded the bodies of two of their comrades, their corpses in that shapelessly limp form that only the dead possess once their spirits have fled their body and the spark is gone. The camp, for all the usual hustle, bustle, and noise of thousands of men talking and going about their business, stopped completely as every single eye turned towards the *Praetorium*, where the wagon had stopped. These were the first deaths in combat that these Legions had suffered; while the 7th, 8th, and 9th were veterans in the sense of the amount of time served, they had not seen any combat to that point. As we learned later, it was our comrades in the 8th Legion, 3rd Cohort that were hit, and it suddenly made what we were doing very real. Instinctively, I moved towards Vibius, to stand closer to him, sharing in silence the burden of lost innocence. This was no longer a game, and we glanced at each other, both of us giving a look that communicated that fact.

The one consolation for all of us was that the Century inflicted several casualties on the Lusitani, well in excess of what they suffered. Still, the camp was the quietest any of us ever heard it that night as we all sat at our fires, choosing this night to stay with our closest companions. Normally, the men would wander from one area to the other to spend time with other friends outside their Century, yet this night, as if by unspoken agreement, everyone chose to spend that time with their tent mates. Even Didius was silent that night, although I was not sure whether it was due to his own thoughts or because there were no takers for his inevitable attempts to fleece others. Whatever the cause, I was thankful for it, being in no mood to hear him prattling on.

Finally breaking the silence, Remus said, "Well, at least they took a few of the bastards with them."

"I was talking to a friend in the 8th," Calienus spoke up, "and they said that there were more than twenty bodies around the wagon. Now that," he finished quietly, "is how a Roman dies. Taking as many of the *cunni* with him as he can."

We all nodded our agreement at this, although to be truthful, we had no idea what we were talking about. The Pilus Prior came up to us and squatted by the fire. We all braced for some sort of cursing for paying too much attention to what was going on in the rear of the column, but none of were prepared for his true purpose.

"Evening, boys."

We all replied automatically, still worried about what was to come.

"How's everyone holding up?"

Whatever we were expecting, this was not it. Without waiting for an answer, he continued, "It's always a shock when you see men killed the first time, I don't care who you are. And that's the one thing that we can't train you for, that moment when you see your first dead comrade."

We all nodded, mystified at this new apparition we saw before us. After the night of our swearing in ceremony, he immediately reverted back to the Pilus Prior that we all knew, hated, and feared, so this human being was something very strange to our sight.

"But if you're being honest, while you're sad, you're also a little bit relieved that it's not you, or one of your friends. Am I right?"

Despite agreeing with this, this time, it was a bit more reluctantly.

"And that's normal. Don't think there's something wrong with you for feeling this way. It doesn't mean that you're not sorry to see good men die when you're happy that it's not someone you know. If they were alive now, and you were the dead ones, they'd be feeling the exact same way." He stood to leave, but before he did, he finished with, "That's why we train so hard, so we have as few of these moments as we can. If I do my job right, none of you will have to feel how the men in that Century are feeling tonight."

Bidding us good night, he left to go to the next tent and talk to them, leaving us even deeper in our thoughts than before.

The next two days were spent in that camp before marching again, it being the custom to take one day off after a few days of continuous marching, although Caesar regularly ignored this later on. Another thing that Caesar ignored was the customary distance and stopping time for the day, preferring to push on for at least two more parts of a watch, so that we often ended up working in the dark to finish the camp, yet this was one of the things that made Caesar as feared as he was, because of the rapidity of his movements. Coupled with his famous lack of hesitation, it meant that his army could appear somewhere long before they were expected, and was a key factor in keeping our enemy off balance. However, I think that the extra day was not just because of the rest, but also because we had suffered our first casualties, and were a largely unblooded

army. Caesar wanted the veterans to have time to talk to those of us who had yet to see battle and try to help us understand what it all meant, as well as prepare proper funeral rites for our first dead without having to rush. I, for one, was eager to get back on the march, because the sooner we reached the barbarians, the sooner we could engage and avenge the deaths of our comrades. Despite not knowing them, they were men who had suffered through the same things I had; the forced marches, the feeling of the *vitus* across our backs, the fatigue of trying to stay awake standing on a wall where you knew nobody was going to attack or make any other kind of mischief. They were brothers to all of us, even if the best I could say was that I had seen them around the camp during our training. Such was the feeling that we had for each other, and that feeling was fostered and encouraged by our officers. It is yet another reason why the Legions are so rightly feared; to hurt one of us is to hurt our brother, and we will have vengeance if that happens.

The mood as we set out on the march again was subdued, yet underlying that was a sense of anticipation. Despite remaining stationary those two days, our scouts had been extremely active, and came back with news that there was a town a day's march away. Judging from the tracks, it served as the source of the mounted men who attacked the Century and the wagon. The news of this find ran up and down the army like a bolt of lightning, with the idea of vengeance putting a sudden urgency into our step. No longer did our Centurions have to curse at us to keep the pace up; indeed, they found themselves in the unusual position of trying to slow us down so that we did not leave the baggage train and the rear Cohorts too far behind.

"Do you think we're going to attack the town tomorrow, or will we assault it as soon as we get there?" Romulus asked this of Calienus, who shook his head.

"There's no telling," the Sergeant replied. "It all depends on whether or not it looks like they're ready for us, I would guess."

This made sense to us, except that he was wrong, but only because we were marching with Caesar. Any other general would have done the prudent thing as Calienus suggested, a thorough reconnaissance before making any decisions, yet other generals were not Caesar. However, we were blissfully unaware of this as we marched towards the village.

I do not know the name of the town, but it was easy to see. It sat perched on a hill that commanded the surrounding plain so the barbarians could see us coming just like we could see them sitting there. At first, it was just a dark spot on the horizon, a speck sitting on a bump that ever so slowly got larger as we marched. All of our eyes were fixated on that spot, knowing that for most of us, we would be facing battle for the first time in our lives. This was not training; this was going to be the real thing, and none of us who had yet to be blooded could imagine what we were about to face. Perhaps Vibius and I, and some of the others with kin that served, had a better idea, yet even we knew that no matter how descriptive veterans were with us, it was going to pale in comparison with what we were about to experience. With the sun moving across the sky, while it did not seem to be any hotter than any other day up to that point, I found that my sweat poured more freely than during any previous day's march. Glancing over at Scribonius, I could see that his face glistened with moisture as well, so I at least knew that if it was not the heat, but nerves, I was not alone. The chattering that was normal as we marched was also less than other days, kept to a few muttered comments between men who marched next to each other; the customary banter and catcalls that men in one Century or Cohort would call out across the ranks almost completely missing, so that the sounds of the clinking and clanking of our gear along with the rhythmic thudding of our feet dominated the air. Slowly, ever so slowly, the village became more distinct and started to take shape.

It was just about two-thirds of a watch before sundown when we were halted a little more than a mile from the town, which we could plainly see now. It had a wooden wall around it, but did not appear to have any kind of ditch or other defensive measures, relying on its position on the hill and the slope that would have to be climbed first to get to the base of the wall before any assault of the town could begin. The wall itself appeared to be about ten feet tall, and while made of wood, the parapet was crenellated, with men clearly seen in the gaps watching us as we slowly spread out before them. The 8th was given the vanguard that day, in honor of the fallen men, so they were arrayed first, in the *triplex acies* formation. We were third in line, just ahead of the baggage train, making it almost sunset by the time we arrived to take a place to the left of the 8th and the 7th, occupying the far left of the line. The *cornicen* sounded the signal for the Legion officers to join the command group, with the Primus Pilus and Tribunes for each Legion moving to where

Caesar's standard was displayed, the red pennant that denotes the presence of the commanding general. Being in the First Century of the Second Cohort meant that we were in the front line, although I was in the last row of the Century, with the Fifth Century immediately behind us, and I could hear them talking behind me, the topic the same thing that occupied all of us. Were we going to attack, this late in the day? We were standing easy, with our gear grounded, the only order given to that point indicating we might be going into battle being the order to unsling our *scuta*, which we rested on the ground in front of us.

Staring at the walls, I examined the men watching us as they moved about, gesturing at us to their comrades, saying the gods only knew what. I remember wondering if what they were thinking was similar to what I was thinking, which was wondering what they were thinking. Still, no matter what was in their minds, they were certainly active, bustling about and starting fires behind the walls, their locations identified by the trails of smoke. That got me wondering what the fires were for, but none of the ideas that I could come up with gave me any comfort.

As if reading my mind, I heard Romulus say, "Maybe they're cooking us dinner."

This was met with a laugh by all of us; I think it was probably more hearty than the joke actually deserved, yet it served to relieve some of the tension as we waited to hear what we were about to do.

I do not know how much time passed, but finally, the Primus Pilus came back, then ordered our *cornicen* to sound the assembly for the Centurions of our Legion, who quickly moved to gather around him to get instructions. As I craned my neck, once again I was thankful for my height as I peered at the group of Centurions, watching them nod in acknowledgement of what the Primus Pilus was telling them. After just a moment, the group of men broke up, and all fifty-nine Centurions came striding back to their respective Centuries.

The Pilus Prior came to us and bellowed in his command voice, "Listen up, ladies, we're going to be making a marching camp, but it's going to be a little different than usual. We're going to create two camps, with two Legions in each camp. We're pairing up with the 9th, which is just coming up now."

He pointed to an area some distance away. When we looked over to where he was indicating, we saw a group of men that are part of the advance party. Their job is not only scouting for campsites, but also to provide any engineering and pioneer work to clear the way for the Legions should the terrain require it. To this point in our march, the terrain, despite being hilly in places, consisted of low scrub vegetation, with only occasional patches of woods that we could easily bypass. It was not until we were in Gaul that I saw the real value these men provided, when we would advance through forests that lasted for days, but here in Lusitania, it was not necessary for them to clear the way. Instead, they would usually have our camp boundaries already staked out and ready for us to start entrenching and building, except on this day, they were held back from their normal task until the army had arrived and Caesar decided what to do. Now, they were using their instruments to survey and mark out our camp.

Continuing, Pilus Prior Crastinus said, "The way it's going to work is that we're going to stay here in formation, while the 9th makes the camp. Same for the other two Legions; one works, the other watches. The one thing that we're going to change is that we're changing to single line to extend our coverage of the ground here."

What this required was the Legion to counter march, in this case to the left, and extend the spaces between each Century so that the second Century of each line could then move forward and to the oblique to fill in the space created. Consequently, instead of three lines of double Centuries, we would have three longer lines of single Centuries. Although it did not provide the depth, it would extend the coverage, making it harder for the barbarians to sally forth and move around our flank. As far as we were concerned, the news could not have been better; no digging, no carrying, no chopping for us!

It was hard for us to contain our grins, but the Pilus Prior saw some of our expressions and snapped, "Go ahead and laugh now, because sooner or later, Fortuna is going to piss all over us."

That killed the mood of joy immediately, because we knew he was right. Not for the first time, I cursed the Pilus Prior and his talent for taking the fun out of any occasion.

It was more than a full watch past dark before we were given the order to fall back and into the camp, and while nothing exciting happened, we still learned a valuable lesson that day. Even when one is standing still, when it is a requirement to stay vigilant and ready to go into action at a moment's notice, it can be just as tiring as making a camp. I, for one, was surprised to find how fatigued I was, but the others confirmed that they were in the same state, making me feel somewhat better. Additionally, we were ordered to have no fires either, confined instead to chewing our fat bacon and gnawing at whatever bread we managed to keep to the side. That night, the guard was doubled, so the prospect for sleep was not auspicious either. All in all, our first sighting of the enemy was proving to be more boring and troublesome than anything else. While we sat in a circle outside the tent, finishing what passed for our meal, the Pilus Prior came by, accompanied by Optio Vinicius. He had just been to the command group briefing, and was spreading the word about what we could expect the next morning, and he called all of the men in our Century to gather in the Century street, then motioned for us to sit down while he talked. As he squatted in front of us, we could just make out his bulk by the light of the half moon and the glow of the few torches that were allowed to be lit along the walls.

"We attack at first light," he announced, causing all of us to stop chewing our food to listen intently. "The engineers are going to be busy tonight making scaling ladders, and we're going to assault the town from two sides. The artillery will begin a barrage a third of a watch before first light and soften up the defenses. I doubt that what we have with us will be big enough to knock down any of that wall because it looks pretty strong, so it'll probably be the ladders that'll get us over the quickest. The 8th is going to use the ram," he was referring to the mobile ram that was broken down and carried as part of the baggage train, "to assault the main gate, which is the most heavily defended. The other two Legions will be support, which is why we're in the camp together."

Suddenly, I understood why two camps were made and, in the darkness, I could just make out Vibius' face and saw that he recognized it as well. Thinking about it more, I realized that the 7ᵗʰ and 8ᵗʰ's camp was directly in front of the main gate of the town, while our camp was arrayed opposite the side of the town where we would be assaulting. Maybe this Caesar did know what he was doing after all.

The Pilus Prior paused a moment to let all this sink in before finishing, "You'll receive more detailed orders in the morning, but I just wanted all of you to know now what was going to be happening. In the morning, we'll assign the sectors of the wall and who'll be the first over it. So get some sleep, because tomorrow is a big day."

With that, he stood and strode off, leaving us to talk excitedly to each other. When I looked over at Vibius, he gave me a tight smile, his teeth shining dully in the moonlight.

"I bet we're one of the first over the walls," he said, his voice quavering just enough so that only I, his closest friend who had known him for all these years, would recognize the fear in his voice. I felt my throat constrict, so instead of answering, I just nodded.

"That just means my first *Corona Muralis*." Didius' voice cut the air between us; neither of us had realized that he was within earshot or even listening.

Feeling the familiar tickle of my anger rising, instead of lashing out, I replied as coolly as I could, "Or you'll be the first man dead."

I could see the whites of his eyes as he glared at me angrily and snapped, "As you could be, Pullus. Don't forget that."

Then he turned heel to stalk away, but despite feeling a little sense of triumph for having rattled him, his words and the warning of Optio Vinicius collided in my mind, sending a shiver up my spine. Was I going to have to watch both my front and my back, as the Optio had warned me?

There was little sleep that night, I suspect, by any of us in the army, with the possible exception of the veterans. The Centurions certainly did not sleep; they were prowling around the camp, checking on the men in their Century, conferring with each other about the coming day. In our tent, only Calienus lay snoring softly, oblivious to our whispered conversations. Vibius tossed and turned for a while, and I could hear him mumbling to himself, while I lay just staring at the roof of the tent, trying to think of other things that had nothing to do with what was happening in just a couple of watches.

Finally giving up his attempt to sleep, Vibius rolled over to face me and whispered, "Do you have it in a safe place?"

Inwardly, I cursed; this was probably the fourth or fifth time he had asked me that question this night. Biting back a sharp retort, instead, I sighed, "Yes, Vibius. I have it in a safe place. It's wrapped in the greased leather bag in the bottom of my pack. The same place it's been the last four times you asked me about it."

I could not resist this last gibe, but fortunately for both of us, and for the rest of the tent section, he was too agitated to take offense.

"I know, I know. I'm sorry I keep asking. It's just that…"

"I understand," I whispered.

And I did; if the truth were known, I had found myself wanting to ask him the same question about my will. As my designated comrade, one of the primary responsibilities we had concerning the other was keeping each other's will in a safe place. Each of us was also responsible for carrying out the bequests made in the will, ensuring that we carried out the last wishes of our closest comrade and friend. We were ordered to draw up the wills in the days prior to starting our campaign, just another somber reminder that this was indeed serious business, and we did so with the guidance and help of our Sergeant, along with the Tesseraurius Cordius, who had experience in these matters. One of the duties of the Tesseraurius, besides keeping the watchword, is to act as the Century's banker, and also in the case where a man lost his comrade, hold the will of the lone man until he found another comrade to do so. Cordius was well liked and trusted by all of us, a critical trait for that position, almost as important as the ability to calculate sums. Both Vibius and I knew our letters, but neither of us had much practice at actually writing a document, a very common fact in the Legions. Some were even illiterate, so instead, they dictated the terms of their will to their Tesseraurius, who wrote it for them. Didius was one of those illiterates, a fact that brought on him much derision and jeers from the tent section, especially since each of us had been subject to his bullying or boasting. Consequently, this piece of information was filed away by all of us to bring up at opportune moments, much to Didius' rage and consternation.

"And you remember what to do?" Vibius pressed, and this time, I could not keep a groan from escaping.

"By the gods! Yes, Vibius, I remember!"

But he would not be satisfied just with that. "Tell me," he insisted. "What are you supposed to do?"

Sitting up, I glared at him, although it was pitch black.

Since he obviously was just not going to let this go, through gritted teeth, I replied, "I'm to take your ashes not to your family, but to Juno and give them to her. Then I'm to tell her that she's no longer bound to you, and has your blessings and prayers for her happiness."

"And what else?"

Sighing, my anger deflated; it was hard to stay that way when you were talking about your best friend's possible death, especially when it was that same friend who brought it up.

"I'm to tell her you died well, facing the enemy. Even if..." I did not finish, because I did not want to.

"Even if it's a lie," he finished quietly. "I want her to always remember me in a good light, Titus. Surely you can understand that."

I nodded, although he could not see me, and responded, "Yes, Vibius, I do understand that. It's just that neither of those is going to happen. I won't have to lie because you're not going to die, and even if you do, you're not going to die with your back to the enemy. It's just not in you."

211

"I hope you're right," was all he said to that and I dropped back down on my cot, willing the time to pass more quickly.

Somehow, I managed to doze off, because when the *bucina* sounded the signal for waking, I about jumped out of my skin. Sitting up, I heard the others rustling about, along with the cries and calls of the Centurions greeting their men that signaled the start of the day. Looking through the flap, I saw that it was still dark, which was not unusual. It was the shade of darkness that told me that we had been roused even earlier than normal. The one change from the night before was that now we were allowed to start fires and actually cook our breakfast. Immediately, the men designated to cooking duty that day began gathering the ingredients from their comrades that would make breakfast. It would be the standard porridge, with salt bacon thrown in, and as many spices and flavorings as could be scrounged up. Soon enough, the smells of simmering porridge sent the signal to my stomach via my nose and, despite my anxiety, I found I was famished. Since our officers evidently wanted us fortified with a good hot meal before battle, I felt obligated to eat, despite my misgivings. My comrades all seemed to feel the same way and, more quickly than normal, the porridge pot was emptied. Once we were finished, the Pilus Prior again summoned us in the darkness, although this time, Optio Vinicius carried a torch, the light from it dancing on the rugged features of Pilus Prior Crastinus, the shadows accentuating even more the hook of his nose. One difference I noted immediately in his demeanor was that it seemed as if the invisible man waving the turd was given the day off, and he looked at all of us with an expression that we had not yet seen on his face. Could it be pride, I wondered? Might this man actually be proud of his Century and the men we were becoming? While the Pilus Prior was in direct command of our Century, he was also the senior Centurion for the entire Cohort, so he called for the entire Cohort to be assembled to ensure that he only had to relay orders one time.

"As I told all of you last night," his voice rang out, "we've been selected by General Caesar to be the assault element on the walls of the town, while the 8th Legion will be conducting a simultaneous assault on their front gate. Our assault is going to work like this. First, Second, Third, and Fourth Cohorts will be first over the walls. The First and Second Maniples of our Cohort, commanded by me, will scale the walls, while the Third Maniple will provide covering fire at the base of the hill. Once we're over, the Third Maniple will follow suit. We'll be followed by the other Cohorts, in numerical order. An artillery barrage will precede the assault, and all the scorpions for both the 9th and 10th are being assigned for our use. They'll station themselves on a small rise a couple of hundred paces away, and they'll be providing close support, only lifting their fire when we begin climbing the ladders. That should make those bastards keep their heads down while we take care of business."

He paused for a moment to let all of this sink in. I cannot say I was surprised that we would be the first over the wall, but it was still a frightening prospect.

Continuing, he said, "There's also been a slight change from what I described to you last night. Instead of acting as our reserve, the 9th is going to march to the far side of the hill, in order to ensure that there's not a sortie by the enemy from the rear gate, or any escape when we take the town."

This last piece of news caused some heads to turn as we looked at each other, aware of the import of what he had just said. It did not appear that we were going to let anyone escape if we could help it. Sometimes, defenders are allowed to flee, in order to avoid facing an enemy that will fight that much harder, knowing that certain death or slavery awaited them. Giving them an open escape route meant that there was an alternative for them, and it would encourage them to give up the fight more easily. However, because these people were technically in rebellion, Rome declaring this region pacified some years ago, these people were not going to be given that option. In such ways are examples made that discourage those people foolish enough to think that they can escape Rome's dominion.

"So tonight, when we're victorious," his eyes narrowed and his voice took on a hard quality, even more than his norm, "and we will be victorious, we'll be spending the night under a roof, in a nice bed, and maybe there'll be a woman beside you. Willing or not," he finished with a wolfish smile. The Cohort burst out into a cheer, then we were dismissed to go don our *loricae* and gather ourselves for the coming trial.

Once we were prepared, we assembled in the forum, both the 9th and 10th Legions, where the Legates for both Legions were standing on the rostra. Legates are the nominal commanding officer of the Legion; while the sub-command is rotated by the six military Tribunes, the position of Legate is more permanent and is appointed by the Praetor, although in Caesar's army, Legates were moved about as well. Both of them gave short speeches, but I honestly do not have any idea what they said. In fact, I have been trying as I dictate this to remember the name of our Legate back then, but for the life of me, I cannot; he was that unremarkable, although I believe that was due more to Caesar's presence than any real shortcoming of his own. Once they were done inspiring us, we marched out of the camp to array ourselves, shortly before first light, where Caesar's design became clear. He wanted these Lusitani to wake up, rub their eyes, and look out to see the might of Rome arrayed before them, ready to strike and wreak a type of havoc they could not possibly imagine. The artillery had been rolled out of the camp earlier and was already in their position, with the ballistae arrayed so that they focused on the front gateway. The scorpions had just finished being pushed up a small hill to the southeast of the town, about two hundred paces away. They were accompanied by a Century to serve as a guard in the event the Lusitani made a sortie to try and destroy the artillery. Back then, each Legion only carried four scorpions apiece, but Caesar put great store in artillery, so when we began the campaign in Gaul, the number of both scorpions and ballistae were doubled. Each of the scorpions has a two-man crew drawn from their respective Legions, and while each of us had practice fired both the scorpion and ballistae in training, those who showed the greatest aptitude were designated as artillerymen, working almost exclusively with the weapons until such time that artillery was no longer called for, whereupon they took their place back in the ranks.

As the sun rose, another facet of Caesar's genius became clear to us. The town's gates were arranged along the customary north/south axis, with the front gate facing north and the rear to the south. In terms of terrain, other than the small hill previously mentioned, there was not much variation, which was what made the establishment of this town on this hill so sensible. Since there was no real advantage offered by terrain; the area immediately surrounding the town out to at least a quarter mile was cleared of vegetation that might hide an advance of a large body of men, Caesar used something else to our advantage. By choosing to assault the east wall, he not only took advantage of the only other high ground in the area, where he placed his scorpions, but arrayed as we were, we had an even more powerful ally in the sun rising behind our backs, forcing the Lusitani to stare straight at it in order to watch our advance. Another advantage, and one that I did not appreciate at the time, but learned to as I gained a better understanding of how men thought, was in the symbolic gesture made by this approach. Caesar chose to ride over to join our side of the assault, partly, I am sure, because he had already spoken to the other element while they were still in the camp, which explained their roaring earlier. The other reason became plain when we saw him sitting on his horse, motionless, his *paludamentum* in all its splendor resting on his shoulders, rippling gently in the soft breeze that was blowing, facing the fort bareheaded, but dressed in his ceremonial armor, a glittering cuirass made of silver and chased with gold with matching greaves. It was as if he was a god, which I now know was precisely the effect he was hoping for, so that as the Lusitani rose that morning and saw before them this glittering army, headed by a man whose very essence seemed to be framed by the sun, it had to be a devastating blow to their morale. Rome had come, led by a part man, part god, and all who stood before him quaked in fear.

Apparently, however, their morale was not damaged enough to see reason. Before launching the assault, Caesar sent a Tribune, under a white flag, to parley with the occupants of the town. We watched him approach warily, stopping about a hundred feet short of the gate, on the rutted road leading into it. Even though the Tribune tried his best to sit stock still, his horse was obviously very nervous, hopping and skipping about and acting very skittish. As I learned later, he had been sent by Caesar with one last offer to submit to Rome, showing their good faith by the payment of a tribute and giving of hostages, the customary measures with such matters. The Tribune sat on his horse, obviously listening as a man stood on the wall above the gate, actually climbing onto the crenellation so he was standing in plain view, pointing down at the Tribune and then gesticulating back towards the town. This man was obviously of some importance, wearing what appeared to be armor made of some sort of golden scales, and a high, conical helmet. He looked to be a fairly large man, although that might have been because he was standing on the wall.

"Come on; let's get on with it," muttered Scribonius, and I wholeheartedly agreed.

Despite being scared out of my wits, the waiting was even harder, and I could only imagine the tension the next time if this parley was successful and the Lusitani in the town gave up without a fight. We would march on, something like this would happen again, and we would again find ourselves arrayed and ready to do battle. As far as I was concerned, it was just time to get it over with.

Luckily for us, unluckily for the Tribune, the parley was unsuccessful. Our first inkling that our terms were rejected came when suddenly, without any warning whatsoever, we saw what looked like a sliver come slicing down to strike the Tribune in the chest, almost knocking him from his horse as he reeled with the impact. Obviously, it was not a sliver but a spear, and from the combination of the height and the obvious strength of whoever threw it, the spear transfixed the Tribune and we could clearly see the bladed end protruding from his back. Almost before this could register, a number of other such darts struck him down from his horse, leaving it to gallop away in a panic, a short spear lodged in its flank, streaming blood. Despite our discipline, seeing the death of the Tribune brought a collective gasp from all of us, and I am sure across all the ranks of men who saw what had happened. Shock was immediately followed, at least in my case, with a terrible anger. The flag of truce was clearly on display; there could be no mistake in what they had seen, but they still murdered one of our Tribunes in cold blood. Even as we were absorbing that act, the gate was flung open. Two men came dashing out and, before we could do anything more than shout a protest, they dragged the bloody body of the Tribune, now looking like a pincushion with multiple shafts sticking from his body, back into the town, shutting the gates. Then, a moment later, the man on the wall reappeared, except this time, in his hand he was waving as a trophy the head of the Tribune, dripping blood and gore from the severed neck. His call of defiance was drowned out by the roar of more than 20,000 men, all of them screaming with rage. It was absolutely deafening; I felt more than heard myself screaming out in inarticulate fury and I could feel the ground vibrate under my feet from the sound. I had reached yet another new level of anger in my life to that point, and it was clear that I was not alone.

Caesar remained motionless, his only visible sign of distress in the clenched fist that he struck against his thigh over and over. It was when he turned to face us, riding in our direction, that we could see his lips thinned in rage, but once he got close enough, it was his eyes that arrested all of us. They were like glittering points of ice, and it was with a start I realized that this was the first time I had been close enough to see the color of his eyes, a bluish-grey that looked like an angry sea. He drew his *gladius*, then slowly waved it over his head to get our attention. We slowly stopped our invective to listen to his words. In the brief silence before he began speaking, we could hear the Lusitani, chanting on their own, working up their own courage since they could have held no illusion what was facing them now. They had cast their die, and were trusting their skill to avert the righteous vengeance that they deserved. I, for one, vowed to myself that they would need more than skill this day.

"Soldiers," Caesar's voice rang out clearly, and even using his oratorical voice, his outrage was plain to hear, and we could tell that it was unfeigned, "you have just witnessed one of the most abominable acts any supposedly civilized nation can perform, the slaughter of a defenseless emissary under a flag of truce." Suddenly dropping his *gladius* and pointing directly at the 10th Legion, he roared, "What do you propose to do about it?"

Our answering cry once again shook the ground, except this time, we replied not just with voice, but by pounding our *pila* against our *scuta* in a rhythmic manner that lasted for a couple of moments before he motioned us back to silence.

"Very well," he called. "I have your answer. Now," he pointed to the wall, "show me your answer in deeds. I will give," with his left hand, he pulled a leather purse that looked as if it were bursting with coin, "one hundred sesterces to the first man over the wall, along with the reward of a *corona murales*."

One hundred sesterces! That was a fortune! How could one man possibly spend that much money? I wondered. I laugh now at my naiveté; I have wasted a hundred sesterces in a single night's debauchery since, but for the country boy from Baetica I was back then, I could not comprehend such riches. Finished with us, he raced off to the 8th to make the same offer, while his command staff distributed themselves among the Legions to take nominal command. My heart sank when I saw none other than Doughboy approaching, and my sentiments were echoed by the muttered curses of the men around me.

"Gods, why us?" I heard Calienus groan.

Trying to remain optimistic, I ventured, "Maybe he'll be smart enough to let the Primus Pilus give the orders."

"*Gerrae*! You know better than that, Pullus."

I shrugged. He was right, but one could always hope. Doughboy marched up to where the Primus Pilus, Pilus Prior Crastinus, and some of the other Centurions were gathered. Even from a distance, we could see the barely disguised contempt on the face of the Centurions, something Doughboy either ignored or was too stupid to see.

"Well, men," he called out in a loud voice, thinking, I guessed, to inspire us with his words of wisdom. "Are we ready to go over the wall and spill some Lusitani guts and get our hands wet, eh?"

"Of course, sir," answered the Primus Pilus smoothly, without a hint of mockery in his voice. "As long as we know that you'll be the one leading us over the wall."

Doughboy's face blanched before he realized he was letting his feelings show.

"Pardon me, Centurion?" he started, but got no further.

"That's Primus Pilus, if you please, sir," the Primus Pilus responded, his voice a mask of formal politeness. "It's just that I worked hard to get here, sir, and well, it's my proper title."

Doughboy's eyes narrowed in suspicion as he glared at the Primus Pilus, trying to decide if he was being toyed with, but the Primus Pilus had been cowing young Tribunes since before Doughboy had been expelled from his mother's womb, and was the picture of rectitude and respect. Obviously deciding to drop the matter, Doughboy started again.

"Forgive me, Primus Pilus. You're correct, of course. Anyway," he cleared his throat, "back to what you were saying earlier."

"Yes, sir," the Primus Pilus replied cheerfully. "As I was saying, we'll follow you anywhere you choose to lead us. Isn't that right, sir?"

Now Doughboy looked nonplussed; how could he answer this in a way that let it be known he had no intention of being the first to anything other than the food line, and not expose his cowardice? Therefore, he apparently decided that silence, accompanied by a thoughtful nod of the head and stroking of his chin, as if seriously considering the remarks, was the best course.

The silence dragged on for a few heartbeats, before the Primus Pilus continued helpfully, "It's just that you're a young man on the rise, sir. Nothing makes a young patrician's career like being the first over the wall. Besides," for this, he turned to his companions, "that sort of thing is a young man's game, isn't it, boys?"

This was greeted by a chorus of agreement, each of the Centurions looking at Doughboy with wide-eyed innocence.

Clearing his throat yet again, Doughboy looked at the ground as he murmured, "It's just that if I'm first over the wall, I won't be able to assess the overall situation, you see? I thought it would be better for me to remain in a place," he looked up at the Primus Pilus earnestly, "close to the wall, of course, not completely out of danger, but far enough back so I can have an idea of what's going on."

The Primus Pilus pursed his lips, slowly nodding his head in thought.

"I do see your point, sir. Indeed, I'm not sure of these things, so you're no doubt correct. I'm sure that you've read many more manuals than I have on the subject." Despite what I guessed was his best effort, the Primus Pilus could not entirely conceal the scorn with this last remark and just barely remembered to finish with "sir."

Doughboy's ears turned a roasting red, yet there was really nothing he could do because there was nothing objectionable in the Primus Pilus' words, despite knowing that it was an insult.

Cutting his losses, he muttered, "Right. Well, then, carry on."

Whereupon he stalked off down the line to station himself in the proper place to avoid the appearance of cowardice, while not exposing himself to much danger. The other Centurions, during this last exchange, were all feverishly studying the ground, but we could see their shoulders shaking with silent laughter, threatening our own composure. When the Primus Pilus turned and saw that we had witnessed and heard the whole thing, his only response was to grin and give us all a wink, destroying all remnants of our façade and we laughed heartily.

Our barrage started immediately after that exchange, the sound of the ballista snapping against the cross bar causing a crash, followed by a whirring sound as if a flight of birds was taking off, and we all looked up to watch the stone arc through the air. The first shot landed short, the stone thudding into the ground with a spray of dirt before its momentum took it skipping to where it smacked into the base of the wall just next to the main gate on the north side, which we could see from our spot on the far right of the line. This was immediately followed by a stone that actually hit the wall, and even from where we stood, we could see the dust fly as the timbers vibrated. One after the other, the stones hit the area around the front gate, and in the pause as the ballistae were reloaded, we could hear the cries of the Lusitani raising the alarm that the assault had begun. It was just about a third of a watch past dawn, and now we would wait while the artillery either did its work, or did nothing more than raise some dust. While we were told to remain in formation, we were allowed to stand at *otiose*, meaning that we could turn, talk to the men around us, and bend our legs and so forth, but not leave our position in ranks. The customary way it is observed is that as long as your left foot stays in position, you can pivot around to talk to the others. I turned to face down my rank and Vibius immediately caught my eye.

With a completely straight face, he asked, "Do you have it in a safe place?"

Reaching down, I grabbed a clod of dirt and threw it at him, then we both laughed. Grabbing my crotch to make an obscene gesture, I answered, "Oh yes, it's in a safe place, all right. It's right here. I used it to wipe my ass this morning."

"You mean you're smart enough to wipe your own ass now?" he shot back. "I guess it's true that the Legions can teach ANYONE if they can finally teach you."

I promised that I would make him regret his words, to which he answered with an obscene gesture of his own.

"All right, you bunch of women. Shut your mouths." This came from Optio Vinicius, who was standing next to me, and I turned in time to watch him yawn, then scratch himself, as if we were standing around camp. "I've heard you two going back and forth about that damn will for too long now. Can't you talk about something else?"

Indignantly, I pointed to Vibius and protested, "Don't yell at me, yell at him. He's the one who keeps asking."

"Yes, and you keep answering him, so who's the bigger fool? The fool who asks or the fool who answers?"

I really was not sure what to say, because with Vinicius, it was always very hard to tell whether he was being serious or not, especially since he looked like the messenger of death all the time. As I was starting to form an answer, I saw just the corner of his mouth twitch in a gesture that I had learned was his version of a smile. Rolling my eyes, I looked back to the front and kept my mouth shut.

The front gate was completely obscured by dust, and while we saw splotches of a lighter color that indicated the wood of the walls was scored, we had no idea if it meant a substantial weakening or just a spot where the bark was knocked off. Meanwhile, we saw the trails of smoke again, at various spots along the walls, and now I could not resist the temptation.

Looking over to Vinicius, I asked, "What's the meaning of the smoke, Optio?"

He looked at me with his deadpan eyes and seemed to consider something before he shrugged, then answered, "I imagine they're heating up some pitch to pour down on us, or maybe some sort of oil."

He saw me shudder at that and asked quietly, "Would you rather have me lie to you?"

I shook my head. "No, Optio. But still..." I did not finish, and he merely nodded.

"I know, boy."

The order of *intente* was sounded, and we immediately snapped to, with our *scuta* up and a *pilum* in our other hand, the second *pilum* held along with the *scutum* in our left hand, which is awkward, to say the least.

Our Primus Pilus strode out to where he could be seen, and called out, "Before we start out, I want everyone in the assault elements to pass their *pila* down to their supporting Maniple. You won't be able to throw them from a range where they'll do any good, and they're going to be useless once you get on the ladders. Give 'em to the boys who'll be supporting you, and they can deliver 'em to those bastards for you."

As weak a joke as it was, we still smiled. Passing mine off, while it felt strange to have my right hand empty, I was grateful to be able to hold my *scutum* cleanly. I could feel my heart thudding heavily and, when I looked down, I was surprised to see my *lorica* jumping slightly with every beat of my heart. As we were passing the *pila*, a wagon rumbled up and, in the back, there were a few dozen ladders the engineers had lashed together. Each Century in the assault elements was given two ladders with the order to place them at least three *scutum's* width apart to deny the defenders massed targets.

The Pilus Prior stood in front of us and called out, "Right, I want my veterans up front to pick up the ladders." As those men like Calienus did so, he continued, "They're going to be the ones carrying the ladders and will be between files so that the rest of you boys can hold your *scuta* up to cover them since they'll have their hands full."

Then the Pilus Prior designated between which files he wanted the men, and those files moved out a little to widen the gaps while still having enough spacing so that they could provide protection. This forced all of us over a couple of steps and we quickly adjusted.

"Now, listen and listen carefully," Crastinus continued, oblivious to the fire of the scorpions that were just starting in preparation for our move to the walls. They make a deep twanging sound when the bolts are launched, and it was hard not to watch as they worked, but I managed to stay focused on the Pilus Prior. "I'm going first up the ladder. Normally, I wouldn't, but since this is you boys' first engagement, you just follow me and everything will be fine. The Optio," he motioned to Vinicius, "will be the first up the other ladder. We'll need one man, one very strong man to brace each ladder against the wall while the others ascend."

Immediately, the men in my vicinity turned to me, and I could feel my face burn. The Pilus Prior looked over at me thoughtfully before shaking his head.

"Not Pullus. I want him up early after me. He's been the best in training, and besides," he grinned, "the very size of him is going to scare half of those bastards to death before he lifts a finger."

I was in an agony; part of me glowed at the distinction I was being given while the other was petrified because it was clearly expected that I would perform valiantly. That feeling of pressure that was almost non-existent once we started the march came flooding back, and I struggled to maintain my composure. For a fleeting instant, the thought of screaming out the fact that I was still underage crossed my mind, sure that if I did so, I would not have to go up the ladder. Just as quickly, the shame of that idea washed over me, and I recognized that, if I were to do such a thing, while it might get me out of being killed in battle, it might not necessarily save my life. Enlisting under fraudulent circumstances is a serious crime; we had been forced to witness the execution of two men, from different Legions, whose identity as slaves were uncovered. First, they were scourged, then executed, and the sense of shame that such a death brought was more overpowering than my fear. Consequently, I just stood there as if mute, hoping my face did not betray the stark terror that I was feeling. Instead of me, Crastinus picked Didius to hold our ladder, who responded with a "Yes, Pilus Prior" that was as close to insolent as one could get and still escape the *vitus*. That was not lost on Crastinus, who glared at Didius before choosing the man for the second ladder, another recruit named Macro. He was shorter than I was, but built very thickly with rippling muscles. As I was turning back to face my immediate fate, Scribonius tapped me on the shoulder.

With a tight smile, he murmured, "Good luck, you lucky bastard. Try not to kill all of them before the rest of us get there."

The smile I returned felt more like a grimace. At that moment, the *cornicen* from the command group sounded his call, followed by the *bucina* from each Cohort, with the standards dipping in acknowledgement of our order to begin the advance. Stepping off, for a moment I was struck by a sense of panic because I was still in my accustomed place at the back of the Century; how was I supposed to follow Crastinus up the ladder from the back? Glancing over to my right, I saw the Optio was next to me, also in his accustomed place, confusing me further. Despite the fact that talking was forbidden when we were advancing, I felt there was enough urgency to risk breaking the rules.

"Optio," I hissed.

My call seemed to snap the Optio out of some sort of trance, because his head jerked around in surprise. Or maybe he was taken aback that I dare talk at a time like this.

He did not rebuke me, however, just asking, "What is it, Pullus?"

"How am I supposed to get from back here," I motioned to our location while trying to maintain my alignment with the rest of the rank and the cover of my file, "to up there?" I indicated the spot with a jerk of my head.

"You follow the file of men with the ladder, idiot," was his response. "The Pilus Prior'll be there at the base of the ladder while the ladder is being lifted. Then you follow him."

"Oh."

Chagrined that the answer was that simple, when I looked over, I was suddenly not so sure it was indeed that easy because they were three files over, putting men between me and them. I was in too much of a state for me to think it through, so I shrugged my shoulders and turned my attention back to the front. The town was looming larger, but the snapping of the bolts being fired over our heads was an oddly comforting sound. I could clearly see men on the ramparts of the wall now, only in glimpses, though, as they were forced to keep their heads down because of the scorpions. Every so often, one of them would risk a quick peek around one of the crenellations to see when we would be in range. Even as I watched, apparently either one of them was a little too regular in deciding when to peek his head out and one of our gunners noticed, or he was just the unluckiest man in the world, because the timing of when he poked his head out and the bolt arriving in the spot his head now occupied, however briefly, could not have been better. In front of my very eyes, I saw the blur of the bolt, then saw the man's head explode, the top half of his skull shooting off to the right while the continuing blur of the bolt, now with what looked like a fine red mist trailing it, went hurtling further into the town. My eyes were riveted to the sight, and I heard the exclamations of the men around me who saw it happen as well, all of us watching as the torso, with the lower half of the man's head still attached, totter there for a moment before collapsing back behind the wall.

"Remind me not to ever get in front of one of those things," Scribonius muttered, and all I could do was nod.

Our front ranks hit an unseen line, marking the spot where we now came in range of their slingers. While not of the same renown as the slingers from the Balearic Islands, they were highly skilled nonetheless, and in the space of just a few moments, we would learn to respect and fear these weapons almost more than any other that the Lusitani wielded. Dozens of men appeared, whirling their slings above their heads, preparing to launch them despite weathering the bolts from a partial volley of scorpions that knocked a couple of the men off the wall.

"TESTUDO!"

That command was roared simultaneously all along the leading line and it was in this first moment that it became apparent to every new *Gregarii* that all of the training and the beatings that came with it possessed a value that could not be overestimated. Even before I consciously thought about it, I crouched down and lifted my *scutum* above my head, since the threat was coming from ahead and above us. If we were exposed to enfilading fire from the side, I would have held my *scutum* across my body, while sheltering under Scribonius' *scutum*. A bare instant later, there was a sound like a sudden hailstorm as the stone shot that the Lusitani used bounced off the surface of our *scuta*, mostly inflicting no damage. Scattered among the rattling sounds indicating no damage done, however, there was another, a sickening thud either followed by a grunt, or worse, by a scream of pain that made the hairs on the back of my neck stand up. Although we kept advancing, we could not move as quickly as we normally would in standard formation, so there was a tradeoff of sorts. Despite being more protected, the amount of time we were exposed to the slings was longer. The first volley did not inflict any casualties on our Century, but after the second rattling of shot, and more shouts and screams, there was a ripple in the formation as someone fell to the ground and we automatically compensated, closing up the spot where the man fell. While I could see a prone figure out of the corner of my eye, I could not see who it was, and I realized with a shock that we were now blooded. We had suffered our first casualty, but judging from the ferocity of the volleys that we were absorbing, it was not likely to be our last.

"Jupiter Optimus Maximus, protect this Legion, soldiers all," someone cried out the Legionary's prayer and, while appreciating the sentiment, I wondered whether Jupiter really cared.

Our advance hampered by the use of the *testudo*, the distance closed agonizingly slowly and, for the first time, I began noticing that my arm was getting a little tired from holding my *scutum* above my head. Glancing over at Scribonius, I saw that the sweat was pouring from him as if he were standing in a rainstorm, his face red from the exertion. Meanwhile, the smacking and thuds of the shot continued, and more times we had to adjust the formation. Then, a man two ranks ahead of me, his arm obviously tiring from holding the *scutum*, let it slip just a bit, enough so that I noticed the crack of daylight that allowed a beam of pure light to shine through as if shot down from the heavens. A sharp-eyed slinger saw that crack too because just a heartbeat later, there was a thwanging sound, slightly different than those I had quickly become accustomed to, and the Legionary dropped to the ground without a sound, not moving. The man in front of me, Papiria was his name, almost stumbled over the body, which would have left several men exposed, but with a curse, he managed to maintain his balance and I resolved not to make the same mistake, forcing myself to look down as I came on the body. I wish I had not; he was lying face up, with one eye hanging partially from its socket, a gaping hole showing between the orb and where the bridge of his nose had been, while his heart still pumped blood in a spray, the bone of his nose apparently carried by the shot into his brain. I felt the bile rise as the ghastly sight was burned into my memory forever and, even today, I can close my eyes and still see him, alive but not, his heart not yet receiving the message that it was no longer needed. Dragging my eyes away now that I had stepped clear of him, one detail tugged at my mind. The rim of his helmet had a huge dent in it, and for some reason, that image occupied my thoughts. Even as we were still moving forward, in formation, I thought about it and finally understood the thwanging sound I heard must have been the shot hitting the rim of the helmet, which in turn deflected it down, into his eye, and through his brain. The helmet was not penetrated and, when thinking about it later, I realized that if we were facing an enemy on the same level, and not occupying higher ground, the chances were very good that he would have been struck a glancing blow, except the projectile would angle up instead of down, and all he would have suffered from it was a headache and ringing ears. Such are the whims of the Fates.

Making it to the base of the hill, we started up, with one thing becoming clear immediately. The distance from the bottom of the hill to the base of the wall was deceptive; the Third Maniple would be forced to move higher up the hill to launch their *pila* than originally planned. Our Century had shrunk even more, and when I anxiously glanced over to my left, my heart sank as I saw that my rank was at least four people narrower than before. Meanwhile, the slingers continued their assault on us, the racket of missiles hitting the *scuta* or occasionally striking something else and scoring a hit almost continuous. I tried to determine how many of the men in my tent section were missing from the back rank simply because they moved up to replace a gap, and how many had gone down themselves. From what I could remember, at least two men in files ahead to my left had fallen, and I thought there might be a third as well, yet that still left one of my tent mates unaccounted for, and my greatest fear was that it was Vibius. What if he were right after all? Trying to shut that out of my mind, I turned my attention back to the task at hand, and, in a panic, I saw that I had dropped my *scutum* a fraction while thinking about something else. Quickly, I readjusted, just in time to feel my arm shudder, hearing the unmistakable strike of a shot as I cursed myself for my inattention and vowed that I would not falter again. We were beyond the base of the hill now, reaching a point where the angle between our *testudo* and the slingers was such that the only way for a slinger to launch a missile at us was by leaning out over the edge of the wall. A couple of them tried and almost immediately were scoured from the wall by the scorpions. That was when they turned their attention to the Third Maniple, and it was like the hailstorm suddenly stopped now that it was their turn to come under fire. From our spot, the predominant sound was now the whirring sound of the slings circling around the men's heads, followed by the whistle of the projectiles slicing into men behind us. Reaching the base of the wall, the Legionaries carrying the ladders immediately moved into action as we moved our *scuta* to the side to allow them room.

Half the men got on each side, grasping the ladder, while the Pilus Prior commanded, "Didius, get your sorry ass up here."

Didius was one of the men who had moved up, putting him a little closer to the front of the formation, but he still had to push his way past the other men of the Century, drawing curses as he jostled them and forced their *scuta* over, exposing them for an instant. Fortunately, nobody was struck down and it became apparent that we were relatively safe from fire, so Crastinus ordered us out of the *testudo* and I dropped my arm, thankful for the brief respite. The ladder team planted the feet of the ladder on the ground, while Didius was moved into position by the Pilus Prior, who grabbed him by his harness and faced him in the opposite direction from the rest of us, with the ladder between him and the Century. Then, pushing him down, he forced Didius to sit, while simultaneously the ladder team walked forward with the ladder and it started to rise. The Pilus Prior then made his way to the base of the ladder once it was raised to a sufficient height.

"Pullus, you big oaf. Get behind the Pilus Prior!"

This came from Vinicius as he made his way past me over to the other ladder team, which was doing the same thing as ours. Startled out of my observation of what was going on, I moved quickly behind the Pilus Prior, just in time for him to look behind him to see if I was there, as I gave a brief thanks to the gods that he apparently had not missed me before this, shuffling in behind him as the ladder was raised.

"Good luck," I heard a man mutter, but I found my throat was too dry to respond, so instead I just nodded. My heart was pounding harder than if I had sprinted the whole way to the wall, and I was sure that if things continued, it would explode right then and there. A different kind of sound added to the cacophony of noise, and I sensed the rapid movement of objects heading towards the walls, looking up to see the *pila* thrown by the Third Maniple slice through the air and into the wall, some striking the Lusitani. Immediately after this were screams of pain, followed by dull thuds of men falling down to the ground off the rampart. Very quickly, another volley landed, with much the same effect. The Lusitani were now huddled behind their walls, unwilling to expose themselves to any more of the *pila*, telling us this was our moment. Didius reached out to grab the sides of the ladder, pulling it taut against the wall so that it would not slip. While watching him do this, the Pilus Prior was already halfway up the ladder before I realized it.

"Get up there, you stupid bastard. We're right behind you," I could not see who it was, although it sounded like Calienus' voice.

Gulping down the huge lump in my throat, I began climbing, taking two rungs at a time in an attempt to catch up while trying to hold my *scutum* above my head. There was still no sign that the Lusitani felt safe enough to peek their heads up to see what was happening, and again I offered a prayer that our luck would hold a few more moments.

It was at this moment that there sounded a horrible scream, something so inhuman that it caused all of us, Roman and Lusitani alike, to freeze. For just a moment, all activity stopped, and I looked in the direction of the noise, which was just dying out, seeing that it came from a man on the other ladder. I say it was a man, but it would be more accurate to say that what I was viewing was merely a large lump of scorched meat. What had been his face was blackened, along with every inch of his exposed skin, which was issuing a thick smoke, like when the fat in meat catches fire, and I suppose that was exactly what was happening. The part of his tunic not covered by his *lorica* was burning brightly, the flames licking up around his head, and covering him from head to feet appeared to be a substance that to my inexperienced eye looked like boiling honey. Immediately, I realized that it was the pitch that they were heating in preparation for just such a moment. However, as much as the scream, it was what the man was doing that I think arrested everyone's attention, for he was still ascending the ladder, very slowly but definitely noticeably, and despite my horror at the sight, I also felt a fierce sense of exultation. This was how a Roman died! I thought. Even dead on his feet, he still advanced, and I imagined that this sight must strike fear and despair into the heart of the Lusitani. We could not be stopped, and as if in answer to that thought, I felt the ladder begin shaking again as the Pilus Prior continued his climb, even Crastinus stopping like everyone else. As Crastinus did so, the other man slowly toppled off the ladder, still in flames and smoking, and I saw the men below scatter out of the way in order to avoid being hit and burned by his body, which in a sense had become a weapon of the enemy's on its own, since anyone touched by it would be horribly burned as well. I started climbing again too, when I was struck by the sudden thought that the man on the ladder had nobody above him. That meant that he was first, so it must have been Vinicius who I just saw incinerated. Just moments ago, I was talking to him about the very thing that killed him, and I wondered when we would next talk again in the afterlife. Maybe sooner than I think, I thought grimly as I peered up to see the Pilus Prior almost at the top. Just then, a Lusitani appeared in a gap in the wall just next to the Pilus Prior; letting out a cry in his language, he used a long spear to try and skewer the Pilus Prior. However, his war cry alerted Crastinus, who dodged out of the way, almost losing his grip on the ladder, which he now clung to with only his right hand. Without waiting for another blow and displaying a speed that astonished me, he jumped up and over the wall, disappearing from sight, then I heard the thud of his borrowed *scutum* as he smashed the boss against the Lusitani, followed by a wild yelp of pain. Even as Crastinus did this, I scrambled the last couple of rungs, then pulled myself up onto the wall where, for the first time, I could see into the town. The parapet of the wall was also made of wood, about ten feet across and crowded with men. All of them were armed, although there was a wide variety of weapons, some of the men brandishing nothing more than hoes and sticks with sharpened points. Nevertheless, there was also a fair amount of men in armor, and these were the men crowded around the area where we were assaulting the walls, the more poorly armed men obviously in reserve.

All of this I took in over a matter of no more than a couple of normal heartbeats as I jumped down onto the parapet before turning to my right, barely in time to meet a wild swing of a Celtic *gladius* with my *scutum*. Feeling the shock of the blow move all the way down my arm, making it go numb instantly, it was only because of my size that I did not stagger backward. For the first time, my opponent seemed to notice my bulk, his eyes going a bit wider. Dumbly, I stood there, allowing him to recover before I did and strike once again, this time in an overhead swing, I guess to try to split me down the middle. Once more, as if of its own volition, my arm went up to block the blow, my body again vibrating from the shock.

"Pullus, you stupid bastard, draw your *gladius* and kill that *cunnus*. Quit messing about." I instantly recognized the voice of the Pilus Prior, and only then did I realize with a great amount of chagrin that he was right; I had yet to draw my *gladius*.

I was ashamed of myself; here I was supposed to be the star pupil and I could not even remember to draw my weapon! Grasping the handle while holding it in the manner Vinicius had taught me, I unsheathed the *gladius* and immediately dropped into the first position, my *gladius* pulled back and blade parallel to the ground. Instantly, I felt a surge of confidence as my body reacted to the familiar, and my opponent must have sensed the change because he assumed a wary expression as I advanced toward him, grimly determined to retrieve my dignity, also remembering that I needed to make room for the men coming up behind me. So far, no more than a dozen normal heartbeats had elapsed, and I heard other men landing behind me as I moved towards him. Suddenly, I lashed out with the *scutum*, catching him by surprise because he was obviously expecting me to make a move with what he considered my offensive weapon, not realizing that to Romans, the *scutum* is as much of one as the *gladius*. He staggered back, but in his attempt to regain his balance, used his own *scutum*, much smaller and round compared to our larger oval, moving it backward in an automatic movement to try and recover by counter-balance. Both of us knew in that instant that he just made a fatal mistake, because I saw the despair in his eyes as I lunged, thrusting the blade while twisting forward with my hips in a perfect training ground thrust. My blade pierced him in the left side, in the ribcage, and he let out a short, sharp shriek before collapsing as I made a perfect recovery. Rather, I tried to, yet I had not been quite as training manual perfect as I thought. One of the first things we are taught is to strike with the plane of the blade parallel to the ground, so that if we do strike in the rib area, it is more likely to slide between the ribs and not get caught in the bone. I obviously did the opposite, holding the *gladius* with the plane perpendicular to the ground so that when I went to recover, the blade stuck in his body, causing me to almost lose my grip. At the same instant, another man, this one carrying a long spear and, with the same type of *scutum*, came charging at me, again forcing me to parry the blow with my own, but unable to counter because I could not get the damn blade out of the other man's body. This Lusitani lunged at me again, and again, but despite being able to block, I was having a hard time maintaining my focus on him while trying to twist the *gladius* free. After his third strike, my blade finally came out just in time to use it to parry his lunge by knocking his spear down while stepping forward and using the boss of the *scutum* to smash him hard in the face. I heard the bone crunch, and he made a choking cry as his mouth and nose filled with blood. I hit him once, twice, then three more times, until his face was pulverized and he fell to the ground twitching. Within the first moments on the wall, I made my first two kills, and I could feel the confidence surging through me as my training took over.

By this time, I was joined by another man, who stood by my side shoulder to shoulder, there being only room for two of us to stand this way on the parapet at this moment with a bit of room to maneuver. There were still a sizable number of Lusitani in our vicinity of the parapet, but they had seen the fate of their two companions and now were not quite as bold. The two of us moved slowly forward, our *scuta* locked together, then I felt someone grasp my harness behind me to brace me in the way we were trained.

"Let's go get these bastards," I heard Calienus say and, realizing that he was the one behind me made me feel even more confident. For the first time since I was on the wall, I became aware of the sounds of battle going on around me; the clashing of metal on metal, the roars of men trying to slaughter each other, the cries of the wounded, and shrieks of the dying. I was too inexperienced to know how the fight was going by the sound; that would only come after several engagements, so I had no idea how the assault was progressing. Moving forward, we stepped over the bodies of the two men I had slain, taking care not to trip as we tried to close the distance between us and the remaining Lusitani. At first, they were content to keep backing up, making half-hearted jabs with their weapons, then one of them looked behind himself and saw what we had seen already; they were running out of room. Immediately behind them was a series of large log columns protruding above the parapet, effectively blocking it off from the parapet on the other side. There was a ladder next to the columns, but they knew as we did that the moment they tried to climb down, we would be on them, and while the wall was only ten feet high on the outside, the actual level of the town was lower by a few feet where they had dug down to create streets and such. This was not a height that would kill them if they jumped, but it would definitely stun or knock the wind out of them, which was just as dangerous. However, this was actually a bad spot for us as well, because now that they knew there was no escape, their only choice was to attack or die. Not that it mattered much in the larger picture; the murder of the Tribune sealed the fate of the defenders of this town, along with the citizens, but first we had to finish what we started. One of the men, a decent-sized warrior a bit older than us, was the first to attack and, in doing so, showed us a characteristic of the Lusitani that I have since seen in other Gallic tribes, with whom the Lusitani are distant cousins. Unleashing a war cry, he lunged forward, a whirlwind of ferocious movement as he slashed at us with his long *gladius*. Both the man next to me and I raised our *scuta* as we were buffeted by blow after blow, each of them sending shocks traveling down our arms that were clearly transferred backwards as we recoiled. Keeping our guard up while watching through the crack between the *scuta*, we waited for an opening, and it soon presented itself. For a moment, the Lusitani dropped his guard as he panted for breath, both his *gladius* and his *scutum* moving just a bit. Like a snake striking, my comrade, who I recognized as a veteran from my Century that was salted into our ranks, thrust his blade through the gap between us, plunging it into the gut of the Lusitani, who let out a gasp of air as if he was punched. Before my mind even registered it happening, the blade was back behind the *scutum* and I looked down to see that fully half of its length was covered in blood. The Lusitani took a step back, began to turn around, then toppled off the parapet, whereupon another man took his place, and it was then that I noticed this strange custom. The Lusitani, much in the same way as the Gallic tribes, have this notion of single combat and, whenever possible, prefer to attack one at a time. At least, that is how they start out; usually, by the third or fourth time we faced them, they learned the folly of their ways, but since this was our first battle with the Lusitani, they still were determined to fight in the manner in which they were accustomed. The next man apparently did not learn anything from watching his comrade, instead coming and swinging wildly at us, making it a matter of a few heartbeats before he was dispatched. It was in this manner that we slowly moved forward, eliminating all of the men on that section of the parapet.

Once our section of the parapet was cleared of the enemy, we turned our attention to the fighting around us. The immediate area was now crowded with Legionaries, yet none of us had made sufficient headway against the Lusitani to enable us to get off the parapet and down onto the ground. While our Century was clearly holding its own, I thought that they would welcome the help of the rest of us in our small group, but I was not sure what to do, so I turned to Calienus for direction and he seemed to weigh the options in his mind. Narrowing his eyes in thought, oblivious to the mayhem that was taking place just feet away from us, he announced, "We've cleared our section, so we could go down the ladder and come back up behind them farther down the wall," and I looked down at the area immediately surrounding us.

It was full of the Lusitani in reserve, and although they obviously did not have the weapons and probably did not have the training of the Lusitani on the wall, they made up for it in numbers, at least as I saw it. However, I would obey my Sergeant, no matter what he said.

"But I think that while we could take most of those bastards, there are just too many to make it a sure thing," and I heaved a sigh of relief at the decision. "So let's go help the boys over there." He pointed to where Crastinus was fighting.

Running along the parapet, we were forced to hop over the bodies heaped there; it surprised me how quickly I was becoming inured to the feeling of wanting to throw up whenever I saw a corpse. Less than a full watch ago, I felt like I wanted to vomit when the Tribune was decapitated, but now I hopped over mangled bodies like they were no more than a log. I have always found it interesting how the human mind works that way. Making our way to the rear of the group of men from our Century who were in the assault team with the Pilus Prior, I grabbed the back of the harness of the man in front of me who twisted in surprise, in turn giving me a shock, albeit a happy one. It was Vibius!

He grinned when he saw me and I returned it as he asked, "Well, how many have you done for so far?"

"Three, and helped with a couple of others. You?"

He looked a little embarrassed as he shook his head, then nodded towards the front and replied, "Those bastards up there won't give me a chance. They won't rotate through like they're supposed to."

Standing on tiptoe, I could see that, indeed, the Pilus Prior was still up front, thrusting away with short, brutal strokes and I could see men toppling over in front of him, most of them either falling or being pushed off the parapet to land on the ground. Next to him was one of the veterans of the Century, a Legionary named Figulus, who was doing the same. Looking down at the growing pile of bodies heaped below the parapet, I saw some of them moving and trying to crawl away, with others being completely still. I tried to estimate how many there were. I thought maybe twenty or thirty, but there appeared to be at least that many men left between us and the rest of the Century that had been led by the unfortunate Vinicius, so that pressure was being applied on both sides as the two parts of the Century moved towards each other, making the results inevitable.

After another few moments of fighting, we cleared the area of rampart that we were assigned, whereupon Crastinus pointed down with his *gladius* at the mass of men standing in what passed for a street in towns like this, although was nothing more than a wide expanse of rutted dirt with puddles of mud.

"Let's sort those bastards out," he yelled so that he could be heard over the noise.

Despite our immediate area being clear, we could see down the length of the parapet to see very fierce fighting still going on, extending all the way to where the wall curved out of sight, following the contour of the hill. There were a couple of spots that looked like the Legionaries were getting the worst of it; whether it was that the Lusitani in command of that local area were made of better stuff, or the men themselves were more organized, I could not tell. I wondered briefly if we would go to their aid, except it became clear very quickly that the Pilus Prior was not concerned with them. Turning to us, he scanned our faces, found someone, and pointed at him, beckoning him to stand next to the Pilus Prior.

"Rufio, you're the acting Optio. If you don't completely fuck things up in the next little while, maybe you'll be Optio for real," he said matter-of-factly, and I was troubled that he did not make any mention of Vinicius. He was the whole reason for Rufio being promoted, after all, yet as I was to learn, those emotions that one feels at the loss of a close comrade are to be put away for later, after the battle, and Crastinus was more concerned with keeping the rest of us alive. Rufio joined him, then Crastinus turned to the rest of us to give us our orders.

"Half the Century is going to go down that ladder," he pointed at the one nearest us, "and the other half is going down that ladder."

He indicated back behind us to the ladder that we were closest to earlier.

"So, Sections One through Five on me, the rest on Rufio. We go when I give the signal. Look around to see if there are any *pila* that can be used lying around here. We'll use them to keep these savages away from the foot of the ladders while the rest of us go down. I go first down my ladder, and Rufio goes first down his. Just make sure you don't end up like Vinicius."

The mention of Vinicius affected us, and Crastinus saw it. "Mourn him later, boys. We still have work to do," he ordered.

Then he sent us on our way and, as we went back the way we came, we looked around the parapet for any *pilum* whose pin had not sheared. One of the things that make our *pilum* so fearsome is its design. It has two pins affixing the iron shaft to the wooden one, with one pin made of iron, while the one closest to the head is made of wood, and is designed to shear off on impact. Also, although the tip of the *pilum* is tempered and hardened, the metal shaft is not, making it bend easily. Combined with the wooden pin, it makes the *pilum* a weapon such that once it strikes something substantial, like flesh, bone, or even the wood of a *scutum*, the iron shaft bends and partially detaches from the wooden shaft at the spot where the wooden pin shears off at impact, making the weapon unusable to throw back at us. The other advantage is that if it strikes the enemy's *scutum*, once again, it will bend, the weight of the *pilum* making the *scutum* basically useless after that.

While we managed to scrounge up about two dozen that were sufficiently undamaged to use to keep the Lusitani at bay while we descended the ladder, it also did not appear that they were overly anxious to meet us. Perhaps it was the nature of the men held in reserve that they were not as aggressive as the warriors who occupied the walls. I think it was just as much that they had experienced a taste of Roman fighting and found it not to their liking. Whatever the case, we gathered quickly as Rufio, still unaccustomed to his new status, tried to decide how we would descend the ladder. Looking around, his eyes caught mine and, with a sinking feeling, I realized what he was thinking.

"Pullus, you were second up, you may as well be second down," he commanded.

At first, I felt inclined to argue, but felt the eyes of my comrades on me, so instead, I simply nodded, not willing to trust myself to say anything. Rufio turned his attention to the others, quickly counting out the order that we would line up and designating six men to remain behind to provide support with their *pila* while we established a presence on the ground, men who had proven to be accurate with the *pila* in training. The Lusitani, guessing our intentions, started to surge forward, but even to my inexperienced eye, I could see that it was more for show than anything. Even so, there were still a couple hundred of them. They stayed just out of range of our *pila*, except there was no way to be sure that they would not charge us when we started down the ladder, and there was only one way to find out.

Rufio took a breath before calling to the men who were providing support, "Watch our backs on our way down."

Immediately, he began descending, back to the Lusitani who, seeing us start down, started their chanting and bashing of their *scuta* all over again. Then, on a signal by a man who apparently was their leader, the enemy began rushing towards us. I was not about to repeat the mistake I had made on the way up the wall, so the instant Rufio cleared the first couple of rungs, I started following him down. There is no real way to describe what it is like to turn your back on a large group of men who want to kill you, and I tried to ignore the shaking of my knees as I made my way down. Rufio made it to the bottom, as did I an instant later, then the man behind me, followed by another, whereupon we took a few steps forward to make room for the rest of our group, standing shoulder to shoulder as the horde approached. Hearing Calienus give the command to ready the *pila*, followed immediately after that by the order to release, we sensed them flying towards the men, now not more than twenty paces away. There were only six of us throwing, so it did not come close to stopping their charge, yet every one hit its mark and the men who went down caused others to stumble, checking their wild advance for just a moment. Then, just as they started their charge again, the command to release was repeated, with more men going down. In the intervening time, another half-dozen of us made it down and I glanced over to see Vibius step into place to my left, where we had just enough time to grin at each other before the mob closed the remaining distance to slam into us. The collision was terrific, and I recoiled backwards from the mass of men who were the first to meet our fragile wall of *scuta*. Feeling my feet skidding backwards, I strained forward, putting all of my weight against the Lusitani screaming just inches from us, so close I could smell their stinking breath. Peeking over the edge of the *scutum*, I locked eyes with a man who appeared to be several years older, with his hair worn long in their manner, pulled back into a knot at the back of his head. His face was decorated with some sort of patterns made with what looked like paint, which combined with his wild eyes and shouting chilled my blood. Desperately, I looked for an opening for a thrust to his face or body because it was impossible to use my *scutum* in any offensive manner, then I felt a hand grab my harness to start pushing against me, least stopping my backward slide. There was one small advantage in the sudden and surprising fervor of the enemy; in their haste to destroy us, they ran headlong into our *scutum* wall, the back ranks pushing their leading warriors up against our line, crushing them against us so tightly they could not wield their weapons with any effectiveness. However, neither could we strike back, forcing something of a stalemate, yet it was one that we would inevitably lose because of the numbers we faced, unless something happened in our favor. Glancing at Vibius, I saw that his face contorted with the effort of maintaining the integrity of the formation, and I could tell that he was rapidly weakening. Something had to be done or we would be overwhelmed, even with the rest of our group now on the ground with us, and it had to be done quickly.

The answer came with probably no more than a few normal heartbeats' of time left before one of us in the front line failed and caused a breach. Instead of disaster, it was one of those accidental events, which, now with my experience in hundreds of battles and skirmishes, has as much to do with deciding the outcome as the tactics and strategy of the generals. The man pushing against Vibius, who looked no older than we were, had been trying to poke Vibius with what appeared to be nothing more than a sharpened stick, thrusting it over the top of Vibius' *scutum* as Vibius hunched behind it, dodging every jab. Finally, in frustration, the man dropped the stick to grab the top of Vibius' *scutum* with both hands, giving a mighty yank, and succeeded in pulling it almost out of Vibius' grasp, exposing my best friend to the warriors surrounding him. Feeling a roar of rage burst from my throat as I saw Vibius about to die and finding a strength I did not know I had, I threw the man facing me off with a huge push, staggering him backwards into his comrades, causing a ripple as the men pushing him from behind were knocked backwards as well. Turning my body, I brought my *gladius* up to strike out at the men threatening Vibius, yet before I could, there was a blur of movement as the man to Vibius' left also saw him in trouble and used the opening created to strike a blow on his own. His blade entered the neck of the man who dropped the stick and was still holding onto Vibius' *scutum*, blood spraying us as the blade was withdrawn just as quickly as it struck. I could not see who was next to Vibius; I reminded myself to find out and thank him later, but Vibius was not out of danger yet as another warrior, this one better armed than the first man, moved his arm forward in a sweeping arc in an attempt to take advantage of the gap that was still there. It is hard to describe events that take place in a matter of heartbeats accurately, yet when in battle, something strange happens, and time seems to stand still. Your mind can track things that are taking place literally in the blink of an eye like they are happening in slow motion, and one at a time instead of simultaneously. All that I am describing here took perhaps five or six normal heartbeats at the most, and still, more than forty years later, I see them as clearly as I see poor Diocles straining to keep up with me! Perhaps even more clearly, since my eyes do not seem to be as sharp as they have been in the past, even a year ago.

Continuing, I saw that Vibius was still in danger, as one of the few men armed with one of the long Gallic *gladii* that the Lusitani favored was swinging it down to cleave him in two. Instead of thrusting at the man, I instinctively swung my *gladius* up in a backhand sweep that started at my waist, with my blade meeting the man's arm just before his own weapon crunched into Vibius' head, who had closed his eyes in anticipation of the blow. My blade severed the man's arm as it moved upward through his limb just below the elbow, the reward being another shower as the severed portion of his arm tumbled end over end, splattering blood and flying just above Vibius' head to smack the man behind him. It turned out to be Scribonius, the arm hitting him dead in the face while the long *gladius* clattered harmlessly to the ground as our friend bellowed out a roar of disgust and, despite the gravity of the situation, I felt a grin on my face. Vibius had recovered at this point, his *scutum* back up in the first position, and he struck a blow of his own, gutting the man whose arm I had removed as he stood there staring dumbly at the stump pulsing blood in rhythm with every beat of his heart.

Once he went down, between his and the man with the stick's deaths, we had formed a small pocket of space, and I heard Rufio roar, "Move forward, Pullus. Use your fat ass for something useful."

Nodding that I heard him, I stepped forward to meet the man who had originally been opposing me, by now having regained his balance to come back at me. I saw that he held a spear, a wicked-looking thing with a large head that appeared to have barbs on it, in his other hand, the small round *scutum* they favored, and he advanced warily. I felt Vibius move forward back to my side; it made me feel secure and allowed me to concentrate on the man who wanted to kill me. Even as my foe moved forward, another Lusitani apparently thought to help him and moved next to him, but my opponent snapped something, causing the second man to look angry and make a gesture before turning his attention to Vibius. Now that my opponent was not screaming and acting like he was possessed by a demon, I could see that there was something different about him than the others; he was better dressed, for one, and there was an intelligent, almost humorous look in his eyes. When our eyes locked, he gave me a grim smile before making a short, mocking bow, then attacked. He was weaving the spear back and forth, and despite myself, I followed it with my eyes, exactly what he wanted. Lunging suddenly, he forced me to move my *scutum* in the direction of the lunge to deflect it, also what he wanted me to do. Realizing my mistake at once, it was nevertheless too late, the head of the spear punching at me as he made a backhand, slashing thrust, causing me to twist my upper body in desperation. My countermove saved my life because instead of striking square, the point struck a glancing blow along my ribs, sliding off my *lorica*, but still knocking the breath out of me. Even with the protection of the chain mail, I felt a searing pain, making me wonder if he had drawn blood as he instantly recovered to launch another attack, which I managed to block with my *scutum* this time instead of my body. The Lusitani struck at me again and again, yet despite regaining enough of my composure to defend against him, I was still rattled and did not try to strike back. Being truthful, my pride and confidence were hurt more than my side as I realized that I had been taken in by the constant praise and the belief in me that my comrades displayed, and had convinced myself that I was invincible. Now, this Lusitani had almost proven me and everyone else wrong. Gripping my *gladius* more tightly, I resolved to make up for my mistake and not do it again, waiting for his next attack. He began the weaving again and I smiled grimly, determined not to make the same error. This time when he lunged, my *scutum* remained still, not moving to meet his supposed target. Instead, I took a step forward to make a thrust of my own in the instant where the momentum of his lunge created a gap between his own *scutum* and the shaft of his spear. The point of my blade shot through that small gap, punching into his body just below his breastbone. This time, I remembered to keep the blade parallel to the ground, then twist it to cause more damage before withdrawing. His eyes widened in shock as his knees collapsed, staring up at me, and I thought, you're not smiling now, are you, you bastard? Vibius, in the meantime, had dispatched his adversary, enabling us to move forward just a bit more, slowly but inexorably giving our section more room to form into a proper formation. Rufio did not have a whistle, so he was forced to bark out verbal orders for us to rotate through, which he did at that point. Vibius and I each gave a heave to the Lusitani we were engaged with before taking the step to the side, allowing Calienus and Scribonius to take our respective places. Backing up, I kept my *scutum* up since I was on the outside of the formation, then fell behind the last man in the group. I had not realized how fatigued I was, but when I turned to speak to Vibius, I found that no words came because I did not have the breath yet.

Finally, I gasped, "That was a close one, neh?"

Vibius was holding onto the harness of the man in front of him and did not answer, keeping his eyes straight ahead, his face flushed with what I guessed was more than effort. He seemed to be embarrassed and I tried to tell him it was of no matter, yet he refused to speak so, irritated, I turned my attention back to what was going on. Advancing across the clearing to the edge of where the first round huts that comprised the beginnings of the town were located, we rejoined the rest of the Century as the Pilus Prior took charge again. We took a moment to collect ourselves and look around; the wall was now breached, and we could see the other Centuries moving down the dirt streets, heading towards the center of the town.

"All right, boys," called the Pilus Prior. "We head down that street." He indicated a dirt track winding in between the rows of cottages that seemed to head in the direction we needed to go. "Keep tight, stay sharp, and by the gods, watch the alleys and spaces between these *cac*heaps. These bastards are regrouping somewhere, but they probably left some men behind to hold us up."

With that admonition ringing in our ears, we began moving down the track, pushing our way into the town. Moving past the first of the native huts like we were ordered, we kept our eyes open for any stragglers or ambushes. Instead of a threat, we saw the women and children of the warriors fighting us and whose fate was being decided as they sat, huddled in abject terror and fear. The sobbing and cries of them as we moved down the muddy street could clearly be heard, and despite knowing that they brought this fate on themselves, I felt my heart lurch at the sights and sounds. We did not run into any resistance, the remnants of the defenders apparently deciding to form up for a last stand somewhere ahead. Although the town was not yet taken, we could already hear the sounds of a city that falls by the *gladius*. It has been a custom since the gods only know when that a town that resists leaves itself open to the complete destruction and sacking of it. Nothing is safe; no property and no person, and we could already hear some of the Legionaries in the other Cohorts begin taking what was now theirs before the fight was finished.

Pilus Prior Crastinus heard it too and commanded, "If one of you *cunni* take so much as a crust of bread until you're told, I'll personally flog you until there's nothing left but a bunch of bloody meat, understand?" We responded, and he finished, "Just because those bastards don't have any discipline, it doesn't mean that we're going to be like them. The Second Cohort isn't a bunch of fucking rabble, got it?"

Again, we answered, except I could plainly hear the bitterness and disappointment in some of the men's voices. Since I had never participated in the sacking of a town before, I had no idea what to expect, and therefore, did not know that I was missing anything, nor did any of my comrades who were *tiros*. Approaching the town center, we heard the clash of arms from other Cohorts running into resistance before reaching the large clear spot that served as their market and assembly area. It was not dissimilar to my town of Astigi, despite the fact it had not been Romanized, making it more native in appearance than Roman. Smoke was beginning to curl up from different parts of the town where the Legionaries had started putting things to the torch. Forming up just at the edge of the town center, we waited for the rest of the Cohort to join up, and they came streaming out behind us, spreading out in a single line. Facing us, about 150 paces away, were the remnants of the defense, perhaps 500 men all told, many of them clearly already wounded. This time, there was not a lot of their screeching and jumping about, just a grim silence as they awaited their fate, except we were just as silent, from our training and discipline, but also from the deep-seated belief that the end was inevitable and Rome's army would be victorious once again. While we waited, the Pilus Prior ordered each of the section leaders to do a head count of their tent section, which was quickly done.

"Anyone seen what happened to Didius and Vellusius?" Calienus asked us.

"I saw Vellusius go down before we got to the wall," Remus replied. Glancing back at Scribonius from my place in the rank ahead, he responded with a shake of the head. "I didn't see it," he said quietly.

"What about Didius?"

Atilius spoke up from his spot two ranks ahead of his normal spot. "I saw him fall off the ladder when we were coming down, but then I got busy."

This drew a laugh from us, the sound carrying over to our enemies, and I clearly saw the anger and humiliation on their faces, since I am sure they thought we were laughing at them. That we were doing so at all, no matter what the reason, clearly rattled them a great deal and I have seen such things many times since. It is part of the Roman mystique, if you will; the fact that we can laugh when death is all around is no small feat, and is yet another reason why we are so feared. What kind of man is it who laughs in death's face instead of shrinking back when it looks at him? I was worried about Vellusius, although it is probably not surprising that I did not have the same feelings for Didius. His death would remove a source of worry on my part, but I was not to be that lucky.

Once the butcher's bill was tallied, we were ordered forward once more, and this time we possessed no *pila* to launch. No more than a third of a watch had passed since we assaulted the walls, and I hoped that we would be finished soon, looking forward as I was to what was about to happen once we were turned loose on this town. First, though, we had to take care of this business and I turned my attention back to the problem at hand. Once we were about fifty paces away, we were halted to have our lines dressed. To our right, arrayed in the same manner, were four Cohorts of the 8th Legion, compared to our five Cohorts, a total of about 2,500 men to maybe 500, and of those 500, many of them were already wounded. Primus Pilus Favonius moved to the front of the line where he could be seen, not only by us, but by the Primus Pilus of the 8th. Next to him was his *cornicen*, who blasted the signal to prepare for assault, causing a ripple of movement as we crouched down and got ready. Glancing over, I saw that the 8th's Primus Pilus was holding his *gladius* in the air in the same manner as Primus Pilus Favonius, both of them watching each other. The moments passed, then the 8th's Primus Pilus, obviously deciding that the tension was raised to the sufficient level, swept his arm down, followed an instant later by Favonius. Even as the *cornicen* blew the signal for the attack as well, the sound was almost drowned out by our roar as we began the charge. Adding my voice, I ran forward, following my comrades as the distance closed rapidly. The Lusitani apparently had decided to stand and meet the charge, rather than try to countercharge to create their own momentum, always a mistake. So much of what happens in a battle hangs on that first collision and standing still is a foolish, or desperate, thing to do. Slamming into the Lusitani, the clash by now a familiar sound to me, it was still difficult to listen to the cries and screams of wounded and dying men. Ignoring those feelings, I held onto the back of the harness of the man in front of me as we settled into the rhythm of battle. Now that we were reunited and working as a Century again, we listened for the Pilus Prior's whistle, so I moved up at each blast, until I was next to go. When the whistle sounded for my turn, I waited for the Legionary in front to push off, then stepped in to see that there were perhaps 300 men left, with a number of bodies lying at my feet and along our front.

The man I relieved had done a good job because the Lusitani he was facing still had not recovered his balance, so I finished him with a quick thrust. There seemed to be a renewed energy in the Lusitani, except it was that of desperation, the courage of men for who all hope is gone and all that is left for them is to die well. When the next warrior I faced came screaming at me, I noticed that he was one of the few I had seen to that point who was fully armed and armored. On his head was a high conical bronze helmet, and he wore the same kind of armor that I saw on the man who slew the Tribune, a series of scales made of bronze overlapping each other, but unlike the leader, his armor was tarnished and had some scales missing. Carrying the long *gladius* and customary *scutum*, he was somewhat darker than the men around him, his face smeared with blood, and I wondered whose it was as he came at me, immediately trying to take my head from my shoulders in a single blow. I took it on the *scutum* instead, but the impact was fierce; this man was the strongest I had faced to this point. It did at least answer whose blood it probably was on his face, that idea fueling my desire to end him and wreak vengeance. As he recovered, I smashed him with my *scutum*, expecting the same reaction that I experienced before, except this man met me boss to boss, blocking the blow, although it sent him back a step. This surprised me, and I told myself not to take this man lightly because he possessed the most skill and strength of anyone I had met in this first battle. For the next few moments, we both bashed at each other, desperately seeking an opening, me for a thrust, him for a slash, but neither of us finding one. Finally, we stopped, glaring at each other, panting like dogs on a hot summer day and cursing each other in our own tongue. Because I was younger, I recovered more quickly, but just as I moved towards him, the whistle blew again and I cursed my luck. One more time that day, my pride was stung and I worried that he would not be around to finish our battle, so I pretended that I had not heard the whistle and kept moving forward. Instead of meeting me, he took a step back and I felt some grim satisfaction as I closed the distance; obviously, he had learned that I was not one to be trifled with.

"Pullus, you idiot. You're too far out in front," I recognized the roar of Pilus Prior Crastinus.

Immediately looking around in surprise, I gasped in shock at the sight. I was several feet in front of the rest of the line; my opponent was not scared, he had taken my measure. He saw I was a young, prideful fool and had drawn me out. Instantly after this recognition, I was attacked by a man to my left, who, fortunately for me, was armed only with a short spear instead of their usual long one. The point of his spear embedded in my *scutum* and it was only because of my strength that I was able to wrench the spear out of his hand while keeping my *scutum* up, despite the awkwardness of having the shaft sticking out of it. My original opponent then saw his chance, leaping at me to slash in a great, sweeping arc, trying once again to separate my head from my shoulders. Desperately parrying with my own blade, the grip that Vinicius taught us saved my life, because the momentum of his heavier blade would have knocked it from my hand if I was holding it in the standard fashion. Even so, my arm instantly went numb and I almost dropped the *gladius* anyway. At that instant, there was a roar of rage and I sensed a blur to my right launching at the man, getting inside his guard before he could recover. There was a flash of a blade, the point punching the man in the throat to go through his neck and out the other side for an instant before being withdrawn. Even before the man wielding the *gladius* hit the ground, I dispatched the owner of the short spear, then stepped back past the front of the line and moved to the back, wrenching the spear out of my *scutum* as I did so.

When I passed the Pilus Prior, he caught my eye and growled, "You and I will talk about this later."

I gulped and answered him, continuing to the rear. There to greet me was Vibius, who said, "Now we're even."

I looked at him in surprise. "That was you? You moved so fast I couldn't tell who it was."

"I've always been faster than you," he shot back, then smiled at me.

Grinning back, I saluted him. "You're right. Now we're even." Then we turned back to the fighting.

It took two more rotations before we finished off the last stand of the Lusitani in the town, but that did not mean the fighting was over, as hundreds of warriors melted into the town, most of them hurrying to their families. That was where they were found; in their huts, weapon in hand, determined to protect their families to the death, which was what they did. While we rested in the town square, Caesar and his command group rode up and we were called to *intente*, the Primi Pili giving their report to him. Once they were finished, he addressed us, sitting astride his horse.

"Comrades," he called us, the first time that he ever did so, explaining why with his next breath, "for that is what you have become today. We have shed blood and had our own shed. Undoubtedly, you will have comrades who have been killed, or may Fortuna smile, been wounded, and that is a bond that can never be broken. Today, we become comrades in arms, the most precious connection any man can share, even more precious than the bonds of family. As a salute to your bravery and as a gift, I give you this town and all that is in it, to do with it as you will!"

Finishing with a sweeping flourish of his arm to indicate the expanse of the town around us, we cheered him lustily before he rode away to address the other men scattered about the town.

The Pilus Prior stepped up to bellow in his command voice, "All right, boys, you heard Caesar. The town's yours."

Cheering again, some more loudly than others, for truly, we new *Gregarii* had no idea what that meant. Oh, we had been told stories around the fires by the veterans, but just like battle, describing it and living it are two different things.

"Here's how it will work," he continued. "You new veterans," we cheered his acknowledgement, however faint, that we were no longer mere *tirones*, "will follow the older men's lead. Do what they do. And you're going to do it," he indicated the path we followed into the town, "in that area we just came through. You take what you can carry and that's it. And don't forget," he added in warning, "that you have to clear the houses before you can take anything. You can hear that the fighting's not over; it looks like a fair number of their warriors are still about and in the houses, so be careful. And remember, the more you leave alive, the more slaves there'll be for sale."

With that, we were dismissed and Calienus called us together, pointing to an area. "Let's get going before these selfish bastards take everything worth taking."

Then he started trotting towards the huts, with the rest of us tagging behind. Vibius and I exchanged a glance, to which I shrugged. I had no idea what to expect; Cylops never talked about this aspect of war to us. I soon found out why. As often as I have done it since, the first time I participated in the sacking and destruction of a town was an experience that will never be forgotten, as much as I try. I also wish I could tell you that the troubling feelings I experienced struck me while we were doing it, yet in the heat of the moment, after facing death and dealing it out, I felt nothing but a wild exultation as I did my share of all that comes with the taking of a town and putting the inhabitants to the *gladius*. As much as I learned of combat that day, I learned as much and more about the darkness that we all carry in our hearts, being tutored in the finer points of pillage and rape. Following Calienus into the first hut, we found a family of four, with nobody to defend them, just an older woman and her three children, all of whom we killed, leaving their bodies where they fell. He showed us where people were likely to hide their valuables; under a loose stone in the hearth seems to be the most common, and how to leave no possibility, however unlikely, unexamined. As we left each hut, we marked it with a symbol, etched into the doorway that designated it as being searched by our Century. It was not until the third hut that we met resistance; a warrior came screaming at Calienus as soon as he kicked in the flimsy door, but Scribonius and Romulus were standing on either side, cutting him down immediately with thrusts to the body. He collapsed, yet did not die immediately, and as I stepped over him, I saw the absolute despair and anguish on his face.

"Well, well, I can see why he was so keen to fight us," Calienus laughed, pointing to a figure huddled in the corner of the one room.

It was a young woman, obviously the man's wife, and Calienus was right. She was a rare beauty and instantly the mood in the room changed as we all looked at her hungrily. She had raven-colored hair, offsetting her smooth white skin, but even with the dirt on her face, it could not disguise the fine nose and high cheekbones, and while her eyes held fear, there was a hint of pride and disdain there that only served to inflame us further. Nobody said a word; nobody had to say what was on his mind because we were all thinking the same thing.

Finally, Scribonius spoke up, saying nervously, "Maybe we should leave her be. She'll fetch a good price as a slave, won't she?"

Calienus laughed again.

"That may be, but that doesn't mean we can't have a taste first. It's not like she's a virgin, right? That was obviously her man we just did for, so there's no harm in taking a sample."

As he said this, he was unbuckling his belt and harness, dropping it to the floor. The woman tried to shrink even further into the corner, it being clear to her what Calienus was about to do. Looking over his shoulder at us, he grinned. "This is one time I'm pulling rank, boys. You can have a go after me, but don't mark her up because that'll hurt her price. Got it?"

Nobody said anything, just nodded in agreement, whereupon Calienus turned back to the woman, who began whimpering in fear. Our Sergeant approached her and she made a desperate lunge to get past him, but he was more experienced at this game than we were. Laughing, he stuck a leg out as she ran past so that she fell to the dirt floor with a thud. I could not seem to tear my eyes away, despite feeling a sense of shame at what was going on, but it was not strong enough for me to try and stop what was happening. Calienus fell on the woman, his weight pinning her down, and I sensed a movement behind me, turning around in time to see Vibius leave the hut.

I followed him, while Romulus and Remus jeered and laughed at me, Romulus saying, "You lose your place in line if you leave, Pullus."

I did not answer, feeling a flush rise to my face. Leaving the hut, I stood by Vibius, who was looking down the street, watching other Legionaries as they carried loot out of the huts, some of it in the form of screaming women tossed over their shoulders. The smoke was intensifying as more and more of the town was put to the torch and, over it all, we could hear the sounds of fighting, women screaming, the harsh laughter and shouts of men sating their lusts.

For a short time, neither of us spoke, then Vibius said, without looking at me, "I can't do something like that, Titus. I swore to be true to Juno, but it's not just that. When I looked at that woman, I saw Juno. How would I feel if that happened to her?"

I did not know what to say, yet I tried anyway. "But that would never happen to Juno. She's a Roman, Vibius. Nobody will ever beat us."

He looked at me with a sad smile, and replied simply, "And that bothers me too."

Resuming our silence, it was only broken when Romulus came out, a huge grin on his face as he buckled his harness back up. "Your turn, Pullus," he called out cheerfully. "We left enough for your share."

I could not look Vibius in the eye as I turned and went back into the hut.

By the time the sun was going down, the town that we assaulted no longer existed, nor do I remember its name. The surviving Lusitani were bound in chains, destined for the slave markets that would send them to Rome and the Republic. Seeing the bound prisoners as they were led away, I was troubled by a thought; was this how Phocas and Gaia had come into my life? It had never occurred to me to ask how they came to be slaves, and I found that thought troubling. All of us were filthy; for the first time, I noticed that my hands were caked with blood, and I remembered thinking that they were sticky at some point during the attack, but it never occurred to me to look down to see why since I was too busy. Now when I looked down, it surprised me to see that not just my hands were covered, but almost every inch of me was spattered with other men's blood, and I dully wondered how long it would take to get it out between the links of my *lorica*. It was only then that I became aware that my side still hurt, so I struggled out of my *lorica*, the effort making me gasp in pain as the dull ache increased to a sharp stabbing pain. Feeling something warm starting to seep down my side, soaking my tunic even more, I did not want to look. Instead, I used my fingers to explore, touching the area gingerly, then feeling around the edges of what was a gash perhaps two or three inches long along my right side. Needless to say, it was extremely tender to the touch, made even more so because the blood had dried my tunic to and around the wound.

Bracing myself, I was just about to yank it free when I heard Calienus call out sharply, "Don't do that. It'll make it bleed even more."

Turning to see him behind me, he was already shed of his *lorica* and headed for the baths when he obviously saw me poking at myself.

Walking up to me, he smiled. "I guess I have to show you new boys everything, including how to take care of yourself."

Looking at the gash, he pursed his lips. "This is more serious than I thought. You're going to need to get it cleaned up and stitched. I can do the cleaning part all right, but you'll have to go to the *medici* to get it stitched up."

I was dubious, to say the least, since I had never been injured to the point where I needed to have anything stitched up, and I was none too keen on the idea. However, Calienus ordered me to go, so I went to the *quaestorium* where the medical section was located.

I wish I had not. This had been a day of firsts, and this was one I wished I had never seen, not just because I did not like to see my fellow Legionaries suffer. The knowledge that it had only been a matter of luck that I was not one of them, moaning in pain while trying to will it away was sobering, to say the least. Or I could have ended up worse; of all the things I learned that day, it was that I was not nearly as skilled and invincible as I thought, and I vowed that I would never take my skills lightly, nor would I ever stop training with dedication and focus. Of all the vows I have made in my life, this is the one that I can say I abided by more closely than any others.

The interior of the large tent was lit with numerous lamps, the heat from them making the atmosphere stifling, not helping the stench, and I was forced to fight back a gag. The aftermath of a battle, whether one wins or loses, is horrible. Some men's wounds are too horrific to describe, so the *medici* are just as busy putting men who cannot be saved out of their misery as they are stitching up wounds and setting bones. Some wounds have to be cauterized, and this more than any other smell made my stomach lurch. Because I was one of the walking wounded, I was not a priority; once I was assessed, I was told to go sit on the ground and wait with others in similar condition. There were almost a hundred men like me, and with a staff of maybe twenty *medici ordinarii*, some of them physicians, although most were orderlies, it meant I was in for a long wait. Finding a spot, I made myself as comfortable as possible, trying to avoid eye contact with the other men around me, not being much in the mood for talking, especially to strangers. Luckily, they all seemed to be of the same mind, so we contented ourselves with trying to shut out the screams of men as their wounds were cauterized or their bones set. Almost as frequently, two orderlies would carry a man out who had not survived, and all of us scanned the faces of the men on the stretchers to see if we knew them. Some of them it was impossible to tell, as their wounds were to their head and facial area.

At one point, I heard a man gasp as the orderlies carried a body out, then heard him mutter, "Well, that makes our tent roomier. Poor bastard."

Finally, I was seen and my wound cleaned, albeit a bit roughly for my taste, except I was determined not to give the orderly a hint of the pain I was feeling as he pulled the tunic from the wound, starting a fresh bout of bleeding. Once cleaned, my wound was stitched up, the orderly obviously proud of his handiwork, but I was an indifferent audience. Just as I was leaving the tent, I heard someone call my name and I looked at the rows of men lying on cots who had been treated, finally seeing someone wave to me. Walking over, once I recognized him, I smiled in genuine pleasure at the figure of Vellusius, lying on a cot with a grin equally as broad.

"Vellusius, I thought we had lost you, old son."

He gestured to the bandage that was awkwardly wrapped around his right shoulder and across his chest diagonally. I noticed that his arm was immobilized as well, and he explained. "I got hit by one of those cursed missiles, right on my collarbone." He grimaced even as he said this. "It broke it, but it also slowed the damn thing down so it just lodged in my shoulder."

"Did they get it out?"

He nodded, making a face. "And that hurt like Dis, I can tell you, but I'm feeling all right now. They gave me some wine and some sort of herb mixed in that tasted like the butt end of a mule, but I'm feeling pretty good right now. Wait, I said that already."

He laughed, and I could not help but join in, partly out of relief at seeing him alive, yet also because of the woozy smile he was giving me.

Turning serious, I asked him, "What about your wound? It's not going to put you on disability is it?"

He shook his head. "No, they said I should be good as new in a few weeks, as soon as the bone knits."

Vellusius smiled the smile of a man who has beaten the system, even if it is temporary.

"You know that that means, right, Pullus? No digging, no guard duty, no marching about." He smacked his lips. "Yes, I could definitely get used to that."

I laughed again and bade him goodnight, promising to tell the others the good news.

"Be sure you tell those thieving bastards to stay out of my stuff. Especially Didius," he called to my retreating back, which I acknowledged with a wave.

Making my way back to the tent, I stopped just long enough to get some porridge dished up from the section pot, then went to the baths to get clean, taking a fresh tunic and loincloth. Despite feeling clean physically afterwards, in some ways I still felt dirty, in a manner that is hard to define. By the time I returned, I was completely exhausted and thankful that we had been given the next two days off from normal duties. The fires from the town still cast a glow that gave the camp an orange pall, which would be intensified shortly when our dead were cremated. I was curious about whether we would be required to attend the funerary rites since it appeared that Didius was dead, given that I had not seen him at the aid tent. I also wondered if the fact that I would not grieve meant that I was a bad person. Getting back to the tent, the others were gathered around, with a pile of loot that was being divided out evenly.

"Pullus," my comrades cried out.

Smiling, I took my normal place next to Vibius, where we exchanged a long look at each other, not saying a word, yet communicating our mutual relief that we were both alive. I told them that I had seen Vellusius, which was greeted by cheers all around and they all laughed when I passed on his last message, except I left out the part about Didius, thinking him dead. Calienus was in charge of dividing up the spoils, such as they were, there being just a small pile of coin. However, most of the valuables were in the form of jewelry of one sort of another, and there was some bickering about the value that Calienus assigned each piece as he distributed it out. I saw the pile for Vellusius, which was going to be watched by his newly designated mate Scribonius. Scribonius had originally been the close comrade of Artorius, but to both Vellusius and Scribonius' relief, Artorius' dismissal from the Legion meant that Scribonius needed a new one, and Vellusius was originally forced to partner with Didius. Immediately after Artorius left, Scribonius and Vellusius approached our Sergeant, who was as aware as all of us the loathing in which we held Didius and vice versa. Didius did not take the rejection well, making his usual dire threats to Vellusius, which so far were unfulfilled. Thinking of that event, it in turn led me to the fate of Didius, and I was unsure how to broach the subject. While the rest of my tent mates knew how I felt about him, I still did not want to make my feelings for him too obvious, especially if he were dead. I noticed that there was a pile for him as well as Vellusius, except that did not necessarily mean anything. It is the custom that in the event of death, the spoils taken would be sent to the slain man's family, if he had one, or put into the funeral fund that is kept to pay for the proper sacrifices and rituals that are observed when a Roman Legionary dies, along with paying for an appropriate monument.

Finally, my curiosity could not be quelled any longer, so I cleared my throat then asked, "So, what about Didius?"

I was not sure what reaction I expected, but it was certainly not the one I got. Nobody said anything; instead, there was a silence where the prevailing attitude, if I am any judge of facial expressions, was one of disgust.

"I'm in here. Why, Pullus? Did you miss me?"

Though muffled, it was still clearly the voice of Spurius Didius, who apparently was in our tent. This puzzled me, but when I looked to the others for the story, they steadfastly refused to speak, in turn looking at Calienus, who tried to ignore them. Finally sighing in exasperation, he said in as neutral a tone as he could manage, "Didius was injured on the way down the ladder. He took a serious fall."

This news was followed by what sounded like a cough, and I glanced over to see Remus staring at the ground with what I thought was a grimace, except that his cough seemed to ignite a fit of sounds. Finally, he could not contain himself any longer and began openly laughing, which as it tends to do, started a conflagration of the same behavior, soon becoming a riot of guffawing hilarity that I was swept up in despite having no idea why.

"Quiet, by the gods, or I'll come out there and gut every one of you," I heard Didius roar, just making things worse as far as the laughter.

Our refusal, or inability, to subside prompted him to appear, but it was the way he did so that ignited a fresh round of laughter. He was hopping on one foot, his other leg dangling off the ground.

"I told you to be quiet or all of you will pay," I know he meant this to be a threat that we would take seriously, except it came out as a petulant whine. "I bet that if any of you had happen to you what happened to me, you'd have been doing the same thing."

I was still unclear on why it was so funny that he was hobbling around, until Calienus finally explained. "It seems that our dear Didius, when he jumped off the ladder, landed on a nail that went into his foot."

Amid the continuing hooting, I asked, "Why didn't he pull it out?"

This triggered even more mirth, as now some of the boys were literally rolling on the ground, tears streaming from their eyes. "Because he couldn't; he was too squeamish." This came from Romulus, eliciting a roar from Didius, who hopped closer to the fire to shake his fist at all of us.

"It was in too deep, I tell you! None of you would have been able to pull it out if it had been in your foot."

Remus got up to reenact what Didius had done. He jumped up to begin miming going down a ladder, but when he landed, he immediately fell to the ground, screeching, "By the gods, I've been shot! I'm dying! Oh gods, the pain... the pain...."

Remus was now rolling around on the ground, clutching his foot, whimpering and carrying on, so that quickly I was laughing as hard as the rest of them.

"I tell you, it was all the way in to the bone." Didius made one last attempt at restoring what was left of his shredded dignity. "By the gods, you'll all pay for your insults....."

Before he could finish, Calienus shot back, "Oh do be quiet, Achilles. Go rest your foot."

And this was how Didius earned the nickname he was to carry for the rest of his time in the Legions.

The next three days were spent resting, cleaning our gear, and mourning our fallen. In our Century, we had lost three men dead, including Optio Vinicius. Vinicius' replacement Rufio had been judged to have avoided messing things up enough to warrant him losing the title, so Rufio became our new Optio. However, there was a surprise for all of us, when the Pilus Prior came to find me lying on my cot in our tent, dozing. I was awakened by a kick to my feet, opening my eyes to see the Pilus Prior standing there, with his *vitus* and the invisible man with the turd back on duty as well. Jumping to *intente*, I tried not to wince at the pain in my side from the sharp movement, but the Pilus Prior had been around too long to be fooled.

"Side still bother you?" he asked gruffly.

"Not much, Pilus Prior. Only when I move suddenly."

That prompted a bark that passed for his laugh. "Well, you'll be doing plenty of that. I've decided to make you our weapons instructor in place of Vinicius. Rufio agreed that you're the best choice."

Stunned, I opened my mouth to protest, then thought better for a moment and shut it. There was a silence as he watched me, and mentally cursing myself, I plunged in anyway.

"That's a great honor, Pilus Prior," I began, but he cut me off.

"I don't give a fucking brass obol if you think it's an honor. It's an order, and the only response I expect is 'Yes, Pilus Prior' or 'Yes, sir.'"

I should have shut up then, yet I couldn't, I just had to keep going. "But, sir, why me? I thought after what happened on the wall when I forgot to draw my *gladius*, you'd realize that I'm not ready for this. Maybe someday…"

I got no further; now the Pilus Prior was truly angry, and he stepped close enough that I could smell the *posca* he had consumed for breakfast on his breath.

"Are you doubting my judgment, *Gregarius*?"

Despite saying this in a deceptively quiet voice, I had learned this was the sign that I had truly angered him, along with addressing me by my rank and not my name. Trying to remain solidly at *intente*, I could nevertheless feel myself leaning backwards as he thrust his face up at mine, although it was even with my chest. It was the disconcerting feeling that must come from a wolf leaping up at your throat, and I could not have been more terrified.

"N-n-no, Pilus Prior." I cursed myself again for stammering like Artorius. "I just….I just…nothing, Pilus Prior. I'll do my absolute best, sir."

Just as quickly, he changed back to his normal hard-ass self and clapped me on the shoulder. "Good, it's settled then. You won't be expected to start training the others until you're completely healed."

Turning to leave, he then stopped to face me once again and said quietly, "I know you can do this, Pullus. I have faith in you, which is why I picked you. I know you won't let me down."

Whereupon he turned heel and walked out, leaving me a mass of confusion. How was it possible to want to kill a man and die for him, all in the same instant? Such is the nature of a great leader that he can inspire those feelings; it was a lesson I never forgot and did my best to emulate when my turn came, however poorly I might have done so.

After our recovery period, we broke camp to continue heading north, and once we were deep into Lusitani lands, Caesar gave the order to start laying waste to the countryside. It was not harvest time, so the crops were still young and green, making them somewhat harder to burn, and we were forced to get inventive. One method was to line us up, with each man standing on a row, armed with his shovel. When we were given the signal, we walked forward, using the shovel to pull out the young shoots by the roots, as we were followed by slaves who gathered them up to use as forage for the livestock. It was somewhat time consuming, but in our Century, the Pilus Prior made a contest of it, offering an extra ration of wine to the first five finishers.

"I joined the Legions to get away from the farm," Romulus grumbled one day as we worked side by side.

"Look at the bright side," I told him. "At least you're not planting crops; you're pulling them up."

"Like that's a big difference."

I laughed as he kept mumbling to himself. The livestock were kept to feed all of us; it is amazing how much an army eats, and I think another secret to the success of the Roman army is that a large part of the effort and organization to sustain the army in the field revolves around feeding us, and truth be known, we ate much better than a lot of us ever had before, me included. For the first time in my life, bread was as plentiful as meat, although I still found it funny that for most of the men, if you gave them a choice between a nicely roasted haunch of beef or pork, or a loaf of bread with some olive oil, most of them would take the bread. My tent mates always gave me grief about my taste for meat, yet I did not mind, because it meant that there was more for me.

However, I do not want to give the impression that our activities in spoiling the countryside went unopposed or unmolested. The Lusitani were experts in hit and run tactics, suddenly appearing out of nearby woods to attack small groups of men, or slow-moving targets like wagons that were sent out to round up supplies of one sort or another. Our losses were small, but it was aggravating and nerve-wracking nonetheless, and it meant that none of us ever really felt we could relax, except when we were in our marching camp. Regardless of this harassment, we continued to march northward, torching every single farm or small village that we found, rounding up the inhabitants to be sold into slavery. As far as loot went, the pickings were slim to say the least, and we began to look forward to another sizable town to take and hoped that the Lusitani would be as stubborn as before.

A little more than a week later, we approached the city known as Conimbriga (Coimbra), which is a Roman colony built on the site of a Lusitani village. The city is near the Muna (Mondego) River, and is about a day's march from the ocean, sitting on a plain at the foot of the hills that ring the city from the south. The scouts reported that this town had gone over to the Lusitani, but without any shedding of blood of the Romans who were living there, which was a bit unusual. Calienus thought that it was a sign that their hearts were not really in it, and the citizens of the town did not want to do anything to provoke Caesar. The word of what we had done to the first town and of our scorching of the land that we passed through naturally preceded us. Thus, when we arrived, the townspeople immediately sent a deputation of the Lusitani who were involved in the rebellion to surrender the city immediately. Caesar accepted the surrender, demanding that hostages be given by the noble Lusitani families, and a fine be paid for rebelling, even if it was one in name only, since it went directly into Caesar's chest instead of being sent to Rome. Thus satisfied, we continued to march northward.

This set the pattern for the next few weeks; we would march through territory, destroying everything that we could not carry or consume, and whenever we approached a town, the example set by our first attack was sufficient to convince the Lusitani to quickly capitulate and offer up whatever Caesar demanded. Initially, this was fine with us, but the monotony of marching and digging, followed only by more marching and digging was beginning to get to us. We began to grumble among ourselves when we were sure the Centurions could not hear us.

"How are we supposed to make any money on this campaign?" was how Calienus put it. "When I marched with Pompey, we took a pirate town or city a week almost, and they were all taken by storm, so we had a share of the spoils. And those pirates were rich!"

It might be appropriate to relate how Calienus' remark pertained to our situation. For as long as anyone could remember, and is still certainly the accepted practice, there is a method by which the average *Gregarius* can expect to enrich himself and begin a climb to higher status, which as I have already related, was very important to men like me. The custom is that if a town falls by assault, the spoils of what is taken from the town in the form of loot and slaves is divided equally among the men who participate in the sacking. However, if a town capitulates on its own, then whatever payment the general demands, whether it be in gold or other forms, particularly in confiscated slaves, goes directly to the general himself. I imagine the logic behind it, although nobody ever bothered to explain it to us, was that it is usually due to the general in command's persuasive powers that convinces a city to surrender without bloodshed, and therefore he deserves all that comes with that. Since, by this time, we had subdued at least a half-dozen such towns in this manner, Caesar had made a tidy sum of money. The gossip at the time was that he had accrued enormous debts, which was one reason why he was so keen to convince the towns to surrender.

"He's the only one getting rich," Vibius grumbled, and I must admit I was surprised, at least at first, that Vibius spoke in this manner.

Before this moment, he had uttered nothing but good things about Caesar as a general and as a man. This was the first time I could remember where he said something critical, although it was not going to be the last, something I would find out, much to my dismay.

"He uses his skills as an orator to talk them out of putting up a fight, just so he can keep all the money," Vibius continued, and just when I was prepared to argue the point, I could see that most of my tent mates agreed with him, or at least seemed to since they were all nodding their heads.

Accordingly, I kept my mouth shut and held my own counsel, except the way I saw it, he was keeping us alive. What was the sense in wearing us down when we all knew that the further north we went, the worse the terrain and the more vicious the enemy? Still, I have to admit that I was beginning to get a little itchy myself for something to break the monotony of what we had been doing. Despite there being numerous skirmishes, and even a couple of engagements that involved more than one Cohort, we had not seen any of that action since the taking of the town. And like any young man, the horrors that one swears they would never want to endure again fade quickly as the days go by, so that by this point, it was not only my scar that needed scratching.

Continuing north, it turned out that Caesar was not blind and deaf to the rumblings of his army, and he took steps to mollify the men. Leaving the 8th Legion behind in Conimbriga to patrol the surrounding area and remind the inhabitants of their promise to him, this left him with the 7th, 9th, and us. After a three-day march, we arrived at the walls of another town and, once again, a deputation ran out to greet him, falling all over themselves to do so. However, they were in for a rude surprise, because Caesar gave them terms that were so exorbitant that it would have bankrupted every person in town. He further insulted them by demanding that whatever slaves they owned were to be handed over to him to dispose with as he saw fit, and if the number of slaves did not meet with his satisfaction, he would demand that the leaders of the town turn over some of their citizens to make up the supposed shortfall. The Lusitani could not agree to this, something Caesar knew very well, and to add further insult to injury, when the deputation made to return to the town, Caesar had them seized and held as prisoners. Consequently, the Lusitani were left with no choice but to fight. Because the 10th was the assault element in our first town, this time we acted as reserves while the 7th and 9th got their chance to attack. The same stratagem was used on this town, with the 7th using the ram on the main gate, and the 9th going over the wall. One difference was that, unlike the first town, this one did not have a natural defense like being on a hilltop, forcing the inhabitants to go to greater lengths to fortify their town, starting with a ditch several feet wide and several feet deep. Implanted in the ditch, on the bank nearest the town wall, were rows of sharpened stakes pointing outwards, while the ditch was half-filled with water that had gone stagnant, and was covered in a green slime. As in the first town, all brush and other matter that could provide even the most modest form of cover was removed, leaving a killing field of at least 200 paces in a swath around the town wall. The wall itself was again made of wood, but was even taller than the first town's since it did not have the advantage of a hill, and was about fifteen feet high. What I found curious was that there were no trees visible in the surrounding area that would have qualified to be included as part of the wall, making me wonder where the ones that made up the wall came from, and in such number. I would have understood if I had at least seen stumps that indicated that this place was forested at one time, but there was nothing like that. I asked Calienus, who shrugged, obviously never having thought of such a thing before.

"I guess they dragged them here from someplace else."

Acting in our capacity as the reserve, we were split into two, five Cohorts each, acting as support for the assaulting Legions. Our section supported the 7th, who were assaulting the gate, giving us a front row seat to watch what the 8th had done from a different view. Positioned where we were, on a small rise perhaps a furlong from the walls and slightly to one side of the gate, it also meant that we could act as judges on how the other Legions did their business, and it would probably not surprise anyone to know that we found them seriously wanting. We were allowed to sit on the ground, still in formation, of course, and watch the artillery go to work. This time, the scorpions were evenly divided between the two sides because there was a significant enemy presence on the parapet above the gate and immediately surrounding it. The 7th formed up, with a Century pushing the ram, once again covered in green hides, which we could easily smell from our positions. As further protection, the hides were liberally doused with water so that the ram was dripping as it was pushed forward. Two tent sections, eight to ten men on each side, pushed the ram forward, with the rest of the Century following in *testudo* creeping along behind it, waiting for a man to fall. Whenever that happened, one of the men in the *testudo* would leave the formation, run to the vacated spot, yank out the fallen man's *scutum* to lay his own on the rack provided on the ram, then start pushing. In this manner, the ram never slowed down for any length of time. To further protect the men, the ram was constructed so that the roof jutted out above them, with the hides working as cover from the missile fire as they approached the walls. On the parapet, there was the usual array of men, dressed in their usual array of armor, or lack thereof, some of them armed with slings and a few even with bows, something that we had not run into before. Our scorpions kept up a steady rain of bolts, occasionally hitting something besides the wood of the wall, thereby consistently forcing the men on the wall to keep their heads down for more than a brief instant.

"They're taking nowhere near the kind of beating we took," sniffed Remus, and we all nodded our heads in sage agreement, accepting as fact something we did not have the experience at that point to truly judge. Meanwhile, the rest of the 7th came forward behind the ram, formed in *testudo* by Century just as we had done, attacking the wall, their form drawing further commentary from the men around me. Consequently, the slingers on the front wall had more of a concentrated target than those along the walls around the town, knowing as they did that the Legion was headed for the main gate. Casualties mounted as the 7th advanced, with men beginning to fall out of their respective Centuries, some of them dead, while most howled in pain. Some of the stricken writhed on the ground, calling for help, but others just lay quietly waiting for the slaves and scribes that worked in the headquarters and who acted as stretcher bearers to come get them. One could sense that these men had been wounded before, and knew that there was no sense flopping about, yelling like a cat set on fire. Once the first men fell, all the joking among us ceased; there was nothing funny about seeing one of our own suffer.

The ram made it to the gate to begin its work, while the rest of the 7th sat absorbing the punishment, waiting for their chance to assault the gate. The air was thick with missiles and arrows, most of the arrows having been set alight and targeted at the ram, inevitably meaning that some of the men at the ram fell to them. A few men suffered the further misfortune of catching on fire, causing them to shriek even more horrifically than the other fallen, and we averted our eyes at the sight as those unfortunates staggered about, a couple of them lucky enough or with enough of their wits about them to run the short distance to throw themselves into the ditch and the slimy water to douse the flames.

Even as this was happening, the ram began to do its work, with the men heaving it back and forth on its sling, and we could see the dust fly with each impact. Naturally, some of the men began to bet on when the massive oaken gate would give way; there is nothing that a *Gregarius* will not wager on, and nothing that he will not wager. Wine rations were the most common, since few of us had any coin with us, even after our spoils from the first town; this bounty was promptly deposited with Cordius, our Tesseraurius, who refused to give any of it back, despite the most urgent pleading, the loudest whining, or the vilest threats. That lack of cash meant that anything else of value was used instead. Besides wine and food rations, turns on duties that were considered easy were wagered the most often. Where the line was drawn was with pieces of equipment, since losing anything because of a bet guaranteed a flogging while the rest of the Century watched. Once the gate finally burst open, one who was unaware might have been taken aback that along with the lusty cheers, there were scattered howls of protest and disappointment, as the men who picked the wrong number saw something precious to them go to one of their comrades. Almost immediately, a new line of betting was arranged, this one on the amount of time it would take before the town was declared taken. It turned out that nobody won the bet, because it took well into the night before the last Lusitani warrior was subdued. For a period of time, we were called to *intente* and there was some debate about whether or not we would be thrown in to help finish the job, with both Tribunes of the assaulting Legions arguing with Caesar against it, claiming that it would dishonor their Legions since they had not been called to assist us. Or so that was the word that spread around, which we took with smug self-satisfaction, nodding to each other as if it merely confirmed what we had known all along, that nothing could be accomplished without the good old

10th Legion coming in and saving the day. Therefore, we were turned away to sit back down and watch the flames grow higher around the town, the yells and cries of men fighting and dying soon accompanied by the chorus of screams of the women who were unfortunate enough to live there.

Once more, we found ourselves staying in one place for a couple of days when it was the turn of the other Legions to nurse their wounds and regroup. Even so, we were being sent out in Century and Cohort-sized patrols while they rested, ranging the countryside looking for both Lusitani and anything worth eating or destroying. Late in the day of our second day in place, our Century and the Second Century was finishing the burning of a farm and surrounding buildings when we were attacked by a mixed force of mounted warriors and infantry. It was only because of the Pilus Prior that, despite being surprised, we were not unprepared, since he had drilled us over and over for just such an eventuality. There is no way to overstate the value of the type of drill that the Roman army does, because it prepares us for just such emergencies, making our reactions as close to second nature as I believe it is possible to get. In this case, the enemy waited until we were finished torching the farm, so that some of the men were occupied with driving the half-dozen cattle while others were carrying freshly killed chickens. Perhaps a third of one Century was thus occupied, while a section scouted ahead on foot and another section acted as rearguard. Caesar's army during this campaign was hampered by a lack of cavalry and it was because of this deficiency that a body of men more than three times the size of our two Centuries could get close enough to try and ambush us. They waited until we were passing through a heavily wooded section, which the Pilus Prior had pointed out to us as a good spot for an ambush as we passed through, something I believe was a factor in our quick reaction as well. Despite this, it was not enough to save some of us, with the attack signaled by a volley of spears that flew out from either side, a half-dozen of them finding their mark among us. The hissing sounds were instantly followed by thuds as they struck the bodies of our comrades, two or three of them screaming in pain as they were impaled, but the others perhaps were luckier, falling immediately without a sound. I caught a glimpse of a man in the front of the formation transfixed through the chest, his eyes staring vacantly at the sky, his spirit already having fled before he hit the ground.

"Form square!"

The Pilus Prior roared this command and we instantly obeyed, even as the Lusitani descended on us from the surrounding woods, their war cries suffused with joy that they had already struck some of us down. Because of the surprise, we had no time to form in our normal manner, with each section arranged in its usual line of march side by side, so I found myself, for a change, in the middle of the line instead of on the end, and at the rear of the formation which was not exposed to immediate attack, although soon enough, the warriors flowed like water around us on all sides. Risking a quick glance, I saw that once again, Vibius was by my side, this time to my right, with a man named Plautius from the third section on my left. That was all the time I had because the Lusitani came throwing themselves at us, using their bodies as just as much of a weapon as any of their spears or *gladii*. They had learned that their best chance to defeat us was to break our formation, and one thing I cannot take away from them is their bravery. There never seemed to be a limit to the number of men willing to sacrifice themselves on our wall so that their comrades would have a space in which to strike at us. Again, the continuous drill proved priceless, when the Lusitani managed to knock a man down a short distance away from me, whereupon he was immediately hacked to death by the howling mob. This was their mistake, because during the time they turned their attention onto the unfortunate Legionary, it gave the man behind him the opportunity to step into his spot. One of our many problems was that we only had a double line, formed in a square twenty-odd men across and two deep, and even in the second line there were a couple of empty spots. It was when we were arrayed in this manner that it was brought home to me that we had lost men in battle already, and any more that we lost would make us that much weaker. Perhaps one of the most difficult things about fighting in square, at least as far as I was concerned, is that you are quickly surrounded and despite the fact you are facing your part of the enemy, you are still constantly aware that there is fighting going on behind you and to the sides, outside of your peripheral vision. Simply put, if there is a breakthrough in those parts, you are very likely to be slaughtered. But one has to have faith in one's fellow Legionaries, just like they have to have faith in you, and for me, at least, it was this knowledge that drove me in striving never to be the one who subjected my comrades to death. This group of Lusitani, while brave, was not particularly skilled and dressed in a slightly different fashion than what we had faced before, a sign that they were from another branch. In quick succession, I dispatched three men facing me, so that it was only a matter of moments before the Lusitani who kept coming had to slow down to scramble over the bodies of their fallen, something that worked to our advantage. My arm began to grow weary, but this is where our training serves us best, because there is no waste motion; unlike our opponents, there is no flailing about, screaming and gnashing of teeth, all of which consume energy. That is why the nature of battle is a series of ebbs and flows; at the beginning, it is all sound and fury, with each side doing its best to kill each other. Inevitably, the energy levels fall, and then both sides will spend a few moments doing little more than stand several feet apart, glare and curse at each other before recovering enough to do it again. However, the only time that the fury of battle is equal to the opening clash is when one side or another begins to smell that the end is near, with one great effort tipping the scale in their favor. It is during this period where the conditioning of the Roman Legionary is most evident; we are generally the ones with the reserves of energy left to make that final push and finish off our enemy.

This day, the battle unfolded in a similar manner. Once we sustained the initial assault, the Lusitani settled into their usual series of rushes of small groups of men, trying first one side of the square, and then the other, which were easily repulsed. In fact, it seemed to be much easier than it should have been, and it was Calienus who first brought it to our attention.

"Something's not right," he muttered from his place in the second rank.

Calienus turned to the Pilus Prior, commanding from a spot in the middle of the square. Lying at his feet were four men who had been wounded thus far, one of them looking as if he would not last the day, which he did not.

"Pilus Prior," he called out.

"What is it, Calienus?"

"Does this seem right to you? I mean, do these bastards seem like they're just trying to hold us in place more than they're trying to kill every one of us?"

The Pilus Prior looked around, taking in each side of the square, his eyes narrowed in thought.

Nodding his head, he replied, "You're right. They're trying to keep us pinned here while they wait. I don't know what they're waiting for, but I don't want to find out."

Then he leaned down to examine the wounded men, speaking softly so that what he said could not be heard over the din. One of the men shook his head, while the others grimaced as they pulled themselves to their feet. Turning my attention back to the front, I saw that it was my turn to step forward while Romulus, who had originally been directly behind me, pushed the Lusitani away before stepping to the side so that I could take his place.

"Right," the Pilus Prior's voice rang out clearly above the din. "We're not going to wait around for whatever these bastards have planned for us, so everyone stand ready. When I give the command, we're going to march out of these woods and try to find some better ground."

As we exchanged nervous glances, I felt a shiver of dread; we had practiced marching in square a great deal, but this would be the first time that we would be trying to do it while in combat.

As if reading our minds, the Pilus Prior called out, "Remember your training, boys. This is no different from on the drill field, except we have these little bastards as a nuisance. Think of them as you would a rock or a log in the way."

This brought a nervous chuckle, one in which I did not share. I have been blessed, or cursed, depending on how one looks at it, with an overly vivid imagination, but there was no stretch of it that I could make that turned these sweating, howling madmen waving spears in our faces into logs that just happened to be strewn in our path. Thinking about this evidently showed on my face, because I heard a laugh and glanced back to see Vibius smiling at me.

"By the gods, Titus, did you just swallow a bug or something?"

"No, I just don't like logs that are waving a *gladius* at me," I growled in irritation, which was compounded when he merely laughed again.

"You're not turning into an old woman, are you, Titus?"

I shot him a murderous glance, but said nothing. We got ambushed shortly after we entered the wooded area, making the fastest way to clear and higher ground back the way we came. The problem was that the relative safety of that high ground lay in the opposite direction of our camp. However, the Pilus Prior decided this was the lesser of two evils, so we began moving toward our refuge. Vibius and the rest of us on what had been the rear of the square now became the front, so for us it was a straightforward march ahead, pushing those Lusitani who tried to stop us out of the way, or cutting them down if they tried to fight. It was straightforward in that sense only; the front rank has to make sure they are not moving too fast for the two sides of the square, who are sidestepping as they move, which is obviously more difficult than just walking forward. The biggest risk was that we would open up a gap at the junction of where our lines met, which could be exploited by the Lusitani. At this point, they were still making a token resistance, losing a few men before contenting themselves with screaming imprecations at us that we could not understand, although we could guess the intent because of the gestures involved. They also hurled the occasional rock, not often, just frequently enough to keep us on our toes. However, as hard as the side files had it, it was even worse for the back ranks, forced to back up the whole way. These Legionaries at the rear of the formation were put under the most pressure by the Lusitani, who were darting in and out, trying to make one of the men take a careless step backwards and fall. All of these factors meant that we could not move very quickly.

Meanwhile, the Pilus Prior and Pilus Posterior of the Second Century, a man named Vetruvius, along with the Optios, Signiferi, and *cornici* of both Centuries all walked within the square, helping the wounded keep up. Pilus Prior Crastinus was calling out the count, with the rest of the officers exhorting us to keep our cohesion, warning men whose alignment was getting too far off and generally trying to make sure we stayed together. The worst part was that if a man went down and was unable to get up, he was left behind, a fate that all of us feared more than a quick death. There had been Legionaries who fell into the hands of the Lusitani during the campaign, and if the tales told about their fates were true, it was not a fitting end for a beast, let alone a man. However, I also know that these tales may have been made up, because if there is one thing that competes with gambling in the heart of a Legionary, it is gossip and lurid tales, the bloodier the better. Finally making it to the edge of the woods, we could see in the distance a large plume of dust hanging in the still air, there generally being no breeze at that time of day. Despite having perhaps a watch and two-thirds of one of daylight left, it now being the height of the summer, we all knew that we were in dire straits indeed if we were forced to stay out overnight without the opportunity of making some sort of camp. Yet at that point, it did not look like we were going to be given the opportunity to do anything of the sort.

Once we entered the clearing, another source of misery came into our lives; while there was no breeze, when we were under the cover of the trees of the woods, we at least had shade, but now there was neither. Almost instantly, I felt the sweat start to form, and before we went more than a furlong, it was running down my face and into my eyes, which I had trouble keeping open because of the sting of the salt in my perspiration. I could not use my arms to wipe the sweat away either; if I moved my *scutum*, I would expose Plautius, still on my left, but if I used my *gladius* arm, the time it took to wipe my brow would obscure my vision. This was just the kind of thing the Lusitani were waiting for in order to make some sort of move or to throw a rock while I was not in a position to duck or dodge. Making matters worse, I was not the only one in this condition, as the curses I heard all around me attested to, but despite this hardship, we continued to trudge along. The Pilus Prior had pointed to the small, low hill that would be where we tried to make some sort of stand about a half mile away. This may not seem like much, but when you are under constant pressure in the way we were, it is the same as making it back to Rome. It was this small hill I was completely focused on, thinking of nothing else when finally someone made a mistake. Unable to see any more, one of the men in the rear rank walking backwards took the risk of trying to wipe the moisture from his eyes, or at least so I was told later by the man next to him. I do not know why, but for some reason, he stumbled and fell, but before he could scramble to his feet, a rock sailed from the mass of Lusitani, hitting him square in the face.

The man next to him started to move towards him to drag him to safety, now that the rear had taken another step or two backward, but the Pilus Prior's voice cut through all of us like a *pugio* as he roared, "You take one step towards him, I'll cut you down myself. He's a dead man! Leave him to his fate!"

I was appalled and, from the look of it, so were Vibius and Plautius, who both muttered curses under their breath.

"*Silete!*"

This came like the crack of a whip from Calienus, adding to our shock and confusion. Meanwhile, once the man on the ground, who was in the fifth section of the Second Century and one of the new men like us, was left behind far enough out of range that we could not protect him with either *gladius* or *pilum*, the Lusitani descended on him. While I could not see, I could plainly hear their cries of triumph as they surrounded him the way a pack of wolves do when they close for the kill, and I said a silent prayer to the gods that he was still unconscious. Unfortunately, the gods were not listening because I was not even finished when I heard him shriek with the kind of pain that comes from the most agonizing of mortal wounds. Despite my attempts to shut it out of my mind, I began speculating on exactly what they were doing to him, his screams continuing for a few moments before, as abruptly as they began, they stopped just as suddenly. We moved just a few more paces when there was a flurry of activity in the surrounding hordes. After a moment, it became clear that one or a group of them was doing something that aroused the rage and frustration of both Centuries, as behind us we could hear the others cursing the Lusitani with a venom missing to that point. I got my answer why when a Lusitani came sprinting within our line of sight, out of range of a *pilum*, but certainly close enough to see and hear him. He was brandishing a spear, on the point of which sat the head of the man they had just slain, and I felt my stomach roil as I fought the urge to unman myself by vomiting at the sight, the blood still dripping from the severed neck, the source of his agony made apparent by the clear visual evidence that he was not decapitated in one clean blow, but in three or four. Still wearing the look of shock and horror that I imagined was his last, his eyes were open, staring at us. They had even left on his helmet and this barbaric display was met with roars of approval from the surrounding Lusitani. Finding myself joining in the cursing, I hurled every vile imprecation I could think of and, as I was doing so, I locked eyes with one of them. This Lusitani was a medium-sized man a few years older than I was, with long hair pulled into the knot that was their custom, bare-chested and armed with a long spear and a small *scutum* made of painted wood. Looking me in the eyes, he grinned and with his spear made a gesture across his throat, then pointed and laughed at me. Staring grimly at him, I marked him as a man for whom I would be on the lookout if I was given the opportunity.

Just a hundred paces short of the hill, it was only then that our front rank took a casualty. It was the man behind Plautius, and he was hit by a rock that skipped off the ground to smash into his shin, shattering the bone, forcing him to fall to the ground clutching his leg. As we marched past him, he reached out, grabbing Calienus by the leg, forcing him to alter his stride.

"Don't leave me," he begged. "For the sake of all the gods, don't leave me with those savages!"

Calienus refused to answer, but the wounded man would not relinquish his grasp, and now Calienus was falling behind in a way that endangered the line, which in turn endangered the Century. From the corner of my eye, I saw a flash of silver; Calienus dispatched the man with a quick and merciful thrust, saying loudly for all of us to hear, "If we break ranks, we'll all die. I'll do the same to you, and I expect you to do the same to me if it's needed."

I did not need any more encouragement to keep my place, trying to shut out what I had just seen. Despite knowing it had to be done to ensure the survival of all of us, seeing Calienus kill one of our own was hard to take. Finally, we made it to the base of the hill, even as the cloud of dust had grown closer, and it now looked like there was a sizable force of Lusitani no more than two miles away. The punishment was not all one way; as we made our way up the hill, the warriors opposite us were now walking backwards up the hill when one of them lunged at us to try striking at what he thought was a weak spot in our line with his long *gladius*, but the blow was deflected easily. As he backed up, however, he tripped over his own feet just a couple of paces away from us, but before he could regain his feet, he was done in with a quick thrust, his death met with a howl of outrage from the Lusitani. Reaching the top of the hill, we underwent a brief struggle with a few of the more stubborn warriors who realized the advantage we would have if allowed to stay on the crest. My chest was heaving from the effort and I recognized this as a good sign; the hill was much steeper than it looked, and any advantage we could reap from the situation helped. Even so, things looked bleak until the gods smiled on us, in the form of the Lusitani themselves.

Once it was clear that we would make the crest, the warriors that had steadily harassed us now withdrew to the base of the hill, seemingly content to watch us while they waited for reinforcements. The Pilus Prior did not waste any time; since we were out on a patrol that included destroying crops and chopping down vines and trees, we had a semi-complete set of tools with us, lacking only a turf cutter. Crastinus ordered our Century to dig a defensive ditch, using the spoil for a makeshift rampart, while the other Century remained on guard. We were told to keep our *loricae* and *galeae* on while leaning our *scuta* and *pila* close to hand as we worked, so if I thought I was hot and sweating profusely before, I was mistaken. As I dug, I watched the water pouring off the end of my nose in a steady stream whenever I bent over, and I wondered dully how long it would be before I ran out. There was no time to even drink, let alone rest, so that before long, I was desperately thirsty. Meanwhile, the Lusitani leaders huddled up in a discussion once they saw what we were doing, with a lot of arguing back and forth, men gesturing first to us and then to the dust cloud, which seemed to remain stationary, although we knew that was impossible. Very quickly, the reason for the debate became fairly clear; there was a sizable contingent in the group that considered it vital to attack us immediately to keep us from erecting a defense, no matter how flimsy. This discussion quickly became an argument that grew increasingly heated, a fact that was not lost on us.

"Maybe they'll kill each other first," I heard someone on guard say, and I thought, one can only hope. However, while they bickered, we kept digging, and I, at least, was thankful for the delay.

Crastinus kept exhorting us, calling out so that we could all hear, "Keep it up, boys. The deeper you dig, the safer we'll be."

The trick was to dig a ditch wide enough where they could not leap across it and deep enough so that they could not just simply step down into it without slowing down. Additionally, the deeper and wider the ditch, the higher the rampart, which half our tent section was erecting as the other half dug. For once, even Didius was not shirking, clearly seeing the danger we were in as much as the rest of us. I was digging, while Vibius was packing the spoil to form a rampart, and it was brutal work, the hardest I had performed at that point during my short time in the Legions. Our shovels and pickaxes were flying as we worked frantically, yet the gods were smiling on us because the Lusitani debate quickly degenerated into a physical confrontation, with warriors clearly dividing into two camps, both sides shaking their fists and doing a lot of yelling at each other. Then, someone pushed someone else and all of us, despite our predicament, stopped to watch as a brawl developed among our enemies, so astounding was the sight.

Even the Pilus Prior stood there, mouth open in amazement for a moment, before snapping out of it and snarling at us, "All right, that's enough of the show. Put your backs into it, you *cunni,* or I'll stripe you good."

We immediately turned to again, smiling in spite of the threat.

By the time their reinforcements arrived, assessed the situation, then arrayed themselves to attack us, it was late in the afternoon, and I had never been as tired as I was at that moment. Even with the tension and imminent danger, I was fighting a losing battle against falling asleep on my feet. More than once, I would feel myself pitching forward, only opening my eyes and averting an unforgivable lapse of discipline less than a heartbeat before I reached the point of no return and fell flat on my face. No matter what I told myself, how horribly I cursed my weakness, I could feel the tendrils of sleep curling around my brain. I was struck by the thought that perhaps dying in one's sleep would not be such a bad way to go and, looking at my comrades, I saw they were much in the same condition. Having finished what preparations we could make, we were now standing behind a parapet that stood chest high for most of the men, yet was only just above my waist. The only saving grace, at least as far as I was concerned, was that it was fairly thick and, despite being low for our tastes, we could still kneel down and be covered from most missile weapons, especially if we set our *scuta* on top of the parapet. Not for the first time, we thanked the gods that the Lusitani did not use the bow very often, and we could see there were only a few scattered in the mass of men who surrounded us now. Calienus, being the most experienced, estimated that the new arrivals numbered between 400 and 500 armed men, adding to the 300 or so that ambushed us, although we had whittled that last group down by fifty or thereabouts. Regardless, they were long odds, of which we were all too keenly aware.

Lusitani were milling about at the base of the hill, flowing around it like a flood encircling us, and once again beginning their pre-battle rituals, the sound rolling up to us, steadily growing as they worked themselves into a frenzy. Speaking for myself and, I imagine, a lot, if not all of the other newer men, I was almost beside myself with fright. Looking around to see that we were completely surrounded by a vastly larger force, I could not see any way to get out of this alive, and I was positive our Centuries were about to be wiped out to the last man. Then, I heard someone laugh.

Turning to see Optio Rufio and Calienus walking towards us, I saw that it was Calienus laughing. He and the other section leaders had been called over by the Pilus Prior to be given their orders, and he was returning to relay to us what we were supposed to do. Yet here they were, acting like they were back in camp, strolling along and having a good laugh, just moments or, at the most, a matter of a couple watches before their death. It astonished me, and I could not even begin to fathom how one could be so lighthearted, knowing they were about to perish.

Calienus came to us, with Rufio going to talk to another group, and our Sergeant called us closer, but before he could speak, I blurted out, "What in the name of the gods could be so funny at a time like this?"

Calienus looked at me, eyebrow raised in surprise. "Time like this? What do you mean?"

Then, waving towards the Lusitani, he laughed again. "Oh, you mean this bunch? Do you really think we're in that much danger, Pullus?"

Feeling my face flush, I knew that I was being ridiculed for some reason, but I was not about to just roll over. "We're outnumbered five or six to one, Calienus. Are you saying that's not cause for worry?"

Nodding, he replied, "You're right, Pullus. We are outnumbered, but numbers don't tell the tale." Without being obvious, he indicated the men below us, encircling the hillside, with a nod of his head. "Do you notice anything, Pullus?"

I was still not seeing what he was, and told him so. "What I see are a lot of men down there who want to kill us."

"Yes, but look carefully. They've encircled us, correct?"

Biting back a sharp retort, instead I merely nodded.

"You want to know why I'm not worried? Because they have us surrounded." Thankfully, I could see that I was not the only one who was puzzled. Sighing, he squatted down, indicating that we were to follow suit. Continuing, he explained, "Now, if they were in one big bunch, I'd be very, very worried. See, I know that each one of us can handle five or six of those bastards each, right? I mean, how many kills did you have on the attack on the town, Pullus?"

"More than that," I admitted grudgingly.

"See, their problem is that they're thinking like warriors, not like an army. I promise you that each one of them has picked one of us out that he's sworn to his gods he's going to kill personally."

This made sense and I was beginning to get a glimmer of where he might be going.

"And like I said, each of us can handle a half-dozen of these bastards. Now," he shook his head and smiled, "what would scare me out of my wits is if they were down there, in a formation like we use, and focusing their attack on just one part of the defenses. And if they had a leader half as smart as the Pilus Prior, that's exactly what they'd be doing right now, so thank the gods that they don't. Because if they hit one area, they'd take a lot of casualties, but it'd be a matter of moments before they'd overwhelm that point in the defenses, and that's when our lack of numbers would really show. No," he finished, "this isn't going to be all that difficult to handle."

Calienus started to rise, then Scribonius asked him quietly, "But how long are we going to have to hold this hill? I see that you're right about the way they're going to attack, but I have to believe that it's a good chance that there'll be other Lusitani showing up before too long."

Calienus nodded. "You're right, and I forgot, that's what I was supposed to tell you before I got off course patting Pullus' ass for him." This brought a round of laughter and, despite being the butt of the joke, I found myself joining in. "The Pilus Prior wanted us to pass the word that we'll probably have to hold this hill through the night and the first couple of watches tomorrow, but since we weren't sent on an overnight patrol, Caesar will know that we're in trouble. The command group also knows where we were assigned, so they'll immediately send aid, probably the rest of the Cohort."

This cheered us up immensely; at least having some sort of finite time where we could expect help was a tremendous boost to our morale. Once Calienus was done, we stood and took our places, ready to face the Lusitani.

Pilus Prior Crastinus had ordered us to construct our defense tightly enough that roughly only half of us stood at the parapet at any one time. Although this lowered the number of *gladii* we could bring to bear, it meant that we were able to be relieved, and would have someone else to step in should we fall. Provided that we did not lose more men than we could replace, I remember thinking. In the center of the ring, we piled all of our excess equipment, forming a last-ditch set of breastworks in the event the parapet was breached and became untenable. Naturally, we were forced to lose the cattle and forage when we marched to the hill, but that just gave us one less thing to worry about as far as we were concerned; their numbers could always be made up. Our breastworks were not much, yet perhaps they would serve, but I prayed that we would not have to find out. Once again, I had chosen to be next to Vibius, who gazed out over the waving, threatening mob with an expressionless face.

Sensing that I was looking at him, he turned to me and asked, "Is it in a safe place?"

We both burst out laughing, causing looks of disbelief and snorts of derision to be thrown our way, but we were oblivious to it, quickly finding ourselves laughing hysterically, neither of us able to stop. Finally, we heard the voice of the Pilus Prior growling behind us.

"I wonder if you two laughing boys would find it funny if I pitched both of you on the other side of the ditch?"

That immediately shut us up, so we turned back to our foe, who were just sending forth their slingers, appearing to number about eighty men.

"Slingers!"

Someone shouted the warning and we automatically lifted our *scuta*, resting them side by side on the parapet, creating an impenetrable wall. At least as long as nobody got anxious to have a peek like last time, I thought, though hopefully everyone had learned his lesson. Recalling the pulverized face of the man I walked over during our assault on the town, I knew that I had, at least. Because the slingers were intent on trying to hit all of us, they too were spread around the base of the hill, making the fire much less concentrated than what we faced attacking the wall of that first town. Still, the sound of the lead and rock missiles cracking against the faces of our *scuta* was loud and constant enough to dominate any attempt at conversation. Instead, we were forced to content ourselves with affecting profound boredom, conspicuously yawning to show our comrades that this was now old news for us, and was nothing to give much thought or worry about. Even so, someone had to peek, except this time, it was someone I knew. Didius decided to try to be sly by peeking around the edge of his *scutum*, but his effort was rewarded by a sharp crack, instantly followed by the hollow ring of something striking metal, whereupon he collapsed in a heap. Immediately, the man behind him, kneeling just a few feet away, crawled over to him, looked into his face, and frowned. Despite my loathing of him, I felt a pang of sympathy, remembering that I had seen a missile do exactly the same thing as what appeared to have happened to Didius.

As all this was happening, Romulus, standing next to Didius, called out, "Achilles is down!"

This elicited a sharp reaction from everyone around us, since we were the only ones at that point to use the nickname.

"Who in Hades is Achilles?" snapped the Pilus Prior as he crouched over to us.

"Er…I meant Didius, sir. Sorry."

"You will be, trust me, you little *cunnus*. I don't care if you call him Aphrodite; next time use his proper name so I know who it is. I don't have the time to learn all your pet lover's names." Turning to the man checking on Didius, he asked, "Is he dead?"

Even I was somewhat relieved when the man shook his head. "No, sir. It looks like it deflected off his *scutum* first, then his helmet, and hit him in the forehead. He's out cold, but he's breathing, and it doesn't look like his skull is broken. In fact, there's not much of a bump here at all."

I, along with all my tent mates, twisted our heads sharply, exchanging glances, and I know we were all thinking the same thing.

However, the Pilus Prior, at this point, was unaware of Didius' history and merely ordered, "Then drag him over to the middle behind the breastworks. Maybe he'll come to and be of some use."

The man complied, taking care not to rise above the level of the parapet since the missiles were still whizzing around. Grabbing Didius by the harness, he began dragging him, prompting me to look over at my tent mate once he was at a point where I could clearly see his face. He did have a mark on his forehead, a red bump, but there was no bleeding and it did not look terribly damaging. Just as the man pulled him over the breastworks and I continued watching, my heart leapt when I swore, for just a heartbeat, that I saw Didius open his eyes before quickly shutting them again. Immediately, I told Vibius what I thought I had seen, and he looked back at Didius, who was still lying unconscious, or pretending to, his lips compressed into a thin line of contempt.

"It wouldn't surprise me at all, the bastard," he said quietly.

"Do you think I should tell the Pilus Prior?"

He considered, then shook his head. "The Pilus Prior doesn't know about the ladder, but what he does know is that you two hate each other, so he's unlikely to take what you say seriously."

I nodded; he was right. Besides, there were more important things to worry about at that moment besides one coward, and it was coming up the hill towards us. After waiting a few moments for the slingers to try inflicting damage, with only Didius being brought to the breastworks, heartening as it was, the Lusitani began marching up the hill. Speaking frankly, I can use the word marching only in the loosest sense, since it was more of a shambling half-trot, replete with the usual complement of screaming and hopping. The slingers, because of their position downhill, were forced to lift their barrage almost immediately to avoid hitting their own men, and the Lusitani were rapidly approaching the range of our *pila*.

"Prepare *Pila*!"

At the command, we assumed the position, our right foot back, right arm pulled all the way back with the shaft of the *pilum* lying on the length of the arm, the hardened point aimed skyward to create the arc that helped it pick up momentum. My arm trembled a bit as I readied my body for the effort, choosing not so much a target, but a spot where I wanted it to land, confident that there would be a man occupying that space when it arrived.

"Release!"

The air filled with the black lines that signaled the *pila* in flight, and as I followed through, it brought me to a crouched position where I could look directly at the Lusitani. To a man, they all looked up, trying to catch the flight of our rain of death, hoping that they could isolate and focus on the one that posed the most danger to them personally. Some of them were lucky, yet most in the front rank were not, with almost every *pilum* finding something in which to bury itself. The thuds of our missiles hitting flesh and wood of *scuta* were punctuated by the screams of the men hit and, in turn, they caused a slight pause in the uphill climb as the wounded men crashed into one of their comrades, knocking him down or staggering him, with the dead men becoming obstacles to step over. It did not slow them long, however.

"First line kneel, second line prepare *pila!*"

I immediately knelt, as did the rest of the men on the parapet.

"Release!"

The *pila* went whizzing just over our heads as we watched them arc and again slice into the advancing Lusitani. Another shudder of more men going down, then we in the front rank stood to fire our last salvo.

"Prepare!"

"Release!"

One of the advantages of being on the hill was that it increased the effective range of the *pilum*. Normally, both lines would not have been able to launch two salvos before we had to go to the *gladius*, but we used all of the *pila* we carried, to maximum effect.

Immediately after we finished throwing our second, the Pilus Prior commanded, "Front rank kneel and draw *gladii!*"

The metal made a comforting rasping sound as the blades left the scabbard, even as the second rank discharged their last volley. Quickly estimating that more than two-thirds of our *pila* had hit a target and put it out of action, whether it was a warrior or a *scutum*, it still meant perhaps 150 men were either out of action or severely hampered with no protection. This might have been enough to stop the attack, except the Lusitani by this time had learned that we only carried two *pila* apiece, and if they absorbed the punishment, they would be able to close the distance to fight us hand to hand. That was exactly what happened; after they took a moment to recover from the last volley, a large man wearing one of the high, conical *galeae* and dressed in the fish scale armor that was common of their nobles, waved his *gladius* in the air, moving it in a circle while bellowing a command in their language, before dropping his arm to point at us, the signal for them to stop their steady advance and throw themselves at us at a run.

"Here they come," someone yelled.

"Oh, really? Thank you for alerting us, Hannibal," Calienus muttered, causing us to stifle a nervous laugh as we braced for impact.

Part of the reason for their delay in the attack was that they had gathered together bundles of wood, or were even using our sacks of forage to throw into the bottom of the ditch, allowing them to cross over without having to climb out of it. Hurling everything they gathered into the ditch delayed their charge, as the thought flashed through my mind that we would have been better served waiting to launch our *pila* until that moment and, I had to acknowledge grudgingly, that the Lusitani might have been smarter than we thought. Crossing over their makeshift bridges, they came at us with the usual crash of *scuta* and *gladii*, roaring their rage at us, smashing against what was nothing more than a wall of thin wood and loosely packed dirt. The wall held, but only just as the Lusitani tried to pull our *scuta* down, clawing at the rims to gain a purchase. A grubby hand appeared in front of my face, curling around the top as I felt the man behind it begin to pull and I suppressed a smug smile, knowing that I was stronger than he was and not worried that he would succeed. Very quickly, the smugness disappeared when just a heartbeat after his hand started pulling another hand, quickly followed by another, began tugging as well, and I could feel my grip rapidly weakening under the added pressure. Gritting my teeth, I brought my *gladius* up to hack at the hands, but even with the awkward angle, I was able to lop off several fingers, their screams of agony accompanied by my cry of disgust as the fingers went flying, one of them striking me in the face while another found its way into the gap between my tunic and *lorica*, where I could feel it sliding down to rest above my belt. Bile rose in my throat, but I could not indulge myself in vomiting since I had bought only a temporary reprieve. Immediately, a spear came thrusting over the top of my *scutum*, which I barely ducked, followed by a second thrust aimed at a different point. This one caught me a glancing blow on the helmet, causing a burst of stars to explode in my head and, for a moment, I felt like I was losing my balance and falling backwards, but the man behind me braced me, shoving me back forward.

"Go on, Pullus; have at 'em."

Shaking my head to clear it, I saw the spear come at me for yet a third time, except instead of ducking this time I grabbed the shaft, thankful that my hand was big enough to maintain the grasp on my *gladius* at the same time even with the Vinicius grip, then gave a mighty yank. Even above the din, I could hear a yelp of surprise as I relieved the Lusitani of his weapon, dropping it on the ground next to me. Their initial assault was starting to ebb a bit; we could tell both by the sound and the fact that the hammering against our defenses was slowing as the Lusitani's energy began to flag. So far, nothing had penetrated, yet even as they fell back a little way down the hill to regroup, we knew that another charge was imminent. During the interval, I debated whether I had time to get that damn finger out from under the *lorica* and took a peek, but I saw that they were about to come back. This time, they chose not to work themselves into a lather; on some signal that we did not hear or see, they simply launched themselves at us again. Once more, there was the smash of bodies and metal, this time accompanied by a couple of grunts of surprise from some of the men who were not paying close enough attention.

"This would have been a good time to warn us, boy," griped Calienus. I suppressed a smile, turning my attention to bracing myself as someone tried his best to kill me.

We managed to stop the second attack. By this time, the sun was disappearing over the horizon, apparently prompting the Lusitani to decide that their best course was to withdraw and rest for the night. Having the advantage of numbers, they could afford to actually build fires and eat, while keeping a small portion of their men on guard at any given time. Unfortunately, we did not have that luxury, instead being forced to keep half the men on watch, with the rest of us chewing our cold rations, then trying to get some sleep before relieving the men on guard. The Pilus Prior ordered no fires, both because there was little enough wood and any light could silhouette one of us who might fall prey to an opportunistic slinger. By this time, Didius, his new nickname Achilles now an open joke in the Century, helped along by Remus' spirited retelling of the event that earned it for him, regained consciousness, if he had truly ever been out. Scribonius came to sit next to Vibius and me while we chewed on some salt bacon, quietly discussing our predicament, and we glanced at him curiously. It was not like Scribonius to horn in on others' conversations unless he had something to say, but when he did, he was not usually shy to say it, yet this time, he seemed to struggle to find the right words.

Finally, he whispered, "Did either of you happen to look at Achilles at all while we were fighting?"

We both shook our heads; the last time I remembered glancing his way was right after they dragged him to the breastworks.

"Why do you ask?" At first, Scribonius did not answer Vibius' question, instead staring intently at the ground, his face faintly illuminated by the half moon and the usual cloudless sky. Finally, he shrugged and replied, "It's just that I could have sworn that I looked his way and he was watching us fighting, just like he was lying in his bunk."

This caused me to straighten up; so I was not mistaken! Excitedly, I whispered back, "I saw it too. I thought I must have been seeing something, but I swore I saw him peeking at us."

Sitting there for a moment, all three of us were clearly unable to speak. The implications were enormous; if Didius was accused by us and was found guilty, he would be crucified in front of the entire army, but not before he was scourged first as an example to all of what happened to cowards. As much as I despised him, I was not sure that I wanted the burden of such a horrible death on my conscience.

With that in my mind, I looked at Scribonius and asked, "What do you think we should do?"

He thought for a moment, then shook his head. "I don't think there's anything we can do."

This did not sit well with me, or Vibius, for that matter, and we both spoke up in protest, which Scribonius silenced with a wave of his hand.

"Think about it, Pullus. It's well known that you hate him, and he you. And it's well known that he threatened you. I went and got Vellusius to split with him as close comrade, so there'll be suspicions about me as well."

He paused to let this sink in, and I realized he was right.

However, I still did not feel right about it. "There has to be something we can do."

Vibius spoke. "There is. But we can't do it now. We'll have to wait until we get back to the main camp."

As I searched his face in the gloom, it bore no hint of what he had in mind, so I accepted this idea with a shrug, as did Scribonius. With that matter temporarily settled, we lay down, pulling our cloaks from our packs to keep out the evening chill, aware that getting as much rest as possible under the circumstances was vital. It was not until I lay down that I was struck by a thought, sitting bolt upright with a curse, startling Vibius and the other men around me.

"What in the name of Dis has gotten into you?" Vibius demanded.

Ignoring him, I quickly undid my harness instead, then climbed to my knees, shaking my *lorica* until something dropped out. Vibius obviously heard something plop on the ground, and asked curiously, "What was that?"

I did not answer; instead, I picked up the finger, then held it close enough for him to see what it was. He squinted as I moved it

286

almost under his nose, then his eyes shot open in shock and he recoiled.

"You bastard!"

He said this loudly enough for others to drown him out with orders to shut his mouth, and I don't think I had ever laughed that hard in my life. Throwing the finger out over the parapet and still chuckling, I lay back down, falling asleep immediately.

Suddenly awakened by the call "To arms!" I opened my eyes to chaos. Men on relief were scrambling to their feet, fumbling for their weapons in the dark, while all around us was the crashing din and cries of men fighting.

"What's happening?" Vibius called out as we tried to make sense of the situation.

Out of the dark, the answer made our hearts drop.

"The wall's been breached!"

Whirling around, I tried to determine where the danger was coming from, but doing so was extremely difficult because of the gloom. Consequently, it took a moment before I could determine where the sounds of battle seemed to be emanating from, and I turned to Vibius who had just finished pulling on his helmet. Indicating he was ready, we began making our way to the sounds of the battle, but the bulk of the Pilus Prior suddenly appeared from the dark, and I felt his rough hand grab my arm.

"Where do you think you're going, you big oaf?" he growled.

"To the fighting, Pilus Prior."

I could barely make out the crest on his helmet moving as he sneered, "And what if this is just a diversion? That's just what the *cunni* want us to do."

"But I thought the wall was breached."

He laughed. "That's just some woman posing as a Legionary saying that. They attacked, all right, but they haven't breached anything yet and aren't going to, unless you fall for a trap like that."

Chastened, I turned back in the direction of where I thought my position was, with him giving me a helping shove to get back to my post. Stumbling back over to our designated area, where those comrades already on watch were still standing, Vibius and I joined them to peer into the dark. A short distance away, we could see the winking lights of the enemy campfires, the Lusitani camping far enough away where it was impossible to determine whether there were men gathered around it.

"Figures those bastards would pull a stunt like this and put us on full alert so we won't get a wink of sleep. Or a bite to eat."

Vaguely, I recognized the voice of a man in the second section, since the first five had drawn first duty, and I sympathized, but sleep was now out of the question, at least for me, so I spoke up. "How about we take over and you boys go get your rations, as long as you promise to come back here quick so we all don't get on the punishment list for deserting our posts?"

I sensed a movement as someone turned to peer in my direction in the gloom, trying to make out who their benefactor was. "Pullus, is that you? That's a splendid idea. May Fortuna smile on you for thinking of us and grant you long life."

I flushed with pleasure as they hurried by, proud of myself for what I had done.

"You do realize that when he's wishing you a long life, it just means that he's wishing the same for himself, since if you live, the chances are good he will too." This came from Vibius, who always had a knack for finding the rat turd in the honey.

"You don't know that," I responded indignantly, "because I may die a week from now, and he might die tomorrow."

"True, but first, we have to get through tonight."

Pilus Prior Crastinus had been right; the attack was a diversion. Apparently, during their council of war, they decided on a different approach than what they used during their daylight attack, instead setting out to do the worst thing that they could under our circumstances, what we had feared since we climbed the hill, or at least since Calienus made us aware of it. As they were making a demonstration on one side, the bulk of the remaining Lusitani, using their skills as hunters, climbed stealthily up to within a few paces of the wall before leaping up with a great cry. It was as if apparitions from the underworld just materialized from the ground, the kind of *numen* that mothers tell young children about to make them behave. Faint moonlight glinted silver on their brandished weapons as they closed the distance to the wall in a matter of a few heartbeats, with the main impact several paces away from me. Even though the Lusitani focused their attack across a narrow area, we could not afford to move to help the others trying to hold them back since the Lusitani in the rear ranks would immediately shift from their spot to flow over the deserted wall like a raging flood sweeps away an earthen barrier. Consequently, we were forced to endure the sounds of fighting, more furious than ever before and, for the first time, we heard the cries of our own men dying, crying out in our tongue as they fell. Gripping my *gladius* tightly, as if it would help me to shut out the sounds, I kept my eye on the area in front of me and I am sure that my comrades were trying to do the same thing. I heard the bellows of the Pilus Prior, along with Pilus Posterior Vetruvius, exhorting the men around them to hold, using a combination of threats and promises as a means to motivate our men to fight ever harder. For the second time that night, we heard the cry that the wall was breached, and I peered hard in that direction, trying to determine whether this was another false alarm. It did seem that this time there was more of a tumult, an impression of a flurry of movement, while the noise changed, sounding nearer than ever before. Gritting my teeth, I turned to head over in that direction, but a hand pushed at my chest.

"You can't leave, Pullus." This was Calienus, and I knew that I should turn back to my post, yet I had made up my mind.

"I have to, Sergeant; they need our help."

"Maybe, but we haven't been given orders to move yet."

"I think that it's too dark for anyone to fully know what's going on," I replied desperately, pushing against his hand.

"So you know better than the Pilus Prior?" This provoked a laugh from Calienus, and I could tell that he was not going to bend. But neither was I, so I used my size once again to bear over him.

"Sergeant, I'm going over there. If you want to have me flogged for it, fine. But I know they need our help."

Pushing past him, I was torn that he did not try to stop me, since a large part of me was screaming at myself to stay put, and I walked perhaps only ten paces when something came rolling out of the gloom to bounce into my legs. Almost tripping and falling, I just managed to catch myself, then moved to kick whatever it was away, but when my foot touched something wet, warm, and yielding, I peered down and again had to fight the urge to vomit. It was a head, and even in the gloom, I could see that there was a Roman helmet on top of it.

I walked into the jaws of Cerberus. It was not a false alarm; the wall in fact was breached and the struggle to contain the incursion created an inward bulge as the Lusitani pushed across the barrier. They were now feeding men into this pocket that their warriors created, trying desperately to exploit the crack in our defenses. Even as I drew closer, it was hard to tell exactly what was going on as men slashed and hacked at our thin line, now reduced to a single line of Legionaries desperately holding them back. The Pilus Prior was bellowing out; locating him from the sound of his voice, I rushed to a spot in the line as far away from him as I could get. I knew I was taking a huge risk defying the latest order I was given, but I reasoned that if things were as bad as they appeared, we were all dead men anyway, and if we turned them back, it would take all of us to do so.

Picking a man, I braced him from behind, causing him to glance back. "Thanks, I was about done in," I heard him gasp.

"When you get a chance, I'll relieve you," I answered and instantly a small voice inside me began cursing myself. What was I volunteering for? Certain death? I could do my part right where I was, the voice said. You're already in enough trouble, Titus old boy, without compounding it by putting yourself in a position where you will certainly be killed. Such is the nature of that voice, one I have learned is in every Legionary, and I suspect in all of us. There seems to be a part of you whose only goal is to keep you alive, at all costs, yet what makes man different from the rest of all the animals is that we can choose not to listen to that voice. Ignoring that voice is what defines us, at least in the Legions. So when I felt the man in front of me make a huge effort, tensing up just before thrusting his *scutum* into the body of a Lusitani to send him staggering back, I took my cue, moving quickly into his place. Panting his thanks, I felt him holding me an instant later as the man he threw off came back, sending a shock up my arm when he smashed his blade into my *scutum*, turning my arm numb. In the darkness, I could not tell much about the man except for his size, which was average, despite packing quite a punch for his stature. He came at me again, his second blow as strong as the first, and I could feel my grip slipping as the numbness spread to my hand and fingers, knowing that another blow like that might knock the *scutum* from my hand. Instead of waiting for it, I took a half step forward, lashing out with the *scutum*, using my boss as the weapon and I was gratified to hear a crunching sound accompanied by a muffled scream as I smashed his face. Stunned by the pain, he was standing there, stationary, making a perfect target for the thrust of the *gladius* that I followed up with and he toppled over, falling on top of what appeared to be a Legionary. My first kill was immediately replaced by another man, his outline in the dark telling me he was slightly larger, except he used his body as a weapon, smashing into me and thinking to knock me back. However, I was braced by my comrade behind me, so when he reached out to grab hold of the rim of the *scutum*, with a grim smile I struck, this time taking the whole hand instead of just fingers. This was the pattern for the next few moments; truthfully, I have no idea how much time went by, but judging from the fatigue I felt when there was a brief respite, it was a substantial period. I was satisfied that there was now a small pile of dead and dying in front of me, the wounded still trying to crawl to safety, making the tangle of limbs and torsos shift eerily in front of me in the moonlight, and if I had not known the cause, I might have thought there was something otherworldly about it. Someone tapped me on the shoulder, the man behind me asking if I wanted to be relieved. Just as I was about to say yes, I thought better of it and shook my head. Thinking back, I believe this was the first appearance of a trait and belief that I developed over the years, which was my reluctance to trust my fate to others if I was able to have any say in it. Part of it was the hubris of youth, to be sure; however, it was also based in a belief I have in myself that I am the best arbiter of my destiny and whenever possible, I should take control of the situation. I will say that he did not argue too hard about it.

The respite lasted perhaps a span of fifty normal heartbeats, certainly no longer, before the assault was renewed and finally our wall of men protecting the pocket from expansion broke when a Legionary fell from a wound and there was nobody to step into his place. Hearing the roar of triumph from the Lusitani, I immediately sensed a flurry of movement as their men rushed to exploit the gap, accompanied by the shout of our two Centurions as they met the enemy from their spot behind us. The clash of metal and the thuds of blows to the wood of our *scutum* wall increased as well, the growth of the pocket meaning that more men could fill it.

"All those on relief on me, at the double!"

This came from the Pilus Prior and the message was unmistakable; the enemy was within our thin dirt wall. Turning to my relief, I gasped out, between exchanging blows with a man who stank of onions, "Here, you take my place and I'll go."

He had already turned to leave, but came back readily enough, patting me on the back to let me know he was there. The onion man, wielding a huge club, swung it over his head in an obvious attempt to inflict a devastating downward blow that would split my *scutum* and dash my brains out at one stroke, but I was ready, launching a simple thrust over the top of my *scutum* before he could bring the club down, hitting him in the throat. Feeling the grating of bone that told me the blade had exited the back of his head, I withdrew as quickly as I struck. In the time it took for him to collapse, I moved aside, breathlessly thanking my relief as I hurried to the Pilus Prior's voice. As I tripped a couple of times on bodies at my feet, one of them uttered a short cry before hurling curses at me as I stepped over him, while I mumbled an apology. I reached a spot where I could make out the Pilus Prior, who was now as engaged as the rest of the men around him. I could not help admiring his form and economy, seeing his blade glint in the moonlight, making a silvery streak in the air as it struck, each blow being rewarded with a scream or gasp of pain and surprise. Then I saw another one of our men go down, alive but wounded, before attempting to pull his body under his *scutum*, dragging it on top of himself as the victor stepped over him while drawing his arm back to drive his spear into the back of the Pilus Prior, who was engaged with another Lusitani. Letting out the loudest bellow of rage that I had ever uttered, it startled the Lusitani just enough that it stayed his hand for the fraction of the heartbeat that I needed to jump across the space between us. Crastinus was just starting to turn at the sound of my shout as, while still in midair, I violated the elementary rule that the point beats the edge, swinging my arm while twisting my body to add to the force and, in one smooth motion, my blade sliced through the tissue and bone that composed the Lusitani's neck. His head flew up in the air as I landed, tumbling crazily and spurting blood in all directions as the torso, the heart still sending a fountain of blood spraying several inches in the air above the stump of his neck, stood for a second, as if trying to decide what to do before crumpling in a heap to the ground. When I landed, it was with one foot striking another body, so that for a sickening moment, I found my arms whirling as I tried to maintain my balance, knowing that if I went to the ground, I was dead. Finally managing to restore my footing, I saw the Pilus Prior peering at me in the gloom, trying to determine who had just saved him, and I gave him a wave and a smile.

"Is that you, Pullus?" he asked, his surprise obvious.

"Yes, Pilus Prior, and you're welcome." I don not know what I was expecting him to say, but it certainly was not what came out of his mouth.

"Welcome, am I? We'll see how welcome I am once I've striped your back, you *cunnus*. I seem to remember telling you specifically to remain at your post."

"But…" I was cut off before I could finish my protest.

"But nothing. Those were your orders and you disobeyed them. Your ass is mine."

Without another word, he turned back to face another Lusitani, parrying a blow as easily as if he were waving his *vitus* around. I was stunned, but I was also angry, so I turned it on the Lusitani. With another roar, I waded into a small knot of men engaged in a desperate struggle, knocking both Lusitani and Roman aside to begin thrusting, hacking, and swinging my *gladius* about, barely registering when I scored any kind of hit except by the shouts or screams of men I wounded or killed. Disdaining the use of my *scutum* for any kind of defense, instead I began swinging it about, smashing into both friend and foe that stood in my way. I felt myself giving way to the anger and rage I felt inside, that instead of gratitude, I faced a flogging from the Pilus Prior for saving his life. It also angered me that these men were trying to kill me, that men like Didius could shirk their duties of defending Rome; it angered me that Juno picked Vibius over me, that Vibius beat me at dice just the night before, and it angered me that my father hated me because in my birth, I had killed the only thing he ever loved. In that moment, I felt the rage surge through me, washing over me in a warm flood, giving me more energy than I had ever experienced in my life. Feeling the blood spattering my face, instead of my normal revulsion, I reveled in it, loving the warm sticky fluid as it started to dry on my skin. Becoming dimly aware that the roars of triumph coming from the Lusitani were turning into cries of alarm, it only fueled me to keep killing and maiming. It was in that moment that I knew I had found my purpose in life; I was a killer, a machine, and there was nothing that could stand in my way and live if I did not wish it to be so.

My next conscious memory is standing alone, panting, my legs trembling and feeling the fatigue so greatly that I could not lift my arms, even if it meant my life to do so. I also became gradually aware that the noise of battle was gone; not totally, but certainly the furious sounds of frantic combat had disappeared. The wider world around me slowly came into focus, and it surprised me when I noticed that I seemed to be standing by myself, so I peered around in the dark until I saw several Roman *galeae* profiled against a lightening sky. It appeared that all heads were turned towards me as I continued my return by noting that the ground around me seemed to be piled much higher with bodies than anywhere else. With my breathing slowing, I felt a slight surge of energy coming back, so I began to move towards my original position on the wall, and was annoyed to find that I had to lift my leg like I was climbing a low fence, except this one was made of flesh and bone, some of which was still moving and emitting low moans. I was unbelievably weary, to the point that all I wanted to do was to sit down somewhere and rest, especially once the memory of the words I had exchanged with the Pilus Prior came back to me. If I was going to be flogged, I wanted to be as fresh as I could get. By this point, the fighting had almost completely ceased; I heard the clash of metal on metal and shouts over where the diversion started, except there was none of the urgency in the voices of the section leaders and the men in that spot. Very quickly, I was surrounded by my comrades, two of them stepping aside to let me through without saying a word, for which I was thankful, because I was barely able to move; adding talking to the burden, I felt sure would cause me to collapse. Steering myself in the direction of where my gear was lying on the ground just behind where I had been posted on the wall, I focused on just putting one foot in front of the other. A slight breeze blew, except instead of being refreshed, I felt clammy and was surprised to realize that every part of my body where open skin showed was wet, and as the breeze did its work to dry the moisture, I could feel my skin tighten as whatever covered me cooled. It must be blood, I thought. That did not stop me from finding my gear, feeling in the dark to count from the end of the pile to where mine would be, before collapsing more than sitting down. Not even bothering to shed my *lorica*, I laid down my *scutum*, then arranged my *gladius* so it was not in the way, removed my helmet, and fell backwards, asleep before my head hit the ground. The fact that I was violating all sorts of regulations and had not been given leave to rest did not even cross my mind.

I was awakened by a kick to my feet, opening my eyes to a blinding sun shining right in my eyes. Jerking alert, I sat up immediately, trying to clear my head a bit as I strained to see who it was standing above me, outlined like a god coming down from the heavens with the sun behind him. It was no god, just the Optio, and his face was expressionless when he spoke.

"Get up, Pullus. The Pilus Prior wants to see you now."

Groaning, partly from the soreness I felt as I got up, but more because of the dread of facing Pilus Prior Crastinus' wrath, I got to my feet, swaying a little, and the Optio put out a quick hand to steady me.

"Easy, Pullus. Well," he shook his head after looking me up and down, "you're quite a sight, but it'll have to do. You all right now?"

Without waiting for an answer, he turned and led me to where the Pilus Prior was standing with the section leaders. I estimated that it was at least two parts of a watch past sunrise, and I was surprised that I was not roused earlier. All of the carnage from the night before was now clear to see, causing my step to falter as I looked around at the mangled bodies and the huge dark spots on the ground where men's lifeblood had left their body to return to the earth. Work parties were carrying corpses and throwing them into a pile of enemy dead, but I was more concerned with the bodies wearing our uniform and I looked around for a spot where they might be laid. Surveying the surroundings, I saw there was one spot with a concentration of bodies much higher than what was strewn around the rest of our makeshift walls, identifiable as well by the fact that they were on the inside of the dirt barrier. I was almost to the Pilus Prior when I frowned; while everyone was still wearing their gear, and there were Legionaries on the wall facing where the Lusitani camp was, there were still a significant number of men who were busy with other tasks. From where I was, I could not see over the wall to their camp to see what the Lusitani were doing, and I was unable to pay any more attention because I was now standing in front of the Pilus Prior.

Coming to *intente*, I saluted in my best parade ground fashion and barked out, "*Gregarius* Titus Pullus reporting as ordered, sir."

Crastinus continued directing the section leaders as I stood there. He was clearly ignoring me, only fueling my sense of anxiety, and I tried not to fidget as I waited for him to turn his attention to me. Once finished with them, the section leaders dispersed, among them Calienus, who was sporting a bandage on his upper arm and a slash along his jaw. Meeting my eyes as he passed me, he did not say anything; the shake of his head was eloquent enough. Once they were away, I continued standing there, trying to tell myself that the shaking in my legs was because I was still tired, but Crastinus continued to ignore me, barking out orders to some of the nearby Legionaries. Finally, after what seemed like a third of a watch, but was probably no more than a hundred heartbeats, he turned his full attention to me, looking me up and down, his face expressionless, the invisible man with the turd again taking the day off. Staring at a spot above him, out of the corner of my eye, I could see the fatigue in his face, the lines etched by the countless days of weather and sun even deeper now than before, with the rings under his eyes making it look like he had been punched in the face. It was the first time I saw Gaius Crastinus as just a man, like me and the rest of my comrades, and not some demigod sent by Mars to torment young Legionaries. When he spoke, it was not in his command voice, but with a tone I had never heard from him before, even the one night when we were sworn in.

"You know, if I were to abide by the regulations, I should have you scourged at the very least, and scourged and crucified at the very worst."

My jaw clenched as the fear caused by his words struck deep into my heart. Besides the pain, the shame and humiliation would be unbearable, and I was already regretting my rashness. Then, a miracle happened.

"But," my heart did another skip, "it wouldn't be very gracious to kill a man who saved my life. Besides," he continued, "it wouldn't help morale, seeing as how you also probably saved the lives of the rest of the Century, not to mention the Second's as well."

Shaking his head, he tried to suppress a smile; his words had already unburdened my soul and I could feel my chest beginning to swell with pride.

"What you did last night, boy, was one of the stupidest things I've seen in all my years under the standards, but it was also the bravest. I told you once that I thought you might have a future in the Legions, and last night didn't change my mind."

Fighting the urge to smile, that urge was blown away like smoke in a strong breeze with his next words. Stepping close to whisper in my ear so only I could hear, there was no mistaking his tone, even at a whisper.

"But if you ever disobey me again, I don't care how decorated or famous you are, I'll gut you myself, and I'll make it look like you were killed in battle and nobody will ever know. Do you understand me?"

"Yes, sir."

It seemed crystal clear to me that this was the only answer I could give, especially since I held no doubt whatsoever that he was completely serious, and capable of doing what he promised. I could handle myself and more with the barbarian tribes, but I harbored no illusions how long I would last with a man like Crastinus. Just as quickly, he switched back to a human being and clapped me on the shoulder.

"Good. And we'll speak no more about it. I know I won't have to."

Making my way back to my section's gear, I passed the area where the bodies of our dead were laid out, and I am somewhat ashamed to record the relief that I felt when I saw faces I recognized, but none from my own Century. There were nine men on the ground, and as I moved on, I saw an even larger group, all of them in varying degrees of distress from their wounds. One man was moaning while the *medici* who was assigned to us did what he could to make him as comfortable as one can be when the only thing keeping one's guts inside their body is a linen bandage. It will be ten dead at least, I thought as I walked past, then I spotted Romulus sitting on the ground, a bandage on his head obscuring one eye. It struck me with dread at the thought that he might be maimed and unable to continue in the Legions, except I was too timid to ask him, so I decided I would ask Remus when I saw him, since he would undoubtedly know. I found my tent mates seated by their gear, eating their morning meal. Vibius, looking up and seeing me, smiled and rose to his feet, then the others saw me, whereupon they too stood. I slowed as I got near; this was not how I was usually greeted.

Vibius stepped forward and, ignoring the gore that was still caked on me and my gear, embraced me, and whispered, "You crazy bastard. If the Lusitani hadn't killed you, I swore I was going to for scaring me so badly. But now when I see you, I'm just happy that you're still alive."

"Me too."

There was nothing more said before the rest of my comrades were on me, pounding me on the back and congratulating me. Only two men hung back; Didius, which did not surprise me, but Calienus was the other, which did, and I was mystified by the reception.

"Everyone in the Century is talking about it," Scribonius explained. "You single-handedly saved both Centuries last night. Those bastards had broken through and it was you who stopped them and saved all of us."

I did not know what to say, but in truth, I was not of a mind to dispute what was said. When you are young and dream of glory, how hard are you going to argue when such honors are laid at your feet?

The Lusitani had withdrawn; they approached under a flag of truce while I was asleep early in the morning asking to retrieve their wounded, which the Pilus Prior granted. They left behind almost 300 dead, out of an original force estimated to be between 500 and 600 strong. My tent mates claimed that there were less than a hundred unscathed, the rest being wounded to various degrees. Our butcher's bill ended up with ten dead, twelve wounded that would return at some point to full duty, and another nine whose wounds were disabling to the point where they would be put out of the Legion on permanent disability. Added to that were the four men we lost when we moved to the hill. It did not matter whether they were killed outright, or had been too seriously wounded like the man who grabbed at Calienus' ankle; once they fell, they were dead men. I was just happy that Romulus was not one of those too badly wounded to continue under the standard, sustaining a serious wound just above his eye, while the eye itself was spared. The scar he carried gave him the look of a pirate or brigand of some sort, except much to our surprise and chagrin, we discovered that it seemed to be a point of attraction to the ladies, who would coo and flutter about him, asking him how he got it. It was not long before some of us were hoping that we could someday be mutilated in the face to enable us to become the object of the same kind of attention.

Even as the Lusitani were finishing up the gathering of their wounded and making preparations to retreat, a column of dust started drifting towards us, the sign that Crastinus had been correct; help was indeed on the way. While we waited for the relief column to arrive, the Pilus Prior sent small groups of men out foraging for wood to build funeral pyres, and some sort of animal, preferably a white goat or sheep, to sacrifice during the funeral rites. Although the latter group came back empty handed, it turned out that it did not matter. As usual, Caesar thought of everything so that when he dispatched the column in relief, he sent along the proper animals for sacrifice, knowing that we would have had casualties. It was also a subtle message to all of us that said he knew the only reason we could possibly be delayed was because we were locked in desperate battle. The remaining men were detailed to dig a pit to throw in the bodies of the Lusitani, with a small number of men standing guard. Between the beating we had just given them, and the sight of the column, Crastinus was convinced that the Lusitani would not do anything foolish and just be content instead to limp off with their tails between their legs. I was exempted from duties as a reward for my antics the night before, yet after a few moments, I could not watch my friends digging without getting up to help, so I pitched in. It also helped pass the time, and gave us a chance to recount the events of the day before. In between shovelfuls, Atilius gave a running commentary on everything that happened as he saw it, with the others adding in their own obol's worth.

"Yeah, I thought we were well and truly fucked," he said as he threw another spade's worth of dirt out of the hole, "because I couldn't see a damn thing and all I could hear was that abominable screeching they do when they attack."

"I was pissed because I'd just gotten off light duty," added Vellusius, still working at a disadvantage because although the bone was healed, he had lost some range of motion in his arm, making activities like shoveling painful. "I thought, by the gods, if I get wounded again and put back in the hospital, I'll go mad." His face was red and he was dripping sweat at a much faster rate than the rest of us, and despite doing his best to hide it, we all saw how much strain this was putting on him. However, when we suggested that he could stand down to let the rest of us dig, he refused. "I've been lying about long enough. I need to pull my weight just like everyone else."

I do not know if it was meant in the way it was taken; all I do know is that immediately after Vellusius spoke those words, every eye shifted to Didius, who as usual was doing more leaning on his shovel than actually working with it. Of course, he noticed immediately and scowled at us collectively, with extra malice towards Vellusius. However, he was wise enough this time to keep his mouth shut. The bump on his head was still noticeable, but only just, and was certainly not enough of a justification to put himself on the sick list, although I was a bit surprised that he did not try.

Atilius, who was sporting a massive bruise on his thigh just above his knee, courtesy of a bouncing rock from a sling and so was hobbling a bit, added, "I got knocked down, and I knew I had had it. 'Atilius old son,' I said to myself, 'if you get out of this one, it'll be because of the divine intervention of Fortuna herself. You better show her how grateful you are if she sees fit to spare you.'"

"Well, she obviously did, so what kind of sacrifice are you going to make?" Vibius asked.

"You know, I've been thinking about that." Atilius stopped digging for a moment. "I don't know what's appropriate. What do you boys think?"

This engendered a debate on what would be a proper measure of gratitude, before we finally decided on a white kid goat.

"How much do those cost, I wonder?"

Scribonius supplied a guess. "I shouldn't think more than twenty sesterces."

Atilius almost choked. "Twenty sesterces! By Dis, I'm not THAT grateful. She'll have to do with something less than that, then."

We laughed at that, prompting a visit by the Pilus Prior to bark at us, saying that if we had breath to laugh, we were not working hard enough. The section all stood at *intente*, faces made of stone and with hearts as pure as the Vestal Virgins' until he stalked off, whereupon we picked up where we left off, just more quietly this time.

The grave was dug, with the grisly task of pulling bodies over and throwing them in the pit falling to us as well, and we paired up. Vibius and I worked out a system whereby we alternated grabbing the legs or the arms, because holding the legs in most cases is the least unpleasant since you are farther away from the gore of the wounds that killed them. Sometimes, though, the bodies were in pieces and we would find ourselves carrying some limbs, or just a torso, which was the worst. The sun beating down ensured that it did not take long for the stench to get to a point where it was not only noticeable, but was becoming hard to bear, spurring us on to finish as fast as we could. Once all the bodies and parts were collected and thrown into the ground, we covered them up with dirt. It is a strange sensation when one looks down into a hole and sees a face staring back up at you, with open eyes and a mouth still set in the expression they were wearing when death claimed them. For some, it was a look of surprise; for others it was a look of terror, and still others a look of pure anger and hatred. It was these last that I did not mind throwing dirt over to hide their visage, while for the others, I felt a sort of sadness as I interred them, and I remember wondering what sights their eyes would be missing from that point on. They would never see their women again, or their children grow up. They would not revel in another sunrise or sunset, or stare into a fire and think the private thoughts that all men have at some point in their lives. But they had chosen their path, I thought, and this was where it led them. Pity is not an emotion in which a Legionary can indulge, and I resolved to myself that I would banish such unseemly feelings from me, no matter how hard it might be.

While we were busy digging the grave and filling it up, the Second Century, now being aided by the Second and Third Cohort that had been dispatched to come to our aid, built funeral pyres for our dead, using the scented oils for such ceremonies that were sent along with our rescuers. The fact that we actually needed no rescue was a source of great pride to all of us, and it gave us a bit of a swagger from that day onwards. The news of our stand spread throughout the army and I would be remiss if I did not add that it was at this point my name first became known to more than just the men in my Legion. Our dead were laid on the pyre, their bodies and uniforms cleaned up, then wrapped in linen, as is our custom. One of the priests attached to the Legion was sent along with the Cohorts to perform the ceremony, and we stood in formation as the pyres were lit and our comrades consumed by the cleansing flames. We had been so busy that none of us had time to clean up our own gear, but that could not be helped and, once the fire died down, their ashes were collected, the ashes from each put into ten urns that would be sent to their families. With that duty performed, we formed up to march back to the main camp. Our Century was given the place of honor, just behind the vanguard, while our wounded were loaded on the wagons brought by the relieving force. As we marched away, none of us could stop ourselves from giving a last glance back at the little hill where we had made our stand. The dirt wall was still there, the breached part of the wall clearly visible, and there was still the normal debris strewn around that signifies a battle has taken place; only the bodies were missing, but one could still clearly see the darkened splotches where men had fallen. It was on that hill that we truly became veterans, and from that day forward, the First Century of the Second Cohort of the 10th Legion was no longer treated as if we were still new *Gregarii*. We had been in the Legions a total of four months and two weeks.

Our return to camp was also the occasion of my first face-to-face conversation with Caesar. Since Caesar ordered that we would stay in the same camp for an extra day, we were given time to clean and mend our gear, which in my case meant a lot of vigorous scrubbing, using a stiff horsehair brush to get the caked blood and gore from between the links of my *lorica*, a process that took the better part of an afternoon by the time I felt presentable. The next morning, after our morning meal and formation that was held whenever we were not packing up to march and where the orders of the day are passed along, the Pilus Prior held me back while dismissing the others.

He looked at me critically, eying me up and down, reaching out to make an adjustment here and wipe off some speck of something there, before he said curtly, "Follow me."

Then he turned to head toward the *Praetorium*, slowing enough for me to catch up and walk beside him, unusual in itself and increasing my anxiety. The thought that perhaps my transgression was not forgiven flitted through my mind, but I instantly dismissed it. I was sure that I would have sensed that the Pilus Prior experienced a change of heart at some point before this, yet that only lessened my anxiety a fraction. For such is the nature of the ordinary *Gregarii* that any type of summons to headquarters is enough to send the stomach down to one's feet and one's heart up into the throat. Even for someone like me, who had decided that he did not want to be just one of the faceless masses of men who were in the Legions, it was still a cause for concern.

"Right, now listen up," the Pilus Prior spoke quietly so that only I could hear. "I turned in my report to the Legate, who forwarded it on to Caesar, who interviewed me himself. He wants to meet you."

It is hard to describe which emotion I felt first, or the strongest between exhilaration and fear. The best way to put it is that it was not dissimilar to the feeling one gets before going into battle, and I swallowed down the lump in my throat.

"So what should I do?"

He looked at me sharply. "Do? You don't do a damn thing. You answer his questions with a Yes, Sir or No, Sir, and otherwise, keep your mouth shut. Got it?"

I nodded, except I was still troubled. "What if he asks me a question that doesn't have a yes or no answer?"

The Pilus Prior puffed out his cheeks impatiently, and snapped, "Then you answer the damn question, but use as few words as you possibly can."

Nodding again, I was about to say something else, but knowing the look that the Pilus Prior had on his face, I kept my mouth shut. Approaching the guards, we were stopped and the Pilus Prior stated our business. One of them entered the headquarters tent, returning a moment later to motion us in. The Pilus Prior removed his helmet, placing it under his left arm, and I followed suit, then he took a breath, squared his shoulders, and marched inside, with me following behind him. The tent was brightly lit with many lamps, and there were a number of scribes, all of them with their own desk, copying out orders of one sort or another. Tribunes were hurrying about carrying wax tablets, looking their normal officious selves and, out of the corner of my eye, I caught sight of Doughboy engaged in conversation with another Tribune slightly younger than he was. I had seen him before, but did not know his name, and made a mental note to ask the Pilus Prior about him. He was a little unusual for a Tribune in that he had an air about him that betrayed a sense of competence, and the few times I was around him, I also noticed that he did not speak to us *Gregarii* as if he thought his *cac* did not stink.

Crastinus and I made our way across the outer room and into the section that acted as Caesar's office, separated by a doorway made from a leather flap that could be pulled aside. I am not sure what I was expecting, but it was not what I saw. Knowing that Caesar was a patrician from an old family, I expected his office to reflect his status and be filled with all sorts of luxury items and ornate decorations. Instead, there was a simple desk directly across from the flap, noticeable only because it was larger than the other two in the room, those against each wall of the tent, and each with its own scribe. Caesar was standing behind his desk, reading from a scroll while simultaneously dictating to the scribes and it was here that I got my first glimpse of one of the things that most people know about him today and made him the greatest man of our age, or any other, for that matter. He would dictate a sentence to the scribe on his left, who would begin writing rapidly, and while waiting for him to finish, he turned to the scribe on his right, dictating yet another sentence on a totally different topic, all the while his eyes never leaving the scroll that he was reading. He only stopped when the Pilus Prior and I approached, with the both of us halting the prescribed distance from his desk to give him our best parade ground salute.

"Secundus Pilus Prior Gaius Crastinus, of the 10th Legion, reporting with Legionary *Gregarius* Titus Pullus as ordered, sir."

Caesar laid the scroll on the desk to acknowledge our salute with the same solemnity and gravity that it was given. For a moment, he said nothing, just inspecting the two of us, spending more of his attention on me as I kept my eyes locked at a point above his head, yet even so, knowing that I was being inspected by the general commanding the entire army ignited in me the queerest feeling I had ever experienced in my life to that point. It was a mixture of pride, apprehension, exhilaration, and not a little bit of anxiety, all while I tried to remember the Pilus Prior's instructions. His inspection done, Caesar smiled, then walked around the desk to face me, doing something that I will never forget.

Extending his hand, he said with a smile, "*Salve, Gregarius* Titus Pullus. The Pilus Prior has told me of your valor in your engagement, and I wanted to offer you my hand in thanks."

I did not know what to do; this was so far out of anything I had contemplated that I was flummoxed, but the habits of a lifetime saved me and, more importantly, Caesar any real embarrassment, as before I could even think about it I extended my hand and we shook hands in the Roman manner, clasping each other's forearms. His hand was warm, and I could feel the calluses formed by many hours practice with the *gladius*. Most importantly, his hand was not like a wet and clammy fish, his grip instead strong and dry. Before I could stop myself, I looked down at him, meeting his eyes, yet despite my horror at this slip in discipline, he did not seem to take any umbrage whatsoever. His eyes carried a measure of warmth that I was not expecting, with none of the disdain I saw in those of men like Doughboy when talking to their social inferiors. It was the appreciation of one fighting man to another, and I am not ashamed to say that in that moment, I became Caesar's man forever.

Withdrawing his hand, he continued, "It's good to know that Rome will be served by young men such as you in the coming years. I fear that she will have more need of your services than either of us would like."

I was confused as to the proper response; this was not a question. Did he want me to comment? The best I could do was to say, "And I'll be ready, sir, whenever Rome needs me and wherever I'm needed."

He smiled again, nodding his head as if I had passed some sort of test. "This is what I wanted to hear. I must confess, when I was told that a young *Gregarius* was being selected as the weapons instructor for their Century, I was a little hesitant to approve. But the judgment of the Pilus Prior has been confirmed in a way that leaves no doubt in my mind."

My chest swelled and, for a brief instant, I wished that by some miracle, my family could be there to hear his words, even my accursed father. Perhaps then, he would relent in his hatred of me, I thought.

Concluding the meeting, Caesar finished, "Well, I just wanted to meet the young *Gregarius* I had heard so much about in the last couple of days. I will be keeping an eye on you, Pullus. I expect great things from you in the coming years."

I did not even try to hide my pleasure. We were dismissed, and I felt I was a foot taller than when I had walked in.

As we walked back to our area, the Pilus Prior grumbled, "Don't go getting a big head now, boy. I'll still knock the *cac* out of you if you mess up."

Despite the harshness of his words, I could tell by his tone that he was as pleased and proud as I was, so all I said was, "Yes, Pilus Prior."

That evening, Vibius, waiting until Didius went wandering off in search of victims to fleece, brought up the subject of what Didius had done.

"I'm not willing to see him scourged and crucified," was how he began. "But we can't let this kind of thing go unpunished."

The moment Vibius brought the subject up, I resolved to keep my mouth shut; it was no secret that Didius and I hated each other, so I knew that anything I proposed would be considered to be based in our mutual antagonism. However, just looking at the faces of my friends, I could tell that they all seemed to be in agreement with Vibius' basic position.

"So what do you have in mind?" Scribonius asked.

Vibius hesitated for a moment, then replied, "I've been thinking about it, and the most obvious solution would be for us to beat him so badly that he'll never consider doing something like that again." Before anyone could voice an objection, he held up a hand. "But," he continued, "I don't think we can do that."

"Why not?" demanded Remus, who of all of us seemed to be the angriest about the matter, which was understandable considering his brother was spending the night in the hospital. "What else will work with that bastard? You know how he is. That's the only thing he understands is brute force."

"And are you ready to answer all the questions that will come when he shows up on the list?" Vibius asked, referring to the twice-daily call for those either sick or injured. "Because I'm not."

Remus seemed about to argue, but then sighed and shook his head.

"No, I suppose not. But it's just…wrong," he grumbled.

"Which is why I don't think he should go unpunished." Vibius took a breath, then came out with what he had in mind. "But if we shun him, and I mean we don't even allow him in the tent and force him to look for someplace else, I think. No, I *hope*," he amended, "that will be enough of a message for him not to do it again."

There was a silence as everyone digested this, then once more it was Scribonius who asked the most important question.

"How long?"

"A month," Vibius replied immediately.

There was an audible sound as more than one of us took in a sharp breath, and I will admit I was one of them.

"A month?" Vellusius asked, his tone doubtful. "I don't know about that."

For the first time, Vibius looked irritated, and he argued, "Anything less than that isn't going to work, I know it!"

"I don't think there's any way to know if it will be or not," Scribonius interjected, once again adopting a tone that somehow kept Vibius from boiling over because he was being challenged. "And," he pointed out, "I think a month is going to draw the attention of Rufio at the very least, and most likely Crastinus. Then there are going to be the kind of questions that we don't want to come up in the first place."

All eyes were on Vibius, and I knew him well enough to see that Scribonius' argument had scored with my best friend. His eyes narrowed and, for a moment, I thought there might be an explosion of argument, but then he gave a hiss in frustration.

"Fine," he said, although he spat the word out; Vibius had never been a gracious loser, although I have no room to talk. "So how long do you think it should be?"

"I think no more than a week," Scribonius replied.

Vibius opened his mouth to protest, but I saw his eyes dart around the circle and he saw what I had seen, that the others accepted this as the term of Didius' punishment.

"All right," he grumbled, but then pointed a finger, moving his hand to include each of us in turn. "But when that turns out to be not nearly enough, don't forget who told you that!"

I finally spoke up, assuring Vibius, "Don't worry. I know you; you won't let us."

That had the effect I was hoping for, as my comrades laughed, while Vibius scowled at me for a moment, before he could not fight it and joined in.

When Didius was informed by us, confronting him as a unified group, for the first time since we had known him, he did not react with his usual bluster. His face turned pale when Vibius, elected as our spokesman, calmly informed him that while we were disgusted with his behavior, neither did any of us want to see him scourged and crucified. I believe that was the first time it occurred to him just how serious an offense he had committed, and much to at least my surprise, he meekly accepted his punishment. And while it did not wreak any miraculous change in him, I will say that he never did anything so cowardly after that.

That was not the only lingering problem after the action on the hill that affected our tent section. As I mentioned, Calienus had been decidedly cool towards me when I returned to my section after the talk with the Pilus Prior the morning after the fight on the hill, and it continued through that day and night. In fact, it was not until the next night when, in frustration, I sought him out and asked to speak to him privately. He was clearly reluctant, but he did walk with me as we moved away from our own tent, which is the only way to get any real privacy in a Legion camp. After silently debating the best way to approach the subject, I decided on the tactic that I say with some reluctance is the most common method I employ when confronting something I consider a problem, head on and swinging away.

"Why are you angry with me?" I blurted out. "What did I do wrong?"

A look of surprise flashed across Calienus' face, but he smothered it quickly.

"Who says I'm angry?" he asked, but there was no mistaking the coolness in his tone.

"I do," I shot back. "You haven't said more than two words to me since the other day."

"That's not true," he protested. "It's been more than that."

"Fine," I snapped. "You've said three words. Is that better?"

While I was at the very least upset, as I hoped, my clumsy attempt at humor seemed to reach him, and despite the fact he clearly did not want to, he chuckled. Still, he said nothing, and I recognized he was not going to, so before I did lose my temper with a man who was not only my superior, but who I respected a great deal and admired almost as much as I did Rufio and Crastinus at this point, I turned to stalk away. Behind me, I heard him utter a curse under his breath.

"Wait," he called out.

I stopped and, with a sigh, he walked over to me, an expression on his face that was hard for me to identify.

"Believe it or not, I'm not angry with you." He paused, then plunged on, "I'm angry with me."

Of all the things I had braced myself to hear, about my hubris, or my refusal to obey his order to stay put, this was the last one.

"With yourself?" I echoed, not understanding in the slightest. "But why? You're not the one who disobeyed an order."

"But I should have," Calienus replied quietly. "I knew it then, that you were doing the right thing." Suddenly, he looked down at the ground as he shook his head. "But instead, I chose to hide behind the fact that we were given orders and stay where I was, rather than jump into a fight where I was needed."

Frankly, I still did not understand, and now, looking back on the other side of this conversation, I often wonder if I was right to continue.

"But...why?" I asked again. "You were doing what you were supposed to do, but if you knew what I was doing was right, why didn't you come with me?"

"Why do you think?" Calienus snapped, looking up to meet my gaze.

Again, I could not identify the look he was giving me, although I can now; it was a look of shame. Shame at what he considered his weakness.

"I was too scared to, Titus." Calienus barely got this out in a whisper. "I didn't know what was going on, that's true, but I've been in enough fights to know that this was a bad one. And," he shrugged as he closed his eyes, "my nerve failed me."

"No," I shot back, probably more sharply than I should have, but I was not about to accept this. "That's a pile of *cac*. Your nerve didn't fail you. You did the smart thing." I could tell he was unconvinced, so I pressed my point by continuing, "What Didius did? *That* is someone whose nerve failed. If he has any to begin with," I could not resist adding, heartened to see Calienus at least give a smile. Now it was my turn to shake my head, and I finished, "Calienus, you did nothing to be ashamed of. By the end of the night, you got your *gladius* as bloody as any man there."

"Not as bloody as yours," he said, and there was a rueful quality that made me laugh.

"That's true," I granted. "But nobody has ever accused me of being smart."

I offered my hand, which he took, and we clasped forearms, saying nothing for a moment.

Finally, I broke what to me was the awkward silence, and said, "Well, at least I'm happy to know that it's not me you're angry with." I turned and started to walk away, heading back to our tent, calling over my shoulder, "Now, let's get back before those greedy bastards eat all the chickpeas."

Calienus did not move, and once I became aware of this, I stopped, turning around again to face him.

"You won't mention this to any of the others?" he asked, his worry plain to see. "Even Domitius?"

"Mention what?" I replied blandly.

Then, without saying anything more, I resumed my way back to our tent. And I kept my word; until now, I never mentioned our conversation to anyone, ever.

Continuing our northward push, the army entered the lands of a tribe known to be particularly warlike and never fully accepting of the Romanization of Hispania to that point. They were called the Gallaeci, and were supposedly a branch of the Lusitani, yet to the *Gregarii* like me, it did not really matter much. They were enemies to be defeated because that was what Caesar and, by extension, Rome, wished, so it would be done. There was one material difference between the rest of the Lusitani and the Gallaeci, and it was in their use of horses. While we had seen and been harassed by Lusitani cavalry before, the Gallaeci took it to another level, specializing in using missiles, either throwing something similar to our *pilum* or using bows. Although this was not unique, what made them different was in the way they would employ their cavalry, their warriors having learned the art of galloping around in a large circle, providing them with the security of constant motion and making them extremely hard to hit. When they were in part of the loop nearest to us, they would launch their missile attack, then keep riding in the loop to repeat it over and over again, until they either ran out of missiles or we found some way to drive them off. By this point in our campaign, Caesar had partially rectified the dearth of cavalry on our side by having cavalry auxiliaries sent to him. There was an *ala* of auxiliary cavalry, consisting of ten *turmae* attached to each Legion, so the *ala* consisted of a total of about 300 men at full strength. The trick was to use our cavalry properly as a screening force and as *exploratores*, but not send them out so far that they could not be recalled quickly to repel attack by the Gallaeci horsemen. The closer we approached the Durius (Douro) River, with the last Roman colony at the time being Portus Cale (Grando Porte, Portugal), the more lurid the tales became of the skill and devastating accuracy of these mythical horsemen. I believe that in every Legion, there is a group of men determined to paint the grimmest picture that they can, and they foretell our defeat and slaughter in every upcoming battle. Why they do so I have no idea, but they are always given more credence than I think they deserve, and as I was to find out a few years later, their dire outlook could infect a whole Legion if the Centurions did not put an end to it.

It was near the Ides of Sextilis, meaning the campaign season was drawing to a close and, in consequence, Caesar picked up the pace of the operations. Portus Cale had been taken by a confederation of the Gallaeci Bracari and the Gallaeci Lucenses, who normally warred on each other, but were now united in their common hatred of Rome, and slaughtered all the Roman citizens who did not flee.

By the time we arrived at the walls, Caesar's practice with the last few towns and cities was well known, so there was never any question, as far as the enemy was concerned, whether or not he would offer terms. To delay the inevitable, they burned the bridge across the Douro, which at that time was made of wood, and it was here that Caesar made a demonstration of his abilities as an engineer. To be fair, it was a demonstration of his ability at design, since it was the *praefecti fabrorum* who actually had to put his design into use. It was not as large or ambitious as his later bridge over the Rhenus (Rhine); still it clearly awed the Gallaeci, who stood watching helplessly from a distance as in the space of a day, a pontoon bridge was built over the river using confiscated boats. On top of the boats, planking was laid of a sufficient strength that a Legion and an *ala* of cavalry could march across to set up a defensive camp protecting the selected site. The main problem of building a more permanent bridge, besides the Gallaeci trying to destroy it, stemmed from the banks of the Douro rising up steeply from the river, with very little flat and stable riverbank on which to build. Much later, a bridge of stone was erected, but at the time, our orders were to erect one that was sufficient to allow the Legions, along with their baggage trains and artillery to pass over, just not one that would take more than a few days to build. One challenge was finding timber suitable for using as the piers to hold the bridge up, but within a half day of our arrival, Caesar had seen what needed to be done. Simultaneously ordering the construction of the pontoon bridge, he also sent several Cohorts and wagons out to scour the area for wood of sufficient size for a more permanent structure. It was found a half-day's march from our location, and it was a good thing that Caesar did not tarry, because fairly quickly the Gallaeci succeeded in destroying the pontoon bridge, sending several fire rafts downstream to run into the boats holding the bridge up. This effectively cut the 9th off on the far bank, not as much of a military threat as it meant that the three days' rations they marched over with would have to suffice. The 7th and 10th were left on the south side of the river as a labor force, while the artillery was set up on the high bank of the Douro to provide covering fire and to keep the Gallaeci from getting any more ideas.

By dawn on the fourth day, the bridge was finished, and even from a distance, it was easy to read the despair of the mounted men who were our constant shadows while we worked and the 9th watched. They made no attempt to attack the 9th in its camp, which was probably a mistake, although it was one that suited us perfectly fine. It was clear to us that they thought that they had earned enough of a reprieve that it would allow time for the Gallaeci Lucenses to send fresh reinforcements down from the north to help them stop us, but the problem for them was that Caesar knew it as well. However slight the delay was, we still had to be quick about taking the town, and it was here that Caesar made another one of his decisions that is a demonstration of his tactical brilliance. Leaving the 7th to besiege the town, he continued the march north with the 9th and 10th to confront the Lucenses separately, trusting the 7th to take care of the Bracari. This was totally unexpected by both parts of the enemy force, and it was no more than two days after we crossed the Douro that our scouts came galloping back to the main column to report that they had spotted the advance scouts of the Lucenses column. Approaching to within sight of their own advance party, for the better part of a third of a watch, the two sides sat on opposing hills no more than two miles away while the Lucenses scouts and what we presumed were their leaders talked over what to do. Not that we were idle; the *cornu* and *bucina* were blaring out orders that told us to array along the top of the hill in a *triplex acies*, although we still were waiting for the 9th to arrive in full since they were marching drag. But as usual, Caesar knew what he was doing.

Just the sight of our one Legion making preparation for battle was enough to convince the Lucenses that they needed to fight another day, and even before we finished shaking out into battle formation, the dust cloud that signaled the location of their column began to rise in the air again as they reversed march to head back north. Resuming our own progress, as soon as we approached the hill from which they had observed us, we saw in the distance beyond that there was yet another formation a short distance behind the original column, traveling on a parallel track that was more to the east than the one that we had been observing. Seeing this other force, Caesar decided to wait and see what they would do, deciding that we had gone far enough that day and ordering us to make a marching camp on top of the hill. It was while we were in the process of making camp that a courier from the first column obviously made it to the second, because they also turned around to head back north, deciding to find better ground, which we expected. What we did not expect was that they would pick an island, or rather, a number of islands.

Over the next two days, we were never able to catch the Lucenses, although I am not altogether sure that Caesar wanted to, given the length of our marching column, strung out as it was because of the terrain. Coming to the Minus (Guadiana) River, it was here that we ran into a challenge bigger than the one that we faced at the Douro. This river empties into the great ocean, and is guarded on both sides by high hills. On the opposite bank, there was a good-sized fortified town, right at the mouth of the river and with a commanding view of the area. Compounding the problem, this was the best area for miles to build a bridge, but was out of the question because of the position of the town. There was no bridge in place; instead, the Lucenses were using a large number of flat-bottomed boats to ferry their army across, and we were greeted by a frustrating sight. Climbing the last hill of the opposite bank just in time to see the last boatloads cross, we could only stand helplessly and curse as, of course, they did not send the boats back. The Minus was too wide and deep to cross by fording; even a pontoon bridge at that location was out of the question because of the vulnerability to the Gallaeci army and the swift current as the river emptied into the ocean. Consequently, we would have to march upriver and Caesar wasted no time in giving that order. We were in the vanguard that day, so Caesar diverted the 9th to send them east up the river, while we now became the rearguard. A cavalry *ala* was left behind to keep watch on the Gallaeci in case they thought to go back across the river and follow behind us. To forestall that further, once we moved up the riverbank and crossed over another hill out of sight from the town, Caesar dropped the 8th, 9th, and 10th Cohorts of our Legion off on the reverse slope, directing them to build a camp. By climbing the short distance up the hill to the summit, sentries could keep an eye on the Gallaeci to make sure that they did not come after us. If they did, there would be a blocking force that could intercept them if they came onto our side of the river, or at the least warn us if they followed on the other side. We knew that we could not keep them from observing our actions, yet that did not mean we had to make it easy on them.

Another ten miles had to be covered before we found a suitable site on which to build, and the one blessing was that the surrounding hills possessed enough timber that we did not have to travel much farther in order to supply the building materials. This bridge took longer than the one at the Douro because we had less manpower. The 8th had been left behind more than a month ago; the 7th was besieging Portus Cale, and my Legion was reduced by the three Cohorts we left to guard the route behind us. Meanwhile, Caesar kept all of the *ala* still with us, busy scouting the area in order to provide us with enough warning in the event of any surprise the Lucenses might care to come up with. Once our camp was prepared, and the artillery that came with us was arrayed to provide covering fire against the opposite bank, we immediately set to work on building the bridge.

For five days, we labored, with our artillery driving off those Gallaeci who came too close. We could not keep what we were doing secret, but we could keep them from doing anything to stop our progress. Some of the auxiliary cavalry had forded the river and stood by to drive off any of the enemy who got too close, or delay an enemy sortie if it came in force. However, for whatever reason, the Gallaeci seemed to be resigned that we would not be denied from crossing the river, an accurate judgment. Once the bridge was completed, we marched across, heading back towards the coast and the fortified town. Along the way, we ran into an attempted ambush, but brushed it aside with few casualties on our side and heavy losses to the Gallaeci. Nevertheless, it was enough to delay us so that we could not begin an assault on the town until the next day. For what seemed like the hundredth time, we found ourselves digging and building a marching camp within sight of a town's walls. Unlike the other towns, this one was more of a fortress than anything we had seen before, with walls made of stone, as were most of the buildings. It was also on the shelf of an extremely large hill, almost at the top, forcing us to climb up in the face of heavy fire. The truth is that nobody, especially the veterans, looked forward to assaulting this place, and the mood was grim as we gathered around our fire that night.

"That's going to be a real bastard to take," Calienus announced quietly.

Even with the ramparts in the way, we could look past them and see the town spread out on the slope rising toward the crest, perched there as if daring us to attack it. We newer men took a cue from the mood of the veterans, knowing that if they were not enthused about the prospects, we certainly should not be ourselves. Nobody answered him; there was not much to say about it. The town was there, meaning it had to be taken because it had not surrendered and we could not leave its inhabitants in our rear as we marched further north.

We should have had more faith in Caesar, because he immediately saw that the very feature that the Gallaeci were counting on, their position on the side of the hill, was also their biggest weakness. The shelf on which the town was built was perhaps two-thirds up the side of the hill, leaving higher ground above them. The opposite slope of the hill was extremely steep, a feature that the Gallaeci were undoubtedly counting on as being precipitous enough so that nobody would try to climb it in order to take a position above the town. They did not account for Caesar's determination and imagination, because that was exactly what he did, or we did. Word was sent out among us, asking for those men with experience in scaling such slopes, and from our two Legions was assembled an *ad hoc* group about two Cohorts strong. They were assigned the task of sneaking out of the camp at night, carrying not just extra *pila*, but a number of the scorpions and one of the smaller ballistae that was broken down, then stealthily making their way to the back side of the hill. Using the darkness as cover, they scaled the steep slope of the back side, despite losing almost a dozen men who lost their footing and fell to their deaths, dragging the artillery behind them and using ropes to pull the pieces up. About two-thirds of the watch before dawn, the rest of us were given the order to assemble in battle array outside our camp, located less than a mile from the town and in clear sight of the Gallaeci standing on the walls, looking down on us as the sun rose. They were greeted by the sight of two Legions arrayed for an assault on the town, minus the two mixed Cohorts who were at that moment just getting into position and reassembling the artillery. Meanwhile, the rest of our artillery deployed and were ready to begin the bombardment of the walls to create a breach. The veterans had assured us that, despite the apparent greater strength of a stone wall, it is actually easier to knock it down with artillery than a wooden wall is, because there is no give in the rock, making it more brittle. Despite finding this hard to believe, we had learned to trust their judgment on these matters since they were seldom wrong.

From our formation, Caesar sent another Tribune under a flag of truce, except this time with an armed escort, none of us forgetting what happened at the first town. That group approached the walls and began to parley with the Gallaeci in the town. We were ordered to keep our eyes turned on the exchange at the gate; Caesar did not want anything to betray the surprise being prepared above and behind them, since some observant Gallaeci who noticed that our heads were turned to the top of the hill might get suspicious. Still, most of us, me included, kept our heads turned to the parley, but nevertheless watched the top of the hill out of the corner of our eyes.

"There they are," someone called out, and although it took me a few heartbeats, I saw a group of men, barely more than dots, appear on the crest of the hill followed moments later by larger shapes as they assembled the artillery pieces.

Finally, one of the men on top of the hill waved what appeared to be a flag as some sort of signal, which the Tribune negotiating with the Gallaeci had obviously been waiting for, because he immediately pointed up to our force on the hill.

The battle for the town was over before it really began. Once the Gallaeci saw our men on top of the hill, with our artillery pointing down at them, they did not even need a couple of projectiles thrown their way to convince them that they were finished. They accepted the terms that the Tribune was offering almost immediately, except they still had one trick to play, as we were about to find out. Regardless of what lay in the immediate future, all of us who were going to be assaulting that town heaved a huge sigh of relief; for once, the idea of survival outweighed the lure of plunder and when the surrender was announced, we all cheered heartily. Meanwhile, the Gallaeci continued haggling with the Tribune about minor details, something the Tribune was too inexperienced to recognize as a ploy. Finally, Caesar grew impatient when none of the enemy came out of the town to surrender, prompting him and his command group to ride over to the Tribune, whereupon Caesar began pointing and gesturing at both the Tribune and the Gallaeci, who were still standing on the wall above the gate.

"Something's wrong," Scribonius mused, "or else Caesar wouldn't be so worked up."

319

As we watched, Caesar jerked his horse around and came galloping back to the formation, giving orders for the artillery to open fire and focus on the gate. This sudden reversal swept through the ranks and we began to talk amongst ourselves, speculating on what could have happened.

"*Silete!*"

The Pilus Prior seemed more irritable than usual, and I wondered if even he was beginning to get nervous about what was going on. With the artillery all concentrating their fire on the gate, it did not take long before it crashed open, one of the doors hanging by what appeared to be a thread from a distance. Immediately afterwards, the *bucina* and *cornu* sounded the advance at the double and the First Cohort peeled away, jogging towards the gates, followed by us, then the rest of the Legion.

"Keep your intervals, you bastards," roared the Pilus Prior as we drew closer, our eyes fastened on the parapets, waiting for men to suddenly pop up and start bombarding us with missiles. Fortunately, it never happened; the First Cohort went sweeping through, followed by us immediately behind them, they fanning out to the left as planned, us fanning out to the right. Immediately, we noticed that the area of the town surrounding the gate seemed to be deserted, except for a few old men and women, along with some people who looked infirm and weak. This town was arranged in such a manner that it was laid out in two levels; the original part of the town was built on the shelf of the hill and was fairly level, then as it grew, a second level had gotten added that was built further up the slopes of the hill. After a quick search of the lower town, we huffed and puffed up the narrow streets to the second level, finding only more old and sick people. All of these we put to the *gladius*, since they held no value as slaves.

It turned out that the only able-bodied men left were the few men on the parapet above the gate negotiating with first the Tribune, then with Caesar. As we descended back down, we saw them by the gate, bound and on their knees, surrounded by the officers and some of the senior Centurions. Despite their state, they looked up at the men surrounding them with defiant expressions, a couple of them even smiling, like they had won some sort of victory, which in a sense, they had. It was only after one of them was summarily executed that the others began to talk, finally explaining how the inhabitants of a town, not only combatants, but all of the citizens who lived there that could walk, had vanished. One of the men indicated a street that was very hard to spot, branching off the larger street on the side of the town nearest the ocean that led up to the upper town. Because of the stone construction, it blended in as part of the wall that the street followed and was not really visible until you were almost on top of it. Sending a Cohort down the road, they came to a sheltered cove, where the boats that had hauled the people across the river had been moored. With the upper part of the hill above this spot dropping off into a sheer face more than a hundred feet above the water, the approach to the drop was so steep that the men on top of the hill had no way to get close enough to look down and see the harbor. It turned out that even before the sun came up to shine on our army ready to assault the town, the Gallaeci had determined that there was no real way to stop us from taking it. Our reputation preceded us and they knew that we would not just go away until the town fell and, once it did, all the people in it would suffer a terrible fate. Therefore, as soon as the sun went down, they began evacuating the place and the only reason the men on the parapet seemed to have a change of heart and ceded the town was because the last of the boats had just pulled away. By the time the last boat that left after the sun came up and reached a point where they might have been seen by our men on the hill, their attention was turned completely on the town, this being when Caesar gave the order to make ready to fire on the town with their artillery. Despite ourselves, we held a grudging admiration for the guile and skill of the Gallaeci, even if it meant that we would have to face these same men again.

The town was sacked, except there was little of value left behind, and we were immediately given orders to break camp to resume our pursuit of the Gallaeci. Those Gallaeci who remained behind to stall us were tortured, but it became clear that they did not know where their compatriots were headed. Since they were under no illusion that they would escape their situation alive, there was no need for them to know where the rest of the tribe was headed. This was not good news, because it meant that we were forced to march along the coast, which in this part of Hispania is extremely hilly. While giving us a commanding view of the ocean and the area ahead, it also meant that our pace was considerably slowed, no matter how hard Caesar pushed us. The end of the campaign season was rapidly approaching, betrayed by the cooler nights and shorter days, and it was our baggage train that slowed us the most. At some point, every man found himself, his shoulder hard up against the back of a wagon, pushing with all his might as the mules and oxen struggled to pull their load up each hill. In many ways, however, going down the hill presented more risk, since there was a danger of a wagon being too heavy for the beasts to control, so we would use ropes attached to the back of the wagon and act as a multi-man brake to keep the wagon from careening out of control down the hill and smashing into other wagons or our comrades. Despite it being a little more than thirty miles from the town to the spot where we finally caught sight of the Gallaeci, it still took the better part of four days to cover the distance.

When we finally found them, there was a collective groan from the entire army. Our scouts had come rushing back with some sort of news, but it was not until we crested a hill and looked down on what lay before us that we in the ranks saw what we were facing. There was a bay, with a deep inlet that crossed in front of us, cutting some few miles deep into the land, the bulk of Hispania being to our right. Out in the bay were a number of islands, three small ones arranged in a row, crossing to our front perpendicular to our line of march, all clearly deserted. Farther out past that were a pair of islands, arranged parallel to our direction, and much larger. One of them appeared to be deserted as well, but even from a distance, the second island, even farther away, was clearly inhabited because of the smoke rising above it that signaled the presence of people. We had to make a sharp right turn in order to follow the inlet around to a point where we were opposite the larger islands and, as we drew closer, more details appeared. The larger of the two islands was shaped like a crescent, with the open end facing away from us, and on the lower hills of the island, we could see fortifications. There were a large number of boats of varying sizes pulled up onto the beach opposite where we stood and it did not take a military expert to know that this is where the Gallaeci had fled from the town. To make matters worse, soon after we arrived opposite the first island, the scouts came back to inform us that further north, perhaps ten miles ahead, was another island that was fortified in a similar manner. We stood watching the low hills of the first island as the command group conferred and the mood was apprehensive, to put it mildly. Very few of us had any experience on the water, making the idea of getting in boats to be ferried over to either of these islands unappealing in the extreme. However, Caesar was not to be denied and, in truth, it did not make sense for us not to finish the job, so we resigned ourselves to our fate and waited to see what we were supposed to do.

Our mounted scouts scoured the area of the inlet, along with another inlet opposite the second island, yet they could not find any craft large or seaworthy enough to ferry us across the water to either island.

"Maybe he'll call off an attack," Vibius said hopefully, a sentiment that I answered with a snort of dismissal.

"Not very likely. We've just marched across the entire length of Hispania; do you really think Caesar is going to be denied now?"

Despite not liking what I said, neither could he argue and he knew it, just answering with a shake of his head as he viewed the expanse of water with trepidation. Caesar's answer to the lack of boats was simple; we would make them. Once again, we found ourselves finding, felling, and dragging back trees that the engineers deemed suitable for our purposes. There were men with experience in shipbuilding who were put in charge of the work, with the rest of the Legions supplying the manual labor. It took a full week, and was done far enough up the inlet that the results of our labor were not visible to the Gallaeci on the islands. While we were involved in this work, those Gallaeci that, for whatever reason, had not joined their comrades on the island did whatever they could to delay us, most commonly attempting to fire the boats at night. They managed to burn one, so after that raid, we kept a constant vigil, forcing a lot of us who worked all day to go without much sleep at night as we stood guard. Despite the Gallaeci's attempts, the work progressed until we had a dozen flat-bottomed barges, each of them able to hold two Centuries and an artillery piece. Meanwhile, the command group worked out the plan for the assault, deciding that our best chance was to cross at night, something that became a symbol of Caesar's, the sudden movement that the enemy did not expect. However, a night attack requires a huge amount of coordination and not a little luck, but as we were to learn, almost as much as his skill, Caesar was renowned for his good fortune and he never hesitated to put his faith in it during tough times.

The 10th was chosen to lead the assault, with the First through Fourth Cohorts designated as the first group the boats would take across, and the decision was made to attack in three days' time, there being no moon starting that night, a *gladius* that cut both ways. It would make our approach harder to detect, but it also meant that the chances of a mistake were much greater. To help guide us a small group of men, using a boat commandeered from somewhere that was small enough to be harder to detect, would row over to the island the night before the assault, then remain hidden during the day. On the next night, at a pre-appointed time, they would light a shielded lantern on the beach only detectable from our spot out on the water to help guide us in. To further the subterfuge, the boats would not be brought down the inlet until after dark, requiring us to hurry to load up then row across to the island, using the lamp as our guide. It would require a minimum of foul-ups in order to be successful, and the fact that Caesar put his faith in us made us all the more determined.

When the night of the assault arrived, helping our cause was a heavy cloud cover, or at least so we thought. However, shortly before the boats were supposed to arrive, it also began to rain, with the wind picking up, blowing off the ocean and directly into our faces. That made the trip down the inlet more difficult for the men selected to row the boats, so they arrived later than planned. By the time they pulled up onto the beach, the wind had increased so that the falling rain was almost horizontal and the waves had become increasingly choppy. Peering through the rainy dark at Vibius, I saw an expression of real apprehension that not even the gloom could conceal, bringing me a bit of comfort now that I knew he was as worried as I was. Both of us were country boys, our first glimpse of the ocean occurring on a training march from our camp at Scallabis several months earlier, while neither of us had been in so much as a rowboat, let alone a flat-bottomed troop transport. Calienus and the other veterans who had participated in amphibious operations with Pompey did their best to put us at ease, but their own looks of concern did nothing to assuage our fears. Being the First Century of the Second, we were one of the first to load up, bringing on board with us two artillery pieces, both scorpions, whereupon we rowed out a short distance, then dropped anchor to wait for the other units to load up. Before much time passed, the violent bobbing made most of us sick, so the gunwales of the boat were lined with Legionaries puking their guts out. I am not ashamed to say that I was one of them; it was not until much later that I got my sea legs, but even then, I did not, nor do I now, like sea voyages of any duration. It took perhaps a third of a watch to load the rest of the Centuries of our four Cohorts into the boats, then we ran into another problem. With the rain getting steadily worse, it became so heavy that we could not see the beacon that was supposed to be guiding us to the island.

"If we can't see the damn light, how can we know which way we're going?" This was Didius' voice, and for one of the few times, I was in complete agreement. "For all we know, we may end up twenty miles out to sea, then what'll happen?"

"We'll all drown, you idiot. What do you think will happen?" Even Calienus' voice sounded strained when he replied to Didius.

Vibius and I, as usual, were standing together and Vibius whispered to me, "Titus, I'm not going to lie. I'm scared to death."

"Me too," was all I could manage before retching again, despite having lost everything in my stomach.

Ignoring the lack of a guiding light, the men at the oars began to heave when the order was given and once more, someone called out, "Jupiter Optimus Maximus, protect this Legion, soldiers all," as we began making our way towards what we hoped was the island.

It took the better part of a third of a watch, with the men at the oars straining all the way, before we got close enough to the island for someone to see the lantern.

"There it is, off to the right," I heard an excited voice call out.

"By the gods, we almost missed the damn island," another voice exclaimed, and there was a chorus of agreement. If we had passed by with the island off to our right, we would have headed out to open sea and certain death by drowning.

"Well, at least we found the damn thing." That was the Pilus Prior, who for once seemed as apprehensive as we were, not bothering to tell us to shut up once. Continuing, he told us, "Listen up, boys. You just saw how long it took us to get to this island. It won't take them half as long to get back because the wind is at their back, but it'll take them just as long, if not longer, to bring up the next four Cohorts. In fact, we'll probably be on this island for at least a full watch by ourselves, so keep that in mind. No heroes; make sure we stay together because it's darker than Pluto's bunghole out here. Hopefully, the boys on the island'll be able to point us in the right direction."

"Pilus Prior, wouldn't it make more sense to wait until the whole Legion is on the beach?"

I do not know who asked that, but I believe that only the total darkness emboldened him to question our orders. What was even more surprising was that the Pilus Prior did not take offense. In fact, he agreed.

"Yes, it would make more sense, but that's not our orders. Caesar has commanded that we begin the assault immediately, and that's what we're going to do. The thing that worries me is that the artillery won't be able to use the combustibles to start a fire in their defenses to give us light, so we're going to have to be very careful and stay in formation. Make sure that nobody gets separated by keeping close enough to each other so that you're touching. If you lose contact with someone on either side, call out immediately so they'll know to close back in and get in contact, but by the gods, keep your voices down when you do it."

Just as we answered him, we felt the bottom of the boat scraping the beach. Without waiting, Pilus Prior Crastinus called out, "All right, boys, let's go give these bastards some Roman iron. They escaped their fate once; we're not going to let 'em get away a second time."

With that, we heard a splash above the sound of the waves lapping at the beach as he jumped over the side, and immediately, we began moving forward as we disembarked. Landing in thigh-deep water, I was thankful for my height because it was shockingly cold; if I had been shorter, the water would have hit a part of my body that never reacts well to anything cold touching it. I was assigned to help carry some of the pieces of the artillery ashore, so I grabbed what was handed to me before turning to wade the few paces to the shore.

Immediately, I bumped into someone, my bigger size knocking him down, and my heart sank when I heard the voice of the Pilus Prior cursing me, my mother, my father, and all my ancestors. Muttering an apology in a voice that I hoped he would not recognize, I skirted past him to get as far away as I could. It was impossible to see anything and the only way that we got organized was by calling out to each other, then following the sounds of voices. This was only possible to do because of the rain and howling of the wind; if it had been quieter, I do not know what we would have done. The rest of the men carrying the artillery pieces stumbled over and we began assembling them by feel. Hearing a curse, I recognized the voice as one of the men assigned as an artilleryman and asked him what the problem was.

"The torsion rope is completely soaked. That means that it's useless."

This was not good news; not only would we be assaulting in the dark, without reinforcements, now we did not even have the help of at least one artillery piece. Immediately, a quick inventory discovered that all of the pieces had the same problem, leaving us without anything heavier than our *pila* to assault the fortifications. Our Pilus Prior made his way over to Primus Pilus Favonius while we all stood there, shivering and miserable, having been ordered to leave our cloaks behind and take only our weapons. One thing that we had to be thankful for was that we were told to leave our leather covers on our *scuta*; there is nothing quite as heavy or as useless as a water-soaked *scutum*.

The Pilus Prior came back a bit later and called out, "Change of plans. We're going to wait until the next Cohorts arrive to see if they had any better luck with their artillery. We're not going to release all of the boats until we find out, so that we can send one back and tell the command group the situation and see what they want to do."

While this made sense, and was something of a relief, it also meant that we had to sit huddled up as close to each other to keep warm and wait. When one is truly, thoroughly miserable, the hardest thing to do is to gauge the time accurately. You are sure that at least two full watches have gone by, only to learn that it is less than a quarter of that, and as we sat there, soaking wet and getting colder by the moment, we occupied ourselves with trying to guess how much time had passed. Of course, it was not long before there was betting going on, which I ignored, preferring instead to sit there, trying to tell myself that this was making me stronger and would come in handy someday. It would turn out I was right, although it was a small comfort, to be sure.

With the arrival of the next boatloads and more men piling ashore, our officers informed the Centurions joining us of the situation. A quick check revealed that the artillery in this wave was in the same shape as ours, so the word was passed to the returning boats of the situation, with a request for further orders. More time passed and, despite my discomfort, I dozed off somehow, because when the third wave arrived, I almost jumped out of my skin, prompting a laugh from Vibius. Just a few moments later, the Pilus Prior returned to inform us that the assault was going to be postponed until first light, and that the next wave would be bringing assault ladders with them so that we could scale the walls of the fortifications. Trying to make light of this news, we told each other that this was old stuff for us; we had done this before and it had turned out fine, except that my stomach, just beginning to recover from the boat trip, began twisting again. However, there was nothing that could be done and at least we would be doing it with some light to help us. Of course, it also meant that the Gallaeci would see us coming.

By the time the Legion was assembled on the beach, with assault ladders, the rain that continued pouring down had caused us to get so cold that we were shaking uncontrollably and were unable to keep our teeth from chattering. When one man's teeth are knocking about the sound is negligible, but when it is a complete Legion, it is impossible to describe the din. Our only comfort was that the wind had not abated, and it served to keep the noise we were making from reaching the ears of the enemy, or at least so we hoped. Huddled together, we tried to stay close enough to create a little more warmth, which was slight. In the meantime, we stared towards the east, in the direction of the mainland and the hills beyond, willing the appearance of the dawn so that we could get started. Nobody really talked much, there not being much to say, each of us retreating into our own thoughts, a characteristic common to all fighting men I have known as they wait to go into battle.

Finally, Vibius nudged me and, when I looked up, I saw the sky beginning to lighten and the Legion beginning to stir, whispers passed along that alerted all of us that dawn was approaching. Not more than a few moments later, the order was quietly passed for us to stand up and get back into our formations, with the men designated to carry the assault ladders making their way over to the pile of them to grab one, then returning to fall back in formation. Once more, I was selected to be one of the first over the wall, although I would not be second, but fourth of the first section. For the hundredth time, I checked that my *gladius* was ready to slide out of the scabbard easily, then fiddled with the cords that kept my helmet firmly on my head. I tried to ignore the numbness in my extremities brought on by the cold and wet, stamping my feet to try to get some feeling back in them, as were most of the men around me. Straining my eyes, after a few moments, I finally made out the outline of the wall in front of us, barely visible but unmistakable.

"Get ready, boys," the Pilus Prior whispered to us. "We'll be going in shortly."

Once the time passed, we were motioned ahead, doing our best to move as silently as possible. There was one hidden blessing about the rain because it packed the sand of the beach and the area beyond it down so that we could walk on it without sinking down or stumbling, something that might have caused us to make enough noise that our presence was detected, even with the wind. Moving quickly into position a few paces away from the walls of the fortification, I saw that we were partway up a low hill. As we crouched, waiting for the command to move, I noticed that I was no longer cold; in fact, a warm trickle of sweat began moving down my back, mingling with the cold rain soaking my skin. Then there was a blast of a *cornu*, followed immediately by an explosion of sound as we all jumped up, roaring out the signal that death was approaching the Gallaeci. As one man, the Legion began running towards the wall. The light had increased sufficiently that we could see the dark forms of the few men standing on the ramparts, and even above our own cries, we heard the shouts of alarm from them as they realized they were under attack. Reaching the wall, I ran to stand behind the ladder group I was assigned to, taking my place behind the men I was assigned to follow over the wall, thankful that I remembered the lessons I learned from the first time I had done this. Once the ladders touched the walls, we scrambled up, still yelling at the top of our lungs, and in a matter of moments, the parapet was cleared of any enemy. Jumping down into the fort, we swept past the crude shelters made of skins and wooden frames that housed not only the warriors, but their women and children, while I could hear the screams and sobs of the women as we cut their men down without any mercy. They were caught completely by surprise; the weather had helped mask our plans and it also contributed to their sense of security, sure that we would not be crazy or stupid enough to brave crossing in such weather. The fight for the fort took less than a third of a watch, although it took longer for us to stop killing anyone and anything in our path. Our Centurions did their best to restore order, but as usual, we had our blood up, and the fact that we had been subjected to the cold and rain, coupled with the rough crossing, did not help their cause.

"The more of these bastards you kill, the less slaves there'll be, and the less money for your own purses, you idiots."

Pilus Prior Crastinus was repeating this over and over as he trotted around, bashing us with his *vitus* to emphasize his point, but it still took quite some time before the slaughter and rape stopped. The surviving Gallaeci were rounded up and put under guard, where they sat on the ground, watched by a Cohort; the women wailing, the children crying, and the men who survived staring at us with undisguised hatred. None of them held any illusions about their fate; they were headed to the slave markets around the Republic, where children would be separated from their parents, husbands from their wives, and families split asunder to feed our insatiable need for slaves. The "lucky" ones would be sent to some household somewhere, and in all likelihood actually live a better life than they had now, although I could understand how they would not see it that way. However, they chose to revolt against Rome, and by doing so, sealed their fate. I was finding that the more I was exposed to this type of misery, the less I was affected by it.

There was now just one island left, north of the fort we had just taken. It was a much larger island and less hilly, so the fortifications on it were more elaborate, with the garrison and people sheltering within its walls in much larger numbers than the first fort. In fact, their works gave every appearance of having been in place for some time, and that the Gallaeci had made even more improvements to the fortifications after their arrival. For example, there was a double wall now instead of a single one, with a defensive ditch in between, sown with a number of obstacles. The outer wall had wooden towers at intervals along it, with sloping roofs and firing slits, making knocking them out difficult, while the inner wall surrounded a low hill that was the dominant feature of the island, and it was within the second wall that all of the defenders and their families were located. The rumor was that there were more than 5,000 warriors, along with another 15,000 people within the fortification, and these numbers did not make us feel any better. Add to that the fact that this was their last bastion and would be the site of their last stand meant that all the signs added up to a very bloody fight indeed. Our casualties during the assault on the first island were extraordinarily light, but we harbored no illusions that we would be that lucky this time. Both Legions still with Caesar would take part in the assault, attacking in two prongs. The 10th would approach from the south, from the general direction of the first island, with the 9th coming from the east, directly across the bay. The news that we would be attacking from the direction of the first island was met with a lot of muttered complaints, since it meant that we had a good distance to go. The distance between the two islands was around ten miles, but even cutting at an angle between the two islands before turning north, we would still be in the water for almost two full watches, a prospect that none of us viewed with any enthusiasm. One blessing was that the weather had broken, with clear skies and calm seas; we could only pray to the gods to make sure that it stayed that way. Another difficulty was that we needed more boats, since this was going to be a two-Legion assault and one of the original boats had gotten too damaged by the rough water. Although we avoided losing any men, the boat itself had to be scrapped, so one more week would be spent building more boats, during which the weather could change again. Every morning, we woke up scanning the skies with a worried eye, hoping that our luck would not run out, also knowing that Caesar was not likely to delay even if it did. After all, we took the first fort in horrible conditions with minimal loss, so why would he delay a second time? So we cut down trees and dragged them back to the beach, not bothering to hide our intentions this time; sawing, hammering, and sweating so that after another week, we had a second fleet of flat-bottomed boats. Instead of using Legionaries to row this time, the Gallaeci men captured in the first assault were pressed into service and forced to row us to kill their comrades and kin. Despite myself, I found I had some sympathy for these men; it must be a terrible fate indeed to be forced to help in the destruction of your people.

The day of the assault dawned with much rejoicing and prayers of thanks that the weather dawned sunny, clear, and calm. In fact, the surface of the water was barely rippled, looking almost as placid as the surface of a small lake. For reasons known only to Caesar, he had decided not to use the same tactic of a night assault; Calienus guessed that it had something to do with the distance that the 10th was going to have to cover, which made sense to us. Even with clear weather, several miles of water is a long distance, and much could go wrong. The Gallaeci had not helped; at night, they restricted their fires to the lower parts of the fort, not up on the hill, so it was almost impossible to see the lights from any distance. Therefore, at dawn, we piled aboard the boats, once again cursing our fate and grumbling about how we were not made to spend time on water. Setting out, despite the calm waters, I found my stomach rebelling, so that before long I was again standing at the gunwales with some of my other comrades, launching my breakfast into the ocean. Those men with stronger constitutions jeered at us, but we were too miserable to take offense. With the island just a black line barely visible on the horizon, we soon grew bored watching it and willing it to grow larger with every stroke, so instead, we began our normal routines of gambling, gossiping, and complaining. Sitting with my back against the side of the boat, I watched my comrades, and despite the seasickness and apprehension of the coming battle, I felt my heart swell with a kind of pride that comes when one has a sense of truly belonging to something greater than oneself. I smiled as Romulus and Remus bickered about something that had happened months before; Scribonius and Vellusius were playing their own game of dice; Calienus and Rufio were having a contest to try to see who could balance his *pugio* on the tip of his finger the longest. Vibius had found a spot where he could stretch out and was lying with his face up to the sun, smiling contentedly as he soaked up the warmth and nourishment of the sun's rays. Despite the fact that we were about to throw ourselves into another type of contest, where the stakes were much, much higher, I realized that there was no place on earth that I would rather be than in this boat, with these men. And there is no amount of money that a man can possess that is worth that feeling.

Finally, after what was a little less than a full watch, we got close enough that the signal was given to the 9th to begin their crossing, since they were required to wait for some time before starting. The plan was that we would arrive at the fort at the same time, although we were going to land at the southern end of the island, about a mile away from the fort. In order for this to work, we had to be almost to our landing point before the signal was given to the 9th to proceed. Once more, I was assigned to help carry the artillery, except this time, I would actually have to lug it across the sand. There was only one problem; there was no sand. Rowing closer to the southern end of the island, we passed by a smaller island that was deserted and had blocked our view of the larger island.

Once past it, I heard one of the men with some experience as a sailor call out in a worried voice, "This isn't good."

The words and tone immediately got us all scrambling to our feet, and we peered ahead. At first, I could not see anything that to my inexperienced eye would cause any concern. There was a strip of white at the base of the island where it met the ocean, and I assumed that it must be the beach that we were to land on. After a few moments, I began to look again, puzzled by something that did not seem right, so I tapped Calienus on the shoulder, pointed, and asked, "Sergeant, have you ever seen sand that white before?"

He looked closely, then shook his head. Before he could say anything, the sailor, having heard my question, answered for him. "That's because it's not sand, *Gregarius*. That's foam."

"Foam? What exactly does that mean?"

"It means that that's not a beach; it's rocks, and the foam is from the water striking the rocks. There's no way we can land there."

Before we could react, he turned quickly to his assistant to snap some orders, who in turn began giving directions to the men rowing, and for the first time, it occurred to me that we were in some danger. Once we cleared the small island, we were less than a half mile from the large one, and in the space between the two land masses, some forces were at work that created a current that was propelling us with alarming speed straight for the rocky shore. In the same moment that

I recognized that danger, the thought struck me that the men rowing held our fate in their hands; they could exact their revenge by refusing to obey the orders of the men commanding the ship, and let us go dashing onto the rocks. They were chained to their benches, so they would undoubtedly die, but they would at least do so with the satisfaction that they were taking a lot of us with them. We were one of the two lead ships, and if we did not correct our course, there was no reason that the other ships following us would not be led to their destruction as well.

Those next few moments reinforced my loathing of being at sea, at the mercy of forces much greater than ourselves and outside of our control. However, the gods smiled on us in the sense that the Gallaeci, who also held the power of life and death over us, were in love with living as much as we were, because they frantically began reversing our course. Slowly, we turned away from the jagged rocks waiting to turn our boats into tinder, managing instead to move up the eastern side of the island. It took us closer to the fort, yet that was another blessing in disguise, at least for me and the others who were supposed to carry the artillery. Finding an area that, while not a sandy beach, was smooth enough that it was deemed to be safe for landing without damaging the boats excessively, we immediately began unloading then moving onto the beach. As we fell into formation to begin the march to the fort, we could see the boats of the 9th disappearing behind a headland that jutted out to our east.

"We're going to have to hurry if we want to be in place when we're supposed to be," Vibius commented, and I nodded in agreement. It had apparently not taken the 9th nearly the amount of time to cross that they had thought it would, so despite our landing closer to the fort, it was evident that we could not tarry if we wanted this assault to have the coordination that Caesar expected. To that end, the Centurions bawled out the order to begin the march and we immediately set out, with a couple of Centuries sent ahead of us to scout out any possible ambush. The ground was fairly level but was extremely rough, causing a bit of stumbling and a lot of cursing as we moved along, the higher part of the fort clearly visible above a line of trees just ahead. At our approach, we heard shouts and the clash of arms as the advance Centuries ran into something ahead.

"First Cohort, on line!"

The Primus Pilus sounded the order, and the First immediately spread out in a line of Centuries, the sounds of fighting growing in intensity and volume as now the cries of men being struck down was added to the din.

"Advance at the double!"

The First started trotting ahead, with the rest of us following, hearing more than seeing the fighting in the trees. A few moments later, the First slammed into the Gallaeci lying in wait and, in short order, the fighting was over. Entering the tree line, we saw several dozen dead Gallaeci, with our own dead and wounded interspersed among them. The *medici* that had come with us moved up through our ranks, examining our men, assessing the casualties, and administering treatment in less severe cases, or a quick slash across the throat for those who were too severely wounded to survive. No matter how often we saw this happen, we could never get used to it, and to a man, we always averted our eyes from the unfortunates whose lives were being ended as we walked by.

Exiting the trees, we were some 200 paces away when we saw the first wall, manned now by what looked like a few hundred Gallaeci. Orders were given to assemble the artillery and I moved with the section of men I was working with to help put together the piece. In short order, everything was assembled and made ready to fire, but we did not begin a barrage, being under orders to wait for the signal from the 9th, consisting of horns and fire arrows shot into the air. Watching to the right where the 9th was supposed to be, we waited to start while the Gallaeci stood behind their walls, taunting us and shaking their weapons in our direction, telling us in no uncertain terms what they were going to do to us. The fact that we reduced their first fort with such ease did not seem to have any impact on them and we stared across the expanse of ground, silent and grim, as they continued to harangue us. Moving back to my place in formation once I had discharged my duties with the artillery, I stood there with my friends, trying to keep from fidgeting as we waited. After a few moments, we finally heard the blasts of the *bucina*, followed by a streak of light as a fire arrow shot into the sky to our right.

"Open fire!"

The command to begin the barrage rang out, and immediately, we heard the twang of the torsion arms snapping forward as the missiles hurtled towards the fort, some of them striking the wall while others either fell short or sailed high to land beyond the first wall. While we brought ladders, the plan was to open breaches in the outer wall and save the ladders for the inner wall. However, the first few volleys were a disappointment, since it did not seem that the barrage was having the desired effect. There was a lot of dust and, as we had seen before, the missiles tore the outer bark off the wooden walls, but that was about all that was happening. After several moments of this, the Primus Pilus signaled a halt to the barrage, then called for a conference of the Pili Priores, while we had to endure the jeers and taunts of the Gallaeci, who celebrated the lack of success. After conferring, the decision was made to concentrate the fire of the artillery on just two points on the wall, instead of the half-dozen that were originally planned. This was not good news for those of us who were going to be charging in through the gap, since it allowed the Gallaeci to concentrate their forces, but there was no real alternative. Immediately, our intentions became clear to them, as in a matter of perhaps a half dozen volleys, the two points on the wall started to fail, with huge chunks of wood and splinters flying from every strike. Our scorpions were holding their fire, since they would be more useful in keeping the Gallaeci's heads down as we approached the walls. Then the work was done; two good-sized gaps torn in the walls, just the jagged stumps of the wood protruding from the ground, with enough room for a section to enter the breach abreast. Through the dust, we could see the bodies of some of the men who were in the wrong place at the wrong time, yet to this point, the casualties had been minimal, on both sides. That was about to change.

The *cornicen* sounded the advance. This time, the Fifth and Eighth Cohorts were selected to be the first into the breach, another example of how the dirty end of the stick is grasped by all of us at one time or another. Second Cohort was consigned to watch as the others began the advance, the scorpions opening fire once the Cohorts were within range of the Gallaeci bows and slings. Despite the barrage, we saw gaps open in the Centuries, quickly filled by other Legionaries moving up to take the spot of the fallen man, their bodies left behind in the wake of the advancing Cohorts. Missiles issued from the wall in a thick flurry, as it appeared that almost all of the men on the wall carried some sort of sling or bow. Our men started to fall more frequently, some of them with more than one shaft protruding from their bodies, obviously making some sort of mistake in exposing themselves, or even worse, one of their comrades made the error and they had to pay for it. Ignoring the punishment, the Cohorts moved forward, the scorpions continuing their suppressive fire, making me wonder how much worse it would be for us if they had not been there at all. By the time the assaulting Cohorts were within fifty paces of the breaches, it appeared that they had lost more than a third of their numbers, the ground behind them now littered with our dead and wounded. On some unseen signal, the Gallaeci launched one last massive volley and, at that range, it was impossible for any missile to miss its mark, while in fact the arrows had enough velocity at that range to pass through one man's body to penetrate the man behind him. It looked like an invisible hand had swept through the ranks of the Fifth and Eighth, and despite ourselves, we let out a collective gasp of shock and grief.

"They're getting slaughtered," I muttered; without thinking, the words came out.

"Shut your mouth, Pullus."

This came from Optio Rufio, who looked at me as if he wanted to strike me down for uttering the words that I was sure all of us was thinking. Knowing better than to protest when an officer had that look his face, I bit my tongue, bitterly cursing him in my mind instead. Both the Fifth and Eighth came to a shuddering stop, their men trying to regain some semblance of order, stepping over the bodies of their friends and comrades to fill the gaps made by their loss. For a sickening moment, they both looked like they could go no further, except in doing so, that essentially spelled their doom because they would be picked apart. Even worse than standing there was the option of retreating; they would be even more vulnerable trying to back up while tripping over all the bodies lying between them and safety. As brutal as it was, their only chance for survival was to move forward.

"Second Cohort, prepare to advance!"

This caught us all by surprise, especially since we had not been selected to be in the second wave.

"Boys, I know we're not slated to go next, but we can't let our brothers take that kind of beating. We're going to double time over there, stop when I give the signal to redress the lines and catch our breath, then we're going to show those *cunni* what happens when you mess with the 10th!"

I honestly do not know if our hearts were in the cheer that we raised with those words, or we were sufficiently conditioned to know when it was expected of us, but we let out a cheer nonetheless.

"Procedite Ite Aciem, Move!"

Beginning the advance, the sudden movement drew the stares of the other Cohorts, along with a thankful wave from the men of the Cohort who were supposed to be next. The Primus Pilus, along with the Tribune assigned to "command" the Legion that day, came sprinting over to the Pilus Prior, who stepped to the side, but ordered us to continue advancing. By virtue of my place on the outside of the column, I could hear the heated exchange between the Centurions and I worried that we were witnessing the end of the Pilus Prior's career. Although we still hated him in some ways, our regard and affection for him had grown strong enough to outweigh any residual negative feelings that lingered from our training. As hard as he was on us, the Second had already garnered a reputation as being the best Cohort in the Legion, a fact that, looking back, now that I have been in his shoes, I am sure he was counting on saving him. That and his utmost confidence in us that we would be victorious and save what was turning into a disaster. As I passed by, I caught the last of their words.

"All I can say is that this better work, Crastinus, or you know what's going to happen."

The Primus Pilus' words were menacing enough, but his tone emphasized the seriousness of the situation.

"It'll work," the Pilus Prior responded simply.

"But what about the second wall? Your Cohort was supposed to assault the second wall, not the first. Who's supposed to do it now?"

"We'll do both," Crastinus answered calmly, before saluting and trotting past me to rejoin the head of the formation.

My heart sank; we were going to have to clear both the breach and then scale the wall?

I was about to say something to Scribonius, but before I could, he muttered bitterly, "I heard the bastard. Well, Titus, it was nice knowing you."

Immediately after the Pilus Prior resumed his position, the command to begin the advance double time was given and we broke into a trot, the sound of our gear clanking and bouncing about, mixing with the tramp of our hobnailed boots slapping the ground. Up ahead, we saw that the Fifth and the Eighth had entered the breach, with it looking like the Fifth was having a rougher go than the Eighth, so the Pilus Prior veered us in that direction. Behind us, I heard a roar, so I chanced a look back to see that another Cohort was starting the advance as well. I wondered briefly if it were the Cohort originally slated to support the Fifth, and if so, whether their Centurion possessed the presence of mind to move to the other breach. If not, then it was going to be a major mess as our two Cohorts tried to jam ourselves into one hole that already had the remnants of a Cohort in there.

Crossing the ground swiftly, just before we got to the point where the first bodies of our fallen were lying, the Pilus Prior halted us to dress the lines. We were going in as a column of Centuries, so that once again being the First Century had its disadvantages. Nevertheless, I cheered myself with the thought that at least I was in the rear rank, the comfort of which lasted just a few more heartbeats before I heard my name called.

"Pullus, get your fat ass up here!"

Moving out of my spot, I trotted up while the Pilus Prior called the names of the other large men of the Century, where he arranged us at the front, intent on using our bigger bodies to increase the impact when we went smashing through the breach. Up ahead, we could see the Fifth fighting for its life, having made a small pocket just inside the first wall, where they were surrounded by what looked like several times their numbers, and even in the short time we watched, we saw our men falling to the ground. Some of them got up again, but others just lay there or tried to crawl away. Once we were set, we were given the command to start out again, and for perhaps the first time in my life, I cursed the fact that I had been born bigger and stronger than most everyone else. I was on the front rank, on the outside right, with the Pilus Prior running next to me as we advanced. One tiny blessing was that the Gallaeci had stopped with the bows and slings and were now down on the ground, fighting it out with the Fifth and the Eighth. The closer we got, the more treacherous the footing as we had to pick our way over the bodies of our comrades, most of whom were still alive and trying to continue crawling away from the fighting. When a man is seriously wounded, it seems to be the overriding urge to move however one can away from the fighting that served to hurt him, and we had to call out to the men to lie still as we pounded around and over them, trying to leap over their writhing bodies. We were not always successful; behind me, I could hear a scream, followed by a curse as someone stepped on one of the wounded, yet we had no time to stop and help. With the distance rapidly closing to the breach, we could clearly see the faces of the Gallaeci facing us as they looked over the shoulders of the Fifth and saw us coming. Once again, the Pilus Prior knew how to maximize our advantage; I could see the eyes of the enemy widen in shock and terror, seeing what to them must have looked like giants from the underworld come to seek their deaths.

"Kill 'em all, boys!"

The Pilus Prior shouted, and when I glanced over, I saw him grin, his lips pulled back over his teeth and his eyes shining with bloodlust as he circled his *gladius* in the air just before dropping it down to point at the Gallaeci.

"*Porro!*"

This time, our roar was wholehearted and I was sure that the gods in the heavens and down below sat up to take notice. Dis was going to have his hands full, I thought as I went smashing into the breach, shouting at the men of the Fifth that the Second was here to save them.

Hearing our cries, the men of the Fifth engaged with the enemy gave the last of their energy to bash the Gallaeci backwards before stepping aside to let us come charging through their lines. Even as we went hurtling past, I glimpsed the fatigue and relief on the faces of the Fifth before I barreled into a warrior, knocking him head over heels. Flying backwards, he struck two other Gallaeci, who in turn fell down in a heap and, before any of them could recover, I stepped up to make three quick thrusts, ending each of them. Our Century came pouring into the breach and, in the space of a few heartbeats, what was a slight bulge no more than a few feet across by a few feet deep now expanded out until our whole Century was inside the first wall. Spreading outwards along the base of the first wall, we kept it to either our left or right as we moved parallel to it, rapidly expanding our position in order to allow the other Centuries to come piling in. The men of the Fifth withdrew, giving us room to add more men and, within moments, the first wall was effectively taken in our sector. Pausing a moment to assess the situation, a quick inventory was taken by the Pilus Prior. There were a couple of wounded in our Century, yet no deaths, a great start, but it was not over by a long shot because we still had to cross the open ground to the second wall.

Some of the more alert of the Gallaeci arrayed further down the wall saw us bursting through and realized that they were in real danger of being cut off, so they began streaming off the first wall, heading back to the second where more of their comrades waited. As we watched, ladders made of both wood and rope were dropped over the side to allow the defenders on the first wall to climb to safety, and the Pilus Prior dispatched two Centuries to hurry over to try to cut them off, but they were driven back by heavy fire from the slingers and bowmen on the second wall. Despite making a good start, we were about to be exposed to another danger; as long as there was a fight going on for the first wall, the missile troops on the second wall dared not fire for fear of hitting their own men, but once we killed or drove off those defenders, the way was clear now for them to open fire.

"*Testudo* by Centuries!"

Despite moving quickly, some of us fell before we could get into the proper formation. Meanwhile, the Pilus Prior of the Cohort immediately behind us did indeed have the presence of mind to shift his attack to the second breach, and shortly after we were finished, they had secured that one as well. Now we had to cross the open ground, maneuvering across under fire, while also negotiating a ditch laced with sharpened stakes and caltrops, nasty devices that consist of two spikes twisted around each other so that no matter how you throw them to the ground, there is a sharpened point sticking up. And we had to do it under fire, while carrying ladders. In other words, a right bastard of a job.

"There's no use just standing here giving them targets to hit," the Pilus Prior said in a manner that suggested he was talking to himself more than he was to us, while we huddled underneath our *scuta*, waiting for the word to advance.

By this point, I was back in my normal spot in the formation, as were the other large men, our Century moving a way out from the wall to allow for the others of our Cohort to form up inside the wall.

"Pilus Prior." This was the Optio's voice, and we strained to hear what he had to say over the din of the lead missiles from the slings skipping off our *scuta*. "Did you notice anything strange about when those bastards left the first wall?"

"What do you mean, Optio? Spit it out, man; we don't have time for riddles."

"What I mean is that they had to negotiate the ditch and obstacles just like we will, right? But did you see how quickly they scampered across? It was almost as if…"

Cutting him off, Pilus Prior Crastinus finished excitedly, "As if they had a path across the ground that allowed them to move like the obstacles weren't there in the first place."

The pride in the Optio's voice was clear for all of us to hear. "Exactly. There has to be a way across where we won't have to worry about that damn ditch. It's further down that way."

And despite our situation, we grinned at each other. We all liked Rufio a great deal, making any success of his good news for us as well as far as we were concerned. The command was given and we began walking slowly, still in *testudo*, along the inside of the first wall. Both the Optio and Pilus Prior, using the *scuta* picked up from fallen men to protect them, as is the habit of the officers in battle, searched for the signs of the path across. It soon became clear to the Gallaeci what we were up to, so they began concentrating their fire on our officers, who were then forced to integrate with our formation for better protection, making finding the path even more difficult. Further compounding the difficulty was the fact that we were also carrying the ladders inside the *testudo*, which is a trick, I can promise you. There was a steady hail of missiles by now, creating such a racket that even as we shouted at each other, it was almost impossible to hear. It was only because the years of drilling made his lungs as powerful as leather bellows that we heard the Pilus Prior cry out in triumph when he found the path, marked by a series of stakes. If the Gallaeci had been smart, they would have pulled them up as they crossed over, but I gave a promise to Fortuna that I would make a sacrifice in thanks that they had not. The Pilus Prior sent Rufio to tell the other Cohort at the second breach what we found and what to look for, while we turned to head across the ground towards the second wall. Despite the hail of fire, we all had learned our lessons well about not giving in to the temptation of taking a peek by shifting our *scuta* even an inch, so we did not lose anyone crossing the ditch. Despite the stakes, we still had to be careful, the path being barely wide enough to accommodate the width of our Century; I grazed several of the stakes with my hip as we passed them. Climbing out of the ditch with our *testudo* still intact, within another couple of moments, we made it directly underneath the second wall. Now it was our turn to inflict some punishment, as some of us waited with our *pila* for one of the Gallaeci to take a chance of leaning out over the wall to try hitting us with a sling or arrow. It only took a few of them getting a *pilum* through the face to discourage the rest sufficiently that we could break out of the *testudo* and begin the process of placing the ladders while some of our comrades covered us with *pila*. Looking back over my shoulder, I saw a line of Centuries, all in *testudo*, following the exact path we had taken, with what looked like the boys of the Sixth Century immediately behind us just climbing out of the ditch. They would move further down along the wall, and we would wait while the ladders were in place at several points before we all went up them at the same time. This gave us a bit of a chance to regain our breath, which we took advantage of, pulling out our canteens and sucking down as much water as we could, knowing that it would be some time before we could do so again.

It took almost a sixth part of a watch for all of the Centuries of both Cohorts to get across the ditch and into place for the assault up the wall. The remaining Cohorts had made it to the first wall and were sheltered just on the other side, safe from the missiles of the men on the second wall. One disadvantage of their position was that the supporting Cohorts could not see us up against the second wall, and therefore would have to rely on the sounds of the horns to know when it was time for them to come across to make their own ascent once we had cleared the wall. While we waited, we could hear the sounds of battle going on over where the 9th was assaulting, although it was impossible to tell what was happening exactly or how it was going for them.

"They're probably fouling it up," Vibius sneered with the disdain one Legionary holds for a Legion not his own. "You know those *cunni* couldn't find their ass with both hands."

I wholeheartedly agreed with him, as did the others.

"Get ready, boys," the Pilus Prior called out to us as he returned from the other Centuries. What makes the job of the senior Centurion of a Cohort so challenging is that he not only has to run his own Century, but he has to ensure that the others are doing what they are supposed to be doing as well, requiring him to be in several places at once, a feat that Crastinus somehow always managed to pull off with what appeared to be a minimum of effort. Every one of us swore that he had eyes in the back of his head and hearing so sensitive that he could hear a gnat fart, and as I was to learn later, in order for a Centurion to be good at his job, it is essential that this be as close to the truth as possible.

For once, I was not going to be one of the first over; instead, I would be bracing the ladder, and although I was thankful that I was given a relatively easy duty, I would be lying if I said that I was not also slightly hurt. Until that moment, I had not realized it, but I had gotten accustomed to being one of the first into any breach or up a wall, and in the back of my mind, I could not help wondering if I had done something to make the Pilus Prior question my ability, or even worse, my courage. However, as I was about to find out, there was another reason he made the dispositions in this manner.

After telling me I was going to brace the ladder, he turned and pointed his *vitus* directly at Didius and barked, "You there, Achilles." He gave an emphasis to the nickname that did not imply that it was a compliment. "We're going to see what you're made of and if you can live up to the name. You're going up first."

Didius turned as white as I had ever seen him, and before he caught himself, started to choke out a protest before stopping immediately when he saw the expression of not just the Pilus Prior, but of all of us. Gulping, he merely nodded and turned away so that his face did not betray his emotions. We all eyed each other, not having to say a word. The horns sounded, the ladders went up, and with another roar, the men of the Second Cohort began the climb. Sitting with my back to the wall, I gripped the sides of the ladder to make sure that nobody stepped on my hands, and in this position, I got a front row seat to see Didius mount the ladder. I wish I could say that I felt some sort of pity for him, but I did not; instead, I experienced a great sense of satisfaction seeing the sheer terror on his upturned face as he climbed, his shaky legs nevertheless propelling him upwards. I very clearly felt the tremors of his body as he ascended, and it was with grim pleasure that I thought, now we're going to see how much is talk and how much is deed.

Immediately following him was Rufio, who gave me a quick grin as he followed Didius up and he called out to me, "I think he *cac*ed himself. At least that's what it smells like."

I laughed, as did the others who heard him, although if Didius heard, he was too terrified to give one of his normal surly retorts. Scribonius went up behind Rufio and I heard the first clash of metal, followed by a cry as Didius got to the top. Immediately, the progress up the ladder stopped and I frowned in concern, exchanging a look with Vellusius, who had just stepped onto the first rung. This was not good; the key to storming a wall is to get as many men on the parapet as quickly as possible, and I wondered if this had happened when I went up the ladder the first time. Being fair, I knew that it was impossible to judge time in moments like this, so it might very well have been the same when I did it, yet it did not seem that way, and judging from the concerned looks on the others' faces, I had to believe that there was a problem.

"Achilles, you lazy bastard," Rufio called, "make us some room up there."

Over the clanging of metal, I heard Didius reply desperately, "I'm trying, damn you!"

"Well, don't try, you stupid bastard; do it!"

Finally, Rufio gave an exasperated growl and forced his way up the ladder, his voice adding to the melee on the wall. In a few heartbeats, whatever had been holding everyone up was taken care of, because the flow of men began again, moving quickly this time. Finally, I was the last one left and I pulled myself to my feet, giving the job of bracing the ladder to the designated man from the Century behind us and followed everyone else up.

The sight that met my eyes was one of chaos, even more than normal in an assault like this, with the Gallaeci flowing down the hill from the town like ants, headed towards the walls, where the men of the First Century were battling the warriors who were still fanatically fighting on the parapet. They were resisting with the desperate courage of men who knew that not only were they the last line of defense protecting their families, they were the last gasps of a rebellion, and defeat would mean the destruction of their people. Caesar's treatment of the Lusitani that he defeated was no secret by this point, and it was this knowledge that kept them fighting long after they should have been exhausted. My heart sank when I saw a number of Roman bodies littering the parapet, and I could only hope that none of them were my tent mates; it was bad enough that they were from my Century. Looking for a place to stick in and help, I saw a small knot of Gallaeci pressing hard against Calienus and Atilius, both of them with their backs to the wall, frantically parrying the blows of the Gallaeci warriors. With a shout, I rushed over to help them, catching the Gallaeci by surprise. One of them turned his attention to me, snapping something to the others, obviously an order to keep up their assault on my two friends while he would handle me. Giving him a savage grin at this sign of his hubris, I beckoned him to come at me. He had a short *gladius*, similar to those that we used, and he wielded it with some skill, but in a moment, I had his measure; he was too aggressive and prone to over-commit and expose himself. Feigning a retreat after one spirited attack on his part, it gave him the encouragement to press me, which was exactly what I wanted. Once again, he made a thrust and overextended himself, so that for a brief instant, his throat was exposed because his arm was too far forward. It was enough, and I relished the look of shock in his eyes as my blade punched through, coming out the back of his skull, then twisted the blade to free it, kicking him out of the way as I did so. His comrades had too much faith in his ability because their attention was still turned totally towards Calienus and Atilius, so I dispatched two of them with quick thrusts to the back before the other three realized what was happening. Now they were caught between the proverbial rock and the hard place, and in an instant, they were all finished.

"Thanks, Pullus," Calienus gasped and I grinned, giving a quick salute before we turned our attention to other targets.

Working together, we moved along the wall, trying to link up with the other Century further down, squeezing the Gallaeci into a smaller and smaller space as we did so, giving them less room to work while increasing our chances of hitting someone as they became more densely packed. Things were beginning to swing in our favor and the Gallaeci knew it, prompting some of them to jump off the parapet to retreat up the hill to form another line of defense. Some of our men kept their heads about them and, on seeing the Gallaeci warriors jumping down, snatched up their *pila*, flinging them into the backs of some of the retreating warriors. As the situation on the parapet began to stabilize, I began looking around for Vibius. When I saw him, a cry of fear escaped my lips before I could stop it.

Vibius was lying on the parapet, his lower body covered in blood as he lay motionless among other bodies, both Roman and Gallaeci. Running to him, I fell to my knees beside him. He was facedown and as I reached for him to turn him over, I saw my hands trembling; I had never been so afraid in all my life about what I might find. Steeling myself, I gently turned him over, a gasp of relief exploding from me as I saw his eyes flutter. He looked up, his eyes fuzzy and unfocused before they finally rested on my face. Seeing that he recognized me, I took this to be a good sign.

"Wha….what happened? Where am I, Titus?"

"You've been wounded," I replied in what I hoped was a comforting tone, but I had my doubts when I saw his eyes widen in alarm. Immediately, his hands began to roam over his body, and I grabbed them, saying as gently as I could, "Don't do that. Let me see. I'm sure it's nothing."

I began by examining his lower torso, his tunic caked with blood underneath his *lorica*, not bothering to hide my relief when I determined that he did not have any kind of belly wound. I found the wound when I examined lower down, a huge gash in his thigh, both in front and in back, a sign that it had been a *gladius* thrust that had gone all the way through. The other good news was that the blade had not cut a major blood vessel, since if it had, he would have been dead by the time I found him. Telling him the news, I watched his eyes flutter in relief.

"Let me go get a *medicus*," I told him, but before I left, I tore off a piece of his tunic to bind the wound, which was still oozing blood, although it was slowing down. I just hoped it was not because he had run out of blood, but he was still conscious, which I took to be a good sign. Jumping up, I looked over the wall to see if the *medici* had made their way this far along yet, then when I spotted one, I called out to him. He heard me and promised to come up as soon as he finished with the man he was working on. Despite the fight raging further down the parapet, I sat down with Vibius to wait for the *medici* to arrive and talked to him, staying as cheerful as I could, teasing him that he was going to get out of all the duties for a while, yet I saw he was still worried.

"Vibius, don't worry. You're not going to die. I've seen enough wounds to know this isn't fatal."

"That's not what I'm worried about, Titus," he said quietly. "I'm worried that it won't heal properly and I'll be dismissed from the Legion."

I had not even thought of this, and just the mention of it sent me into a near panic, since I could no more imagine being in the army without Vibius than I could grow wings and flying. Refusing to listen to him, I told him firmly that this was nonsense, and if he continued thinking like this, I was going to give him a good thrashing. After he recovered, of course, I amended hastily, and I think to the relief of both of us, the *medici* arrived, so I left Vibius with him to continue fighting, promising that I would come see him as soon as I could. Turning back to the sounds of battle, I looked for our Century before hurrying off to join them, leaving Vibius behind for the first time since we had been friends.

Fighting continued to rage, the accursed Gallaeci refusing to recognize the inevitable, and the battle soon degenerated into a series of smaller, more private fights involving at the most dozens of men on both sides. All sense of tactics and cohesion were gone as the situation reduced itself to its simplest denominator, that of men trying to kill each other for reasons that they could no more fathom at this point than they could express them. When I found the Pilus Prior, he was surrounded by a knot of men from my Century, so I hurried over to the group.

Catching sight of me, he called out, "It's about time, Pullus. Get over there," he pointed to a spot where some of our men were being hard pressed by a larger group of Gallaeci, "and sort that out."

Sketching a salute, I ran over, jumping into a wild melee that resembled a tavern brawl more than any type of set battle. Men were simply bashing each other with both *scutum* and *gladius*, not even bothering to look for an opening or in any other way using their heads, merely trying to batter their opponents into submission. Resolving that I was going to be more logical about this, I waited as I watched two combatants who appeared to be evenly matched, looking for an opening where I could provide some help. After exchanging a series of blows, both the men stepped away from each other, panting from the exertion, their eyes only on each other. Seeing my chance, I stepped in quickly to dispatch the Gallaeci with a quick thrust. The Roman, I believe it was a man named Numerius from our Century, yelled at me in protest.

"I almost had him, Pullus. You didn't have to do that."

349

I looked at him as if he had gone insane; this was not a contest or a training exercise, a point I reminded him of, not mollifying him in the slightest. "Next time, you worry about making your own kill and not wait until I soften someone up so you can just step in and take the glory," he insisted.

I did not know how to respond, just looking at him with my mouth agape. Shaking my head, I turned my attention back to the fight, wondering if I would find someone more appreciative of my help.

Our effort to clear the second wall and move away from it took most of the day. First, we would clear a section, with the Gallaeci falling back into the relative safety of the lean-tos and shacks arrayed on the slopes of the hill, but then they would reorganize and rally before we could move out from the wall. They would come rushing back and, more than once, we found ourselves with our backs literally to the second wall, fighting desperately to maintain our formation and not get slaughtered piecemeal trying to claw our way back up to the parapet. After a couple of setbacks like this, we kept a reserve force standing on the parapet who would first fling whatever *pila* they found to help relieve the pressure, then use the discarded longer spears that the Gallaeci favored, stabbing down at the enemy over our heads as we fought. In this manner, we never had to face the prospect of trying to withdraw back over the wall, although it was a close-run thing. During one particularly vicious encounter, I was slashed down my right arm just as I was parrying a thrust from a spear, an opportunistic Gallaeci next to the man I was fighting lashing out with a short blade, scoring my arm from the elbow to just an inch or two above my wrist. While the cut was not particularly deep, it felt like someone poured liquid fire in a line down my arm; even now, as I am dictating this I can see the scar clearly, although it has turned white with age. Despite myself, I let out a yelp of pain, then gritted my teeth and took savage delight in gutting the man who cut me, laughing brutally into his face as he dropped to his knees, his eyes on me as he died. The blood from the wound ran freely for some time before it clotted; a wave of dizziness struck me after a few moments and I was sure that I was going to collapse on the ground at the worst possible time. Somehow, I found the reserves needed to maintain my footing, once again feeling the rage start to flow through me, giving me a burst of energy. Snarling like a wild animal,

I bashed an older warrior with the boss of my *scutum*, shoving him back to give me room to move forward while thrusting and slashing at any patch of bare flesh that I saw. The men around me began roaring their own war cries, feeding off the renewed energy as our group began pushing back away from the wall, moving steadily forward. Other smaller groups saw us and fought their way to us so that after several moments of non-stop fighting, we had gathered perhaps half the Cohort.

The Pilus Prior saw our group and made his way to us, using us as a rallying point and, while he had the horns sound the command to form on the standard of our Cohort, I took the time to try binding my wound, taking the neckerchief worn to keep our *loricae* from chafing our necks off a dead Legionary, Plautius as it turned out, then with some help, tied it around my arm. It was a bit restricting, although I was fairly confident that once we started fighting again I would not notice, which is what happened.

Meanwhile, the 9th had made their way to a point where they had begun firing the shelters and other combustibles. The wind, picking up in the day as it is prone to do in that part of the world, had begun to whip its way up the hill, sending a pall of smoke in our direction that was irritating yet not thick enough to obscure our vision. The Gallaeci, seeing us rally and form up, gave their own commands so that a large number of their warriors clustered together, ready to oppose our progress up the hill.

For however many times only the gods knew by this point, the Pilus Prior waved his *gladius* in the air in a circle, before dropping it down and pointing at the men opposite us, bellowing, "Kill those bastards!"

Again, we responded with a roar, rushing forward. Finally, however, we could sense that this was the final push; the last fort, the last bunch of the enemy, the last battle of the campaign before we could rest. For some of us who dreamed of such things, it was also the last chance for glory, meaning that I was at the head of the Second Cohort as we smashed into our enemy.

Once it was all over, it was easily our hardest and bloodiest battle to date, which, given the circumstances, was fitting. The

Gallaeci fought like lions, and at some point in the final battle to finish off a last pocket of resistance, I found myself feeling very sad that we had to slaughter such worthy opponents as these. It is a feeling that I have had several times since. In fact, there have been times where I found I have had more regard for the men I was killing than some of the men I was fighting with, and I know that I was not alone. On that day, we destroyed the Lucenses branch of the Gallaeci as a fighting force, or at least we thought we did, although they have proven to be a most resilient enemy. In the space of thirty years, they regained enough strength to cause the Imperator Augustus troubles that found the Legions marching once again over terrain that I had as a teenager. However, at the time we marched under the command of his adoptive father, we pacified the province, bringing the Lusitani and the Gallaeci to heel and ending the revolt. When all was said and done, the 10th Legion lost more than 200 men killed, with an equal number wounded severely enough to be dismissed from the Legion. In our Century, out of the original ninety-one men that made it through the final training and marched out of the camp in Scallabis, there were seventy-four left on active service; twelve men had been killed outright, including Optio Vinicius, and four had to be sent home. None of them were my tent mates, although five of us had been wounded to one degree or another, myself suffering two wounds, though neither of them were serious enough to see me on the sick and injured list. Vibius took a month to recover, and was left with a slight limp that showed up on cold days or at the end of a hard day's marching, but otherwise, did not slow him down. The day after we took the last Gallaeci fort, the leaders of the resistance who were still alive came to camp to surrender to Caesar, throwing themselves on his mercy at a ceremony where we were paraded to watch the spectacle, which we enjoyed immensely. There are few things more satisfying than seeing an enemy humbled before the eagles of the Legions, and it was an event that never diminished in pleasure for me over the years, except when they were fellow Romans. We, the 9th and 10th, marched back south, to be met by the 7th, who had reduced Portus Cale and pacified the area, before continuing our movement until we met the 8th, still guarding their area of Lusitania for the weeks we were pursuing the end of the rebellion. It was in late September that we marched into Scallabis, to be met by adoring crowds, our standards wreathed in the traditional garlands that denote victorious Legions, with Caesar leading the procession. The 10th was given the place of honor on the march into the city, beginning a long relationship with Caesar as his favorite and most reliable Legion, a fact that we were quick to rub in the faces of the other Legions. This favoritism was the source of many a brawl in the inns and wine shops of the places we were quartered through the years. We spent a month in Scallabis as the wounded men recovered, before marching to Corduba.

Word shot through the army like lightning that Caesar was being awarded a triumph in Rome, and the rumor was that he would be taking the entire army with him to enter the city. Almost as quickly, the word changed, as it is wont to do in an army, although this rumor had the added weight of turning out to be true, at least partially. We were then told that, rather than taking the army, Caesar would be taking the more senior Legions, meaning the 7th, 8th, and 9th, leaving the 10th behind. Supposedly, the idea was that, over the next years, we of the 10th would have our chances to celebrate triumphs, but I can tell you that it did not set well with us. The day before Caesar and the other Legions left for the march to Rome, near the end of October, we were paraded for one final formation in front of the Praetor, where awards for individual bravery were handed out. It was on this occasion that I won my first decoration, a set of phalarae for my actions on the hill when we had been surrounded.

My only warning was the night before, when the Pilus Prior bashed me with his *vitus* because he judged the coat of varnish on my harness was lacking, and he asked, "What if by some miracle you happened to be chosen to be decorated, eh, Pullus? Would you really embarrass the Cohort and the Legion with that sorry job?"

"No, Pilus Prior."

And I applied another coat of varnish to my harness, although I was sure that when I was finished, it looked exactly the same as when I started.

That formation the next day was a glorious affair, one of the reasons Vibius and I had joined the army. All four Legions, arrayed in formation in dress uniforms with the horsehair plumes, those of the army previously earning decorations wearing them, with the Centurions standing in front of their Centuries. The weather was glorious and I wished that my sisters and Gaia and Phocas were here to see what was happening, but I had no time to send word to them. I was one of about thirty men from the 10th Legion to be decorated, including two other men from my Century, Rufio being one of them. Two men were awarded the *corona civicus* for saving fellow Romans from certain death, and while this award is the simplest, it is the most prized. The award itself is nothing more than grass plaited together to form a simple crown, yet what it represents is the highest honor one individual Roman can win. Pilus Prior Crastinus was awarded the *corona murales* for being the first over the wall in the assault on the first town, his third such award. Although he could have left it to one of the Tribunes in command of the Legion that day, Caesar chose to personally award all the decorations, despite it taking more than a full watch for all of the Legions. Even though he must have talked to more than a hundred men being decorated, he still remembered most of their names, including mine.

"*Gregarius* Pullus, I'm happy to see that you survived your first campaign. From what I heard, that's an exceeding accomplishment, given your habit of always being in the front."

I did not think it appropriate to mention that most of the time I had been at the front, I was ordered there by the Pilus Prior; there are some things that generals do not need to know. Instead, I felt the heat rise to my face and all I could manage was a mumbled thanks, which he was gracious enough to ignore. Despite being at *intente*, I found my eyes moving down to the silver disks that make up the phalarae, each of them emblazoned with a symbol of the Legion, in this case, the bull. By the end of my career, the phalarae would bear the likeness of Octavian and his wife, or of Caesar, but at the beginning of my time under the standard, it used the symbol that was identified with the Legion that one served with when winning it. At the same time as the individual awards were given, decorations were given to individual Legions and Cohorts for valor of special significance. These awards are discs like the individual phalarae, but they have no special engraving and are larger than the individual awards, and are attached to the Signifer of the Cohort. Second Cohort was awarded two of these decorations, more than the other Cohorts, each of whom received one, a fact that only served to fuel the rivalry and resentment of the other Cohorts, which we did nothing to lessen in any way. The final blessing we received from Caesar came in his closing remarks to the army, where he singled out the 10th for special praise, saying that if he ever had need of a Legion in the future, we would be the first to be called. There is no way to describe the effect of these words among us and I think that day, perhaps more than any of his subsequent actions, Caesar won the loyalty and affection of the 10th Legion, something he would use to the fullest in later days.

The next morning, Caesar left for Rome, followed by the Legions he had selected to march in his Triumph in Rome, who would march at a much slower pace than Caesar did. As fast as Caesar moved with an army, he was even faster when traveling on his own, with only his personal entourage, lictors, and bodyguard. He had made it to Corduba from Rome in twenty-four days, and there was no reason to believe that he would move any slower on the way back. The other three Legions marched off with him, and while we still held some resentment, it turned out that they marched a long way for nothing. Once Caesar arrived in Rome, he was faced with a choice of entering the city in triumph at the cost of running for Consul, the custom being that no general under arms could run for the Consulship. Supposedly, the idea behind this was that the voters would be unduly influenced by the presence of armed troops. Therefore, the 7th, 8th, and 9th ended up being sent to winter at Aquileia without ever setting foot in Rome, a fact that pleased us to no end. The rest of us were given orders that now that Hispania was pacified, we would be marching east to what would become not only our winter quarters, but our home base for the next two years, Narbo Martius (Norbonne). None of this was known to us at the time; all we knew was that we would be spending the winter somewhere else. Before we left, we were allowed a week of leave, staggered over the next month, and so it was around the Ides of November that Vibius and I found ourselves making our way home, a trip that for at least one of us was something to rejoice about, since Vibius was going to see Juno. So was I, but that was more painful than pleasurable; yet I was looking forward to seeing her as much as Vibius was, despite the pain.

We came swaggering into Astigi, wearing our full dress uniform, minus our *scuta* and *pila*, of course, but wearing both of our blades. I took great care to polish the phalarae to a high sheen and, truth be known, I was looking forward to showing off to Juno, letting her see for herself who the better man was. Almost as soon as those types of thoughts crossed my mind though, I would feel ashamed, yet at the same time, I seemed unable to control my mind from going in that direction. Both of us carried our personal items in our packs slung from our *furcae*, loaded with souvenirs and some of the more interesting booty that we had earned in this campaign. Vibius was particularly anxious to give Juno a rather exquisite gold necklace, inlaid with enamel and semi-precious stones, including topaz that Vibius swore would match her eyes. I was dubious; I thought her eyes were more blue than green. However, I was smart enough to know that arguing the point with Vibius might give him an indication that I was paying attention to the color of Juno's eyes, and nothing good could come of that, so I held my peace. For my own part, I brought a couple of bracelets for my sisters, a brooch for Gaia and a gold armband carved with an intricate pattern of leaves and such for Phocas. For Lucius, I brought nothing but myself and my scorn, and the determination that I was going to rub in his face the success I had made of myself, still some months short of my seventeenth birthday. I will say that, even after all these years, the feeling we both got when we walked into Astigi's forum, all eyes suddenly upon these two bronzed and hardened warriors, is a memory that I still savor. Particularly since some of the first people we ran into were our old nemeses Marcus and Aulus, who still spent their days skulking around the town, picking on people weaker than they were. These were the two boys who I once caught dumping Vibius headfirst into a bucket of *cac* that some citizen had neglected to dump out, surrounded by a small group of other boys who they had intimidated and awed into following them about. Using my size and strength, I thrashed Marcus and couple of other boys, while Vibius almost killed Aulus with a rock, and there had been bad blood between them and Vibius and me ever since. Neither of them ever adopted a trade; at least, that is what we were told later by Juno, and yet they always seemed to have enough money to keep them well plied with cheap wine and in the favor of the few whores who lived in Astigi. What I always found strange was that they still managed to attract a small crowd of toadies and minions, weaklings who sought the protection and approval of Marcus and Aulus by being as vicious as they could get away with. Vibius and I stopped to talk with the woman who we had once bought our weekly meat pies from and who had been involved in my incident with the farmer Aulus Plancus, basking in her adoration and the admiring glances of all the females in the area, not minding that most of them were old enough to be our mothers. As we were chatting, I caught sight of the two, standing off to the side, surrounded by their pack, and it was their bad luck that I happened to look up when Marcus was pointing at us and saying something that the others thought to be the funniest thing they had ever heard. Our eyes locked, and I saw the color drain from Marcus' face. That should have been enough for me, but it was not.

I nudged Vibius and when he looked over, I nodded in their direction and said quietly, "Apparently, there's something about us that amuses our old friends. I think we should go over to say hello and find out what's so funny. I'm always in the mood for a laugh, aren't you, Vibius?"

He grinned at me, and replied cheerfully, "Absolutely! Excuse us, ladies; we need to go catch up with some old friends."

As he turned to join me, I saw the looks of alarm on the faces of the women we were talking to and I thought to placate them. "Don't worry, ladies. They're old friends of ours. We just want to catch up."

"Don't take me for an idiot, Titus Pullus," sniffed the meat pie vendor. "I know exactly what kind of 'friends' you are with those two, although I can't say that if you killed them, anyone here would shed a tear. I just don't need our place of business being torn to shreds, that's all."

Giving her a look of complete innocence, I made my eyes as wide as I could, not fooling her a bit. Walking casually over to the group, none of them seemed to know exactly what to do, choosing to look to Marcus and Aulus for an indication. For their part, we had stared across our *scuta* into the eyes of our enemy enough to read exactly what was going through their minds, and it was not that different from what we had seen in the faces of Lusitani and Gallaeci. Their instinct was screaming at them to make a hasty retreat, while their pride was cementing their feet in place, suiting us just fine.

"*Salve,* ladies," Vibius called out, causing both Marcus and Aulus to flush with anger and embarrassment, yet both of them wisely bit back a retort.

Instead, Marcus tried to sound pleasant as he responded. "*Salve,* Pullus and Domitius. It's good to see you back safe and sound.

We've heard of the licking you applied to those savages up north. I'll bet you both saw plenty of action, neh?"

I felt myself smiling; I can guess that it was not very convincing. "You could say that," I replied coolly. "But at least we faced real men. Better than anyone we've beaten before."

I knew how insulting this was, yet somewhere along the short distance walking over to them, I went from wanting to humiliate them mildly to deciding to provoke them enough to give me an excuse to kill them. All of them, if I could find enough of a reason for it.

I saw the look of surprise flit across Vibius' face as well, but he instantly quashed it and, like the good friend that he was, waded in by my side. "Yes, Marcus. Titus is telling the truth. The men we killed make everyone we ever faced before that look like their mother's afterbirth."

Both Marcus and Aulus went white with rage and I saw Aulus' hand move to his belt. Underneath his tunic, concealed from sight, I could make out the outline of a *pugio* of some sort, and the smile on my face widened as I realized that I might be getting my wish. Vibius continued as I watched and waited. "So what have you...*boys* been up to since we've been gone? Been beating up on cripples?"

Finally, Marcus could take no more, although as I look back, I truly wonder if he realized just how much danger he was in the instant he uttered his next words. "Why don't you ask Juno what I've been up to?" he shot back. "She and I have gotten to be very...close."

I did not even see it happen; as I've said before, Vibius was always much quicker than I was, but even for him, this was the fastest I had ever seen anyone move. Before I could blink, Marcus was standing rooted to the ground, eyes open in shock as the point of Vibius' *pugio* pushed into the soft area just at the base of Marcus' jaw where it met the throat. Vibius pushed hard enough that a trickle of blood began to flow down Marcus' throat, and despite himself, I heard Marcus whimper in fear. If it had ended there, it would have been enough to keep Marcus and Aulus from misbehaving, at least for the whole time we were on leave, but then Aulus had to do something stupid. Seeing his hand closing on the hilt of his *pugio*, while I was and never would be as quick as Vibius, I was still very fast, so before he had gotten his blade halfway out of his scabbard, I pulled my *gladius* to make a perfect thrust, blade parallel to the ground and aimed at more or less the same spot where Vibius had pinned Marcus, except I did not stop at his throat. The point exited the back of Aulus' skull, striking the side of the building where they were standing, burying itself an inch or two deep into the wood. That mark would remain there for the next several years before the building was torn down and replaced, the blood staining the wood around it, reminding me of that day every time I came home. As my blade struck, there was a collective gasp and a couple of the toadies let out a shout, while Marcus' whimpering became a moan of fear, and the air filled with the smell of fresh urine as he lost control of his bladder. Aulus' eyes remained open, bulging out as they stared at me while I watched his *animus* flee his body, a sight I had seen happen so many times before in the previous months, and his *pugio* clattered to the ground, making the loudest sound to this point. He remained standing only because I supported him on the end of my blade, and I reveled in the feeling of strength as I maintained my form, my arm out and parallel to the ground, with Aulus more or less dangling from my *gladius*. After a moment, I quickly withdrew my blade and he collapsed in a heap, while I became aware of the heavy silence of the crowd around us, yet I refused to act concerned. Somehow, I knew our future rested on how we conducted ourselves in the next few moments; if we behaved like we had done something wrong, then the chances were high that we would have trouble. However, if we acted like we had done nothing more than defend ourselves, and in a sense we had done just that, then I was sure all would be well. Acting deliberately, I wiped my blade off on Aulus' tunic, my nose wrinkling at the smell as his body lost control of its functions and his bowels emptied. Any shock Vibius felt at what I did he instantly covered up, seemingly realizing the same thing, that this was all going to hinge on the next few moments.

I said loudly enough for everyone to hear as I bent down to pick up Aulus' *pugio* and waved it in the air, "Your friend should have been more careful who he tried to kill, Marcus."

Helping our cause was the stark terror, not only on Marcus' part, but on his half-dozen followers, none of whom seemed inclined to point out that we had started the argument. Behind us, we could hear the beginning of talk, followed by the sounds of feet running towards us. I turned, quickly but with deliberation, sheathing my *gladius* while holding onto Aulus' *pugio*, in time to see three men of the city watch come trotting up, stopping when they saw two Legionaries standing in front of a body. The oldest one, a man of about forty with a long white scar down the side of his face, approached us, hand on the hilt of his own *gladius* while taking pains to show that he was not inclined to pull it.

"What happened here, Legionary Pullus?"

I remembered his name was Cornuficius and that he had been a member of Pompey's Legions that retired in this area, deciding farming was not to his liking and taking the job as commander of the city watch. We had spoken a few times, but I held no opinion of him one way or another, and he seemed to be of a like mind.

Pointing down to Aulus, I responded calmly, "This man was stupid enough to try pulling a *pugio* on me. I killed him before he could use it."

Eyes narrowing, he stared at Aulus' body, then looked me in the eye, obviously sensing that there was more to the story, but I was not willing to say anything more until I was asked. By this time, Vibius had dropped his arm, although he still held his *pugio* in his hands, never taking his eyes off of Marcus, who was just now seeming to come out of his trance. I realized that for all their bluster and swaggering, neither Marcus nor his gang, and certainly not dead Aulus, possessed any experience in this kind of deadly action, and in fact this was probably the first time they ever faced a sudden death or seen one of their own die violently.

Turning his attention to Vibius, Cornuficius asked him quietly, "And what's your part in this, Domitius?"

Vibius shrugged, although he still did not take his eyes off of Marcus. Nodding at Marcus, Vibius replied, "This man insulted my betrothed. I took exception to it and, as we were talking, it's like Titus said. Aulus decided to pull his *pugio*. Titus was quicker."

His voice was flat, without emotion, a simple recitation of facts given in the manner in which we were trained; no flourishes, no commentary, just a plain and simple action report. It was a method of communicating with which Cornuficius was clearly familiar and he nodded as if it confirmed his suspicions. I thought we were in the clear, when finally Marcus came out of his trance.

"That's a lie! I said no such things. This one," he gestured at Vibius, "just went crazy all of a sudden, right in the middle of a nice conversation. We were catching up on old times, and I was congratulating both of them on the job they did to those rebels up north, when out of nowhere, he tried to stab me!"

Seeing Vibius' jaw tighten, I threw up a hasty prayer that he would not lose his temper. Despite his obvious anger, his voice was calm as he retorted, "If I had wanted to stab you, citizen, you'd be dead."

Cornuficius nodded. "That's true enough, Galba." It was not until that moment that I realized that I had known this boy Marcus, for I could have never have thought of him as a man, for something like seven years, yet never knew his last name. "If Domitius wished it, you'd be as dead as your friend there."

Ultimately, Marcus' and Aulus' reputations for trouble was the clinching argument that this was not the cold-blooded murder that Marcus claimed it to be. Compounding his problem was the reluctance of his followers to voice support for his side of the story. I have no doubt that there was a part of each of them secretly glad to see them both get their comeuppance in some way; bullies like that do not lead through personal inspiration, they rule through fear, so I was sure that each of the minions had run afoul of either or both of them at some point. For his part, Marcus disappeared a couple of days later, never to be seen again. And for our part, let us just say that although the townsfolk were friendly enough, they gave us a wide berth.

Leaving Vibius behind in town, I left with a promise that we would get back together in a couple of days when we were going to go see Cyclops and my sister. For perhaps the thousandth time in my life, I found myself plodding down the road towards my farm, yet despite the fact that I was now a man wearing the uniform of one of Rome's Legions, I found my heart was still in my throat. In many ways, it was still like being a ten-year-old boy who lost the bag of nails he had been sent to fetch having to go home to face the consequences. Angrily, I shook my head, chastising myself for such silly feelings. I was now over six feet tall, and had added more than ten pounds of muscle just in the few months I was away. The sun had turned my skin even darker brown than it was the day I left, while my hands and feet were encased in calluses so thick they were almost like iron plate. My chest glittered with decorations I had earned and in the purse from my belt dangled more gold in coin and jewelry than I had ever seen in my life. The *gladius* on my hip had seen the death of many men, not to mention women and children, a fact that I preferred not to think of then or to this day. My helmet was polished to a high sheen, as was my *lorica*, oiled and gleaming in perfect repair, with all the damaged or lost links replaced. The horsehair plume was freshly cleaned and re-dyed a perfect shade of black and I was wearing my best tunic. And yet, for all that, I was still a young boy with a knot in my stomach going home to an uncertain fate.

Seeing Phocas before he saw me, I realized with a start that he was old. The moment the thought crossed my mind, I chided myself. I had only been gone for a few months; there was no way that he had aged that much in such a short time. Of course, that meant that he was old when I left, except that I had not seen it until this moment. When I say he was old, he was all of forty-five or forty-six, but when you are a teenager, that is truly ancient, and I have no doubt that my perception was also due to the fact that I had been surrounded by mostly young men for the last months. Even the Pilus Prior, who I was sure was of a similar age to Phocas, was only twenty-eight years old. Nevertheless, I stopped for a moment to watch him, feeling a tightness in my chest as the unbidden thought came that, slave or not, I wished with all my heart that Phocas were my father, that desire quickly followed by the prickling of tears welling in my eyes. Horrified, I blinked them back, telling myself savagely that I would not shame myself like this. As I regained my composure, Phocas apparently sensed that someone was watching. He straightened up and turned to peer at me. He frowned when he saw the Legionary standing in the road, and I could clearly see a look of worry flit across his face, no doubt wondering what troubles could have brought such a man to this farm. This brought a smile to my face, relishing the idea that I had changed so much that I was not recognized. Finally, the frown slipped from his face as recognition of who stood before him dawned, yet even then, he seemed unwilling to trust his eyes.

Taking a step forward, he asked tentatively, "Titus?"

"Who else would be coming to see you, you silly man?"

With that, he ran across the yard to greet me with a proper hug before turning to call to Gaia. She was working in the kitchen as usual, her hands red and raw from her work, and like I had with Phocas, I caught myself worrying at how tired and careworn she looked. Still, she was instantly alongside Phocas, pulling my head down to smother me with kisses, which I made a great show of protesting, but secretly loved.

It was hard for her to find a spot on my cheek because of my helmet and finally, she said crossly, "Take that thing off, Titus, so I can give you a proper kiss."

My smile grew broader as I pulled it off, automatically placing it under my left arm as I was trained, while the two of them continued to fuss over me.

"By the gods, boy, you look like Mars himself." Phocas grasped me by the arm, looking me up and down with such pride that once again I felt the threat of burning tears.

Instead, I forced a laugh as I shot back, "I'm better looking than Mars."

His eyes turned to my phalarae and despite having no real experience of such things, he knew instantly they meant something special. Indicating them, he looked at me with a questioning gaze, and I nodded proudly. "I won those for bravery, during an engagement up north."

If I was expecting a reaction, it certainly was not the one that I got from Gaia, whose smile immediately disappeared at my words. "Bravery? Bravery? What kind of men's nonsense is that? You mean you did something foolish, didn't you?"

I opened my mouth to protest, but Phocas shook his head with a wry smile. "Don't try to argue, Titus. That's one battle you won't win."

Almost as quickly, her irritation vanished as her examination of me moved her eyes to the scar down my arm, which was still pink and angry. She let out a cry as she grabbed it, running her hands along the length of the cut. "Titus! What have they done to you? How did this happen?"

Her eyes filled with tears, and now I could not help myself as my vision clouded. I was home with people who loved and cared for me, and there are few finer feelings in the world.

I postponed meeting Lucius for as long as I could, letting him sleep off his afternoon drunk while Phocas, Gaia, and I caught up. From the two of them, I learned that Valeria was expecting a child and experienced a strange thrill at the idea that I would be an uncle, something which, to that point at least, had never once crossed my mind. Livia had not become pregnant yet, but was, by their account, ecstatically happy with her husband. Lost on none of us was that both of my sisters' sense of joy was in no small measure due to their being away from this place, but we did not speak of that. Instead, I told them of the adventures I had been having, sanitizing it for both of them, deciding that telling them everything would only make them worry even more. As I talked, I ate some of Gaia's porridge and the memories of happy times came wafting up to me with the scent of her cooking. I gave them the gifts I had chosen for them, along with a fairly large sum of money, telling them quietly to put that someplace where Lucius would never find it. And it was then that I told them my plans concerning them.

"I think that, in a couple more years, I'll have saved enough to buy you your freedom from Lucius." Their look of stunned surprise and happiness made me feel ten feet tall, yet almost immediately, it was replaced by one of such extreme sadness on the face of Phocas that I wondered if I had made a serious blunder.

"Titus, there are no words to thank you for what you're trying to do, but your father will never agree to this."

"Why?" I asked indignantly. "I'll give him more than enough money to buy two slaves to replace each of you." When you are young, the world is so simple and problems so easy to solve. Still, Phocas shook his head sadly. "You could give him money to buy ten slaves for each of us, Titus, and it wouldn't matter."

Looking to Gaia for support in arguing with Phocas, I saw in her eyes the same sad emptiness. "He's right, my darling boy. It has nothing to do with the money."

"What does it have to do with then?" I demanded, although a voice inside me told me that I already knew the answer.

"It has to do with the idea that it's something that you desperately want. You know your father has no love for you, Titus. What you don't know is that his hatred has grown in leaps and bounds since you left. There isn't a day that goes by that he doesn't curse your name."

I was stunned, although I do not know why, unless it was because I still entertained some childish fantasy of winning my father's affections by great deeds. The knowledge that his hate for me had only grown in my absence smothered the last spark of hope I nurtured that somehow things could be made right between us, and I felt the coldness return to my heart, seeing in the reflection of Phocas' and Gaia's gaze that it was clear to see in my expression.

"Then," I spoke slowly and deliberately, "I'll give you your freedom another way."

At first they did not understand, then a look of horror and...something else flashed across Phocas' face. "Don't speak of such things, Titus."

He said this with an urgency that surprised me. I knew that they would not jump at the idea, at least at first, so I decided to drop it, sure that they would warm to it in time. The fact that I could very coldly contemplate the murder of my own father was not lost on me, but I shrugged it off, thinking that what I was just told severed the last thread of obligation I held towards him. If he hated me so, I would return the favor, and I was a much more deadly enemy to have than vice versa, so I dropped the subject for the time being and moved to safer topics.

Lucius finally came staggering out into the main room, his eyes in their usual bloodshot state; as his bleary vision focused on me, he gave a grunt of surprise, and I was gratified to see a look of some fear on his face. Sitting there, I looked at him steadily and when he did not speak, I forced myself to adopt a tone that I hoped sounded pleasant.

"*Salve,* Father. It's good to see you so…well."

Continuing to stare at me, he said nothing for what seemed like half a watch, before blurting out, "What by Dis are you doing here? I thought we'd seen the last of you." Before I could respond, his face screwed up in suspicion and he continued, "You didn't get thrown out of the Legion, did you? Well, if you did, it wouldn't surprise me, but you can't come back here."

Before I could stop myself, I leapt up and stepped toward him, my hand going to my *gladius*. The movement was not lost on him and he gave a yelp of terror as he stumbled back, then immediately lost his balance, crashing into a heap on the floor. He stared up at me, the fear and hatred clear as he made no attempt to disguise his true feelings, and I know that my face reflected the same thing.

"No, old man. See these?" I tapped the phalarae. "I won these. You know how I won these?"

Leaning down, I made sure that our eyes were level before I spoke, more softly this time, my tone only serving to increase the menace. "I won them by killing a lot of men, Father. I've shed the blood of more than a dozen men, all of them better than you. You'd do well to remember that."

"You impudent whelp." His lips curled back and I could see that his teeth were rotting out of his mouth, accounting for the stench that emanated from them. "I am the *pater*..."

Before he could finish and before I had any conscious thought, the *gladius* was in my hand, the sight of it causing him to become a cringing dog in the instant it took me to draw it.

"You're a drunken, mean, little man," I cut him off. "And you'd do well to remember that. I'm the head of this family now, by the right given to me by this," I brandished the *gladius*, relishing the abject terror that it evoked, "and I'll take that right if you say one...more...word."

I gestured with the *gladius* back to his room. "Well, I think we've caught up. You can go back to your room now."

Staggering to his feet, he looked like he was thinking of arguing, a thought that evaporated from his head in the time it took me to point back to him with my blade. He made to leave, but as he stumbled away, I called to him. Turning to look at me, I smiled sweetly at him and finished, "And if you even think for one moment to take your anger out on them," I jerked my head in the direction of Phocas and Gaia, who were standing as still as statues, "I'll find out from my sisters, and I'll come back and show you one of the tricks I learned about how to flay a man alive. Then I'll tan your hide to use as a cloak and your shriveled ball sac will be my coin purse. Do we understand each other?"

As I said this, I realized with equal parts satisfaction and unease that I meant every word I said. From the expression on Lucius' face, he knew it too. Gulping, he nodded, then exited the room.

The confrontation with my father had ruined the mood of homecoming, so I declined the chance to stay the night. Although I was fairly sure that my father would not have the courage to try anything while I slept, I did not feel like sleeping with one eye open. Hugging the both of them and promising that I would write this time, since I had not done so while on campaign, I left them standing at the edge of our property, tears streaming down their faces. After waving to them once, I refused to look back, not wanting to risk becoming a blubbering fool in front of them. Deciding then to head for Livia and Cyclop's farm, despite it meaning that Vibius would not come with me, I calculated I would get there after dark, not that I was worried about being alone at night. In fact, I somewhat looked forward to the thought of some bandit or bandits being unlucky or stupid enough to pick me for easy prey in the night. After all, I told myself, it had been more than a month since I last saw any real action, my confrontation with Aulus hardly qualifying in my mind, and I did not want my skills to get rusty. Even as I thought that, though, I knew that I was lying to myself. It had nothing to do with my skills; the feelings one gets during battle can be as crippling a habit as the hold wine had over my father, and like one in the grip of Bacchus, where the lack of the grape causes a violent reaction of the body, so too does the lack of action to a warrior. Such is the feeling one gets when there has been no violent action that your whole being craves that kind of stimulation, like you are starving of some nutrient. I was now infected with the disease, and it would haunt me for the rest of my life. Yet I was only dimly aware of the deeper meaning of all this as I walked down the road, whistling one of our marching tunes. Passing around Astigi, I did so after deciding to give it something of a wide berth because of what had happened earlier. As far as I knew, we had escaped any kind of trouble, but I held no desire to find out differently by stumbling into the arms of the city guard. Walking along, I contemplated what I would do if indeed there were some problem with what I did that day, and decided that I would have to take whatever action necessary to ensure that Vibius and I could escape back to camp, then put my faith in the army protecting its own. There had already been several incidents where Legionaries had either severely beaten or killed civilians and to my knowledge, none of them received any punishment. The army's view is that if a civilian is stupid enough to tangle with a Legionary, perhaps they are not meant for this world to begin with, and looking at it rationally, from Rome's point of view, there is more value in a Legionary than there is in the ordinary citizen. As long as one did not go about killing patricians or equestrians, a soldier could be fairly confident that they would be able to avoid the normal consequences associated with murdering someone.

Making it to Cyclops' farm about a third of a watch after dark, I stopped some distance away from the house and hailed it, because in those days, walking up in the dark was a risky proposition, particularly with a man like Cyclops. I was pleased to see a light emanating from the window, telling me that they had not yet retired, and after a moment, I saw the familiar face of my brother-in-law peer out from the doorway.

"*Salve,* brother," I called, and for the second time that day I could see someone's face wrinkle up as they tried to determine who was calling them. Fortunately, it did not take him long, his face creasing in a smile when he recognized me. To get Cyclops to smile was enough of an accomplishment in itself, and it was just another pleasant moment of my return home.

One more time I found myself fussed over, although it was almost completely done by Livia, Cyclops content with a firm handshake and slap on the back. And once again, I sat at their table while Livia rushed about making something to eat, ignoring my protests that I had eaten not long before, as I recounted my tales to Cyclops. While still sanitizing my recounting, I was less circumspect with Cyclops than with Phocas and Gaia, until Livia let out a gasp at one of my anecdotes, whereupon I reined in my tongue once more. Cyclops and I exchanged a look as he rolled his good eye, shaking his head at the squeamishness of women. It is truly a mystery to me how women can go through the toil and bloody business of childbirth, yet the talk of lopping off some barbarian's head gets them all aflutter. I suspect it is one of those things I shall have to ask the ferryman, or some of the wise men with whom I will be spending eternity. When Livia asked me if I had been home yet, I responded as briefly as I thought I could get away with, concentrating on my time with Phocas and Gaia, and only mentioning that I had seen Lucius. I was thankful when she did not press, but I could see by her face that I had not fooled her. Livia went to bed, but Cyclops and I stayed up through the night, and despite being happy to see my sister, I was also thankful for the opportunity to talk more freely about all the things I had seen and done, because I had questions that I felt only Cyclops could answer. I related to him how Gaius Crastinus spoke highly of him, and his face flushed with pleasure.

"Crastinus is a good man," he said as he stared thoughtfully into his cup of wine. "You can learn a lot from him."

"I already have," I replied, "but I sometimes have trouble deciding whether I hate him or love him."

Cyclops smiled. "That means he's a great leader, because you respect him out of equal parts love and fear. And in a place like the army, you have to have both."

I could see the sense in this, and I said so. We spent the rest of the night drinking and trying to keep our voices down as we talked, with less and less success, until Livia threatened us with imminent bodily harm if we did not go to sleep.

Waking the next morning with a pounding head, despite the pain, I had to smile. It was good to spend time with Cyclops, this time as a man who finally understood all the things that he had been telling us. I have come to the conclusion that trying to describe battle to someone is much like trying to describe the act of sexual congress; no matter how imaginative one might be, the description pales in comparison to the actual event.

As I bade them farewell, now headed to see Valeria and her husband Porcinus, I thanked Cyclops for all that he had shown me. "It's because of you that not only have I survived, but I've done well," I spoke honestly. I could tell this pleased him, and he surprised me with a bear hug and a kiss on the cheek.

"I'm proud of you, Titus. I think you have a great destiny in the Legions."

To say I was pleased would be an understatement. Kissing Livia, I waved goodbye as I started down the road, wondering if I could make it to Valeria's farm before dark. It had taken more than a day to escort her to Porcinus' farm on the day I delivered her to her new married life; this time, I wasn't in a wagon with my sister, so I was confident I could make it, and I did, actually arriving well before sundown. For the third time, I went through the ritual of hugs, kisses, and concern over my scar, yet I must say that this time was the most enjoyable. Valeria looked radiant, which I heard is how pregnant women were supposed to look, but I was scared to hug her for fear of hurting the baby.

"Titus, you're not going to break me." She laughed, although I was still not convinced.

And for the third time, I was stuffed with food; I ate more in the last two days than I had the previous week, but it was still good to have so much food before me. Porcinus never served in the army, and although I liked him well enough, there was not a lot to talk about with him since I held no interest in farming, but it was the thing in which he was most involved, so not much was said between us after the initial pleasantries. Besides, I was more concerned with talking to Valeria, yet I found for some reason that my reluctance to share details with the other people in my life about all that I had seen fell away with Valeria. I had always been completely honest with her about everything, and this time was no exception. To her everlasting credit, she did not flinch when I told her the things I had done, things like with the woman at the first town we assaulted; she just listened. Once I was done, it was well into the night, and when I bedded down in the main room, she came to kiss me on the forehead, just as she did when I was a boy. I remembered how the last year or two, I had done whatever I could to avoid it. This time I did not mind so much.

The day before we were to return to camp, I went back to Astigi to spend time with Vibius and Juno. It was clear that their feelings for each other were not changed, and in fact, had grown stronger. It was painful for me to watch, but it was also nice to see how happy Vibius and Juno were with each other. Watching them part was more upsetting than I imagined it would be, partly because I wished it were me that Juno was so distraught to see go, but also because I could only hope that one day someone would feel the same way about me. It also made me even more conscious of my obligation to Vibius to keep him alive so that he could return to his true love. I was envious of the obvious pride that Vibius' father had in his exploits, boasting to his friends about his son the Legionary and his great bravery, yet in this I was happier for Vibius than I was sorry for myself. Saying farewell, we made promises to write that we knew we probably would not keep, although I will say that Vibius certainly made a better attempt than I did. In those days, I had little interest in writing, or reading, for that matter, although that would change, partly because once I rose through the ranks, it would be required of me. However, another reason for my increased interest, especially in reading, had to do with what we were about to face now that the campaign was over, an enemy that would prove to be one of the most formidable that any soldier faces, no matter how many battles and campaign seasons they face.

When we made it back to camp, we found that the orders to break it down and begin the march to the northeast to our new home had been issued, so there was a swarm of activity. Vibius and I had agreed to say nothing of the trouble we had experienced in Astigi, trusting in the Fates that word would not reach the ears of the Pilus Prior or any other officer, and it never did. The chatter of the men catching up on their various adventures during their respective leaves helped make the tasks of breaking the camp down less onerous and, within two days, we were ready to march, the only difference being that instead of burning down the camp like we normally did when we marched, this camp was left intact, manned by a small guard left behind, along with a portion of the *medici* who tended to the sick and the men whose wounds were not yet healed to the point where they could travel. To my mind, and to those of my comrades, the fate of these poor souls was worse than death itself, for they existed between the two worlds. They had survived the initial threat of death, but were now lingering on, not getting better or worse as the days crept by. Some of them finally showed up at Narbo, but even fully recovered, they were never the same, and I think the idea of suffering this kind of fate scared me more than actually dying did. The march itself took three weeks, with the weather becoming bitter as we moved north along the coast, rapidly growing colder than anything most of us had experienced. This was far different in climate than the Hispania of our birth, despite the fact that we were still in the province, for the most part. Neither Vibius nor I had ever been this far north, so we spent every night wrapped in our cloaks and wearing our extra tunics, but still our teeth chattered most of the night. Being close to the coast as we marched did not make it any warmer because an icy wind blew off the water to further our misery.

We arrived in Narbo at the beginning of Januarius; it was very late under normal conditions, but there were no plans for us in the immediate future, which of course we had no way of knowing. The beginnings of what would start out as a camp had been begun by the advance party and, over the next weeks, it was transformed into a small city, our tents replaced by wooden huts, still organized around our tent sections, except with wooden floors and a solid roof. The walls were made of planks that we whitewashed, then filled in the cracks, making solid little structures that helped keep out the cold. The outer walls of the camp were initially also made of wood, but gradually, they were replaced by walls of stone, although that was yet to come. Once the camp was finished and deemed to be suitable to be a permanent base, the lustration ceremonies were held, along with the renewal of our oath of loyalty to Rome. We were led to the camp by one of the Tribunes who would serve with us for this year as the senior Tribune, while a new batch of more boy wonders arrived from Rome. Thankfully, the senior Tribune was not Doughboy, who had returned back to Rome to follow the *cursus honorum*; he must have stumbled along the way because we never heard of him again. The Tribune that remained behind to serve as the Senior Tribune was the one that I took notice of earlier who had seemed to have his wits about him, and in the intervening time, I learned his name, Gaius Trebonius. Now, it is a name I curse and hope that Cerberus is cracking his bones as he shrieks in agony and torment, because he was one of the slayers of the great man. However, I was happily ignorant then and was content enough to have one of the boy wonders who seemed to know what he was doing lead us, or more importantly accepted what he did not know and allowed the men who did to do what was necessary.

That was when the secret enemy first showed up, an enemy that we had been warned about by the veterans, except until we faced it, we did not know exactly how vile a foe it is. In reality, it was a combination of two different enemies, working together. They are the twins of despair known as boredom and illness. Once the camp is finished for winter and all the resulting tasks are complete, there is not a whole lot for an army to do, despite the Centurions doing their best to find things to keep us busy. Unfortunately, a substantial number of duties that are considered punishment duties, such as the cleaning of latrines, are reserved for Legionaries who fall afoul of the many rules and regulations needed to ensure the smooth running of the Legions. For those of us who stayed out of trouble, as hard is it might have been to do, that did not give us a lot to occupy our time. A good number of us, by virtue of skills we acquired before joining the Legion, had been given the status of *immunes*; Vibius, for example, worked in the leather factory, making and repairing all the various bits of leather gear, like our harnesses and the tack for the livestock. I had the status of being the weapons instructor after the death of Vinicius, yet there is only so much training one can do in a given day. Therefore, a good number of the men filled their spare time with the pursuit of wine, women, and gambling, each man putting the three vices in their own order. Fairly quickly, I observed that those pastimes carried their own sets of risks, and more often than not, when a Legionary fell afoul of the regulations, it was a direct result of one or a combination of those three. In our tent section, there were two men who seemed to find themselves on the wrong side of the Pilus Prior's *vitus*, or even worse punishment, on a regular basis. One received more official punishment, while the other's tended to be more unofficial in nature, and more likely than not was at the hands not of the officers, but from his fellow soldiers.

Atilius was a type of soldier that I came to know well during my time in the Legions, and is a fairly common sort in the army, having an extreme fondness for wine and by extension, the joys of revelry and debauchery that tend to come with it. He possessed a talent for finding drink under the most unlikely circumstances and was quick to take advantage of his finds, although I never once saw him drunk when his lack of sobriety meant that it endangered himself, or more importantly one of his tent mates or the Century. However, once the rigors and dangers of a campaign were left behind, Atilius was one of the first over the wall in search of Bacchus. Compounding the problem for Atilius was that he possessed no skill, other than fighting, so he did not have the status of *immunes*, which would have occupied more of his time. He was the type to start out as a happy drunk, but as the night progressed, some evil *numen* would inhabit his soul, and anyone participating in revels with him was guaranteed to find themselves in some sort of melee, particularly when there were men from another Legion around, or even worse, civilians. For reasons I never discovered, Atilius hated civilians, which was not a real problem when we were tramping about the countryside. But Narbo, for example, was a well-established town by this point, replete with all the hangers-on that can be found in every town in the Empire that has a Legion present. Pimps were a special problem for Atilius, although in the interest of accuracy, it would be more precise to say that Atilius posed a real problem for pimps. Early on during our time in Narbo, I made the mistake of accompanying Atilius, Romulus, Remus, and Vellusius on a night on the town. I will not go into detail other than to say I found myself shivering in a ditch that I later found out was used exclusively for the drainage of waste, as I attempted to avoid attentions of the provosts and a party of particularly angry associates of a man that Atilius had thrown headfirst through a wall. Now, I liked a good brawl as much, if not more than any man, particularly because I tended to win. However, I could see fairly quickly that my goal of raising myself up from my current status, both in the sense of promotion in the Legion and the even larger one of improving the lot of myself and my descendants, might be permanently damaged if I continued to attend Atilius' romps.

No more than a month had passed at Narbo before Atilius found himself confined to the camp, with a portion of his pay taken, not to mention the thrashing he was given by the Pilus Prior that left him with an especially prominent black eye. However, if any of us hoped that this would serve to warn him off the path he was taking, they were in vain. His second offense happened no more than a week later, when he was caught trying to sneak back into the camp shortly before dawn. Because this was his second offense, the punishment was more severe, and he was given ten lashes, fortunately not with the scourge but the regular lash, and put on latrine detail for a month. This did serve to curtail his activities for a couple of months, and when he finally regained the chance to go back out in town, he was more circumspect, for a while anyway. Regardless, Atilius was destined never to reach above the rank of *Gregarius* and was not even considered for duty as *immunes* because of his problems with wine and debauchery.

The other miscreant in our group did not run afoul of the Centurions, his crime being the type that goes unreported and never appears in his permanent record. By this time, gentle reader, it should not surprise you when I reveal the identity of this individual, and I recognize that at this point you may have suspicions that I am being somewhat unfair to the man. I assure you that if anything, I am being kind. Didius loved to gamble, but more than he loved to gamble, he loved to win, and was not one to scruple much over how he did it. His favorite game was dice, and his gravest crime was that he was too stupid and greedy to know that it did not take long for others to suspect that his winning streak might not be attributed to the many sacrifices he supposedly made to Fortuna as he claimed. Yet he did have a certain amount of skill, because for the greater part, the most that he aroused was suspicion since nobody could quite catch him in the act of cheating, as it were. Until one day in early spring, when his run of "luck" expired, courtesy of an "accidental" jostling of his person just as he was making a throw, a bumping that caused the extra pair of dice he was hiding in his other hand to fall to the ground, followed down immediately by Didius himself. It was only because Romulus and Remus were there to intercede that he was not beaten to death; there are few crimes considered more heinous to Legionaries than cheating a fellow soldier, in any fashion, at just about anything. The only exception to that are attempts made to get out of any kind of extra duties of some sort; the ability to do so is universally admired by every soldier I have met, until you gain the *vitus,* of course. Even then, I found I held a grudging admiration for the ingenuity that some of the men under my command displayed in their attempts to avoid shoveling manure or some such. And it was due to the fact that, as much as we may have despised Didius ourselves, he was one of our tent section that required Romulus and Remus to come to his rescue. Now one might think that, under the circumstances, a man who found himself rescued under such dire straits would express gratitude to his rescuers, and view himself as forever in their debt. Perhaps the fact that Didius expressed no such gratitude will be an indicator that when I speak of him, I am not judging him too harshly. Not only was Didius ungrateful, to hear him tell it, the brothers had stopped Didius from exacting revenge for the unfair accusations made against him by thrashing the half-dozen or so men who had set upon him. The fact that his face was massively swollen, his nose now going in a different direction, with the rest of his body covered in greenish-purple bruises, was a contradiction, if one were to listen to his words. Apparently, however, he was simply lulling his antagonists into a false sense of security by allowing them to appear to beat him senseless, and was just about to unleash his masterstroke counter-attack when the brothers so rudely interrupted. It took the intercession of Calienus to keep the brothers from finishing the job that the other men had started, with both of them making a solemn oath, swearing on Jupiter's Stone that they would never come to his rescue again, no matter what the circumstances. For my part, I must admit that I took some vindictive pleasure in paying particular attention to some of his sorer spots during our weapons drill, in which he had to participate because of an awkward situation, at least for him. Didius could not exactly present himself for the sick and injured list, since the circumstances of his condition would prompt a series of questions that he really had no wish to answer. Despite his protestations of innocence in the matter, Didius was at least smart enough to know that on the face of it, the evidence was not in his favor, so there was a relatively good chance that there would be some official punishment. Because the penalty for cheating a fellow Legionary at anything is extremely severe; it is not uncommon for men to be sentenced to death for particularly egregious offenses, Didius' reticence was understandable. Much later in my career, there was a case of a Tesseraurius who stole the money of the men he had been charged with banking and the punishment for him was the same as when a unit is decimated, except that nobody had mixed feelings about beating him to death. Therefore, Didius was forced to perform his normal duties, including giving me a chance to beat him senseless with a *rudis*, something I enjoyed immensely.

Every morning, either in winter quarters or in garrison, starts with a formation, where the orders of the day are announced before everyone goes about their business. The winter had passed, the spring had come and gone, and we still performed our normal duties, with no prospects of action. In short, the situation was disgustingly peaceful. We still did our forced marches twice a month, so we maintained a certain level of fitness, but to keep Legions honed to a sharp edge for long periods of time is practically impossible. No matter how hard the Centurions tried, those of us stationed at Narbo lost all of the edge that we gained during the campaign in Lusitania. However, one man was prospering; we followed the rise of Caesar's career with great interest, jumping onto every scrap of news about his fortunes. Other officers came and went, but the army, particularly the 10th, thought of themselves as Caesar's men, even in those days of inaction. Rarely a day went by where his name was not mentioned, a fact that I imagine the other nobles who were assigned to command us at that time did not particularly care to hear.

It was during our first year at Narbo that Caesar was made Consul, and what is now referred to as the First Triumvirate began ruling Rome, and by extension, my life and those of all of my comrades in the army. Because of the quiet state of affairs, many of the men started relationships with women in the town, and despite marriage not being allowed, they took wives in everything but name. These men were easy to spot, all of them being exceedingly anxious to be secured from duties for the day so that they could rush back to town to be with their women. Naturally, it was not long before the women got pregnant and families began to sprout. These *de facto* families, no matter what their legal status, would be a regular feature of our lives and the officers almost always turned a blind eye, their only requirement being that the small army that followed the larger one as it marched never impeded the progress of the Legions. Many of these women would help their men carry their loads for them, trooping along behind the Legion marching drag, putting in just as many miles as we did and, in many ways, enduring more hardships. As much as I cared for Juno, I was hard pressed to see her living like that, and I was glad that Vibius resisted the temptation to send for her, because I knew that she would come without hesitation.

The second enemy struck towards the end of our first year in Narbo, in September, during the Consulship of Caesar and Bibulus, although for all intents and purposes, Caesar ruled alone, since Bibulus despised Caesar so much that he refused to serve with him, prompting the joke that this was the Consulship of Julius and Caesar. An illness swept through camp, a horrible affliction that saw men dying while spewing the most noxious fluids from almost every orifice of their bodies. Even all these years later, I still find myself questioning the Fates about the justice of allowing men to live through battle, only to be struck down by some invisible phantom, denying all that it strikes from the clean death that a soldier deserves. As I have mentioned before, our tent section, while suffering from wounds, had escaped the loss of one of us in battle during the campaign against the Lusitani. We were not to escape unscathed from this enemy, however. Remus contracted the affliction, dying after only a few days, at the end deliriously calling for his mother and telling her that he was done with his chores. Romulus sat next to him, clutching his hand and weeping, begging him not to die, while the rest of us frantically made sacrifices to every deity we could think of, all to no avail. The illness raged for weeks, striking fully a tenth of our numbers, and killing well more than half of those afflicted. The doctors and *medici* did what they could, which was little more than making men as comfortable as possible, with the rest of us searching for anything that would help us ward off the horrible disease. There was a small industry of quacks and false healers who made a small fortune off of all of us, me included, peddling amulets and potions that they swore would save us. I took to wearing the claw of a hawk around my neck, which a man who claimed to be Greek swore would protect me from the ravages of the disease. While I am of a mind to sneer at this, I am still here many, many years later, so there is a part of me that thinks perhaps it was not such quackery, after all.

Although this was the first such outbreak I would witness, it certainly would not be the last, and because I tend to try and observe the world around me as much as possible, by the third or fourth time this type of disease struck, I had noticed some similarities in conditions. Even after I witnessed other afflictions, notably the plague, strike armies while out on campaign, this particular disease never seemed to occur while we were on the march. It only happened when we stayed in one place, and it seemed to be only after a period of months in that place before it struck. It also seemed to strike those who were less fastidious in their habits and used the baths or otherwise cleaned themselves less often than the others. I am not inclined to speak ill of the dead, particularly those I consider friends; however, Remus was notorious for not bathing, and even his brother would chastise him severely for it, to no avail. Not once did I speak of these ideas to Romulus, or anyone besides Vibius, for that matter, but when I finally made the rank of Centurion, I earned a reputation for forcing my men to bathe more often than most of the other officers, for which I took a fair amount of teasing and ridicule from my fellow Centurions. Until, that is, I pointed out after a sufficient period of time passed that I consistently put less men on the sick list, and suffered far fewer losses when this particular disease would strike, whereupon the others followed suit.

Only now were we down to the more traditional eight men in our tent, or our hut, in this case. For a period of several days, there was a sense of tension among us as we waited for another of us to be struck down, but we luckily did not suffer another loss. Despite getting an idea of what caused this affliction, I have never understood what makes it stop, but it does, seemingly leaving as quickly as it arrives. Before long, our routine was back to normal, with the life of the Legion in garrison continuing as if nothing had happened, leaving only grieving comrades and brothers behind to wonder at the unfairness of it all. For his part, Romulus was never truly the same after that, like a part of him had been torn out of his soul, which perhaps was not far from the case.

However, that is all of this tale I will tell now; I must take some time to rest, and poor Diocles looks more than ready for a respite himself! There is still so much to relate, about Caesar and what even men who were not there consider to be the greatest feat of arms, not just in our history, but of all time, the conquest of Gaul. And it is with great pride that I can say that I was there, marching with Caesar.

Commonly Used Terms

Cac- Unsurprisingly, this is the slang term for shit.

Conquisitore- A minor official charged with the raising of a Legion, once a *dilectus* was called by a Praetor, Consul or ProConsul. In the Imperial period, these positions were much sought-after because of the opportunity for enriching oneself through bribery. During Caesar's time, when the raising of Legions was much less formalized and haphazard, the position was temporary and not as lucrative.

Dilectus- The actual call for enlistment of a Legion. During the early Republican period, Legions were enrolled for single campaign seasons, a practice that soon fell by the wayside as Rome's expansion became more aggressive. Very quickly, the term of enlistment expanded from four, to six, then ten and finally, sixteen years. Although there is no definitive evidence for when this actually began, in Marching With Caesar, the assumption is made that it starts with the first Legion raised by Gaius Julius Caesar, and that was the 10th Legion. This is because the subsequent Legions raised by Caesar, starting with the 11th Legion, were enlisted for a term of sixteen years. Also, it was almost exactly sixteen years after their formation that the 10th mutinied because their discharges were due.

Edepol- An exclamation of surprise, used by Roman males.

Galea(e)- The helmet worn by Roman Legionaries. *Galea* is the singular.

Gerrae- Similar to *Edepol*, but was not commonly used by the upper classes. This term is similar to the American Northeast "Get the fuck outta here".

Gladius(ii)- The term used for the short, stabbing sword that was the primary weapon of the Roman Legionary. Back then, it was also commonly referred to as *gladius Hispaniensis*, or Spanish sword, so named because it was adopted after Rome's conquest of Spain, and they saw firsthand how devastatingly effective it was. This sword would be their primary weapon from its introduction as the Legionary's weapon, in the Third Century B.C. to the Late

Empire, in about the Third Century A.D. when a longer sword started being used.

Gregarius- This is the shortened version of the rank *Miles Gregarius*, the first and lowest rank in the Roman Legion. It is akin to the modern day Private.

Immune- An *immune* was a Roman Legionary with a particular skill that was deemed vital to the running of a Legion. Unlike their modern counterparts, a Roman Legion was required to be self-sufficient as much as possible, needing only the raw materials to make the implements and weaponry needed to wage war in the Roman fashion. An example of an *immune* would be an armorer, or a leather worker. This was a rank immediately above that of *Gregarius*.

Intente- The Latin command for "Attention", the military command to assume a position of alert readiness for the following command.

Numen- A disembodied spirit or force, *numen* were perhaps the most ancient supernatural form, and as such were much more simplistic and primeval.

Paludamentum- The scarlet cloak worn by Roman commanders of at least Legate rank.

Pilum(a)- The Roman javelin, the design of which is explained in the text. *Pilum* is the singular.

Porro- The Latin command that signals a Legion to begin the assault.

Praetorium- Both the headquarters tent in a Roman military camp, and the residence of the Praetor of a province. In camp, the *Praetorium* is the first tent erected, in the center of the camp, and all the dimensions of the camp were measured from the *Praetorium*.

Probatio- The status for those who have enlisted but not yet started the training in the Legion. While a minor distinction, it was an important one, and represents the need for some sort of hold over a recruit during the period of time it took them to travel to wherever the Legion was being trained, then waiting for the training to begin. This is supposition on my part, but is based on my experience as a recruiter in the Marine Corps. Fundamentally, the reason is pretty simple; while needing to retain some sort of hold over new recruits, it wasn't very likely that they would be subjected to the harsh discipline of the Legions right away, when they were being escorted to their training camp.

Pugio- The dagger worn by Roman Legionaries. Although it was ostensibly their backup weapon, in all likelihood it served a variety of purposes; cutting leather thongs, slicing bread, etc.

Quaestorium- Next to the *Praetorium*, the most important location of a Roman military camp, as it held the quartermaster. It was located next to the *Praetorium*.

Salve- Common form of (formal) greeting. Equivalent of "Hello".

Scutum(a)- The shield used by the Roman Legions. *Scutum* is the singular.

Silete- Latin for silence, this is the more polite way to ask someone to be quiet.

Tacete- The Latin equivalent of "Shut the fuck up".

Tirones- This is the term used for recruits enlisted in the Legions who have actually begun training. This is a distinctly different class than *probatio*, and assumes that the recruit has actually begun the training that was required to become a member of the Legion.

Vitus- The twisted length of vine stick that was a symbol of the Roman Centurion. Even out of uniform, Centurions would carry the *vitus* to let others know their status.

www.ingramcontent.com/pod-product-compliance
Lightning Source LLC
Chambersburg PA
CBHW051523250626
47156CB00001B/201